Gabriel King was born in Cornwall, raised in Warwickshire and now lives just outside London with two cats. Previous works include the highly acclaimed *The Wild Road*, *The Golden Cat*, and most recently, *The Knot Garden*.

Praise for Gabriel King

NONESUCH

Also by Gabriel King

The Knot Garden
The Golden Cat
The Wild Road

NONESUCH

Gabriel King

ARROW

Published by Arrow Books in 2002

1 3 5 7 9 10 8 6 4 2

First published in the United Kingdom in 2001 by Century

Arrow Books
Random House Group Limited
20 Vauxhall Bridge Road, London SW1V 2SA

Random House Australia (Pty) Limited
20 Alfred Street, Milsons Point, Sydney,
New South Wales 2061, Australia

Random House New Zealand Limited
18 Poland Road, Glenfield
Auckland 10, New Zealand

Random House (Pty) Limited
Endulini, 5a Jubilee Road, Parktown 2193, South Africa

The Random House Group Limited Reg. No. 954009
www.randomhouse.co.uk

A CIP catalogue record for this book is available
from the British Library

Papers used by Random House
are natural, recyclable products made from wood grown in
sustainable forests. The manufacturing processes conform to
the environmental regulations of the country of origin

ISBN 0 09 929710 8

Typeset by SX Composing DTP, Rayleigh, Essex
Printed and bound in Great Britain by
Bookmarque, Croydon, Surrey

For Philippa.

Acknowledgements

Thanks must go to all at Century and Arrow for their enthusiasm and care, but especially to Kate Parkin and Kate Elton, Ron Beard and Cassie Chadderton.

'Love built on beauty, soon as beauty, dies'
John Donne
Elegies No. 2, 'The Anagram'

'The grave's a fine and private place,
But none, I think, do there embrace'
Andrew Marvell
'To His Coy Mistress'

Prologue

ON HIS WAY into the church a little before eight one bright Monday morning, Francis Baynes, vicar of St Mary's-in-Ashmore, stopped to watch Anna Dawe ride her bicycle towards him and thought what a gift her energy was to the world. Thoughts like this could still surprise him, as if he believed himself not quite mature enough to have them. At the same time, it was impossible to deny, they made him rather pleased with his own progress. He thought of himself as a vessel which had barely begun to fill up.

Anna Dawe's bicycle was notorious throughout the parish. You saw it everywhere, an old black ladies' sit-up-and-beg equipped with the hub gears and worn skirt savers of another age. Its bleached wicker baskets were always full of shopping. It was as unforgiving in use as an old donkey. Nevertheless, she rode it everywhere and when Francis Baynes caught sight of her that morning the machine was moving freely enough, rattling down the hill past the almshouses to pick up speed on the steep stretch past the Green Man. By the time Anna shot out into Church Lane, he estimated later, she had achieved a brisk twenty miles an hour. It was idiotic of him, given this, to wave his arms and step into her path. For a moment they stared at one another in horror, neither quite able to wrench free of the moment. Then, a comical expression of concentration on her face, she swerved around him; while at the same time he stepped back smartly into the protection of the lych-gate.

'Anna!'

'Can't stop. No brakes. Come for tea, Francis. Come at three!'

Banking with a kind of desperate athleticism round the bend at the corner of the churchyard, she was gone. Her shoulder had actually brushed his. Certainly he had been close enough to smell her perfume, something flowery and light-hearted. He raised his hand to wave after her; then, looking round as if he expected to be observed, dropped it suddenly and made his way through the gate.

History, they say, makes for a crowded churchyard; and Ashmore had seen the Saxons come and go. There were graves everywhere, long, eroded wafers of Horsham slab interspersed with stubby plaques of bland grey South African granite, as shiny as the paintwork of an expensive car. Laminated and flaky, emerging at contentious angles from the turf, the oldest stones clustered by the flint-knapped walls of the church, where a massive yew, the candles of which had enlivened a hundred winters, helped shelter them from the wind. Francis Baynes never tired of this quiet corner of his parish. It caught a little sun, even in December, and on late summer evenings the liquid song of a blackbird could be heard from the branches of the tree. Since the good weather began he had made it a habit to spend a few minutes there every morning. He was a diffident man and often felt he had more to offer his dead than his live parishioners. At any rate he liked to begin the day with them.

He bent down to scrape lichen off one of the stones. 'Wife of', he read; then, on the next, 'Hys lovinge sister'. Here lay crowded together the stalwarts and notables of a thousand years of village life, the Millers, the Clements, the Rose Popes and, above all, the Herringes, Ashmore's most powerful family, whose ancestor Joshua had built the great house Nonesuch in 1482. Herringe influence, uncontested for four hundred years, had waned sharply after the First World War – the family appearing to withdraw, rearrange itself subtly, shift the focus of its attention elsewhere – then further in the 1980s as incomers flooded the village with new money. Would it be eclipsed altogether by the recent bizarre events at Nonesuch? Or would Stella Herringe's cousin, John Dawe, be able to turn things round again?

In life the Herringes had prospered. In death they had imparted to the turf around them a dark, healthy gloss. 'Sir William Herringe', Francis read, 'He meeteth hys maker with a keene eye.' Not far off lay the mother of William's great-grandchildren, Clara de Montfort Herringe. Time had erased Clara's dates but spared capriciously her curious epitaph: 'A woman of great self-knowledge'. Clara – who had chosen to be buried alone despite the predecease of a perfectly good husband and whose portrait, done by a pupil of Holbein, had hung in the Long Corridor of Nonesuch until quite recently – was Francis's favourite Herringe. The portrait, which he had seen only once, a few weeks before its destruction, had shown her dressed in brocade, decked with pearls, holding a stringed instrument. Her eyes had seemed to catch at his, frank with greed, used to power. 'What a monster!' he had thought agreeably, thankful he would never have to deal with her. A little under half the Herringe graves harboured women. And here was a curious thing: they were a long-lived family, but until Stella's death in the unexplained fire that destroyed much of Nonesuch, the women had always outlived the men.

'Stella Elizabeth Clara Herringe, 1947–1999', announced her headstone. There were a few unseasonal flowers in a pot at the foot of the grave, arranged, Francis guessed, by Anna Dawe. To him they looked defeated, but he doubted Anna would see it that way. Her strength of character lay in her optimism. The grave itself had yet to settle completely, the turves fitting together over Stella Herringe with a haphazard air, raw and unfinished-looking: something Stella, always so perfectly turned out, would have hated. Appearance had meant so much to her, reputation less. Bizarre rumours, generated in the socially heated village atmosphere after the fire, still entertained the evening drinkers at the Green Man – cruelty to animals, a clandestine laboratory discovered deep inside the old house itself, death forestalling the prosecution of the woman but not of her successful cosmetics business. (This last item had actually made the television news, some months after the main event, puffing Ashmore up with a questionable kind of pride. It was like having your own murderer.) Even before the fire there had been rumours of tension between the two women over Anna's relationship with John. Stella Herringe, Francis was sure, would have shrugged it all off. 'But a grave like a building site, darling,' he imagined her saying, 'is something else again.' She had been a difficult person, who often reminded him of her own greedy-eyed ancestress; but he had to admit he had rather liked her.

Francis dusted the dry grey particles of lichen from his fingertips and sighed. After a moment he consulted his watch. Passing through the cool shadows of the lych-gate, he looked carefully both ways before he left its shelter. The road was empty; though, crossing it, he experienced a sudden clear memory of the morning's near disaster. He heard again the sad clank of the approaching bicycle. He heard Anna's sudden intake of breath. 'No brakes!' she had called. 'Can't stop!' For a moment, as she pedalled away from him, sunlight had struck through her yellow dress to give him a glimpse of her long legs and leave him in confusion. Francis Baynes was a little in love with Anna Dawe. What this meant to him as a man he was unsure. What it meant to him as a servant first of God, then his bishop and finally of the parish of Ashmore-under-Crowbury was clear enough. It meant the harrowing of his soul – or, at any rate, a considerable agitation of that entity. He shook his head, shut the lych-gate and set off into the village at a penitential pace.

He was twenty-six years old and, as one of his kinder parishioners put it, 'still rather feeling his way'.

Chapter One

The weather was just warm enough for Anna Dawe's daughter Eleanor to sit out on a picnic blanket under one of the great Nonesuch cedars, where – to the amusement of one parent and the discomfort of the other – she could spend her time profitably annoying a large marmalade cat called Orlando.

'Oof,' said her father. 'I felt that.'

Eleanor was belabouring Orlando with an old plastic doll's head she had found somewhere in the rich chaos of the house. The cat would bear her attentions stoically for a while, then move away and sit down somewhere else, the fur on his back twitching with discomfort. Eleanor would promptly follow him and begin again. You could see that he was as much embarrassed as anything: this wasn't correct behaviour, his body language seemed to suggest, for a human being, even a small and sticky one. Eleanor, he felt, ought to know better. Eventually, he got to his feet, stretched and stalked off in the direction of the house to see what the builders were up to. Orlando got on well with the builders.

'I wish we could do something about those two,' Anna said. 'They should be such good friends.'

John Dawe shrugged. Though clearly amused, he was not quite as interested as he might have been in his daughter's behaviour. The garden table in front of him was littered with the plans, invoices and lists of building materials which had filled his life since he and Anna had begun to reconstruct the house.

'She'll grow out of it,' he said carelessly. 'As for the cat, he's good with the kittens. He'll never hurt her.'

He looked at his watch and got up. 'I'm off.'

'Oh, but must you? Francis Baynes is coming to tea.'

'Francis! He's more your friend than mine.'

'He'd be hurt if he heard you say that.'

'Hm,' said John. 'Well, I haven't got time today. We're having an argument about the plaster for the Long Corridor. Do I want cow dung in the mix –'

'John! How appalling!'

'– or can I do with something more modern?' He grinned and for a moment looked rather boyish. 'I want cow dung, of course,' he admitted. 'It's the real thing.' His grin vanished abruptly and he ran his fingers through his hair. 'After that I talk to the bank and try to persuade them to fund the next stage.'

'Oh dear,' said Anna. 'No fun at all.'

'Not much,' he admitted.

She touched his hand and he gave her a smile. Despite their problems, she thought, they still managed to maintain the love they felt for one another. Though sometimes it took more main- tenance than John seemed to have time for. New fathers, she had read, often became a little difficult to reach. Finding life harder than they had expected, they brought into play that well-known masculine ability to focus on problems rather than people. On his way into the house John knelt down and had a conversation with his daughter. He said something to her and Anna could see him stroking an imaginary Orlando. Nice cat, nice cat. You see, nice pussy cat. They stroked the absent cat together for a moment. Then Eleanor banged it on the head again. John's bark of a laugh disturbed birds from the cedar. He held out his hand. The little girl appeared to offer him something, which she snatched away at the last minute with a giggle. They played this game until he tried to take it from her anyway, to be warned off with an offended shriek.

Like father like daughter. Eleanor had a passion for objects. Thousands of them had already passed through her fingers (not to say her mouth). Of these, some had occupied her for ten minutes, others a day or two. Her more lasting obsessions had nothing much in common but Eleanor herself. One of her own shoes, a rag book featuring leopards and lions, and an old nail brush had replaced one another in her affections in the space of a month. But the plastic doll's head, with its curiously smoothed-off features and partly bald skull, seemed to have a staying power the others did not. Eleanor roared if you separated her from it at night; she roared if she woke up without it in the morning. It was constantly covered in loving spit. She introduced it to her dinner. She rolled it in the well-drained earth of the Nonesuch flowerbeds. She banged Orlando on the head with it. (None of the other cats would put up with this; indeed, if they could help it, none of the other cats would remain within arm's length of Eleanor for more than thirty seconds.) During the day, if you tried to take it off her, she wept real tears.

'It's time we got firm about that thing,' Anna said.

John laughed. 'Rather you than me,' he told her.

'It really is a bit disgusting, John. Can't we lose it one evening when she's asleep?'

'She'll have forgotten it in a week,' he said lightly.

'It really is a bit disgusting.'

He laughed and turned away.

Anna shaded her eyes. 'Don't be so offhand, John,' she called after him.

He stopped and looked back at her – the deep shade of the cedar made it hard to judge his expression – then walked off, his gait managing to convey the kind of puzzled, slightly hurt impatience men do so well when they want to avoid talking about something. He looked rather like Orlando.

Now why did I say that? Anna asked herself. *I've spoilt a nice afternoon.*

'These days we only ever use each other's names when we're irritable,' she found herself confiding to Francis Baynes an hour or two later; and immediately wondered why. It was the dog collar, perhaps. In some lights it made him appear older, in others so young that the ten years separating them made her feel old enough to be his mother. 'I'm so sorry,' she said immediately. 'It must be boring to be the recipient of people's confidences just because of your job. You must feel as if you have no real existence of your own. Like a postbox.'

'I'd miss it,' he assured her, 'if I couldn't come here and talk.'

Anna didn't really hear this. 'I'm not being disloyal to him, you know,' she said. 'It's just life. Babies. Renovations. No money. All that. He has a hard time of it since Ellie arrived – it's rather knocked the dreamer out of him.'

'Babies?'

'Well. Baby.'

Francis received this with his patient smile. 'I'd like some more tea,' he ventured, 'if there is any.'

'It will be tepid at best,' Anna warned him.

They were sitting in deckchairs on the lawn, a comfortable litter of plates and knives and jars of jam between them on a weathered old folding table. The sun would soon slant down behind the cedar, filling its branches with glimpses of light. Her face mysteriously transfigured, as if in her dreams she had to concentrate very hard on something wonderful, Eleanor was asleep in the buggy. She really could be the most beautiful little child, Anna thought. It was worth everything just to see her there. Instinctively detecting a window of respite, Orlando the cat had returned to curl up on the picnic blanket. He kept one eye open and his left ear twitched at each clink of the milk jug.

11

Francis tried his tea, made a face. 'How are you getting on otherwise?' he asked.

'Oh, as best we can. We live in the two or three rooms we've managed to finish. The rest is a mess.' John thought it was fun, but it was a bit too like camping for Anna, a bit like camping out, or being a student again. She had enjoyed it to start with, as part of the fierce excitement of being with him, but it was going on too long now, with no end in sight, and she had suddenly begun to feel haunted by the old building. Two years ago, John's cousin Stella, maddened with jealousy by John and Anna's relationship, and believing herself to be the reincarnation of one of her own ancestors kept young by cosmetics made from the placental material of cats, had tried to kill them both. They had watched her burn up in the fire that followed. Thinking of this, she said suddenly to Francis, 'It's odd, though, you know; apart from Stella's apartment, which was completely burned out, the effects of the fire seem quite random. A whole floor will have smoke damage, with two rooms somewhere in the middle of it completely untouched. You'd hardly know anything had happened. Don't you think that's strange?'

Francis spread his hands. 'I know nothing about fire,' he said politely.

She recognised his mood. He didn't want to talk about Nonesuch, or Anna's marriage. He wanted to talk about Anna. He wanted her to gossip about her inner life, so that he could gossip about his. To tease him she said, 'The latest problem, apparently, is an

12

argument about authenticity in the Long Corridor. Did you know that in the fifteenth century they used cow dung to bind plaster? John is all for it, of course.'

Francis only smiled.

'I mean, cow dung,' she persisted.

'Just look at those cats,' said Francis, refusing to rise to the bait. 'Aren't they beautiful?'

'Francis, you're so transparent!'

Nevertheless, he was right. They were beautiful. And odd.

After the fire, Nonesuch had become home to a score of cats, many of whom had known no other life than that of the laboratory animal. Exhausted, perhaps, by the effort of escape, the majority of them had fled no further than the grounds of the house, where they avoided human beings and kept a kind of cat parliament in the rhododendrons that flanked the curving drive. You saw them running pell-mell across the moonlit lawns at night. Who knew what they were up to there? You surprised one of them stalking a wood-pigeon in the herb garden in the early morning – it treated you to an unafraid, measuring, somehow ironic look, as if to say 'I know you' and then it was gone.

They were characters and Anna loved them. But without doubt the most notable of the Nonesuch cats were Lydia, a lovely, large, ornamental-looking beast with dense gold fur, who belonged to John Dawe, Lydia's three almost-grown kittens and a long-legged tabby female, which seemed to come and go at will, and which, because of the

13

characteristic crest of fur on its head, Anna called Tufty. Tufty helped with the childcare, while Lydia endlessly groomed herself (or allowed herself to be groomed). Together they made a sort of family and Nonesuch seemed to hold no terrors for them – though you never saw them anywhere near the ruins of the Painted Room or the old hidden courtyard. It was this ensemble that had drawn Francis's attention. They came stalking across the lawn in a line, swinging their heads from side to side like big savannah cats, Lydia at the front and Tufty bringing up the rear. Somehow this didn't look as comical as it might have. The kittens walked with a louche swagger. Their mother's body was long and gleaming in the horizontal light. Orlando blinked with pleasure and got up to greet her. She let him touch noses, but as soon as he tried to rub the side of his head against hers he was cuffed round the ears for his pains. Her stand-offishness was a family joke.

'Poor old Orlando,' Anna said. 'He's taken such beautiful care of those kittens and this is all the thanks she ever gives him. They don't even look like him.'

'Are you sure he's the father?'

Anna, who sometimes wondered the same thing, said with a certain asperity, 'I don't see who else it could be, Francis. Anyway, he loves them and they love him.'

'We haven't seen much of the tabby lately,' he said.

'She's away for days at a time now. I wondered if she had a new interest somewhere in the village. But

14

she always comes back. It's curious, but she still seems closer to Orlando than his wife.'

Francis looked amused at this. 'Is wife quite the right word here, I wonder?'

Just then, Eleanor woke up and began to howl. The cats, including Orlando, melted away as if they had never been. Anna hauled her child out of the buggy, turned it over and sniffed its nappy. The message was clear.

'Oh dear,' said Francis, and looked at his watch. He could be comically uneasy around the baby. 'I think perhaps I'd better go, too.' Having said it, he seemed reluctant to get up.

Anna felt sorry for him. He had not had his talk, and now he would go off and eat baked beans on toast for supper in the kitchen of a vicarage as draughty and unwelcoming as an aeroplane hangar. She suspected she was his only friend in Ashmore. She said impulsively, 'Stay to dinner! Won't you?'

He seemed tempted for a moment, then shook his head. 'I must be off.'

'Well, if you must.'

With the baby tucked firmly under her arm, like someone securing a piglet, she saw him to his Rover.

From the driving seat Francis craned his neck to look into the sky. The air towards Ashmore was full of liquid silvery light, but despite that he shivered suddenly. He wound the window down. 'It will be a cold night,' he said.

Anna waved the Rover down the drive. 'Say goodbye,' she told the baby. 'Wave!'

Eleanor howled.

I can only come at night, Izzie says, away from the eyes that pry. Little walls have big ears, she says, oh yes they listen all the time don't think they don't. So that's when she comes and I go to her then. I'm not to mind the night and I don't so it's busy busy busy looking for her in all the hidden places I know and some of the ones that aren't hidden at all. Busy busy, I'm in the long place or the short one. I'm up, which can be an effort, and down, which can be an adventure. Busy busy busy. I'm out there smelling the smells in the dust. The night is your friend, Izzie is always saying. I ask why but I only get wait and see, wait and see. Izzie says I am going to find out one day who I really am. Then we'll see what happens, she says. We'll see what happens then. (We'll see what happens to her.)

Some hidden places are more difficult to reach than others. They are a long way. They're shadowy and scary. They smell bad too. I say, I can't go here I've honestly tried and tried Izzie I really have but she says, do you want to be a cooked thing in a pot, or be given diseases, so up I go as fast as I can. Izzie says there, you see, you could do it after all, but we don't find anything anyway and she goes away for a long time and won't speak. It will soon be light and I don't know what to do. Izzie? Izzie? It's cold and no answer and I have to find my own way back. Izzie says you stupid thing, listen to me never do that again, then she says well done you are my coddled egg, you are my perfect quince (which I don't know what that is). One day you'll know, she says, my quince, my perfect little shallot. You'll know.

The Long Corridor was plastered, more or less authentically and only a day or two behind schedule. The bank said yes, the work could go on, though they were, they had to admit, a little worried by some of Mr Dawe's figures . . . Eleanor, meanwhile, grizzled. She sucked the doll's head and made flirty eyes at her father. When he wasn't there, which was most of the time, she grew increasingly difficult to manage. Changing a nappy became a nightmare; feeding, always a tussle of wills, left the kitchen looking like a Jackson Pollock. 'Well, don't eat your bloody Moulinexed vegetables then,' said Anna who, seeing her husband only at breakfast and when they fell exhausted into bed at night, had become sexually frustrated and short of temper. The cats got under the feet of the builders and came back covered in plaster dust. The builders traipsed mud and lime and sand along the hall from the big main doors. It was bedlam. Anna rejected it all and on the comforting hotplates of her Aga boiled the kettle to make tea for her friend Alice Meynell, who had come down for the afternoon from Cambridge.

Alice looked around at the dust and disarray. 'I'm impressed,' she stated. Then, 'Come and have a drink at the Green Man.'

Anna looked at the kitchen clock. 'Perhaps not,' she said. 'Ellie will wake up in a moment and I'll have to feed her.'

'Do it at the pub.'

'Alice, I still breastfeed her in the afternoons.'

'Well?'

'Oh, yes,' said Anna. 'Tits out in the Green Man. The Women's Institute will love that.'

'You don't want to take any notice of them,'

advised Alice, who at twenty years old had no need to.

Alice's cropped tops and pierced navel were rarely seen now behind the bar at the Green Man. Cambridge took up her time and for the holidays she had a boyfriend in New York. He was twenty-three, a physicist from the Santa Fe Institute who gambled on Wall Street in his spare time. Her recent affair with Max Wishart, a concert violinist, had ended amicably, both parties feeling rather pleased with themselves. Alice developed a taste for baroque music. Max bought a motorcycle. (Alice promptly exchanged hers for a faster one. When their visits to Nonesuch coincided, which was quite often, they could be heard from miles away, racing one another along the Drychester Road to the dismay of sensible people everywhere.) Neither of them talked about the day they had pulled Anna and John out of the fire, burned and suffering from smoke inhalation – although on the first anniversary of that event Max had brought with him some bottles of Pol Roger and all four of them had lifted their glasses in a solemn, companionable silence. Remembering this – and remembering how the face of the dying Stella Herringe had seemed to swim away from her into madness and smoke, down into the bitter reek of burning varnish, the fatty smell of melted cosmetics and that other smell, which came perhaps from the very fabric of the Herringe identity and could only be described as that of time itself being consumed – Anna thought how good it was to be alive, even though your daughter was sometimes a bit careless with your nipples.

'Anyway,' Alice was saying, 'if you don't like it, get her on to the bottle properly.'

'She won't let me stop.'

'Won't she, now?' Alice bent over Eleanor's carrycot. 'I wouldn't have that,' she said softly. Alice, you sensed, wouldn't have anything she didn't want. Life was too short. 'Not from you, you rum little bugger,' she told the baby. Then she said in amazement, 'Look at those little fingers!' and, 'Hey, I think she smiled at me.'

'No,' said Anna. 'You're wrong there. She only smiles at her father. Later she will marry him and they will live happily together, having first confined me to an attic.'

'That's her plan, is it?'

'Yes. Luckily for me she's a late walker. Actually, I'm a bit worried about that too. She can crawl well enough to make Orlando's life a misery, but however hard we encourage her she doesn't seem to be interested in anything else. All the other village toddlers are, well, toddling. We must be doing something wrong.'

Alice wasn't willing to accept this. 'Kiddies sometimes don't walk until they're two or three,' she said. 'Others are at it as early as eight months. It's the same with talking – the books tell you stuff, but that's only a guideline. My sister's boys were prattling on before they could crawl. It's the TV. God knows when they first said the words "Ryan Giggs".'

'Oh Alice, are you saying she's a late talker too?'

'The last thing you want to do is get competitive about it.'

Anna sighed. 'I'm sure you're right,' she agreed. 'At least she sleeps well. Touch wood, we've got past those awful nights when all she did was scream and scream when we tried to put her down.'

'Sip of whisky cures that.'

'Alice!'

'That's what my old gran used to say.'

'We would never do that nowadays,' said Anna primly. 'Nowadays we give them a spoonful of Calpol instead. That is, if we haven't drunk it ourselves.' And, while Alice was laughing at that, 'Come on, then, if you can put up with my driving we'll go down to the Green Man.'

John had always refused to own a car, but when Eleanor was born and it became plain they couldn't manage without one, he had reluctantly bought an ancient Volvo 244 which they called 'the Tank'. Its paintwork, originally bronze, had weathered to a dull brown colour and it went round corners like a narrowboat; but as he said, it was dependable and you could move building materials in it too. It was amazing the loads you could ask that suspension to take. It was all heart. Anna, conventional enough to doubt that material things had hearts, fetched the shopping home in it twice a week. She used it to take Ellie to the clinic in Drychester. Eleanor gurgled to herself whenever she saw the Tank. She loved it.

'Which is a good thing,' Anna explained to Alice, looking both ways and then both ways again as she inched out of the drive and into Allbright Lane, 'because I don't. I'm happier on my bicycle, really.'

'I can see that,' said Alice. A little later she added, 'Even a Volvo'll go faster than this' and was silent then until they passed the rectory at St Mary's. 'Wasn't that the new vicar?'

'He's been here two years, Alice.'

Alice craned her neck to look back through the rear window. 'I think he wanted you to stop. Weird bloke, but quite fanciable in a way.'

'Is there anyone you don't fancy?'

'I'm not that keen on Ryan Giggs.'

Eleanor chortled and smiled, and waved coyly out of the window at imaginary passers-by.

Francis Baynes had indeed been trying to attract Anna's attention. Something odd had happened to him and he wanted to talk about it –

He had woken early, to one of those still, wet mornings when even the birds are thoughtful and silent. Rain was hissing down quietly on the knapped-flint walls of the rectory garden. Everything seemed to be meditating. From his bedroom window Francis could see the church, a ship anchored on a quiet green swell, graves bobbing peacefully around it like rowing boats. Pausing between the dresser and the bed, he caught sight of a figure beneath the yew. It was Anna Dawe, tidying the little pot of flowers at the foot of Stella Herringe's grave. His heart lifting, he wrestled with the sash window, which had been painted shut by a previous incumbent.

'Anna!' he called.

No reply; and when he looked again he saw it wasn't her. He felt foolish. How had he made such a mistake? The air was soft with rain, but perfectly clear. His eyes were good. Not twenty yards away, the unspeaking figure was caught as if in a photograph: a woman in early middle age, of healthy appearance, taller than she had first seemed, dressed in brown, head tilted alertly to one side. Suddenly she seemed to look straight at him, and this brought him back to himself. He leaned precariously out of the window. 'Can I help you?'

Instead of answering the woman drew herself up and began to walk away along the side of the church, her gait somehow stiff and graceful at the same time. Francis hurried downstairs. The rectory hall, gloomy despite its gloss-white wainscoting, smelled of floor polish and mice. He opened the door; light poured round its edges like a chord played on an organ. By the time he reached the churchyard it was empty. He stared down at Stella Herringe's grave. Something brought that woman here, he thought. She came for some kind of help. Though it had no basis whatsoever, this idea returned to him with different levels of force throughout the morning, filling him with nervous energy, so that when Anna drove past and he failed to catch her attention, he found it hard to go back into the rectory and work on his sermon. Composition, though, is demanding and some time during the long afternoon it wore the edge off his excitement. Towards tea, he thought briefly of calling Anna to ask if some Herringe relative, staying at Nonesuch, had visited the grave that morning. But other things intervened and he forgot.

Night.

Anna Dawe woke up suddenly, convinced that something was wrong with her daughter.

She was unable to do anything about this for a moment. Her limbs didn't seem to be connected to her brain, ideas were slow to transcribe themselves as action and a dull buzzing filled her head. She felt as if her dreams were unfinished. They had been full of rain and high winds, costumes she did not recognise from her waking life, encounters which, unresolved in sleep, now seemed to animate the room she slept in, passing like smoke across the walls and the looming Jacobean furniture. They were ancient dreams. If she went back to sleep they would slip back into her head and begin again.

'Eleanor?' she said eventually. Her own voice seemed gluey and distant. 'Ellie?'

'I'd prefer walnut inlays,' said John. Flinging out one arm, he turned over. 'It's a problem,' he admitted.

'John?'

He chuckled. He was fast asleep.

Anna got up and went to look in the cot, where Eleanor lay awkwardly, body facing one way, head the other. She had kicked off her covers. Her skin was hectic, her breathing stertorous, her hands hot to the touch. Perhaps she had a light infection. She clutched the old doll's head so tightly to her cheek that it had left a faint indent there.

'Hush,' said Anna absently. She removed the top

23

blanket, rearranged the others. After a moment, the child gave a small sigh, moved one hand as if pointing, relaxed.

Anna folded up the blanket. It's too warm in here, she thought. It made all three of us dream. In a room too warm you thought of fire. After the things that had happened to Anna in this house, the idea of fire was never very far away from her, day or night. She looked down at her hands and saw the faint scars in the moonlight. *I healed well*, she thought. *John healed well, too. Considering what we went through, we both healed well.* When she bent over the cot again, the doll's head caught her attention. Bland, pretty features barely broke the rounded symmetry of its face; its counterweighted eyelids opened and closed fractionally with the child's breathing; a few blond nylon hairs still adhered to its pink scalp. It must be forty years old, she thought, I wonder whose it was. She stared at it for some time and then, back in bed, tried to remember when she had last owned a doll of her own. In the effort of this her anxiety ebbed slowly away and with it the memory of her dreams.

The next morning at breakfast she said, 'You know, the weird thing is this: when I first woke up I thought she wasn't there. I thought that when I looked I would find the cot empty.'

She wasn't sure she had his attention. Both of them were exhausted in the mornings, just from the wear and tear of it all. He had drunk three cups of coffee and now he was trying to read the editorial page of the *Guardian*.

'John?'

'What?'

'I said, when I first woke up I was sure she wasn't there.'

He laughed. 'Chance would be a fine thing,' he said. He leaned over to where Eleanor, trapped in her high chair and growing bored with breakfast, had begun to insert chocolate Rice Krispies into her eye. 'Chance would be a fine thing, eh, Ellie?'

Eleanor offered him a smile of monstrous bonhomie, then opened her mouth to let him see its half-chewed contents, by which he dutifully pretended to be appalled. 'Kidgie,' she said.

Anna said, more loudly than she had intended, 'John, you might listen.'

He put down the paper. 'I was listening,' he said. 'It was just a dream. You woke up from a bad dream.'

She stared at him. 'You never used to be so cavalier about people's dreams.'

'That was in the days before I became a proud father. When all my time was spare time.' He laughed. 'Dreams are for single men.' When she didn't rise to this he took her hand. 'Are you all right, Anna?'

'I am when you notice I'm here.'

He looked at her puzzledly. 'All this is for you,' he said. 'It's for us.'

She touched his hand. 'Is it?' she asked. Then, seeing his hurt expression, 'I know it is. I know.'

They stared at one another for a moment, then he said, 'Well, talk cuts no timber. I'd better get back to it.'

Later that day Anna abandoned Eleanor to the less-than-tender care of Alice Meynell and drove into Drychester to see Dr Martha Russell.

'Do you ever dream of past lives?' asked Anna.

It was an old question, she knew. She asked it every time she came here. She felt trapped by its ironies, in this place where the truth could never be admitted. She stared out of the consulting room window into the little brick courtyard below, where a fine grey rain was falling on the minute beds of rosemary and thyme, the tubs of hostas. After the broad, ancient gardens of Nonesuch, this planned, trimmed, achingly new little space looked less like a garden than an architect's diagram of one.

She shivered a little, thinking of the contrast, then went on, 'Do you think that's possible?'

Dr Russell seemed to consider this for a moment. 'In a sense,' she said, 'that's all we ever dream of. Dreams are a way of revisiting a problem, a relationship. An event.' She gave Anna time to respond to this and, when nothing was forthcoming, continued, 'Or else they are about the fear of revisiting it. Dreams really are intimately caught up with past lives: our own.'

This sounded so complacent that Anna didn't know how to reply. She made an irritable movement of one shoulder, as if shrugging off someone's hand: I don't want comfort. 'I didn't mean that.'

'I know,' acknowledged Dr Russell gently.

Martha Russell was a tall, rangy woman, a little older than Anna, who, growing bored with the management of a 'holistic' practice in Fulham, had left London and turned her attention to post-traumatic stress disorder. She had treated Anna for the lingering psychological effects of the fire at Nonesuch; then, because it seemed clear to them both that the two things were connected, for the bout of depression which had followed Ellie's birth. She was unmarried and a compulsive amateur archaeologist. At weekends she could be found in green padded waistcoat and shabby if rather elegant cargo trousers, pottering about between the longbarrows and circles of standing stones that litter the downs above Ashmore, accompanied by her huge dog Otto. The wide-screen TV in her consulting room was often switched on to show silent video footage of local excavations with which she was involved, as if in a metaphor of her profession, which was to bring to the surface the deep archaeology of her patients' lives. She smoked unfiltered American cigarettes, one of which she now lit. 'So how is it,' she asked, 'with John?'

'You're a doctor,' said Anna. 'But you smoke. How can you possibly reconcile those two things? I mean, I don't mind. But –' It was her turn to leave a pause.

' "Reconcile"', said Martha Russell evenly, 'is an interesting word. So how is it going with John?'

The two women laughed at one another. Over the next hour the rain settled in, beading the triple-glazed windows of the consulting room, falling steadily into the courtyard. Smoke rose from the doctor's cigarette. Dim sounds of traffic filtered into the room from Drychester High Street. Anna felt calmed by all this. Once every session, a moment of inner stillness arrived and she felt that Martha Russell was a help after all; although Martha Russell could never understand – could never be told – what had really happened at Nonesuch.

'I want him back,' Anna said. 'The man I met.' She laughed. 'I know how that sounds,' she continued. 'I know people change and move on. And he probably feels like that about me. After the fire, and the death of his cousin who was so important to him, after the baby, after all the different things that have happened to us, we're both different people. But I loved him when he lived on his canal boat and got angry about things no one else understood, and argued with people about dreams over the supper table.' She tried to add something more to this list, but could only think about the smell of him in bed at night, so she finished, 'I wish he were writing his book again. He was overpowering, then, and a bit obsessive. But I loved that about him. I loved his extraordinary energy –' She shrugged. 'Does this make any sense?'

'What are you trying to tell me?' asked Martha Russell gently.

'All he cares about now is his house and his daughter,' Anna whispered. 'And sometimes I'm just bored by him.'

'I think you're angry too.'

'He doesn't trust me. Since the depression I had, he doesn't trust my judgement. He would never admit that, or put it that way. I suspect he doesn't even feel it that way. He's too nice. But essentially he hasn't trusted me since then. We're avoiding all these feelings between us. I get involved with Ellie. He gets involved with the house. There's nothing really wrong. But everything's wrong.'

'And –?'

'I don't know. It undermines my confidence that he doesn't trust me. Before I came to Ashmore I was in money –'

'Such an odd way to put it. Don't you think? "In" money?'

'You know quite well what I mean. I worked for an international bank and I could make five hundred thousand pounds a year in bonuses alone. I'm not boasting about that. It was just a fact of my life. When I met John he was living on someone else's money, on a narrowboat, writing a completely impractical book about dreams.'

'You rather resent that,' said Martha Russell. 'And yet you want him to be the dreamer again, you miss the dreamer he used to be.'

Anna shrugged. 'I didn't say I wasn't complicated,' she said mulishly.

'Neither did I, dear.'

'Anyway, this isn't about that. I spend all day with Ellie – blaming myself for her bad behaviour and feeling like an unnatural mother because he doesn't have these difficulties with her; while he spends all day worrying about the cost of walnut panelling. And at night we're further apart, not closer together.' She contemplated this. 'I won't give up,' she said, as if the doctor had asked her to. 'I love him. I love him from the bottom of my heart, however silly that sounds. I don't give up easily on things. It's too easy to walk away from a relationship these days. People have made it too easy.' Having come close to saying what she meant, but not quite close enough, she looked at her watch. 'Time's up.'

'How convenient.' Martha Russell laughed.

On her way out, Anna paused. 'I've been coming here since the fire,' she said.

Martha Russell nodded.

'Once a week. At first John had to drive me, even though his hands were burned worse than mine. But now I drive myself.' She stared at the doctor, as if that had been a question. When no answer came, she added, 'You saw me through the post-natal depression. I got over that too. I'm strong. I've always been in charge of my own life.'

'What, then?' enquired Martha Russell eventually.

'I feel as if I'm well again. When can I stop coming?'

Martha Russell smiled. 'You'll stop coming when you want to.'

Before she returned to Nonesuch, Anna decided to shop. Afterwards, in the Waitrose car park, beneath a lowering sky, she found Francis Baynes cramming carrier bags into the back of his Rover. The light was the colour of sulphur; large, isolated raindrops spotted the tarmac. People were running to their cars and slamming the doors.

Francis had bought cans of ravioli; cheap toilet rolls in numbers. 'I have to make economies,' he explained when he saw her expression. 'In fact, I shouldn't even be shopping here.'

'I promise I won't tell.'

They stood there looking at one another for a moment. Francis asked, 'So how's life?'

'Oh, I hate my life at the moment.'

'I don't think you do,' he said. He glanced at his watch, then at the sky. 'Come and have tea somewhere.'

'You mustn't let me take up your time –'

'Think of it as a pastoral visit.'

They found seats in one of the Shambles cafés. As soon as she had ordered, Anna said, 'I wouldn't mind if only John seemed a bit more –' She couldn't think what. 'Oh, I don't know. Connected.' She had always hated women whose troubles came out easily, over meals with people they hardly knew. It was a kind of emotional promiscuity. Nevertheless she went on, 'A house is for living in, not running away into.'

Francis stirred his tea. 'Is that what you think he's doing?'

'Yes, I do.'

'The baby's tiring you both,' he pointed out. 'On top of that, John has money worries.'

'I have them too,' protested Anna.

'Of course. But we are trying to see his side of it here.'

She laughed despite herself. 'Francis, your profession is showing.'

He gave her an interested look. 'Do you think it is?'

'Don't be disingenuous.' She refilled his cup.

There was a brief silence, then he asked, 'Do you get much help from the Herringes?'

'God no,' said Anna. 'It's John's house now – it came to him through Stella – and so it's down to us to find the finance. In fact, when he went to his trust fund for help, they advised him to sell. The Herringe money's all gone offshore and the big family players with it. They're more interested in the NASDAQ Index than their own history. They described the house as an "asset".'

'It must have been insured.'

'The insurers will only go so far. And it's a listed building. That means no one could complain if we let it fall to bits – but once we decide to restore it, everything has to be done properly. There are grants, of course, but –' To make ends meet, Anna had sold her cottage in Ashmore; and though there hadn't seemed much point in getting rid of John's narrowboat – it wouldn't fetch enough to be useful – she knew the *Magpie* would go in the end. For some reason this thought made her even more despondent. 'We depend rather a lot on the bank,' she admitted. 'If John would let me work –' She shrugged.

Francis swilled the dregs of his tea round his cup and examined them with the care of a fortune-teller. He looked up. 'So you don't see any Herringes at Nonesuch?'

'Once in a blue moon,' she said. 'I think there was one down here at Christmas. John had to sign something and they always make a production of that.'

'"A blue moon",' mused Francis. 'I sometimes wonder about the English language.' He looked at his watch. 'Oh dear. Now I really should be somewhere else. Come and talk to me whenever you need to.'

'I will, Francis.'

'Promise?'

She smiled up at him gratefully. 'I promise.'

Busy, busy, busy. Long and short places wide and narrow places, places up and places down. Some places are colder than others but Izzie says we have to be busy about them anyway. Up and down dark and light dark and darker. Looking looking looking. Izzie said you may not like the dark but you surely like the places and she called me her little squirmer. I said nothing.

Soon I arrived at a place. The riddle of it is this, it is quite easy to get to though it is very hard to find. Izzie says some places are realer than others. She laughs and says, You could be forgiven for not knowing which is which. One day, she says, I will know everything again.

Chapter Two

'WAKE UP!'

A sharp dig in the ribs made me catch my breath. 'Wake up, Orlando!'

I opened one bleary eye. Sunlight fell into it, as sharp as an unexpected twig. I blinked the haze away and squinted. There sat Lydia, pursing her mouth. This I could tell not because I could see the detail of her expression – she sat with the light behind her so that it made a golden glow of her fur: an attitude adopted out of both vanity and sun worship but by the disapproving set of her head. It was an expression that had become habitual whenever she regarded me. Time had not improved our relationship. 'What?' I muttered, my eyes closing again.

'You're moaning in your sleep,' she said crossly. 'I wish you'd stop it. Moaning and striking out with your paws. It's really quite infuriating.'

I struggled for consciousness; failed. It was like falling down a dark rabbit hole, this sudden jolt back into the dream. A pair of feet – as neat and white as any rabbit's – fled before me again, darting around corners, disappearing down impossible perspectives, until I was left only with the impression of a shock of tabby fur above the white; a sharp tang of female scent. The scent was that of an intact queen, her mark as familiar as my own and yet as strange as a bird's. My feet twitched in their phantom pursuit and I opened my mouth to call after her –

Another dig, this time, painfully, in the kidneys; a hiss, 'You're doing it again!'

I woke up properly this time, heart thumping, though it was hard to tell why. A sensation of despair hung over me, like a small and personal cloud. Something was lost, something very dear –

'Honestly, Orlando, you're worse than the children. How in the world am I supposed to catch up on my beauty sleep with you tossing and turning and groaning away like that? It's so incredibly selfish of you.'

And before I could even think to retort – for it had been I who had taken her three little darlings bird hunting that morning till my feet were sore; I who had admonished them for making too much noise while their mother dozed in the marjoram; I who had played with them till they were so exhausted they had fallen in a heap – she had turned her back on me, shifting unceremoniously backwards with one of those exquisite golden haunches until she had pushed me entirely out of the pool of sunlight we had until that moment shared, leaving me swallowed by cold shadow.

Within moments she was unconscious and snoring.

I lay there, but try as I might, sleep evaded me. Perhaps it was the chill in the air, or the stertorous drone of Lydia's breathing that prevented me; or perhaps it was my unwillingness to give myself back to the dream. I had been experiencing this same flicker of images, this by-play of events and sensations, in subtly different guises, for the past several days and nights, and whenever I awoke it was to anxiety and a hollow and unfocused dread. It was the sort of sleep that leaves you feeling less rested than when you laid your head down in the first place, so I was not unhappy to abandon my attempt.

I sat up and stretched, and considered Lydia's snoring form. She was still beautiful, I thought with a certain detachment, despite the kittens, despite her recent obsession with food of all kinds and the consequences of that greed. I noted the way the dark ticking of that golden fur added definition to the smooth muscles, the long flanks, the elegantly coiled tail; though her beauty no longer had the power to make me catch my breath or stumble over my speech; no longer sent me howling, hot-eyed and furious, into the rhododendrons from yet another slight or rebuttal. The sharp peaks and deep valleys of my grand passion had been worn away into some vast and limitless plain, eroded down and spun away as fine dust under the climate of her selfishness. But here I was, still at the manor house with her and the girls, and I did not altogether know why.

After all – as my friend Millefleur constantly

reminded me – the kittens were not even mine. Whose they were was the subject of much conjecture. I had more cause than most to hazard a guess at how they might have been conceived, but because Lydia, in her usual superior manner, refused outright to discuss the matter, she had earned the enmity of the local gossips. 'She always was a proper little madam,' they would say, reminding each other of her flirtations with those erstwhile jack-the-lads who used to hang out on the canal banks on sultry summer nights and were now solid young cats, just beginning to spread around the midriff, with convoluted family ties and several families of their own.

'Not what you'd call choosy . . .'

'If she'd take one, she'd take all.'

'A complete tart, if you ask me.'

Which reminded me of something Millie had once said; though during the intervening two years I had never seen her treat Lydia with anything but friendship and compassion. Even so, she kept on nagging at me to leave.

'Have a break, Orlando. Take to the wild roads,' she would advise me, the little tuft of fur on her head that was so like a jay's crest bobbing with her impatience. 'Leave Miss High-and-Mighty to get on with it for a while. Come with me. I've found this extraordinary rocky little dell that runs down to the sea, full of lily of the valley and sweet briar. In the summer it's so warm that the air steams around you; and in the winter the stream freezes over so you can stand right above the fishes and watch them swim beneath your feet. There are voles as big as rats there, and rats as big as kittens. Come and chase them with me!'

But I would shake my head sadly and watch her bound across the lawns, to disappear with a flick of the tail into the animal highway that ran down by the old yew hedge. One minute she was there, the white patches of her fur contrasting sharply against the dense, dark foliage, with her head turned slightly towards me – the greatest concession she would make to bidding me farewell – the next she was gone; vanished from sight as if she had winked suddenly out of existence. Which, to all practical purposes, she had: for to travel the wild roads is to travel in dimensions other than those that are obvious to the eye.

. I do not think it was even Lydia that kept me at Nonesuch. Yet neither was it the big house – with its gaping rooms and the disturbing smell of the old fire – or its grounds, which were infested by the cats that had existed here all their sad lives, both breathing and dead. Nor yet was it because of Nonesuch's human occupants, though Anna had fed and sheltered me since my first days and I felt nothing but fondness for her. I liked the dark man with the careful hands, who had for years been Lydia's feeder; and even the child intrigued me as much as it annoyed me, clutching at my tail with those hot, sticky paws babies have, or cheerfully banging me on the head with its toys. No; there was something else that kept me from charging blithely into the nearest highway and barrelling off to the sunlit coast or the heart of some distant, dappled wood: something that had caught me as firmly in its toils as any spider catches prey in its web. There was a mystery here that haunted my dreams and plagued the edges of my waking thoughts, and I knew that until I had hunted it down and caught it wriggling by the neck, I could not rest.

Lydia made a grumbling sound and twisted up against me. She had started to dream. I could tell this not only by the way her nose was twitching, but because I could *see* the substance of her dream appear in the form of a pale golden ball in the air above her head. There it rose, trembling as if shy of the world, and in its centre the matter of her dream twisted and pulsed, like frogspawn in its translucent gel.

I leaned forward and gazed into the globe. Of all creatures, only cats have the ability to see another's dream; of cats, only a dreamcatcher and then only through a trick of birth. My grandfather had been a dreamcatcher, and his before him, and so it went, always skipping a generation. Old Hawkweed; Granfer. Strange how I missed him, when for so long he had been my bane . . .

Lydia's dream hung there, a paw-span or two above her head, for a few moments – offering me the prospect of a cat's pink tongue licking ice cream off a carton lid; then jaws crunching down on a virulent-looking orange snack dropped by a child's hand and finally a golden muzzle pressed down firmly into a bowl of 'seafood delight': Liddy's favourite tinned treat.

And then it popped, just like a soap bubble. Liddy's dreams were always like this – hazy and fragile – as if her inner life had no more faith in itself than to focus on where the next meal was coming from.

I smiled. For all her complexity and fractiousness, she was blessed with the simplest of dreams. I sometimes wondered – or perhaps consoled myself with the thought – whether it was because she knew I could see into the very heart of her world that she was so awkward with me.

Unlike the kittens. They were fascinated by my gift.

'What was I dreaming about, Uncle O?'

'Could you see me?'

'Did I fly?'

The questions were constant.

In the early days, when they were no more than a few weeks old, I would often amuse myself by sitting over them as they lay in their affectionately tangled heap and watch their dreams forming. At first they had been vague and broken: inchoate images of teats and noses, toes and tails; barely recognisable versions of the world of which they were trying to make sense. Tall dark shapes with waving arms: trees, or humans? Flickers of light before a dark background – the swift passage of bird, bee or butterfly? Something huge and fuzzy that could have been anything from a cat's head seen up close to a person's looming hand. Now, though, their dreams were the usual dreams of young cats: as boisterous in sleep as they were when

awake; chasing
siastically (they wer
all) some ghost meal
gathering in the whiskers

They always cheered me
life. They ate it all up.

Abandoning Lydia, I trotted o
in search of their hiding place.

I found them some minutes later, tucke
the roots of the big cedar where I had on
the dream that had interrupted my one an
night of sexual congress with their lovely mo
They were all curled together as was the
preference, in an endearing jumble of furry limbs.

That fur! I could never quite get used to it. I had
seen nothing like it on any cat in the village. It was a
short, dense blue-grey – the colour of an August
thundercloud, or the wing of an elderly nuthatch. It
was regal and striking, and as far from their
mother's showy gold as you could possibly get.
Liddy, in a moment of unusual amity, had once told
me a little about her parents, no doubt to establish
her social superiority over my own questionable
origins. Her mother, Nefertiti, Flower of Egypt II,
had been a pedigree Abyssinian who had won
prizes at cat shows up and down the country; her
father, Coromandel Ozymandias, a seal-point
Siamese. It was from these two that she had
inherited her mystique and fabulously exotic
colouring, she had informed me, with no apparent
sense of irony. And a golden-furred mother and a

These
s; not
three
them
their
d and
their
had
had
bella
erina
reat
med

and tussling; eating so enthu-
e their mother's daughters, after
hat you could see the saliva
on their chins.
up, the girls. They loved
across the garden
d in among
e chased
d only
her.
ir

...beside them and curled my tail comfortably around my feet. It was hard to tell them apart, when they lay all tangled up like this. Cat had an odd little bony lump on either side of her head just below her ears, as if she had decided to grow horns there and then given up on the project, and Letty a pale star in the middle of her forehead, as if someone had deliberately set about decorating her; but all three of them had their heads turned away under their paws, so there was no sign of these markings. Belle's fur, in certain lights, was a shade darker than her sisters' and she had one white foot – but how to tell whose foot was whose in this great heap?

Even their dreams were hard to distinguish.

A welter of tiny golden globes were even now

bobbling around above the three of them, bumping into the serrated bark of the tree, blundering into one another and bursting in tiny little explosions of air that only I could hear. Like their mother's, their dreams were pale and shimmering, lacking the hot, fiery edge that denoted a dream that might do damage, and even on closer inspection they yielded up little further detail that might help me tell them apart. Even the subject of their dreams tended to similarity – blue paws, blue-grey muzzles, blue tails – for if the girls did not dream of themselves, they dreamed of their sisters, almost to the exclusion of anything else. Peering closer, I could make out a chase going on in one globe; a tussle with a length of pink wool, which I recognised as part of an unravelling garment that someone had brought for the child Ellie only last week, and which Letty and Cat had stolen. In another globe a small brown bird skipped and fluttered, darting here and there to avoid a questing blue paw. The first one drifted away, only to be replaced by another offering a glimpse of milk in a bowl, bubbles rising where the greedy dreamer had immersed her face in it.

Another globe had been obscured behind its fellows all this while, but now, as one of the kittens – a glimpse of that little fawn star identifying her as Letty – stirred and yawned, her dream popped out of existence, leaving the other open to my view. And as if revelling in its sudden exposure, it swelled a little and glowed brighter, revealing a dark orange corona that flared along its circumference. I leaned in closer. No grey-blue fur here, but a kaleidoscope of colours, all as sharp and vivid as those that showed themselves on the big black metal box that John and Anna would sometimes sit in front of in the evenings, the one that made voices and animal speech and birdsong, even though it gave out no scent of other life.

I squinted, then drew back, alarmed. The dull glint of a cage had caught my eye, the bars gone from silver to a brutal grey, where years of anxious faces and paws pressing against the metal had worn away its sheen.

No cat likes a cage, even in another's dream – and I had seen such cages before. I dreamed of them still, on those bad nights, especially in the middle of winter, when the aches came upon me and I smelled again the char of wood; the singe of fur. Fascinated and horrified in equal part, I watched as a hand came towards the bars. I saw how its long pale fingers with their oddly shiny nails – opalescent pink and white-tipped – made complicated motions with the device that controlled the door of the cage; saw how the latch at last sprang open and the hands came in, fingers spread like an owl's talons when it stoops for a mouse, ready to grasp and to carry away. I saw how the hands came towards *me*. Unable to help myself, I shied away.

The view changed. Now I was confronted by a human face, far too close for comfort. It was hard to gather detail from that blurred impression, but what I could glean made the cold trickle through me as if I had swallowed an icicle. I knew those green, green eyes, the way the hands felt, tight and uncompassionate about my ribs, as if a bruise or two would do no harm; for it was not me she wanted . . .

I struggled.

The face went away, to be replaced by those white hands coming at me with black webbing trailing between the fingers; and this image was superseded by a sense of struggle, of force employed, of constriction, and then I was looking down at my own paw, stretched out tight and flat against a white surface, mesmerised by how the black strap cut into the grain of my golden fur –

'Uncle O!'

My head shot up.

'Uncle O – you were spying on our dreams again!'

Suddenly they were all awake and the tangle of limbs had resolved itself into three handsome young female cats, all trace of kittenhood gone from those lithe blue-grey bodies, mocking black lips and alluring orange eyes. I shook my skull to dislodge the image.

Letitia, forehead and star all ruffled and spiky from being squashed up against her siblings, came over and butted at me affectionately. She sniffed. 'What's the matter, Uncle Orlando?' she said softly, regarding me with her head on one side. 'You smell afraid.'

I blinked. 'Nothing,' I lied smoothly, though I was taken aback by her perspicacity and by the fact that somehow, *somehow*, one of the girls appeared to have the ability to channel her mother's nightmares. But two years of hiding my true feelings from Lydia had not gone to waste.

'Nothing at all.'

I said no more about the dream at the time; there seemed no use in it. It had rattled me, certainly, that sense of capture, of defeat, of incipient horror, especially coming out of the blue as it had and from a youngster whose life till now had been marked by no greater tragedy than the temporary loss of a catnip mouse. Besides, there was no way of telling – from their demeanour, at least – which of the girls the dream belonged to; they were all as blithe as ever, apparently untouched by the shadows it had cast in my mind, and I had no wish to alarm them.

Or make them think you stranger than they already do, a small voice reminded me. Uncle Orlando, doing his weird thing again. Foolish as it may seem, I cared about how the girls perceived me, preferring to appear to them solid and genial and trustworthy, as opposed to disturbed and tetchy and somehow adrift from the world, and this also had some bearing on my decision to let the matter lie. But over the days that followed I found myself returning again and again to those dark images as to the itch of an old wound that can be relieved by a swift rasp of the tongue, a scratch with the claws. The sight of those eyes had left me anxious and jumpy in a way I had not been since the weeks immediately following the fire.

A few days later I decided to go and visit the Besom in an attempt to understand why such dire images were haunting me again and, I hoped, to put them to rest at last.

*

46

I owed Millefleur for my recent acquaintance with the Besom. She was an odd old soul who lived a couple of miles out of Ashmore village, but she was the best listener and the wisest cat I ever met. Millie had run into her on one of her many journeys away from Nonesuch and had returned one evening about a year or more ago, brimming over with enthusiasm for her new friend, saying that at last she'd found a cat who knew about the world and its ways, and that I should go straight away to see her and 'get my head sorted out'. Of course, that had just served to make me bristle.

'She'll be another of those poisonous old gossips,' I had retorted to Millie's suggestion. I was still stinging from the rumours about Lydia's pregnancy. 'Another old biddy with time on her paws and nothing better to do than spin tall tales.'

But Millefleur had been insistent. 'You need someone to talk to. Lydia's hopeless in her state, I'm obviously not good enough for you' – she shot me a direct look that made me wince – 'so why not unburden yourself to a wise old cat who's seen it all? You can't just sit here and mope; it's not healthy.'

Which was easy for her to say, I thought bitterly; she hadn't seen what was in the witch's secret room, hadn't witnessed her nearest relatives coming to grief right in front of her eyes, helpless to do anything to save them; and since she wasn't a dream-catcher, she hadn't been able to see the dream that had done such violent damage to Ashmore and its inhabitants, a dream that could distort place and time, a dream that had the power to wrap you about

47

with fiery tentacles in which you were sure you could spy human hair, human eyes, human teeth . . . There was only one other cat in the world with whom I could have shared the cold shivers of my daytime reveries, the sudden clutch of terror in the middle of the night, the awful surreal flashes of memory – and that was my grandfather, dead, long dead.

And that, paradoxically, had been what had persuaded me in the end.

'You'll like her,' Millie had persisted in her characteristically blunt and determined fashion. Like a digging mole, Millie went straight through obstacles as though they deserved to occupy no space in her world, attacking them with a mindless energy that could leave you mentally bludgeoned and as weak as a worm in her wake. 'She knew old Hawkweed. Rather well, I'd guess.'

So I had been persuaded out of the grounds of the old house for the first time in several months. During that time I had rather neglected my duties as the local dreamcatcher, but to no obvious ill effect in the world. I think it was partly a reluctance to use the wild roads that had held me back; the thought of venturing once more into regions that could play such tricks on you, could foster monsters and turn your sense of direction, your entire understanding of local geography, inside-out and upside-down, had been my greatest anxiety of all, and so that first time Millefleur had walked with me we had taken the human highways of Ashmore out to the isolated cottage where the Besom made her home.

Even such a simple journey – plodding one foot before another down the long miles of sun-warmed road – was hard enough. Everywhere we went we were assailed by scents and sights that would signal to anyone else that daily life was continuing as normal, but to me they were powerfully unwanted reminders of the very nightmares I was seeking to dispel. The simplest of smells – the burned oil from the rumbling vehicles that passed us; the scent of a gardener's bonfire, all wood smoke and licking flame – transported me back to the fire at Nonesuch, making me tremble and slink into the long grass at the roadside, my joints weak and my head buzzing.

When we passed the cottage I had lived in since my earliest days, I remembered clearly how Dellifer, our nurse, would lie – a great, thin bolster of a cat – stretched out along the windowsill of the bedroom at the front of the house, just where the afternoon sun struck through the tendrils of clematis and climbing rose; but just as that peaceful scene was establishing itself before my eyes, it was abruptly displaced by the sight of her body – just as long and limp as if she were in repose – stretched out across the road where the witch's car had struck her, a single line of bloody mucus dribbling from her nose. That was not precisely the last I had seen of old Dellifer; but that final image I kept firmly pushed away into the back of my head.

Two people were out in the front garden of the cottage as Millie and I walked by on the other side of the road. They took no notice of us, caught up as they were in their task: they just kept shouting to one another and laughing, and as they did so, another plant would go flying through the air to join the heap of debris they were collecting there upon the brick path. I saw the rambling mint that had run riot through the cranesbill and giant daisies and had even tried to get involved with the hawthorn hedge, defeated at last, in a wilting pile by their car, a gleaming silver object with no roof. Trays of brightly coloured pansies and begonias were arrayed on its back seat and balanced precariously on its bonnet. The overgrown rosemary bush lay on its side next to the car, the earth already drying on its disinterred roots. Even from the opposite side of the road I could smell that hot, aromatic odour, the scent of summer and roasting lamb; we always knew when Anna came out to pick a sprig that we would be in for a treat of titbits that evening . . .

Then they started rooting up the leggy old lavenders that Anna had tended with such care, among which my sister Vita and I had played, chasing one another neatly in and out of the woody stems until we were overcome by the heady aroma of the herbs and fell asleep together in the same tangle of paws I so loved to see in Liddy's girls . . .

I had felt my heart leap painfully and hurried on.

The pond – an almost opaque green in the strong light – was as tranquil as you could imagine. Half a dozen ducks promenaded serenely around the fringes, each on separate trajectories that seemed designed specifically to avoid crossing another's path, as if some tacit agreement had been made that afternoon not to squabble or break the peace in any way. The willows swept down to the water like living curtains: between them, a heron had watched us pass with its cold yellow gaze.

Despite the beauty of the scene I had not lingered. My last sight of the Ashmore pond would remain indelibly etched on my memory: the perfect white of the frozen surface marred by the crazed hole through which Hawkweed, my granfer, had vanished; the sight of the clawmarks on its circumference where he had tried to drag himself up again; the glow of his single orange-gold eye staring up at me from beneath the murky water. I remember shivering, for all the late summer sun.

By the time we reached the Besom's cottage I had felt as shaky as a new-born foal, but Millie had no patience where others' infirmities were concerned. 'Don't lag, Orlando,' she'd chided. 'I haven't got all day, even if you have.' She'd become quite abrupt with me since the night and day of those traumatic events, as if she had deliberately grown a hard and brittle skin over her heart to ward off any trace of the affection she had felt for me; but sometimes I could catch her out of the corner of my eye watching me, her face all soft and yearning. If I could only have loved Millefleur life would have been good to us both. But, for all the stupidity of it, I was still in Liddy's thrall.

We had wormed our way through the prickly holly hedge and there, crouched in a pool of shadow, watching lines of ants crossing the broken flagstones, had been the old cat. I had been disappointed by her at first, with her bony head and dusty coat. I'd been expecting someone more impressive: a big cat, perhaps, or one gifted with great charisma. But the Besom was small and neat-looking, a little sunken at the haunches and cheeks, and her eyes were glazed with age.

'Orlando, this is Ma Tregenna,' purred Millie. The two of them had exchanged brief cheek rubs, then Millie promptly left, casting a sharp glance over her shoulder at me. I knew that look. It said as plainly as speech: 'Put away your disbelief and behave politely.' It was a look as chiding as any you'd give a kitten.

The old cat had greeted me politely, explaining that I should follow her round to the back garden, which was quieter. She had warned me not to tread on the ants. 'There's rain coming,' she'd said cryptically. When she spoke, a soft, rasping cough punctuated her words, as if she had fur caught in her throat.

The little garden behind the cottage was a haven for cats, overgrown as it was with briars and ferns. I loved it at first sight. It was all I wanted from a garden, it defined the very idea for me. Bees rumbled lazily from rose to rose and hoverflies hung almost silent in the air above us, before whizzing away at high speed to suspend themselves a few feet away, as if eavesdropping on our conversation. Suddenly I found I could talk, and talk I did, all that afternoon.

She had hardly uttered a word until I finished, other than to encourage me to continue, or to clarify a point in the story; and at last all she said was, 'Have a sleep now, Orlando. Feel your eyes closing, and have a proper old snooze.' And I had suddenly found myself exhausted, as if all the time I had been with her I had been fighting back a weariness that went even beyond my bones, and had fallen into a long, deep sleep.

As I slept, I had dreamed. I know this, for she told me so. She had sat there beside me, amid the brambles and briars, as the sun dipped over the distant downs, and watched my dreams forming. And when I woke, she told me what she had observed.

For the Besom was a dreamcatcher, too.

I had not until then realised that a female cat could be a dreamcatcher. It had shocked me to think of a young queen out on the highways, chasing down and ripping apart the evil dreams of humankind, putting herself in the way of danger and discomfort – for such had always seemed to me a measure of masculine prowess and pride, the thing that set me apart from my fellows and gave me a private pleasure when they boasted of their own tame experiences of the wild roads. It was yet another failing of my own imagination, I suppose, but I was learning all the time.

Old Ma Tregenna (a title she preferred to Millie's rather less respectful name for her) was to prove a fine, if eccentric, teacher. She had not, like my grandfather, ranged far and wide via the vast network of wild roads, chasing dreams, fornicating and fighting across the country. No, she had lived and worked on the edge of Ashmore all her life – or should I say, all her lives? – accumulating wisdom and observing the world in her quiet, thorough, unsensational way. She had never settled with a mate in this life, at least, though when she spoke of my grandfather it was with a wistful nostalgia and a certain gleam in the eye; nor had she had kittens of her own, as a result of some cruel trick of nature, though she admitted to having fostered a dozen or more of those abandoned by their mothers in harder times, and I suppose I sought her out in place of my own lost mother. In the months in which I had sloped off from Nonesuch to talk to her, my own dreams had become less troubled and I had found in me the strength of purpose to return to the wild roads of Ashmore as its dreamcatcher. I had thought of my world returning to its natural shape, my life resuming a rhythm of peace and domesticity, punctuated only by my night-time duties.

But the image of the witch's green eyes and her strong white hands flickered before my vision even as I lay dozing on the lawn, as I ate from my bowl, as I watched the girls play, and I knew that if I could not dispel it I would go quite mad.

I found the Besom curled up at the foot of a quickthorn, one ear to the ground, apparently fast asleep. However, even before I could address her she said, 'Get on over here, Orlando. En't no need to tiptoe.' And her pouchy old eyes were suddenly fixed on me with the acuity of a hunting cat.

She was always doing this sort of thing. It no longer phased me, though at the beginning I had found it most disconcerting.

'I need your advice.'

'A dream?' she asked, head cocked, interested now.

I did not bother to ask her how she knew. So I told her what I had witnessed – the cages, the poor, desperate cats awaiting their turn in that cold white room; the straps and the table. I finished simply with, 'What I don't know is whether it came from the girls, or if it was always in my own head; whether it's something or nothing; a memory or something I made up.' I took a breath. 'What I don't know, and have got to find out, is whether it's just an echo of old horrors, or an omen of some kind.'

The Besom said nothing for some moments. Then she gathered herself into a sitting position, her spine as straight as a foxglove's, her paws ranged together as neatly as the disposition of her thoughts.

'Cats, as a species, are a mite superstitious,' she stated calmly.

I stared at her, disappointed, again. Clearly, she thought me a fool to disparage my fears so casually. 'Oh,' I said dully. 'Yes, I suppose we are.'

She laughed: a rusty hinge of a sound. 'For good reason. For cats, things en't simply what they seem. Just think – all them lives, time after time after time, and whenever we come back, back come shades of all them old lives – shadows of old events, old fears, all formless and detached from what caused them in the first place. It can make us nervy about the littlest things, things them with no imagination – dogs, say, or sheep – wouldn't hardly even notice. To those who look only as far as their nose a toad is just a toad; the shriek of an owl is only a mating cry and the sight of a magpie mantling over a maggoty old rabbit en't no more than a bird with its meal. But when you've lived a few lives and carried them images with you time out of time, you got a bit of a tendency to make connections quicker than others; you're going to sense danger where others just keep drifting thoughtlessly into its path.

'Something has started this dream off: something from now, however innocent it might seem. What you seen was not your own dream. And it wuzn't just an old echo. You say you thought it might be one of the kittens?'

I nodded.

A silence fell between us, during which the white membrane over the Besom's old eyes shuttled back and forth at an alarming rate. At last she said, 'I knew a blue cat, once.'

I frowned. 'Oh, yes?'

'Oh, yes. He wuz right handsome, he wuz, a really gracious old chap, even if he was a foreigner of some sort; had a fine set to his head, he did, and these amazing eyes – colour of a bee's belly, as I recall – all soft and hazy gold.' A little pink tongue flicked out over her black lips. 'He had an odd way of talking, but he wuz very refined; had a son taken on as the dreamcatcher in Drychester after old Figgis passed over and his grandson fell dead of the flu. Can't quite remember the lad's name now: must be gone fifty seasons or more . . .' Her brow furrowed; then she shook her head. 'Ah well, it'll come back to me, most likely at an inconvenient time. He'd made his escape from some posh pedigree breeding place, determined to catch all those dreams he kept seeing, and the others thinking him off his head; but it wuz *his* grandson was the curiosity. There was some scandal attached to *that* one: they kept it hushed up, they did, never spoke much of him, said he'd "gone away" somewhere. But I knew better.'

She leaned forward. The sun beat down on us. In the distance I could hear a blackbird shouting threatening insults at an intruder. I stifled a yawn. Was it always the province of old folk to reminisce like this?

'Witch's familiar, it wuz whispered, he became.'

My head shot up. 'What?'

She gave me her gap-toothed grin. 'He wuz blue, too; ran in the family; finest of bloodlines, for those who care about such stuff and nonsense. You said the mother wuz golden-furred, did you not?'

I nodded.

'And the girls –?'

'Blue-grey; definitely blue.'

'Ah. Does Lydia ever speak of her trials?'

'No.'

'And you've never seen her dream of such things?'

'Never. All she seems to dream about is her own comfort.'

The old cat gave a twitch of the shoulders; more a tic than a shrug. 'Can you blame her, Orlando? Do you blame her for that?'

I supposed I did: for she never dreamed of me. To deflect this line of questioning I said, 'But why should one of the girls dream Liddy's dream?'

Ma Tregenna patted my paw. 'The bond between mother and daughter always lies deep, lad; deeper than love, some say deeper than thought.'

'But why now?' I persisted. 'What has caused this dream? They all seem so contented . . .'

'Something must've changed,' the Besom mused. She considered this statement for a moment, then added, 'I don't suppose any of them has eaten the weed, have they?'

It was a little yellow plant she meant by 'the weed': simple mouse-ear hawkweed that grew in the wild places of the world and carried the Great Cat's own message to those chosen as her dream-catchers. But I hadn't seen any of the scruffy hawkweed plant growing in the lush and artificial grounds of Nonesuch. I shook my head slowly. 'No, no, I don't think so.'

'Then think, Orlando; something must have happened to draw this dream out into your sight. Think what changes there may have been.'

I thought. I racked my memory. The builders were in at Nonesuch – robust-looking men in dusty overalls who carried heavy things around between them and talked a lot. They had clumped about the house in their big boots, while John followed them with his notepad and pen, but they had done very little in the way of work yet. The only real impact they'd had, as far as I was concerned, was the welcome change in diet they brought with them: I particularly enjoyed the foreman's tuna sandwiches. But their comings and goings had caused no great anxiety and I could not believe that their cheerful presence could have triggered a dream of old horror.

'I'm sorry,' I said at last. 'I can't think of anything.'

The Besom looked deflated. 'Ah well,' she said. 'Keep your eyes open. Come and see me again if one of the girlies has another dream.'

'I will.'

'And bring me some more of that feverfew next time.'

I'd had a bit of this herb caught in my fur a couple of weeks ago, and Ma Tregenna had plucked it off and chewed it up with remarkable alacrity for such an aged cat, claiming that it was good for 'her ticker'.

I turned to leave. It had been little Ellie who had stuck the feverfew on me; that and a bit of goose-grass for good measure; and since that hadn't seemed to affect me too greatly, she'd lately taken to belabouring me with a horrible old doll's head she'd found somewhere in the house. It smelled old and mildewed, though there was no sign of actual mould on it, and I had taken an entirely dispro-portionate hatred to it. (Though if you have a small child hitting you with its favourite toy, you, too, would most likely find it abhorrent.) She must have sensed this, for she kept the thing with her all the time and whenever I was near, would grin from ear to ear and start to chatter at me, eyes open so wide it was almost as if she thought she could communicate with me by the sheer force of her tiny will, before bashing it at me with all the strength she could muster.

'Tell me,' the Besom said suddenly, breaking into my reverie. 'Are the inhabitants of your house sleeping well?'

I considered this for perhaps a second. 'No,' I said thoughtfully. 'No, they're not. Just recently they haven't been sleeping well at all.'

Chapter Three

THE WORK CONTINUED. They took up the floor of the Great Chamber. Part of the east wall was ripped out and rolled steel joists inserted temporarily to support its sagging Dutch gables. Everywhere you went you bumped into builders drinking cups of tea, or experts arguing over how to replace the sixteenth-century *glace bombée* in the Long Gallery. The cats, growing used to this, became involved. They poked their noses into buckets of plaster – which the builders called 'gobbo' – and, venturing halfway up ladders, got stuck and had to be encouraged down with promises of tuna mayonnaise. John's preoccupation with the works reached new heights. Eleanor, out of sorts, shrieked all day and refused to be bathed except by her father. Feeding her had become a grim war of nerves, fought out three or four times a day from entrenched positions in the kitchen. Anna tried everything. Eleanor rejected it.

'John,' said Anna one morning, struggling with baby rice and mashed banana, 'we have to find a better way to do this.'

No answer. Barely seven o'clock and he was deep in a cellphone conversation about some recently restored formal garden in Hampshire. 'That's right,' he kept saying. 'Completely overgrown.' He would listen for a minute, then say 'Yes', or repeat, 'Completely overgrown'. It drove Anna mad.

'That's it,' she told him, the next time Eleanor spat out the baby rice. 'I've had enough. She's your daughter, you feed her.'

He took the child absently, tucking her under his arm like a bundle of old magazines. 'Hang on a minute,' he said to the phone.

'John, you're dropping her!'

He looked down, hitched Eleanor up on to his hip, then wedged the phone against his ear with one shoulder so that he could spoon up some banana and rice, and offer it to her. Eleanor, reduced to swollen-faced fury only a moment ago by exactly the same item, beamed up at him and ate it with relish. He didn't seem to notice. 'The yews', he said, 'had grown out to such a point that they had to cut them down. It was more like woodland than a garden. But this is the thing. Hang on –' More rice. Eleanor opened her mouth for the spoon, looking sideways at Anna from under his elbow. 'This is the thing: when they did cut them down and clean out the scrub, the exact lines of the garden were still underneath. Every line, marked out in the stumps of yew. Yes, isn't it? I mean the purity of form that argues! Every line still distinct and perfect after three hundred years.'

Eleanor looked up at him and laughed.

'Oh, I've got no patience with either of you,' Anna muttered. In fact, she loved to see them like that, father and daughter, and to feel 'This is my family. Mine.' She got out the Dettox and wiped the kitchen surfaces. She threw things energetically into the washing-up bowl. They had a perfectly good dish-washer, but sometimes she just liked to stand with her hands in the warm soapy water and stare out of the kitchen window. She watched Orlando lead the kittens across the kitchen garden in perfect line astern. When they walked with their mother, she thought, they prowled along like fashion models; but when they walked with Orlando, they walked with a quiet dignity. Anna dozed on her feet for a minute or two, musing on this, aware of John still talking on the phone while his daughter pulled at his sleeve and made approving noises on the edge of speech.

'The knot garden? No, not yet. I've got to do something about it soon. What? No, it's not that good an example. If you ask me, Joshua Herringe had all the ego of the time and none of the cleverness. And Stella's death left it very gloomy. Very gloomy indeed. It's rather overgrown now.' There was an interruption at the other end. Then John said, 'To be honest, I think I'm going to have it ripped out.'

Anna would always remember this statement because of what happened next. 'Oh damn,' she heard him say. There was a fractional pause, a brief slithering noise, and then an astonished shriek.

He had dropped Eleanor.

The baby lay staring upwards for a moment, then opened her mouth in outrage. Somehow she had fallen under the kitchen table and by the time Anna reached her she was rolling about down there, bright red in the face with surprise and anger. Whatever else, her lungs still worked. Huge tears were squeezing themselves out of the corners of her eyes. Anna, fearing a depressed fracture of the skull, hauled her out, gave her the kind of unceremonious examination mothers learn early in their careers, then rocked her to and fro until shock turned to self-pity and she began to calm down.

John could only look on, mortified and shaken, while from the kitchen table his cellphone, still connected, made tentative noises of enquiry. 'She just seemed to wriggle out of my hands,' he said.

At this, Anna's temper deserted her. Picking up the cellphone, she threw it as hard as she could at the nearest kitchen wall, where it burst. 'What a bloody useless thing to say!'

'Anna –'

'That's the problem,' she shouted. 'Your bloody cousin was the same. She always had one of those things clamped to her ear.' And then, by a logic even Anna couldn't quite follow, 'You care more about the house than you do about your own daughter.' The moment this was out of her mouth she regretted it, for fear she had made it true.

John Dawe stared at her for a second, then knelt down quietly and began collecting up pieces of phone. There seemed to be a lot of them. He wrapped them in newspaper and put them carefully into the kitchen pedal bin. 'I'm sorry,' he said. 'It was unforgivable of me.'

'I'm sorry too,' Anna said miserably.

But the accident had frightened her, so she let him leave the room, and fought down the impulse to run after him and make up; and for the rest of that day they avoided talking to one another.

Anna woke from a dream of loss, into the ancient silences of Nonesuch. It was some time after three. She was sweating. The room felt close and airless, as if someone had hung it with coarse black fabric – as if the dream had come back into the world with her. The heat made her sit up and call out, 'John? Eleanor?'

No answer.

'Eleanor!'

She jumped out of bed and looked in the Moses basket. It was empty. The baby was gone. She put her hand up to the side of her head. *Oh God*, she thought, *Now we've lost her! I can't believe this, I can't believe it* – 'John!'

She shook him. She switched on the bedside lamp. 'John, for God's sake!'

Anna looked in the Moses basket again. Empty. A search of the room revealed nothing. A search of the room. What did that mean? Only that she went round and round until she blundered into a wicker chair, draped with cast-off clothes, which bounced across the floor and into the bed. 'John!' Even that didn't wake him. It was like a nightmare. It was like a charmed sleep. She had the feeling that everything was happening in a very small space of time, that suddenly she would find the baby and realise that only two minutes had passed since she opened her eyes. Soon she had been round every wall, opened every cupboard. She had looked under the bed. She had pulled out drawers. Back to the cot. Nothing. She stood there swaying, thinking, *this room is so hot, it's so hot*. Then she was out in the corridor, calling 'Eleanor! Eleanor!' and there was nothing there either. 'Eleanor?' Temporary low-wattage bulbs, strung on loops of heavy rubberised cable dimly illuminated the sixteenth-century panelling. There were stepladders at intervals; a dust sheet moved in a draught.

I don't know what to do, thought Anna dully. How could you lose a baby? And after everything else that had happened!

'Oh John,' she called, going back in, 'please wake up!' She shook him.

He groaned and flung out one arm. 'What time is it?' he asked.

'John, the baby!'

This got him out of the bed, yawning and rubbing his eyes. 'What's the matter with her?' he enquired. 'She looks perfectly normal to me.'

Anna stared into the Moses basket. There was Eleanor, exactly as she always looked at night: the doll's head clutched to her cheek, her thumb in her mouth, a frown on her face as if sleep was an effort she might at any minute begin complaining about. 'But –' said Anna. 'John, I –' She was so puzzled she could barely speak. Then she laughed. 'Do you know, I've spent the last five minutes looking for her everywhere.' She shook her head. 'I must have had a dream.' She shivered. 'It was very real.'

John stared at her. 'I had nightmares too,' he admitted. Then, to her surprise, he took her in his arms. 'I'm sorry Anna. I'm sorry about the row.'

'I'm sorry too. I didn't –'

'I know –'

'I didn't mean to –'

Their relationship – begun in unique circumstances, then driven through its first few months by an edginess and anger that could only be described as historical – had suffered more than its fair share of reverses. But nothing as bad-tempered as yesterday's encounter had happened between them before. They weren't used to disliking one another so thoroughly. It was hard to get back from that. In the end he pulled her on to the bed and suddenly, Eleanor or no Eleanor, they were kissing frantically in the hot room.

'I love you.'

'I love you too. Hold me. Hold me.'

Next day it was dull and damp, the kind of weather that makes you feel uncomfortable inside your skin. The cats eyed Anna as if it were her fault; they hogged the Aga. The builders trudged from room to room, opened their newspapers and argued listlessly over the transfer of this or that footballer. Even Eleanor seemed subdued. At breakfast she allowed herself to be fed without a struggle, but if there were no tantrums, neither were there any of those sudden delighted smiles, which so illuminated Anna's day and which sometimes seemed to her the only real reward of motherhood. By eleven o'clock Anna found herself at a loose end for once, wandering about the house with the baby in her arms, saying fatuous things like, 'And this is a clock.'

At lunch, John asked, 'Could you go through the stuff from the Small Wardrobe? I doubt there's anything worth keeping, but someone ought to look at it, just in case.'

Anna was glad to have something to do. 'But if they're family things,' she suggested, 'you should find time to go through them yourself.' She wasn't even sure where the Small Wardrobe was, though she thought it might be on the third floor. 'There may be decisions I can't make.'

'Oh, just put aside anything that looks interesting.'

'Could you be a bit less specific?'

He received this irony with a vague look. 'I think the builders have already cleared most of it out into the corridor,' he said.

They had.

On a line of graceless 1950s dining chairs, the moquette-covered seats of which had been the sport of many a long-vanished cat, Anna found piled a set of velvet curtains stiff at the folds with dust, an old Dansette with its accompanying collection of thoroughly unmemorable 45rpm records still in their dog-eared paper sleeves. If you wanted incomplete board games, empty photograph albums, or a broken Fred Perry tennis racket forty years old, this was the place to come. Careless of the perished electrical flexes and faux-crystal glasses wrapped clumsily in yellowed pages of the *Daily Herald*, Anna put Eleanor on the floor, where she could introduce her doll's head to the joker from half a pack of playing cards, and began to sort through the junk, picking up an item here, another there. It didn't seem much. Ten minutes later she was wondering if the builders had moved everything out of the Small Wardrobe after all.

'Play nicely,' she instructed Eleanor and popped her head round the door.

The Small Wardrobe – annexe of some eighteenth-century bedchamber long remodelled and absorbed into the body of the house as two or three other rooms – turned out to be larger than many an Ashmore cottage parlour. It was empty but for some scraps of carpet in a corner and a crushed-looking Bally shoebox from the 1970s, which had been left behind on the beautiful uneven old wooden floor among scuff marks from the builders' boots. Anna stared around. 'If there was ever a Large Wardrobe,' she would tell John later, 'it must have been the size of a tennis court –' then bent down quickly and picked up the shoebox. Its lid was secured by brittle old Scotch tape the colour of tobacco, and it rattled when she shook it. One way or another it fitted the criterion 'anything that looks interesting', so she tucked it under her arm, separated Eleanor gently from the rubbish in the corridor and took both of them back to the kitchen, where she set them on the table together.

'Gargh,' said Eleanor, beaming sunnily. She belaboured the shoebox with her doll's head, as if it were a kind of inanimate version of Orlando.

'Gently now,' Anna told her, snipping the Scotch tape carefully with kitchen scissors. Up came a faint smell of dust and old paper; a fainter smell of perfume. Inside she found three black-and-white Kodachrome prints and the semi-naked, headless body of a child's doll. 'Good grief,' she said.

The photographs were yellowed, stiff, curled up as if they had been left too long on a windowsill in the sun. The first two featured a small, elegant-looking convertible, parked at the side of a country road. Fields stretched away to gently rolling chalk downs, into the high flank of which had been cut long ago a white horse. The car was a Mercedes. There was no one in the view and as a result it had a kind of bland tranquillity.

Two adults and a little girl looked out at Anna from the third print. Their feet were firmly on the churned-up sand of some sunny yet deserted English beach, but everything behind them was bleached to grey: not even the faintest horizon line remained. They didn't seem disorientated. The woman wore a full-skirted dress with polka dots; the man a white shirt and flannel trousers. Their child – she assumed it was theirs – stood between them, sodden swimsuit sagging round its plump little thighs, its stare bold and direct. One hand shaded its eyes, while with the other it offered to the camera the doll whose body now lay in the shoebox. Anna turned the print over. Alan and Joan, someone

70

had pencilled on the back long ago, then another name, then, Southsea. There was a date too faint to read, although the year might have been 1952.

Anna put down the picture and took the body of the doll out of the shoebox. Something made her lift it to her nose – she expected the smell of salt, but there was nothing. She turned the doll over, moved its limbs, rubbed her thumb across the plastic. It was like all those old toys – dimpled, plump, articulated at shoulder and groin. The manufacturers had smoothed off the other joints to a gesture, so that its limbs were a collection of approximate, babyish shapes, and coloured it a flesh tint no flesh had ever achieved. It wore, with a modesty difficult to understand, a pair of knickers originally white and now grey with dust. Anna examined it thoughtfully, then held out her hand to her daughter. 'Ellie,' she said, 'will you lend Mummy your baby a minute?'

Eleanor, recognising this ploy as the beginning of a hundred desperate bedtime skirmishes and wondering perhaps how evening had crept upon her with such stealth, looked round puzzledly, clutched her doll's head and gave a desolate howl.

Anna sighed. 'Never mind,' she said. 'Mummy doesn't really need it.'

Mummy didn't. The head so clearly belonged to the body and she had known that since she opened the shoebox. The question was, how had they become separated? The question was, how had Eleanor found one and not the other? The question was, what were the odds against them turning up together again like this, in her and her daughter's

71

life? *History*, thought Anna, as she considered the photographs again, *is certainly a strange old business*. There was the doll, fluttering eyelashes and all, on Southsea beach in 1952, whole for perhaps the last time. Anna had the idea it might have been the last time the family were whole, too. She couldn't say why. Alan and Joan, whoever they were, owners of a Mercedes convertible, stood awkwardly together in the sunshine, looking very 1950s and middle class. The doll was endlessly offered to the camera. An offshore wind, brisk and impersonal, had got under its gingham dress. It still had all its flossy nylon hair. The question was, perhaps, who are these two people, with their strained smiles and expensive car?

There was no question about the child. The child was Stella Herringe, seven or eight years old.

Anna rubbed her eyes.

After a while, trying and failing to remember when the doll's head had first turned up in her daughter's sticky hand, she asked, 'Ellie, where did you find your baby?'

Eleanor, always glad to be included in things, cocked her head on one side. 'Ootie!' she said with a wide smile.

Some places are realer than others, Izzie says, and we have to learn the difference between the two (she means me). Look at me, Izzie says, and tell me what you've seen. Because if I can't trust you mark my words I'll never tell you who you are. Then it's coddled egg again and my little shallot and so on until she says to me, have you found it

yet? and I say no. I say, I'm tired of things, and Izzie says,
a raw little tadpole like you? You'll not get tired of things
until I tell you to. Cross me and I'll slip you down like an
oyster don't ever think I won't. When Izzie is angry her
voice gets right inside you.

Things. There's so many of them. I've known about
them since before Izzie came although I didn't know what
they were. I didn't know anything then. I didn't know I
was alive. (You don't know you're alive now, Izzie says.
She says, be glad of that.) Most things are only one thing
but not these. They are all different shapes and some of
them shift about in front of you like water. The beauty of
them, Izzie says, is that they're never the same twice. It's
what frightens me about them too. They're not the same
twice. And they're not the same Here as they are There. (If
you know where There is. Izzie knows, and soon I will. I
have to find them so I will know things. I have to find
them so I will know who I am.) How will I find the right
ones? I ask. You look through all the things in this house,
and you try them all she says. You try them all my little
naked oyster until you find the right ones. The right ones
are the real ones they have shadows in the other place.
They're the ones we need. Off you go now.

So I'm off again up and down round and about looking
this way and that for all the different parts of Izzie.

And Izzie is often with me as I go.

Night.

Francis Baynes stood motionless in his bedroom –
which, it had recently occurred to him, was as bare
as a cell – with his dog collar off and his hands raised
to his neck. The top half of his body was swivelled

awkwardly towards the window, while the lower half faced the tallboy where he kept his clothes. He had on his reading spectacles. The bedside light projected his shadow on to the white wall, where it seemed frozen and graceless. After some time Francis moved. His hands dropped. He turned fully to the window and stared out at whatever had caught his attention. For a moment it seemed he would rap on the glass, pull up the sash, call out. Instead, he quickly and quietly left the room.

A minute or two later he was looking out over the graveyard from the darkness at the back of the lych-gate. Dirty moonlight fell on the Herringe graves and on the bent back of the woman he had seen there. She was planting flowers. That was what he thought: she was planting flowers at the base of one of the old headstones.

'Excuse me?' he called.

She straightened up. He felt her white face focus on him as emptily as a satellite dish. Her eyes were as reflective as a cat's. She began to raise her left hand, in which she held a pair of grey gloves. It was a gesture preliminary to speech.

Francis stepped out of the shadows, vibrating like a wire. 'Yes?' he said.

She was turning her whole body towards him, as slowly as the dancer on the lid of a musical box, when a motorcycle burst into the village from the direction of Drychester. The sound of its engine, compressed by the cottages on either side, funnelled down towards St Mary's, echoing off the front of the church as a jittery, coughing roar. Its headlights sent the shadows of the gravestones racing nervously across the grass. The machine itself was in view for less than a second, boring down on its front suspension as the driver braked heavily, threw it round the corner of Pond Lane under the astonished gaze of two cats on a wall and accelerated away hard enough to lift the front wheel off the road. Francis glimpsed narrow shoulders slick with coloured leather, a twist of stainless-steel exhaust pipes. Then it was gone.

When he turned his attention back to the woman in the graveyard she wasn't there either. The motorcycle had pulled the darkness apart and it was as if she had vanished into the hole it made. He approached the grave, knelt down and placed his palm flat to the damp grass, not knowing what to expect. It was the same as ever. The earth was unturned. What had he interrupted? What was going on in his graveyard? He got to his feet, rubbing his hands on the sides of his trousers.

If he tilted his head he could still hear Alice Meynell's huge yellow Ducati, already a mile away in the lanes up towards East Owler. Otherwise, the night was empty.

He looked at his watch.

Half past two.

Up at Nonesuch, Anna slept fitfully, between dreams of an old Mercedes convertible. The black-and-white photographs, the shoebox, the doll, the things she had found that afternoon, had kept her awake long after John drifted off. She had watched him – noting how he gave himself up to sleep like a boy, quickly and at an odd angle, one leg tucked up – until at a little after midnight she slipped into an unconsciousness the internal architecture of which was a single large empty space. By 3 a.m. the headless body of the doll had begun to turn over and over just behind her eyes. She snapped awake.

Anna Dawe had had enough of the past and the things she knew about it; events had made her feel that, generally, the world would be better off without a past. The room was hot again, she was sweating and she could also feel sweat on John's bare back where they touched. She propped herself up and greedily drank some water from the glass by the bed. As soon as she had had enough, she let herself fall back under the weight of sleep as if she were falling underwater. In her second sleep she dreamed less specifically, but woke not long afterwards in the grip of a fierce anxiousness, as if something had been going on down there under the water she would rather get away from.

Oh no, she thought, not again. She jerked upright, threw off the sheet. 'Ellie!'

The bassinet was empty.

'John! John!'

This time he woke instantly. He groaned and fumbled with the water glass, but Anna had emptied it. 'What?' he said. 'What is it now?' But this time Eleanor had gone and they could both see that, and neither of them could find her. They turned on the bedside lamp and blundered round the bedroom in its yellow wash of light – independently, but each with the numb methodicalness of someone who doesn't really know what to do, saying, 'Well, she's certainly not here' and, 'It seems stupid but have you looked in the wardrobe?' This speech wasn't really addressed to each other. They were caught up in their separate anxieties and if they felt anything for each other it was the kind of impatience people feel when they are in a panic.

'She's not here,' said John eventually.

'I know that. I said that. Oh John, what can have –'

'I'm going to look around,' he interrupted, as if he didn't want her to ask the rest of that question, couldn't see the point of having it asked at that moment. 'You stay here. I'm going to look around, because she must just have crawled out into the passage.'

'John, she's barely a year old. How would she do that? Why?'

John took Anna by the shoulders. 'Just please stay,' he begged, 'in case she comes back.'

This was a persuasive idea and raised her hopes. Even so she didn't intend to wait in the bedroom biting her knuckles and trying not to cry. She followed him out into the passage, but as soon as they got out there she became profoundly depressed. The temporary lighting cable hung in loops. Something about these loops – the blackness, the rubberiness, of the cable – made her feel a little sick. As before, the builders' ladders projected long expressionist shadows on the walls. It was hot. It was empty. Nothing good could ever happen there. Anna went back in and sat on the bed.

'You go,' she said after a moment, though he already had.

After five minutes in which nothing happened she went to the door. The lights had gone out, though there was a faint glow at one end of the passage where it turned abruptly to the left, as if you were looking into a kitchen lit only by a partly open refrigerator door. 'John?' she called. She couldn't see anything.

Then her eyes seemed to adjust, or perhaps it was her brain that adjusted. Lurching towards her, silhouetted against the dim slur of light, she saw a little figure. She knew that gait, she had seen it a thousand times: it was the gait of a toddler, some child no longer in the first flush of learning to walk but not yet blasé about the process. Naked except for a pair of pull-ups, rocking a little to keep her balance, on came Eleanor Dawe. The doll's head was clutched tightly in her hand. As soon as she noticed her mother, she sat down and babbled in the middle of the floor. Behind her came her doting father, who called, 'Anna! Look! She's learned to walk!'

Anna stared for a moment, her heart more puzzled than lightened, then swept her daughter up. 'Ellie! Oh Eleanor, Eleanor, you bad girl!'

She burst into tears. Eleanor gave her a speculative look, then she burst into tears too.

John put his arms round both of them. 'Shush, shush,' he told the child.

Anna sniffed and said, 'We could have lost her.'

'Come on, Anna. You should be pleased. There's no harm done. She's taken her first steps!'

Anna stared at him. 'Come down to the kitchen,' she said.

'But –'

'We'll never sleep now. Come down to the kitchen. I want to show you something.'

They sat by the Aga until it got light. Anna made cups of tea, emptied the shoebox on to the table and showed him, item by item, what she had found, while John leaned forward with his elbows on his knees, trying to look alert. But he was only puzzled and, if she wasn't careful to occupy his attention, he fell asleep where he sat. His face was slack, black with stubble. *I don't suppose I look any better*, thought Anna. She touched his arm. She felt sorry for him, but she felt sorry for herself too. More than that. She felt frightened.

'Don't you find it a bit upsetting,' she asked, 'after everything that's happened to us? Something from the past just turning up like this? Aren't you worried about Eleanor?'

'She's just an ordinary little girl.'

Anna took his cup away from him and put her hands on his shoulders. 'Look at me,' she encouraged him. Something else had occurred to her. 'John, she kept it from us.'

He laughed. 'She's barely a year old,' he said. 'You said that yourself.' He shook his head. 'I don't believe that for a moment.'

'What else would you call it?'

'She's just a little girl who's learned to walk on her own.' He smiled over at Eleanor who, enjoying the novelty of being awake in the middle of the night, was sitting in her high chair looking interestedly around the kitchen. 'She's just a clever little girl,' he told her. To Anna he said, 'You're tired and you're letting things get out of proportion.'

This was more than Anna could bear. 'Oh, don't be fatuous, John. It's the third time this has happened! And look at her. Look at the way she walks.' She shook her head, trying to think of a way to convince him. 'For God's sake, she's been walking around the house night after night while we were asleep, with this bloody thing that belonged to Stella Herringe in her hand.'

John acknowledged this reluctantly. 'I admit it's a bit odd, but all that is over, Anna. We've finished with Stella for ever. She's down in Ashmore church-yard and she can't affect us from there.' He took Anna's hand. 'I love you,' he said, 'and I love Ellie, and I love this family we make. I want to go forward now. I don't want the three of us to be tied to something that happened in the past. I'd rather just forget about it.'

'You'd rather be in denial,' Anna accused. 'We've lived before, John, God knows how many times. It was you who made me see that. Our lives aren't our own. They belong in some way to the past. And that's where this disgusting thing has come from.'

John looked uncomfortable. 'It's only an old doll's head,' he pointed out. ' "Disgusting" seems rather a strong word. And anyway, she doesn't even seem to have it now.'

'Eleanor?' asked Anna.

John said, 'Where's your baby, Eleanor?'

They looked all over the kitchen for it, but it had gone.

Eleanor watched them with delight. 'Izzie,' she said.

Chapter Four

SPENDING TIME WITH the Besom always made me feel more complete, more calm; as if I went to her all ragged with worry and she licked me back into shape, both inside and out, just the same way the Great Cat did with her child, the world.

I trotted back to Nonesuch that afternoon at double my usual pace, a new sense of purpose propelling me along like a following wind. Not only, I promised myself, am I going to pay better attention to everyone's dreams; but I am going to confront Lydia once and for all about what happened to her. It's not right that the kittens should be disturbed by her nightmares.

But if I had been entirely honest with myself I would be forced to admit that it was not solely for the sake of the girls' quiet rest that I was determined to hear Liddy's confession. I thought that perhaps when she had finally shared her ordeal with me, the experience of talking about her pain might bring us closer together. She had been so distant with me. It was breaking my heart.

When I got back to the manor house, however, Lydia was nowhere to be seen. Nor was Millie. I looked in all of Liddy's favourite sleeping places: underneath the marjoram, on top of the car, under the car, in the linen basket on the first floor of the house, on the bed in Anna's room, under the table in the kitchen. But I could find neither scent nor fur of her. I ran in and out of the house, getting under everyone's feet, till I got myself into a state and completely wasted the Besom's calming effect.

Eventually, I found the girls – all three of them together, as usual – jumping in and out of the low hedges of the knot garden at the rear of the house. Lydia and Millefleur were curled up in a pool of sunshine at the foot of the old orchard wall, watching them lazily. I hated this area and I'd thought Millie did, too, since she had been present when I had fought the worst dream of my life there. But she just looked up at me, her eyes narrow in the sun, then laid her head once more on Liddy's snoring shoulder and went back to sleep. I felt faintly let down, disappointed by the lack of greeting.

The intricately planted foliage of the knot garden had become overgrown, the formal patterns blurred and indistinct. It seemed I was not the only member of the household who avoided this place, for the rest of the garden was tended by Anna with meticulous care. I shuddered. The last time I had set foot in this horrible, artificial, woman-made place my world had been dark and savage. If I closed my eyes, I could still see the dream – its fiery corona, its cruel, snaking tentacles, the hair and teeth – for it was here I had run it to ground after it had killed my grandfather and wreaked irrevocable damage on the wild roads of Ashmore. It was here, in this knot garden, that it had finally given up its ghost and seeped away into the chalky red dust . . .

'Uncle O, what's the matter? You look funny.'

I came back to myself with a thud as if dropped from a great height. Letty stood in front of me, regarding me with concern. 'Were you having one of your turns, Uncle O?' she said sternly, in a tone an older cat would reserve for admonishing an errant child or a wayward, infirm and ancient relative.

I gave her a hard stare and addressed myself to Caterina and Arabella: 'You two! Squash! Beetle! Out of there, now!'

The two sisters stopped in mid-leap and turned to consider me, their faces blank with disapproval, as if to say 'You can't tell us what, and what not to do; you're not even really our uncle, let alone our father'. In that instant, I felt myself wither inside, but the moment didn't last.

'It's Uncle Orlando!' Cat shrieked, stating the obvious, and came scuttling through the maze without once touching the sides, like a lizard on a mission.

'It's fun in here, Uncle O,' called Arabella, not to be left out. 'You can hide and jump out.'

Oh yes, I thought hollowly. *I know all about hiding and jumping out here.*

'You shouldn't play in there,' I said weakly. 'It's dangerous.'

Belly rolled her eyes. Then all three sisters exchanged a glance, a glance that shared between them a single, unspoken message: *It's all right, it's only Uncle Orlando being a bit mad again. Take no notice. Humour him.*

Letty tutted. 'Oh, come along, Uncle O. It's only plants and stuff.'

It was. What could I say? There was no place in their lives for the bygone mysteries of Nonesuch. 'Well, it is,' was the best I could do. 'Take my word for it.'

Caterina came over to me, all long legs and flirty eyes. 'Where've you been then, Uncle O? Mum was looking for you earlier. She was cross you weren't here and Millie wouldn't tell her. It seemed like some big secret. Is it? Will you tell me?' she wheedled. She leaned in close to me, as intimate as a calling queen. Then she recoiled. 'You smell a bit weird.'

'I've been to see a friend of mine,' I said and left it at that. Let her make of it what she would. Perhaps if she thought I'd been off gallivanting with one of the local girls she'd tell their mother. Perhaps Lydia would even be jealous. I found myself wishing the Besom smelled better.

But Cat was not to be put off so easily. She stuck her nose rudely into my ruff and took a deep breath. 'Pooh!' She sneezed. 'It smells like old stuff – all musty and dusty.'

Old stuff. I couldn't imagine Ma Tregenna would be thrilled by that description. I pushed Cat's inquisitive young face away with a firm paw. 'Mind your manners, young lady. Anyway, where I've been is no business of yours.'

'Shan't tell you my secret, then,' she returned with a sniff, all hoity-toity. She did so remind me of Lydia, sometimes, and not always when she was behaving at her best.

'Don't, then,' I said, feigning unconcern, knowing this was more likely to infuriate her into confession.

She did, in fact, look highly miffed. Her sisters, meanwhile, bored by our exchange, had started a new game in and out of Liddy's and Millie's paws. I saw something scurry through the grass between them: it seemed they were about to surprise their mother and Millefleur with a large beetle. I saw Cat watching them, evidently torn between her anxiety at being left out of any fun that might be going and her need to show off to me by unburdening herself of her 'secret'. Eventually pride won out. 'Come with me, Uncle O,' she said, shouldering me towards the knot garden. And with that she was off, leaping over the straggling box hedge border, to disappear into the greenery.

I reared up on my hind legs, but that dull blue-grey was remarkable effective camouflage amid the dark-green shadows. With a muttered curse, I jumped in after her, returning to the place I had sworn never again to set foot in. The moment my feet touched the ground on the other side of the border I knew I was somewhere I should not be. At first I was enveloped by the strong smell of the herbs planted there: germander and hyssop and rue, pungent and peppery in the evening sunlight. It had always puzzled me why humans would set such strong-smelling plants in such close proximity. Their noses must be weak indeed, not to be overcome by them as I was: my head felt as though it would burst from the sensation. But as I went further into the heart of the knot garden, on Cat's trail, the aroma map changed. Even with the recent scents of the girls floating above the ground and among the leaves their cheek glands had brushed as they ran, I could smell the witch there. It was a smell I could never forget: rank and fetid with the stink of canker and rot and terror, and that foul ointment, sickly sweet, over it all.

I gritted my teeth, held my head as far off the ground as I could and still see where I was going, and went resolutely after Caterina, cursing her 'secret' with every step. She had taken a convoluted path to a point just east of the centre of the maze. It was here I found her sitting, grooming herself unconcernedly – clearly unfazed by the violent histories this place held.

'You took your time,' she said accusingly, as if I had deliberately made her wait. 'I thought you'd gone off to play with the others.' Her eyes glowed green in the shadows.

She knew instinctively that she was my favourite of the three, but even that assumption didn't always hold jealousy at bay.

'As if I'd do that, Squash,' I replied, forcing myself to sound more jocular than I felt. 'What have you got to show me?'

In response, she turned her back on me, dipped

her head and began to scrabble furiously among the roots of the box that formed the wall of the pattern where it had forced us into the closed end of a loop. Little puffs of chalky dust swirled up into the air as she worked. I watched the muscles rippling in her hindquarters with what was not entirely parental approval. She was a handsome little beast, just like her mother. And, like her mother, she knew it.

A moment or two later, she sat up, triumphant. 'Look.'

I came to stand at her shoulder. At first, in that gloomy, lightless spot, I could make out nothing but what appeared to be a large lump of flint, pale and calcified, lighter than its surroundings, solid and deeply unexciting. But when Cat stepped back to give me a better view I saw what she had unearthed.

It was Ellie's doll's head.

I leapt away as if scalded.

Caterina laughed. Adults were so stupid some-times. 'It's only the baby's toy,' she chided, pushing past me again. She got some of the thing's hair in her teeth and hauled it out into the light, where it rolled about disconsolately. Its horrible mechanical eyelids rattled back and forth over those unnerving blue eyes as if it were winking at us.

I could smell the age and decay on the thing: worse now than when Ellie had come after me with it on those many occasions on which she had loved to torment me. I recalled the way she would make a beeline for me, the head outthrust in her chubby fist, nonsense pouring from her mouth and her green eyes flashing with unholy glee. Choking, I struggled for breath, trapped in the signature of that smell. Then the world had tilted again and I was somewhere else: in Nonesuch, I thought, running down endless darkened corridors whose perspectives kept canting and shifting as if trying to shake me into a corner and trap me there. All the time the walls closed in on me. There was glittery stuff in the air and it was cold – as cold as any wild road – and I could hear voices . . .

The cat, Izzie, the cat, take him by the tail!

A child was laughing.

Then I felt something on my face, something hot and firm. Something was holding my head tight. I opened my mouth to howl –

A tongue was licking furiously at my eyes and muzzle. Sharp little claws dug into the skin of my cheeks to hold me still. 'Uncle Orlando,' a voice kept saying as if from a great distance. 'Wake up, wake up!'

A flicker . . . a blur of blue. Caterina sat back, coming suddenly into focus for me. Her eyes were round with panic. 'What's the matter? You were moaning so terribly.'

'The doll's head,' I said weakly, as if that explained it all. I pushed her aside thoughtlessly. Repulsion made me efficient. Holding the offensive thing at arm's length, I pushed it back into the roots of the knot garden and batted earth over it in a paroxysm of disgust. Even so, filaments of its pale hair continued to stick defiantly out of the dust. Turning my back on the doll's head, I dug energetically with my hind feet till my muscles burned. When I turned back, it was gone from view.

I sat back, exhausted in body and spirit.

Caterina was regarding me with bewilderment. 'But it was *my* secret . . .' she began.

'It's our secret now and it must stay where it is,' I said sternly. There was no explanation I could offer her for what must seem my mad behaviour. 'And you must never play here again, nor let Arabella or Letitia do so. It's a bad place.' I shuddered.

Instead of railing against this apparent unfairness, Cat looked inexplicably sympathetic. 'Is that why you had a bad dream?' she asked innocently.

I stared at her. 'Bad dream?' I echoed stupidly.

'I watched it,' she said matter-of-factly. 'It was like being in your head. You were running down the Long Corridor in the house and some tall white people were after you. One was a man and the other a woman, though they were both wearing long dress things. The man had a lot of hair and that was white, too. The woman was called Izzie and she had nasty eyes, and you were more scared of her than you were of him. The air was all shiny –'

'Caterina!' My voice was more severe than I'd meant it to be. She stopped abruptly. 'You could see my dream?'

She nodded, puzzled. 'Of course. I can see everyone's dreams. It's fun.'

I groaned. *Did I never learn anything*? I thought savagely. The Besom had all but told me exactly this, with her rambling tales of the refined old chap whose son became dreamcatcher of Drychester, the scandal surrounding his son, the one with fur as blue as Caterina's, and Letty's and Belly's. *Poor Lydia*, I thought then, as the pieces fell into place. Mated to a witch's familiar. Poor Squash: inheriting a burden like my own. *It always skips a generation*, the Besom had said. *Dreamcatching: it gets passed from grandparent to grandchild, oblivious to gender or convenience.*

Sharply, I said to Cat. 'Have you been eating a yellow weed?'

Something flickered in those green eyes. 'Might have done,' she conceded mulishly.

'Show me your paws.'

She frowned and held one out to me. All around the toes, where her coat was anyway of a lighter shade, the fur was faintly discoloured, an indistinct, urinous yellow against the blue. I let it go again in disgust. With myself. How could I have been so unobservant? A young cat with the gift, right under my nose; one, moreover, who had initiated herself into the mystery and seemed entirely at ease with her unnatural abilities.

'Oh, Squash,' I said miserably. 'You're a dream-catcher, too.'

That night I found it hard to sleep. I had come to the kitchen later than the others: my duties as the local dreamcatcher meant patrolling the highways at dead of night in search of damaging human dreams to hunt down and destroy. The dreams that escape from people in the small hours towards dawn are the worst, I find; so I had evolved a system which meant making two rounds: one, which I had just completed, in the early hours of darkness, and the second just before dawn; which meant I could snatch a few hours' sleep in between. There was only so much damage a bad dream could do in a few hours out on the wild roads, I reasoned. Tonight, on the first round, there had been little to catch out on the highways. A couple of mating dreams; an odd one in which an endless herd of cows stepped out of a hole in the plaster of an old wall; some chase sequences involving formless monsters – in other words, the usual harmless stuff of Ashmore's nightmares. I never bothered to catch and eat the obviously innocuous ones – the flying and swimming dreams, the shape-changing ones, the dull dreams that involved a lot of talk and faces in close-up. The cows, for instance, I had almost left alone as a harmless oddity; but you can never be too careful. Sometimes the odd ones can take a turn for the worse; and who wants to spend their night chasing a herd of dream cows down the highways, growing all the time as they escape their restraining membrane? It was easier, and safer by far, to catch it and swallow it down while it was still small and manageable: that much I had learned from my grandfather, the previous incumbent.

Now, the first round of my duties done and with no barrier to the worries that had been pressing on me all evening, thoughts chattered around my head like a flock of starlings, stupid and noisy and insistent. Why wouldn't Lydia tell me about the dead witch's cat who had fathered her kittens? There was no shame in it: she had been forced. Was she really so embarrassed that she could not speak of it, even to me? Or did she despise me so much for not rescuing her in time that she bore me a terrible grudge and was using her distance to punish me?

What dreams had Caterina witnessed? Blood flooded the skin of my face at the thought of some she might have seen; dreams of mine in which her mother was the centre of every atom of my attention. No wonder she never took me seriously, always laughing and mocking, and falling into that flirtatious manner with me . . .

Then I started to think about the doll's head and how it could have found its way into the knot garden. This flummoxed me entirely. I had rarely seen little Eleanor without this toy. She cried when Anna took it away from her; she slept with it in her cot at night. So it seemed unlikely that one of the big people had managed to remove it from her without there being a terrible storm of wailing and protest, which one of us cats would surely have heard and made comment on. The cry of a baby is quite the most invasive sound in the world, impossible to ignore, no matter what type of creature it is. But if it had not been one of the adults, how it had got there was a mystery; for surely no baby could crawl all the way around the house and into the knot garden? It was desperately puzzling. It made my head hurt to think of it. If I thought about it too hard, I was rewarded by a vision of the head rolling along under its own volition and that made little ripples of fear run down into my stomach.

I changed position, rolling off the mat in front of

the Aga and on to the warm brick floor. There, I came to rest against another furry flank. *Lydia's*? I wondered with a brief thrill; but no: her characteristic snores located her beneath the kitchen table. Turning my head till it was awry, I could make out quite a pile of cats there: it seemed the girls had joined her. So it must be Millefleur, then, I thought comfortably. As if in response to my thoughts, she purred and stretched, and the fur of her flank gently brushed against mine. It cheered me to feel her friendly presence. I had one ally amid all the turmoil, at least. I had yet to tell her of Caterina's discovery, since she had been in Liddy's company all evening and I did not want to cause concern; but I consoled myself that I would discuss the mystery of the doll's head with her the following morning. Millie was a shrewder cat than me and more perceptive by far. *What a dreamcatcher she would make*, I thought ruefully. But she was the daughter of a dreamcatcher; it would be one of her kittens who was destined to walk the highways.

At last I fell into a light doze and as I slept I dreamed. It was not a pleasant dream, being a reprise of the disturbing vision that had visited me in the knot garden. I was back in the corridors of Nonesuch again, lost and pursued; but ahead of me another cat ran, a cat who knew the labyrinth of passageways well, for it darted along taking one turn after another, and I knew that if I managed to keep up with it I would surely evade the white people behind me.

I had never seen a cat so fleet of foot; its white

paws flashed like beacons in the gloom: follow me, follow me! The effort I had to make in order to keep my guide in sight made my lungs burn. Along the Long Corridor we ran, until at last I sensed a falling away, a sudden absence and, when I turned, I found my pursuers had vanished; defeated, or bored with the chase.

I turned back and ran on, hoping to catch up with the white-pawed cat to thank it for its aid, but although I increased my pace and put my head round every open door, there was no sign of it, except for a brief whiff of a scent in the air of the hallway. I knew that scent. It hovered there around me, tantalising in its familiarity.

Then I woke up.

Someone in the house had cried out. At once, all my fur was on end, as if my skin were more alert than the rest of me. The cry came again: the baby, I identified, and thought little of it. Babies are always waking alone and hungry in the night. I was about to settle down, when the pitch of it intensified. I knew the sound of that cry: a child woken from a nightmare. Wearily, I hauled myself to my feet, stretched carefully, anxious that I might unnecessarily wake Millie. There was no need for concern there, though: she had gone. *Off on one of her night-time jaunts*, I thought. *Perhaps there'll be a warm vole or two for me later*.

Up the stairs I went and met the dream coming down.

It hung in the darkened air, a glowing golden ball, its edges flaring uncertainly. It was small, as dreams go, but I did not like the look of that corona. Where it touched the night air, the gold ignited into a fiery red and then to a darker colour yet. It was only a few feet above my head. *With luck*, I thought, *and an acrobatic leap, I may even catch it before it makes for a highway and then I can go back to sleep*. But as if it sensed my intention, the dream soared upwards and disappeared at speed, drifting through the wall of the front hallway and out into the garden.

I cursed my slow reactions and pelted into the scullery, where John had installed the cat door out of which we came and went at will. Once outside, I took my bearings and scrambled round to the front of the house, in time to see the dream coasting across the garden, towards the tall yew hedges. There was a small wild road that started down there, one that cut through the village to Ashmore Common, where any number of highways came together in a great tangled confluence. If it got that far, I'd spend the rest of the night hunting it.

Across the lawn I fled and straight through the middle of the rhododendrons, careless in my haste.

I stepped on something warm and pliant, which in turn bubbled and hissed.

'Ow! Watch where you're going, you great clumsy lummox!'

It was Grizelda, one of the cats who had escaped the Nonesuch laboratory; a generously proportioned female with a soft, spreading, brindled belly. She and a dozen more survivors were still to be found wandering the grounds of Nonesuch, as if, despite all the horrors the house had held for them, they were too afraid to venture further. Sometimes Anna fed them. But sometimes Belly and Letty, egged on by Lydia, stole the food and brought it back for their mother. If she couldn't eat it all, she would hoard it till it became inedible. It was Millie who had informed me of this, and I was still trying to find a way to broach the subject with the girls and, indeed, with Liddy.

'Sorry!' I called back over my shoulder. 'Dream to catch.'

'Rude boy. Clear off, then!'

None of them could see the dreams I chased: they all thought I was, as Griz put it, 'a bit touched'.

I caught up with Ellie's dream just as it slipped into the highway. Without pausing to make an elegant entrance, I leapt after it. The wild roads are curious places: travelled only by the animals and invisible to the eye of all others, including birds and humans, they channel the life force of the world. The highways feel inimical to life, so Great Cat gives us access to our most primal selves when we travel on them, so that the smallest of tabby cats can be transformed into huge, barred tigers, whether sabre-toothed or Siberian; into jaguars and lynxes, leopards and caracals. In the world that is visible to the human eye most cats appear as innocuous as I am – a marmalade cat of medium size – but like me each of them has a great cat lurking inside, in order to withstand the hardships in that raw and primal world. Cruel winds blow constantly, filled with flurries of snow and shards of ice, no matter what the season outside. Hawkweed had always said the

Great Cat kept them so cold to encourage us to run: *Speed makes heat, laddie,* he'd say to me, *and heat is life.*

The dream globe was giving off a powerful heat of its own. Now that it was on the highway, its corona was burning brightly. I would have to catch it quickly, or it would begin to damage the fabric of the road. Virulent dreams can burn a hole right through a highway, allowing all its energy to drain away, lost for ever. The more that happens, the more creatures sicken and die – at first the small ones, with few reserves to draw upon: the shrews and the sparrows, the mice and the dragonflies; but then it is the rabbits and the foxes, pets and ponies, owls and cows. And if the balance is fatally changed – if too many bad dreams pollute the highways with their freight of greed and guilt, violence and lust – then folk start to perish, too. I took a pride in the health of my domain. Since I had vanquished the witch's dream, we'd had no trouble in Ashmore.

It was an inexperienced dream, this one. Babies' dreams, though they burn brightly, are often slow and uncertain, as this one was. It bobbled against the roof of the highway, easily in reach of my great paws. As a lion, I leapt; as a lion, I knocked it down and caught it in my jaws. It was always the best moment for me, savouring my transformation from small domestic cat to great cat as I sprang for my prey and felt my huge teeth close down upon it, caging it in my mouth. I bit down, expecting an easy swallow.

But the dream resisted. I felt it pulse, trying to force my jaws apart. It was strong – far stronger than

I had expected – and cunning, too: for it went slack and lifeless a moment later and as I took a great gulp of air to wash it down, it slipped rapidly out into the highway winds once more and, catching a powerful blast of air, evaded my flying claws.

I chased it in earnest then, angry at my gullibility. My granfer would have been furious with me. But at last it was caught in an eddy, which trapped it against the wall of the wild road, and I hooked a claw through it and threw it to the ground. There, I stood on it with all my weight and pressed my muzzle to its shining membrane, curious to see what was giving this little dream such potency.

Inside, distorted by the curve of the dream skin, I saw this:

A little girl, standing with two adults on a long, flat expanse of bright sand. The sun beat down; I could feel the heat of it through the membrane. In the distance, where the beach made a great sweep around a bay, water washed in and out, the startling, electric blue of a summer damsel fly. The big people, fully clothed, had their arms round one another, utterly absorbed. The woman leaned into the man and they kissed. The child stared at them, its green eyes hard with resentment. It wore a single thick, wet piece of fabric out of which arms, head and legs emerged, pale and chubby, its skin all goosefleshed from the onshore breeze that ruffled its dark hair. In its hands it clutched an object. I squinted at it.

And then I shuddered. Part of the object I recognised; though the last time I had seen it, it had looked very different: older and broken, worn away by a passage of time.

It was a doll, perfect in every detail. It had a full head of bright golden hair and blue eyes with black-lashed, rocking eyelids. With its gaze still fixed upon its parents, the child shifted its grip on the doll. There was a sudden wrenching motion and the head came away from the pink plastic body. With a silent scream, the child flung the head away from it with all the force of its not inconsiderable will and ran up the beach, fat tears bursting over its crimson cheeks. The head hit the woman hard on the breast. Her hands flew to the place where it had struck, her mouth a perfect 'O' of shock. She turned to say something to the man, but he had his back to her now and was running after the child.

Then I sensed something else, as if a shadow lurked behind this seemingly harmless dream. I could feel another emotion underlying the small jealousy of the child, powering the nightmare along.

I bit down hard and tasted the dark gloat of satisfaction I had intuited there. As I did so, the scene on the beach began to slip away, as if someone had tilted a glass and let its contents slop over the side; and suddenly there was the child again, older now by a year maybe, all dressed in black, amid a dozen grown people, all in similarly sombre garb. The adults talked in low voices, but I could not hear what they said; even so, the meaning was clear enough. The woman was dead, dead of a lump in the breast. Once more I saw the doll's head propelled by malice and some dark thing I could not understand, striking the woman's chest again and again; the picture reversing and repeating, and all the while the child hid its face in the scratchy wool of her father's trouser leg and smiled and smiled with vicious, secret glee. I could feel her thought forming, even as I began to swallow: *I did it then. Perhaps when I am stronger I can do it again . . .*

Revulsion shivered down my spine. I gulped and choked on the foul stuff, gulped and choked again. The dream fought me, but I took it down, mouthful by grim mouthful, until it was gone. It left a taste behind that was as bitter as wormwood.

I stayed on the highways till dawn, then made my way wearily back to the house. I needed to talk to Millie about the doll's head and the dream. She would reassure me it meant nothing, I told myself. Children are jealous beasts, just like kittens and cubs. We all harbour vile thoughts, which come and go as fleetingly as whim. The imperative of this need to hear Millefleur's sensible voice drove my exhausted feet up the lawns, across the drive, under the car and in through the cat door. I found Liddy and the girls in the kitchen; all asleep except for Cat, who was sitting with all four paws pressed neatly together like the ornament of an ancient foreign cat that Anna kept on the mantelpiece.

'Where's Millie?' I asked softly.

'Oh, she went off for a wander somewhere last night,' Cat returned blithely.

I scrutinised her. 'When last night, exactly?'

'After supper.'

I frowned. 'Are you sure?' I remembered the warmth of her body, the way the fur of her flank had tickled against me with each inhalation.

Cat laughed. 'Silly old Uncle O! Of course I'm sure, I walked down to the gate with her to see her off. She said to say goodbye' – her voice dropped guiltily – 'but I forgot and fell asleep.'

My heart began to thud.

Then who was the cat who had lain against me in the night?

Chapter Five

THEY SECURED THE house with child-proof gates. This made things difficult for the builders, who were quick to complain and almost immediately began leaving the gates open for easier access to the upper floors. Anna seemed to spend her time arguing with them. When this produced no result, she was reduced to going round every couple of hours to make sure the gates were shut. She complained to John. John preferred, he said, to be kept out of arguments of this kind. He had to maintain some sort of relationship with the people doing the real work.

Anna stared at him. 'I do real work,' she said and stormed off. 'Bloody men,' she complained to Alice Meynell later. 'What are they like?'

'The pits,' said Alice. 'If you want my opinion.'

Part of the trouble was that Alice's physicist had proved to be as free a spirit as herself. While Alice admired this quality in a man at the end of an affair, she wasn't so sure about it at the beginning of one. Also, he had recently decided to spend two weeks of the coming summer in Baja without her, on the grounds that he wanted to do some thinking about turbulence in hydrodynamic systems. 'That means he's going surfing,' Alice explained. She was losing her patience with him, she said. 'I'm thinking of becoming celibate anyway.'

'Of course you are,' Anna agreed.

Alice lifted her head and sniffed. 'Anna, I think you need to change your baby.'

'I wouldn't change her for the world,' said Anna. 'Oh, that. You wouldn't like to do it, would you? If I go anywhere near her with a nappy there'll be bedlam.'

'Nobody in their right mind would like to do it,' was Alice's response. She approached Eleanor, pretending to hold her nose. 'Pooh,' she said. 'Nasty pooey little girl!' Eleanor, whose sense of humour was exactly what you'd expect in a child not yet two, found this highly amusing. She giggled accommodatingly and allowed herself to be swept up. 'Want to know something weird?' Alice asked Anna when she had finished.

'What?'

'I saw the new vicar in the graveyard the other night. It was quite late and he was hanging about out there on his own.'

'It's his graveyard,' Anna pointed out.

'He was talking to himself.'

'I'm sure he wasn't,' said Anna, who thought him capable of it.

'Excuse me, I had him bang in the headlights. I could see him talking quite clearly and there was nobody else there. I'd have seen more,' she admitted, 'but things got a bit out of shape on the bend into Pond Lane. If you come off the throttle too quick the Ducati just seems to stop dead. I haven't entirely got the hang of that yet and I didn't want to bin it in front of him. Well, you don't, do you?' She chuckled. 'Out there with his dog collar half off, chattering away to himself.' She concluded with a kind of confused piety, 'I suppose you have to expect it of a vicar.'

'Poor Francis.' Anna sounded vague. 'You probably frightened him to death. I must get him round for tea this week.'

'Good idea,' Alice confirmed. 'Invite me too.'

Anna was amused. 'Find your own vicar, you barefaced slut. You're not sharing mine.'

'Ooh,' said Alice to Eleanor. 'Hark at her.'

Anna allowed herself the dry smile of motherhood. 'By the way,' she advised, 'that nappy's on back to front.'

'Oh. Damn.'

Eleanor cackled and wriggled about.

Anna really didn't intend to share Francis with anyone.

What the friendship offered her wasn't clear. She certainly had no religious faith. In the end, she had to admit, it was the attention she liked. She liked having him as a confidant. *What's wrong with that*? she asked herself, but she knew the question wasn't honest. She was perfectly aware of his vulnerability where she was concerned – he was attracted to her but barely even knew it himself, which for a man is always the hardest kind of attraction to manage. In the end she pretended it didn't matter. Francis needed someone to talk to and so did Anna.

He turned up that same afternoon. 'Just on the off-chance', he said, 'that you were here.'

'Where else would I be, Francis?'

She sat him down on the lawn and made him hold Ellie while she buttered some cheap scones he had bought from the village shop. 'You can read to her. She sometimes likes that.'

Francis said 'Ah' and stared rather helplessly at *Ant and Bee*. Eleanor, who had seen through him the moment he arrived, squealed with laughter and clutched at bits of his face.

'Don't let her do that,' Anna advised him. 'Look, I'd better take her. Pour the tea if you want something to do.'

This didn't fit Eleanor's plans. She opened her mouth to let them know about it. She held on quite hard to Francis's cheek.

Francis, at a loss, fumbled about in his pockets for something to distract her. 'Look,' he said. 'Look!'

It was a shiny black lacquered box, about three inches by two, with complicated formal designs of intertwined flower stalks in a cream-coloured inlay. He offered it to Eleanor. 'It's a music box,' he told her. And indeed, when he opened the lid, a faint, tinkly rendering of 'Für Elise' filled the air, like someone playing the piano a long way off. 'I found it in some builders' rubbish by the front door,' he told Anna. 'It's rather too nice to throw away, I thought. Well?' he asked Eleanor. 'What do you think?'

Eleanor stared. Acquisitiveness struggling with caution in her expression, she released her grip on his cheek and allowed herself to be taken away. 'Für Elise' wound itself down, the last notes dripping into the air with a reluctant sweetness. Anna felt for a fraction of a second as if she were in a sepia photograph of some late-Edwardian afternoon, saw herself with some surprise as a sweet-faced girl with a cloud of dark hair under an enormous hat. Eleanor stared up at Anna, then back at Francis, who continued to hold out the music box until it was silent. Eventually she reached out for it, but even then she looked puzzled and shy.

'Say thank you to Francis,' Anna recommended. 'Oh, thank you, Francis.'

Eleanor, finding this hilarious, gave a brief raucous laugh and banged herself with the box. Two or three more notes of music issued from it, then it was silent again.

Francis was in a strange mood. 'I love St Mary's,' he said. 'But it's a waste. Empty, day after day. It ought to be sold off.'

'Francis!'

'It's what my bishop would say.'

'He doesn't believe it any more than you do.'

'No,' Francis was forced to admit, 'I don't suppose he does.'

'Then you're both being silly. Pour the tea.'

'Still, it's a way of acknowledging a truth about the Church. Every stone in one of these old buildings is impregnated with the mystery of religion. But people don't want that any more – not even bishops want that. The blood, the body, the act of sacrifice, the strangeness that sits so firmly at the centre of Christianity. All that's gone. And once you secularise the Church, what's left?'

Anna, who had hoped for one of their quiet afternoon chats about her life, was bemused and a little irritated. 'I don't know. Helping people.'

'Helping people is social work, not religion.'

'What do you want, Francis?'

He spread his hands. 'I want the mysteries,' he said.

'You're alive in the wrong millennium. Eat your scone.'

'The heart of what we believe is unfathomed,' he persisted. 'Still quite dark and unfathomed. No one wants to admit that any more. Their lives are too comfortable.' He shrugged. 'I'd prefer atheism to comfort.'

Anna, who had no idea what he was talking about, glanced at the sparks of sunlight falling through the branches of the cedar. She looked at her daughter, who sat on the picnic blanket gnawing half an unbuttered scone. She looked closely at Francis Baynes and sighed. The expression of dis-satisfaction that turned down the corners of his mouth made him seem even younger than usual. *Relationships*, she thought, *especially these kinds of relationships, have their responsibilities as well as their rewards*.

'What's made you feel like this?' she asked.

That evening she complained to John, 'Francis is in a very odd mood. Alice says she saw him talking to himself in the graveyard. And I couldn't get the slightest sense out of him today.'

'Only today?' John enquired.

'Don't be cruel.'

They turned on the television to catch the early news.

In the morning John had a letter to say that the bank had changed its mind about funding the renovations further. He stared at it for a long time, then balled it up in a sudden but controlled gesture of disgust and placed it on the table. 'Well, that's that, then,' he said, staring at the Aga.

When Anna tried to uncrumple the letter, he added, as if he were talking to a child, 'Oh, for God's sake just leave it alone.'

Anna drew back her hand, but not before she had read the words 'business plan'.

When Anna arrived for her appointment, the television was on in Martha Russell's office. It was hard to know what to make of the blurred, rainy, hand-held-camera images that came and went hesitantly across the screen. People, including the doctor herself, carried things to and fro. Someone held up a theodolite, someone else a spade. There was a jerky change of scene and a deep hole appeared on the screen, its sides chocolatey and steep. Then a close-up of someone's hands, big male fingers with dirty nails offering to the camera two or three small pieces of dried-up-looking wood or leather. From this the camera moved to a kind of sieve, full of similar objects, the wet sheen of which made them look even more unpleasant.

'What on earth is this?' Anna wanted to know.

Dr Russell laughed. 'Some of the contents of an Iceni lavatory,' she said. 'A midden, really. Part of a site at Barton Orcas up near Waverham on the downs. There's some quite exciting stuff there. It's a just pre-Roman settlement, but we're finding religious objects much, much older. It looks as if the locals had quite different beliefs from the rest of the Iceni.'

Something about this made Anna shiver. 'I hate the past,' she said. 'All those things hidden in the ground. I've seen it on *Time Team*, of course.' Suddenly she heard herself say, 'Dr Russell, I think my baby has been wandering about the house for weeks at night, while she pretends to us that she can't walk.'

Martha Russell gave her patient a long and considering look. 'You'd better sit down and tell me what happened.'

This Anna did. 'I don't know where to turn,' she finished. 'It seems so unnatural.'

'Not at all rare, though,' Martha Russell told her. 'Children can be frighteningly manipulative. They hide their development for all sorts of reasons. I have a friend forty years old who still remembers quite clearly keeping it to herself that she could walk. When you ask her about it, she says, "I knew that if I admitted I could do it, I would have to do it

all the time. They would stop carrying me about."
She kept it up until she was four years old. She made
them carry her about until she found her own
reasons for walking.' She gave Anna a careful look.
'That isn't some case history in a book, dear, it's a
real event.'

Anna stared at the TV screen, where the rain had
begun to fall harder and, in long shot, three or four
people were seen struggling without much success
to erect some kind of temporary cover above the
excavation. She watched their efforts for some time.
She had dreams like that, where life was a struggle
in the rain and mud for purposes you couldn't quite
understand.

Dr Russell let the silence linger for a moment, then
lit one of her American cigarettes and turned off the
TV. 'You know that you aren't the first mother to
feel this,' she suggested.

'I know. I do know. Ellie is a perfectly normal little
girl. She's headstrong, a bit tantrumy, the way lively
and intelligent children often are. I love her, don't
mistake me. Even her difficulties can be rewarding.'
Anna shook her head. 'And she's so beautiful. And
most of the time she's so lovely to be with. It's just
that sometimes –'

'You'd like a little more help.'

That wasn't what Anna had meant at all. She
seized on it anyway. 'John should help me more. Yet
when he does, I resent him. He makes it seem so
easy to be with her. They get on so well together. I
do all the work –'

'– and then they shut you out,' said Martha

Russell with gentle irony, 'and never a word of thanks for your sacrifice?'

Anna shrugged helplessly. 'Yes,' she whispered. 'I suppose that's what it is.'

Later, they talked about Francis Baynes.

'He's a dear friend, but he thinks he's in love with me,' Anna said. 'I try to keep him at arm's length, keep the relationship light, but sometimes it's hard.'

'Do you feel it's entirely healthy to encourage him?'

'Of course I don't!' Anna snapped. Then she continued more quietly, 'Of course I don't. But I need him. I need someone to talk to.'

'You talk to me,' Dr Russell reminded her.

'A friend,' Anna said. 'I need a friend.' She knew this was evasive. She had Alice Meynell as a friend. That wasn't what she lacked, not really. 'Oh, I don't mean you're not a friend.'

The doctor smiled. 'Yes you do,' she contradicted. 'But there's nothing wrong with that.'

'Anyway,' said Anna. 'Now he's acting rather oddly and I'm beginning to feel responsible for that too.' She made a gesture with her shoulders, as if trying to free herself from a net someone had thrown over her. She looked down at her lap, then up at the doctor. She felt her lip quiver. Was she going to cry? 'Everybody depends on me –' she heard herself say suddenly.

'Yes?' Martha Russell encouraged.

Anna shrugged and would not go on.

But on the way home, dithering in the face of the fast local traffic, she completed the sentence she had begun. '– when all I want is someone I can depend on. When all I want to feel is safe and loved!'

The next week saw him increasingly withdrawn. He avoided the builders, rarely answered the phone and came to bed only after he thought Anna was asleep. During the day he spent his time staring at the screen of his laptop, or pottering around aboard the *Magpie*, which he had put on the market. About everything else he was bitter and resentful. She found it hard to comfort him. At the beginning of their relationship this would have bewildered her; now she saw that withdrawal helped him process his frustration and left him to it. Herself she comforted with domestic tasks. Nonesuch was suited to that kind of therapy. Filled with a dreaminess amounting to melancholy, she washed up, made beds, sorted linen, wrote lists, told herself *I must buy stamps and bread*.

One morning at eleven o'clock she looked out of the bedroom window to see a large car making its almost silent way up the drive towards the house. It was the silver-grey colour of the rain and there were two men in it. The way they sat, or perhaps the way they dressed, reminded her of something, though she couldn't think what. She watched the car – a Mercedes – until it slipped from view. She heard tyres on the gravel as it pulled up in front of the house; the discreetly engineered European slam of doors; then voices raised in greeting, one of which she thought was John's. A gust of wind shook the cedars, small rain pattered on the window.

'Your daddy's got visitors,' Anna said over her shoulder to Eleanor. 'I wonder who they are.'

Eleanor, dependably a chatterbox in the mornings though she never said anything recognisable or coherent, chose not to answer. She had been too quiet for some time, except for the heavy catarrhal breathing which signified deep and often deplorable involvement. Anna turned from the window to put a stop to whatever was going on and found her daughter sitting in the middle of the great bed, bent over Francis Baynes's musical box. She was staring at it as if she had never seen it before, struck dumb perhaps by the perfection of it, while with a tentative finger she traced the inlays on its polished black lid. Her expression was one of such concentration that Anna felt she had no right to speak: it would be like breaking into the private moment of an adult. *Children are amazing*, she thought. *They're such people.*

After a moment Eleanor looked up. 'Aaaah,' she said.

'Yes. And it would be even better if you let me wind it up.'

Eleanor produced a brilliant foxlike smile; clutched the box firmly to her narrow little chest. No chance of that. Possession, she indicated, was worth more than music. Anyone could tell that.

Anna sighed and looked at her watch. 'Well, I want to know who the visitors are even if you don't.' She held out her arms. 'Come on, let's go and see. It's nearly lunchtime anyway.'

*

114

In the event, John kept his guests busy. They went round the house, floor by floor. Then a second, slightly less expensive vehicle arrived, proving to contain John's bank manager and everyone went round again. This took an hour. By the time Anna bumped into them, hands were being shaken in the hall and you could already imagine the cars speeding off, quiet and wraithlike, to Drychester and beyond. Indeed, the bank manager had gone out to his, leaving John to finish his goodbyes to the two tallish young men from the Mercedes. They were polite, quietly spoken, dressed in identical charcoal-grey suits tailored downstairs at Paul Smith in Covent Garden. They smiled at Anna with the ease conferred by a good education.

'Mrs Dawe. Hello. I'm Mark and this is Oliver. I'm sure you remember us.'

Anna ignored the outstretched hand. 'I'm sure I do,' she said. 'Tortured any animals for profit lately?' No one seemed to hear that, so she raised her voice. 'John, what's going on here?'

'And this is Eleanor, is it?' asked Mark.

Oliver said, 'What a lovely baby.'

Eleanor simpered at him; overcome by faux shyness, she buried her face in Anna's chest and clung like a limpet. Anna stared at John in horror over Eleanor's head. He made some sort of temporising gesture, which Mark and Oliver could hardly have missed. 'She's certainly that,' he told them, walking them through the big doors. 'Are you sure you won't have some lunch?' Anna wanted to scream but common sense made her hang back and watch, inarticulate with anger, until he had got the two of them down the steps and into their vile car. She felt as if her home had been violated, her baby threatened in some unspoken way. She sensed something coming towards her purposefully from a long, long distance off. Her skin crawled with that feeling.

'How dare you?' she said, after John had watched the Mercedes drift off down the drive. 'How dare you have those two in here?'

John was defensive. 'Look,' he said, 'I know how you must feel –'

'No, you don't, John. Or they wouldn't have been here.'

'– but they came with a perfectly good offer.'

'Offer?' She had to sit down. 'What do you mean? You haven't –'

'I haven't said yes to anything.'

'Good, because you're not going to. Everything awful that happened in this house, they were in it up to the hilt. They helped Stella Herringe turn foetal material into cosmetics. God knows what else they helped her do. And it didn't stop with her death. Engelion still exists and they still run it. Or had you forgotten?'

He rubbed his eyes as if she had made him tired. 'Of course not. But they represent the Herringes, too,' he said patiently. 'They came here with Estate backing and a rescue package that might suit everyone.'

She stared at him. 'The Estate? What's it got to do with them? You own this house!'

116

'Like it or not I'm a member of the family –'

'Oh, you are, are you?'

'– and I have to consider their views. Mark and Oliver want to lease Nonesuch as a management training centre for their people. As part of the deal they'll split the cost of the renovations with the Estate. It's a good solution. The bank gets its money. The Estate feels it has an asset again. And most of the year you and I have most of Nonesuch to ourselves.'

'You mean we'd be caretakers in our own house.'

'Let's see what else we could do.' He sounded angry. 'Sit in it until it falls down?'

'Give me six months in the City and I'll buy us another house,' she promised. 'Do you think I couldn't?'

He touched her hand. 'No,' he said with a smile. 'I think you could.'

She pulled her hand away. 'Then for God's sake let me! I mean it. I won't take a penny from Engelion. And neither will you.'

'Anna, they were prosecuted and they cleaned up their act.'

'They got off scot-free, the way all those companies do. A fine they can easily pay, some minor board member sacked at a press conference, a convenient name change. People forget, business goes on as usual. You've seen the same TV footage as me.'

'What do you want?'

'I want justice.'

'Anna –'

'I don't want paltry fines followed by crocodile tears and repositioning of the product in the market.

117

What do they call themselves now? English Garden House of Beauty?'

'I don't think it's that bad. I think they called it "English Lion" or something. They left me a brochure –'

'Oh, shut up, John. You know this isn't right.'

He knew. He looked crestfallen. Eleanor – who, bored since the departure of her admirers, had squirmed impatiently throughout the whole exchange – offered him her music box, then burst into tears when he didn't seem to notice the gesture. In the rather quiet and strained few days that followed, she kept it as close by her as she could. She continued to refuse to have it wound up. Any music that came from it now was fragmentary, incidental. Anna, meanwhile, sure that nothing was as it seemed, acted exactly like a cat whose territory had been disturbed. Her fur was up, her skin twitched. Rehearsing these anxieties, she prowled the corridors as if she suspected Mark and Oliver were still around and hoped to catch them unawares. As anyone who has been burgled will report, none of this was necessarily conscious. Later, Alice Meynell disturbed her in the kitchen, orating fiercely while she ironed perfect little baby clothes of Eleanor's, 'I despise you and everything you stand for.'

It was a moment before she noticed Alice. She shrugged, as if to say, 'Everyone talks to themselves. So what.' Then something caused her to ask, 'Which would you prefer, Alice, freedom from the past or freedom from the future?' As if it were possible to have either. 'I hate the past,' she added, when Alice only stared. 'I bloody hate it.' As if that could explain anything.

'Cup of tea?' suggested Alice.

Izzie says I must be careful where I put things. Putting things away is almost as difficult to learn as finding them in the first place. You're here and there waiting and listening on the stairs sitting in some moonlight on a landing with the smells of mice coming up between the boards. There are a lot of places to put things. A lot of bolt-holes, says Izzie, a lot of rat holes but only one safe place for each one thing. It isn't just a matter of hiding them my little onion. I should know (and she laughs) I put the safest thing away and you'll be older than you are before you find that my girl. Older and wiser, she says, and laughs again.

Won't you have a shock, too, she says. I did. When I saw what I had to do.

When Izzie comes her voice is beautiful. She is often singing a song. She is telling me something already so I miss the beginning of it. She tells it as a story, she sings it as a song. One song is about a very beautiful woman who was forced to kill her own baby.

Ashmore, early morning. Sunshine lay weightless on the fronts of the Victorian almshouses. Eaton Terrace smelled of fresh bread and cut grass. Rooks, up early to see what could be had, planed in widening circles against a clear blue sky. Francis Baynes stood with his hand on the lych-gate to watch Anna Dawe's marmalade cat, its fur full of light, slip across the churchyard on some business of its own. 'Hello, Orlando,' he murmured and clicked his tongue.

The cat, halting for a fraction of a second, looked back over its shoulder at him, blinked its intelligent yellow eyes and disappeared among the head-stones.

Francis smiled and went on into St Mary's. There, he put on his vestments and prepared for Early Communion, which he had reinstated along with the old Book of Common Prayer when he took over the parish. No one had complained because no one ever came. Although he regretted this, Francis rarely allowed it to depress him. He was less a tradi-tionalist, he knew, than a romantic. He had never regretted that, either.

This morning, when he had finished, and put away the cup and paten, the church seemed filled for a tantalising moment with a kind of liquid gold, some glorious substance that permeated the spaces between the very molecules of the air. He loved St Mary's when it was lit like this, from within. Its bareness seemed elegant, willed, proper. Its empti-ness made of it a vessel. But after a moment or two it always reverted to the church he knew, smelling strongly of lilies and wholesale wax polish, and echoing to the faint sound of a tap dripping in the vestry. Ordinary light cut across its columns and pews. Francis sighed, tidied the pamphlets in the rack by the door, and – casting one more glance towards the east window before he turned to leave – saw he was not alone after all.

While he was busy with the pamphlets, she had

slipped quietly past him and now stood at the other end of the nave, at the base of one of the great cylindrical Romanesque piers. He had not heard her at the door. Yet here she was, unspeaking, tall, dressed in brown, carrying her grey kid gloves in one hand and a few flowers in the other. The light from the side windows fell across her. She brought to the cool air of the nave the smell of earth and St Mary's was suddenly resonant with a faint full chord, as if someone had played barely audible notes on the organ.

'What do you want?' whispered Francis Baynes, while some inner voice leapt to answer, 'The mystery! The mystery!' and the woman from the graveyard turned her face towards him and vanished.

All the rest of the day he went about his parish business puzzled and frustrated. By midnight, returning tired yet restless, he found it impossible to settle to anything. The weather had turned and it was raining. He put on his coat, stood for a few minutes in the empty graveyard as if waiting for something; then, getting into his little Rover, hurried it up on to the downs, where he parked and stared out across the rain-dark valley at the Queen Anne chimneys and curiously angled gables of Nonesuch, thinking and thinking, while the wind raced the clouds through a moonlit sky the colour of fish scales.

'Quite dark,' he whispered to himself.

When he got back, the door of the vicarage was

blowing open and someone had turned on a nightlight in one of the upper rooms. He stood there at a loss in the darkened hall. He could hear someone moving about up there.

'Hello?' he called.

No answer.

He started to climb the stairs, but caution made him stop again a few steps up. 'Hello?' Though it was electric, the nightlight seemed to flicker momentarily, as if in a draught. This is ridiculous, thought Francis Baynes. If I'm not afraid of God, I shouldn't be afraid of anything else. 'Hello?'

'Hello!' said the woman in the brown muslin dress.

When he looked up, she was standing at the top of the stairs looking down at him. There was a welcoming smile on her face – she was welcoming him to his own house – and her gloves and flowers were nowhere to be seen. The gloves were off. It was almost dark. He felt that she had changed in some way since the morning. Her body seemed heavier, untidier; her face was less ethereal. Francis found himself thinking she looked more real. Almost, he said to himself, more alive. And then, for no reason he could think of, more established.

He made his way uncertainly up towards her. 'I'm sorry,' he said. 'I –'

What had he meant to say? He had no idea why he should apologise to her. But as soon as he got close to her, a wave of heat seemed to roll across him and he forgot all that. She smelled of earth, flowers, musk. He saw now how low the brown muslin dress was cut; how it seemed to offer him her breasts, heavy in the half-dark. She smelled of sweat. She held out her hand, but he couldn't take it and only stood there as shy as a boy. Because what did he know about her? And anyway, he had an erection suddenly hot and painful in his trousers and he felt that she knew it. He didn't know where to look.

'Francis!' she said. 'That's your name. Francis.' She laughed. 'Isn't it? Well, look, Francis,' she said, holding out her hand again, 'I don't bite. Not always.'

Her hand was hot and dry. She led him into his own bedroom. There he saw, in the dim illumination of the nightlight, that she had taken the entire contents of his kitchen cupboards and refrigerator – a week's groceries bought guiltily at Waitrose that morning – and strewn them over the bed. Two large tin loaves and half a dozen eggs. Fair Trade tea bags and Café Direct. A pound of mild cheddar cheese. Eight pounds of potatoes. Pork pies. Tomatoes, celery, peppers. Rhubarb and gooseberries. Liver and kidneys. Dried pasta shells. Two doughnuts.

Francis stared.

'I'm afraid I started without you,' she said. 'Oh, Francis, isn't it wonderful, just to be alive?'

There was salt everywhere. She had ripped open the milk cartons, and spilled HP sauce and raspberry jam over his bedspread. She had stripped the plastic off the wrapped stuff.

She had taken a bite out of every single item.

'I'd forgotten quite how wonderful it was,' she said.

Francis stared at her. He saw now that she had food round her mouth. Plum juice and ketchup had trickled down her neck and on to the upper part of her breasts. The smell of her had become over-powering. He felt more and more like an adolescent. At the same time he felt like himself, angry, con-fused, more sexually aware than he ever wanted to be. He stared up at her in the constantly flickering light. Somehow, he managed to do that. 'Who are you?' he made himself ask.

She answered, 'You know me. I was in the groves when they murdered Actaeon. I was in Egypt and Persia. I starred in *The Golden Bough*. They called me Diana, they called me the Moon. Later they burned my followers all across Europe. I'm earth to your fire, Francis. If you have any. I'm from far away and long ago; and I'm from around here too. They know me on the downs. This village knows me. The family know me, they always knew me very well – I was on their ground before they built there. You needn't worry.' She went on, 'I'm the answer to your mystery.' Then she laughed. 'Or not so much the answer, Francis, as the mystery itself. You do want to know, don't you? Haven't you always wanted to know? That's why you need me. That, and –' Here she looked meaningfully down at the front of his trousers. 'That's why I chose you. That's why you're so lucky.'

'I –'

'You were waiting for me. You were always waiting for me.' She crooked her finger. 'Come here,' she said. 'Come to Izzie.'

When Eleanor Dawe woke in the mornings, a little chuckling delightful stream of lalage woke with her, a commentary on her life and doings. Listen from a distance and you could be fooled, until you realised that the words were not words at all, but only the sounds that words are made from, timed perfectly to the rhythms of the voices around her. You recognised her mother's voice; her father's. Then, with a little start of surprise, the intonations of Alice Meynell or even Francis Baynes. In the mornings, Eleanor teetered on the edge of speech but never quite jumped in. John and Anna encouraged her by talking to her endlessly. Anna read to her from her favourite book, *Around the World with Ant and Bee*.

John greeted her, 'Hello Eleanor,' forming every syllable with exaggerated care. 'It's Eleanor. Hello, Eleanor!'

Unsure how to respond, his daughter looked dubiously from one expectant parental face to the other, then down at her Lion King dish where it lay on the kitchen table ready to be filled with Rice Krispies. Breakfast, she saw, might depend on humouring them. She managed a placatory smile.

'Gidgie,' she said, pointing to the spoon.

'Spoon, Eleanor. Spoon.'

They were delighted and disappointed by turns. They marvelled at how close she got to language, without quite discovering it. Ironically, they remained frozen in their attempts to communicate with each other.

Mark and Oliver had returned to Nonesuch more

than once. But so had the bank manager and, although negotiations continued and the building work slowly recovered momentum, it was clear no deal had yet been struck. John kept the details to himself. This enabled Anna to maintain an uneasy truce on the subject. Underneath, though, she was still raw. They both were. Nonesuch was rarely mentioned, but they quarrelled over everything else – politics, Eleanor's bedtime, whose turn it was to put petrol in the Volvo. Then John refused to take the *Magpie* off the market.

'You're doing this to spite yourself,' Anna accused him. 'And me. You don't really want to sell her.'

' "Her"?' he said. 'It's a boat, Anna.' And then more gently, 'I don't see what other choice I have.' He passed one hand tiredly across his face. 'I've thought and thought about it. We just need money, any money we can come by.'

She looked at the floor. 'You don't want this,' she persisted. 'What would you get for her? Peanuts. Enough to fund a week or two's work. You're just angry with everything.'

'And you're just being sentimental,' he accused.

She didn't know how to answer that. All she had achieved was to make him more angry and lose the ground she had gained. Eventually she whispered, 'Someone has to be.'

'Things move on, Anna.'

The bleakness of this upset her further. 'I loved our time on that boat!'

He shook his head. 'I loved it too,' he said. 'You know I did. But –' He held her gaze for a moment, looking helpless and miserable. Then he shook his head, folded up the *Guardian* and pushed back his chair. He was always going somewhere else. That was how their life was now. 'Don't you remember?' he asked. 'We did nothing but fight.' He stopped in the kitchen doorway as if he might find some way to soften this, then shrugged. 'Nothing changes, does it?'

'John!'

When he had gone she whispered, 'You don't believe any of that.'

She couldn't stop trying to fetch him out of himself, though she knew these panicky acts only drove him further in. The builders, meanwhile, began some of the exterior work, with a corresponding increase in mud and noise; and Mark and Oliver wandered elegantly about, looking at ordinary household items as if they were brand new and rather clever. Anna heard their voices. She stayed in the kitchen until she could watch their car float away down the drive; while John, temperamentally incapable of sharing his rage and guilt, took refuge in his 'office', an old linen press on the second floor where he had telephone, fax machine and Anna's two-year-old desktop computer set up in a litter of estimates, invoices and half-empty cups of coffee. Anna was reluctant to pursue him there because other rooms on the same floor had been used to store salvaged fittings from Stella Herringe's apartment. Nevertheless she went up one rainy, lonely afternoon, and took Eleanor too because when he was like this Eleanor was the only lever she had.

She found him with his chair tipped back, stroking Orlando's three daughters – who, house-bound by the rain, were padding about on the desk, purring and knocking down anything that looked important. Orlando, meanwhile, sat on the window-sill, looking detached and a little forlorn.

'I'm sorry,' she said and opened her mouth to say more.

'No,' he said. 'Don't. Don't. I'm sorry too.'

They studied one another uncertainly.

'I brought Ellie to visit her grumpy father.'

He smiled. 'So I see.'

'But she fell asleep.'

'I can see that too.' He cleared some files off an old leather armchair. 'Do you think she would be comfortable here?'

'I think she would be very comfortable there.'

'Because it seems a pity to wake her up.'

'It does. It does seem a pity.'

They looked down at her together. 'She's ours,' he said, in tones of deep proprietary satisfaction. He gestured towards the desk. 'And what do you think of these cats?' It was as if he had just found them.

'I think we have the most beautiful cats in the world.'

'Hm,' he said. 'Come and stand by the window.' They stood by the window for a moment looking out. 'This garden –' he began.

'It's a beautiful garden, John.'

He put his arm round her shoulders, and – when she turned in towards him to feel his steady warmth, which always made her want to curl into his chest like a cat – looked down at her and concluded gently, 'So. Between us, you and me, we're in danger of spoiling a very good thing.'

Anna hid her face against him. 'I know,' she admitted.

He smelled of Pears soap. She could feel his heart beating. 'Hold me,' she begged. Then a little later she said something less distinct, which made him draw in his breath and lay her down on the chilly floorboards. The cats purred and trod around them. Anna pulled up her skirt; the wind threw a handful of rain against the windows; the Nonesuch cedars bent their heads. The light was pale grey, gentle but merciless, encouraging clarity in all things. 'Fuck me, John,' she heard herself whisper in a rush of love and bleakness. 'Oh yes, fuck me.' And she wondered, in the instant before she slipped into the willed oblivion of it, how much longer they could use this to heal themselves.

Anna woke suddenly, lying on her side. John had spooned himself round her while he slept. Her hip was sore. She detached herself gently from his enclosing arm and stood up to look out of the window while her hands busied themselves independently about – adjusting, dusting down, tugging at her skirt and cardigan. The rain was heavier; the sky darker and racing with cloud. Something grumbled over the horizon. A storm was on its way, but it was the room that had the thundery look, a kind of brown tint to the air which hung around the computer console, the littered papers and half-empty cups. The computer fan hummed, though the screen was dark. The telephone rang once, then stopped.

John slept on. The cats had gone.

So had Eleanor.

Anna called her daughter's name. She looked under the chair, behind it. She looked under the desk. She bit her lip. It was a room too small to hide in.

The passage outside had an institutional look, acquired during the Second World War, when two or three tall drab rooms along its length had housed for a short time the officers of a local bomber squadron. Anna had never entered those rooms willingly, even before the fire, because they had still seemed to her to smell of the boot polish, hair oil and thin beer of that earlier occupation. But there was no sign of Eleanor in the passage and now one of the doors hung open just far enough to admit a toddler. Anna stopped and listened. She could hear a voice from inside, diminutive, pitched high, oddly conversational.

She pushed the door. 'Ellie?'

Stella's things were piled up against the walls, Jacobean chairs, a cracked slate dining table from Heal's, bits of chrome and bolts of water-damaged brocade, a senseless jumble of furniture and fittings thick with the reek of scorch and damp. Left to herself, Anna – still unnerved by anything that reminded her of the fire, or the events preceding it – would have had this dismal stuff destroyed. Eleanor Dawe had no such qualms. She was sitting in the middle of it all, her legs straight out in front of her, the musical box clutched firmly in one little fist, looking up at everything with wide delighted eyes. She was chattering away to herself just as she did in the mornings – except that now the stream of lalage rushed and bubbled with real words. She seemed to have remembered everything anyone had ever said to her.

'Naughty girl,' she said; and, 'baby, baby, little baby.'

Several times she said, 'What a pretty girl.'

Anna, who recognised many of these phrases because they were her own, stood by the door, as much entranced as disconcerted by the accuracy of the imitation, not daring to interrupt in case Eleanor lost the hang of it. Eleanor, though, wasn't in need of help. She paused magisterially. There was a sense of a gear shifting and she was off on a kind of sing-song recital, picked up effortlessly in mid-flow, 'an to the big hole in the wall, an oops a daisy, oops a daisy, the little girl's fell, oh she's fell over, an it's a big hole . . .' Suddenly her tone changed again and she said, 'I've been down to Portsmouth today. The traffic was vile.' She added, 'When we got there it was full of people in cheap sports shoes.' This, with its effect of a conversation between two dull middle-aged men in the bar at the Green Man, was bizarre to hear in the light, high voice of a toddler.

'Eleanor!' Anna said. 'Eleanor?'

'. . . an dark places an light – haughty-taughty, naughty girl – an up we go little girl, up we go . . . an oh do pay attention Alice . . . an such a lot of stairs, lot of stairs, people on the stairs . . .'

Anna felt something like panic. 'Eleanor, stop now. Stop!'

It was too much. It was too soon. But Eleanor just kept on talking as if Anna weren't there – as if, now she had the hang of it, she would never stop – and eventually Anna walked up to her and picked her up and shook her. 'Eleanor!'

'– and berries,' finished Eleanor with satisfaction.

She gave Anna a sideways look. Then she shook herself suddenly. Her face turned red and large tears rolled down it. A ripe smell filled the room.

'Oh dear,' said Anna. 'Nappy alert, I think.' She turned Eleanor over. There was no need to sniff. 'Come on,' she continued, relieved to have something ordinary to deal with, 'let's clean you up and show you to your daddy.'

Eleanor, unable to see anything in it for her, took this gloomily.

'Cheer up,' Anna advised her. 'You can talk. You can talk!'

Eleanor blinked and offered Anna the music box which, all along, had been trickling its sweet, distant rendering of 'Für Elise' into the dusty air.

They found John sitting on the floor of his office, engagingly crumpled and bleary, rubbing his jaw and yawning with the air of a man who has only just woken up. He had fastened his grey Levis and Oxford cloth shirt, but they looked as though he had slept all night in them. He needed a shave. Anna's heart went out to him, in a rush of love and excitement. 'Look,' she said. 'I mean, listen!'

'You should make up your mind.'

'Go on, Eleanor!' urged Anna. Eleanor, somewhat recovered, smiled blandly, pointed at her father, then held out her arms to him. She remained resolutely silent. 'Oh, Eleanor, how disappointing!'

John eyed them both. 'What's disappointing?'

'John, she can talk. I found her chattering away to herself –'

'Found her?' asked John.

Anna blushed. 'She must have crawled off while we were –'

'Ah.' He smiled. 'That. What responsible parents we are.' He rubbed his face again, looked down at himself puzzledly, then round the room. 'Have I been asleep?'

'Oh, John!'

He examined Eleanor. 'Well, she's not doing it now,' he stated. 'Are you sure? It's easy to mistake that babble for words.'

'Gidgie poes,' Eleanor contributed obligingly; and to that she would add nothing.

'Oh, well,' said John. 'You must have misheard.'

'I suppose I must,' said Anna, who knew she hadn't.

On the way back to the kitchen to make tea, Anna poked her head round the door of the storeroom. Some of the furniture she remembered from her very first visit to Nonesuch. She had rather admired it then, but now it filled her with the same disgust as the concrete pens of the experimental cattery, which had been awaiting demolition since Stella Herringe's death. She shivered. It was so hard to escape the past. And then, she was still puzzled by the afternoon's turn of events – though less now by the suddenness of Eleanor's plunge into language than by her subsequent retreat from it.

Chapter Six

NIGHT AFTER NIGHT I woke and felt that phantom cat beside me. I smelled it in the air; I felt its hot breath on the back of my neck. And while I never sensed that it meant me harm, I was beginning to dread letting go of consciousness, for fear it would show itself to me, after which I knew I would never be able to sleep again. It was a dead cat, of that much I was certain, for it left no footmarks, it took no food, it made no sound. It was a ghost from my past and it was haunting me.

Millie did not return, in all those nights, nor in the long days afterwards. I had taken, on occasion, to hanging around the wild roads down by the gate, sniffing for her scent; at other times, isolated without her and bored with my own company, I would go out in search of her, knowing it to be pointless, but driven by a powerful, unspoken need. I could not talk about my fears with Lydia, who regarded all I did and said with imperious indifference; and anything to do with dreams and dreamcatching as my own personal madness. And I dared not involve the girls, especially Caterina, who had started to pester me about taking her on the highways to learn my skill. I had been an unwilling apprentice, myself, and that had been before I had known the horrors I had in store. Now that I was well apprised of the worst that dreamcatching had to offer, I would not wish it on another living being, particularly one I held so dear.

So I wandered the house and its environs list-lessly, taking in all new changes: how the moorhen chicks down on Ashmore's pond had grown to fit their absurdly large feet and now scuttled every-where, obsessed by the search for food so that they might grow larger still; how the midges swarmed at twilight and the dragonflies quartered the heavy, humid air to hunt them down; how the hard green berries on the bramble bushes gained a blush of colour that attracted the little birds, the finches and sparrows; how the grass on the common grew increasingly sere and scorched as the hot weather continued, till it was as tawny as the fur of the new rabbits who fled across it in the hot summer nights, pursued by a russet creature who looked very much like a fox I had once known. I watched with interest how Anna and John put up white metal gates at the entrance to all the stairways in the house; but if they were meant to keep us out, they were entirely ineffective: for the girls who, though lithe, were still too large to squeeze through the rails, merely treated the gates as a means of providing them with many hours of hurdling entertainment and some-where to stage fights in which the bars made for interesting obstacles to batting paws.

The only visitors to Nonesuch in this time – other than the builders – were the young woman who rode a loud, noxious-smelling machine and clumped around in huge leather boots (we all kept out of her way, though she was not deliberately clumsy) and the man from the church, who kept turning up, it seemed, when John was not here. The last time he had come, he had given the baby an object, a small thing all shiny and black with flowers on it, that chimed and clanged when its lid was lifted; but despite the gift, I could tell it was not the baby that drew him here; I saw how his eyes followed Anna's every movement, especially when he thought she was not aware of it. Cats are very watchful of their humans – 'jealous as a cat' was not phrased without reason – so I, in turn, observed him closely, for as far as I was concerned he had no place at Nonesuch, nor with Anna. If she belonged to anyone, I reasoned, it was to me, for I had come before all the rest; it was me she had fed every night of my life; it was with me she curled up when the baby was asleep and John was working. And it was I who had led her rescuers to her in the midst of the fire, and not without some risk to myself. My whiskers have never been straight since.

One day as I stood my watch at the gates, other visitors arrived, and this time neither on foot, nor on the noisy two-wheeled monster; no, these visitors came in a huge silver car which growled its way slowly up the drive, crunching the gravel under its great wheels, until it came to a halt in front of the

house. I scampered across the lawns in time to see
two men in identical clothing climbing out of it, to be
greeted by John, who seemed pleased to see them. I
was less sure; the smell of them was vaguely
familiar: a scent found once and never since identified. It was so faint as to be illusory; but I have a
good nose. I followed them in, intrigued. They were
quiet and polite, and appeared to offer no threat as
they strolled around the house with John, peering
into this room and that; but then another car came
up the drive and John left the men and went downstairs to meet it. He stayed outside for some time
talking with the new arrival, his voice drifting up to
us as if from a great distance. As soon as he had
gone, the men changed their demeanour, much as
cats do when entering a wild road, taking on their
primal, wild forms to suit the inimical environment
in which they find themselves, a place which
demands the precise deployment of every natural
sense to ensure survival and well-being. Their
identical smiles faded away and they became alert
and watchful. They fairly bristled with anticipation;
I could almost imagine that their features had
become sharp and weaselly, as if trying to sniff out
something that was lost.

One of them said something softly to the other,
who turned at once and walked quickly away, disappearing down the long corridor and round the
corner. Of course, I followed him at once. This was
my domain and he was trespassing. Even so, he
appeared to know his way around, despite all
Nonesuch's mazelike passages, half-landings and

little stairways, and soon we were down on the ground floor again, in the room that gave on to the knot garden. The scent of the witch was still strong in here, even though all her furniture and belongings had been removed. I watched him as he walked the bare boards, patting the walls here and there, as if he expected something to be concealed there. He opened the solitary remaining wardrobe that had been too large to get through the doors but, finding it empty, closed it again, furtively quiet, as if he had no wish to be found. I heard John's voice, closer now as he led the latest visitor into the great hallway. The man stiffened at the sound and his head came up, like an animal sensing threat; then he walked quickly across the witch's chamber, slipped out into the dark corridor and doubled back to the upstairs room, in which he and his companion had been left, by a different route from the one John was taking even now, moving so swiftly and silently all the time that I found it hard to keep him in sight. By the time I arrived, he and the man who looked so like him were standing together at the window as if innocently admiring the view over the knot garden; and John arrived a second or two later with a large man in a brown suit.

'Ah, Orlando,' John declared with a grin, sweeping me up in his arms. 'My little tiger.' He turned to the men at the window. 'I think he's keeping an eye on you,' he said, laughing.

I heard him laugh and it annoyed me. I do not like to be picked up. I struggled and squirmed out of his grip. As I did so, I looked up: the two men were watching me intently, their eyes narrowed and calculating; but by the time my paws had hit the floor, they were laughing, too.

As I walked off down the corridor I could feel them all watching me, their gaze a crawling weight on my back, their laughter like the bark of hounds. The fur along my spine twitched with the sound of it. It was all I could do not to run; but dignity is important in such circumstances. I made it to the top of the stairs, where the new white gate had been left ajar; then, knowing myself to be out of their sight line, I fled down the stairs and into the kitchen. There I found Lydia lying on the rug before the stove, which Anna kept going even in the hottest weather, as if for our comfort alone. She lay on her side, exposing the pale golden fur of her belly, her eyes half closed, her pink tongue just visible; the very picture of somnolence. I threw myself down beside her and wished for the thousandth time she would let me lay my head down on that great, soft expanse and show me a little kindness. Sometimes all you need in life is just a touch of comfort.

Liddy, however, was not going to provide it. She sat up in a huff and looked at me down her long nose. 'What's the matter with you?' she asked, though the tone of her voice implied she was far more irritated at being interrupted than interested in my state of mind.

'Some men just arrived,' I told her lamely.

'I saw them,' she said, surprising me. She did not look as though she had stirred from her lazing spot all day. 'The two who look like one.'

I nodded. 'I don't like them. They do not belong here.'

She laughed, a short cough of a sound with no mirth to it. 'Ah. You'd be surprised at how well they belong here,' she said cryptically, but she would not explain her remark further, and after a few moments turned her back on me to signal that my audience was at an end, settled herself comfortably and went back to sleep.

The next week they were back; and for several days after that. I could smell them throughout the house, for wherever they went they left a scent trail that was both attractive and repellent at the same time. Humans have distinctive odours and, though they wash in water and spray themselves with chemicals to disguise them, they cannot hide their true scents from the nose of a cat. John's smell was strong and complex; salty and tangy when he had been working hard; warm and peppery the rest of the time. Anna's changed from day to day, depending on her mood. When she was angry she smelled hot and sharp, like the ground after a lightning strike. When she was contented she smelled a little like Lydia: aromatic and heathery, with a healthy under-scent of warm earth. But when she and John mated her scent became rank and musky. Then the pheromones would get into the bones of my head and buzz there like a message.

The baby's smell was different again: elusive and deceptive. I could never quite keep it in my head, nor fix it in the scent map Hawkweed had tried to teach me as a way of making sense of these things. When she had first been born, Ellie had smelled as sweet and buttery as a just-opened hazelnut; but some time in the weeks afterwards that aroma had gone, to be replaced by some-thing less wholesome – not the usual small-creature whiffs of faeces and urine they have not yet learned to clean themselves of – but a faint scent redolent of age and must, like something that has been kept for a long time in a closed and airless place. Then that, too, was gone; or if not entirely gone, faded into the background as the baby's new scent formed; and this new scent was a strange half-echo of Anna's at mid-moon, when her blood was hot and she moved as sinuously as a queen on heat. It was a disturbing scent for a child to have. And it affected others more than it did me.

I watched the two men who looked like one admiring her as John carried her around. She would show them her new toy – the black tin box that Anna's friend had given her – stretching out her hand to them, then, when she had their full attention and they reached out to join in the game, she would take the toy away, burying it between her and her father, as if it were their prize, their secret. She giggled. I saw how she watched them over his shoulder when he walked away, how she enraptured them all.

She did not smell the same when Anna held her, I noticed. The musky scent would recede, as if she could exude and retract it at will. I never felt very comfortable in her presence and not just because she liked to hit me with her toys.

142

One week, the hot weather gave way to steady, driving rain. I sat on the windowsill of the upstairs room in which John spent much of his time clacking away at a desk and divided my attention between watching the girls chasing the crumpled balls of paper John had obligingly thrown around the room for them and observing how the raindrops were so heavy that they made even the big leaves of the rhododendrons bounce under their weight. *Poor Griz*, I thought, *not much shelter under there from weather like this*. I had just jumped down from my perch with the idea of showing Grizelda and whichever others of the cattery survivors were under the bushes with her the way into the shed with the broken door – shouldered just so, the door would swing open a few inches; enough to admit a quick cat, though getting out was always rather more of a palaver – when Anna came into the room, carrying the baby.

At once that heady scent filled the air. Even the girls – who had given up on the paper game and were now wandering desultorily around the desk, knocking things off it – seemed to notice it. Their heads went up. Their noses twitched.

One by one, they slipped light-footed from the table and gathered about me. 'Play with us, Uncle Orlando,' they wheedled.

Belly rubbed herself against me. Letitia hurled herself at my feet and began cleverly to juggle one of the paper balls beneath my nose. Cat leapt up on to my back and bore me down to the ground, whereupon they all joined in so that I could hardly breathe for the riot of scent pressing down on me (and because they were crushing my ribcage).

I knew the scent of calling females only too well. Of all scents, it was the one that made me saddest. It brought back memories. I remembered how Millie had smelled, that night under the moon, when she had offered herself to me, as wicked and as sweet as you could wish, her white belly fur almost luminous in the starlight, her eyes glinting with promise. But I – stupid young simpleton than I was – had run away, as if afraid of such a gift. And I also remembered Liddy's scent on that fateful night on the houseboat – how should I forget? – when the dream had interrupted our one and only attempt to mate. Even the memory made me dizzy. She had never forgiven me for choosing the dream over her; I knew that now. She probably never would.

Lydia –

The scent in the air was a powerful reminder to me that I was not playing my role in propagating my species.

'Off with you!' I cried and disentangled myself with some difficulty from the heap of pretty limbs. 'I'm only a poor old fellow: no match for you three hoydens.'

And while the two humans lay down on the floor together and began their mating dance, and the girls trod about them, I fled down the stairs, determined to confront my love once and for all.

I found her at the food bowls. She had finished a dish of chicken in gravy and had just started crunching her way through a bowl of dried pellets. She stood there, her head angled to roll the food between her molars, her jaw working furiously. It was some seconds before she noticed me: the smell of that dried stuff is so strong it can make you oblivious to any other scent.

'Liddy –' I started.

She leapt backwards. The bowl went over and pellets shot everywhere.

'Now look what you've done!' she seethed. She started to bat the food into a heap with her front paws. 'What a waste,' she muttered. 'Can't let it go to waste.' She buried her face in the little pile she had made and tried to eat it down, but without any support to hold them in place, the pellets skittered away across the tiles.

'Liddy – Lydia – stop, please.'

I put myself between her and the remainder of the food. She sat down abruptly, looking beset.

'Lydia, I need to talk to you. I really must.'

'About what?' she said rudely. 'What's so important it has to interrupt my meal?'

'I want you to tell me what happened to you here, when the witch had you captive,' I said all in a rush, determined to get the words out before I lost my nerve.

An unreadable expression passed across her face. 'I don't even want to think about that time. It's past and gone, and I have my girls.'

'I feel,' I said, bracing myself, 'I feel as if you blame me somehow. For not being there. For not finding you in time –'

She laughed. 'You? You think you could have stopped . . . what happened to me? You think you stood a chance against *her*? You're mad, Orlando! Being a dreamcatcher has addled the few wits you were born with.'

My heart was hammering in my head. I could feel more words boiling up. 'You see, Liddy, the thing is . . .' Could I say it? Her face did not invite me to continue. But I knew that if I did not say what I had to say, I would never manage it at all and would regret my failure to do so. I took a deep breath and blundered on. 'I still love you, Lydia, after all this time and even though you've been so . . . cold to me and have shown me no encouragement at all, I still care for you and I want to be with you properly. We could have kittens of our own –'

She looked aghast. 'Kittens?'

I nodded dumbly. 'I would love kittens of my own, kittens with you, Lydia. I love your girls – they are wonderful. Letty is a minx and Belly is a bit of a pawful but –'

'Don't call them that!' Her eyes flashed at me. 'They have proper names: Letitia, Arabella and Caterina. They are not common cats, for you to call them such ridiculous things.'

'But the girls like their nicknames, Liddy,' I said carefully, not sure what point she was trying to make. 'They never use the long forms if they can help it.'

'Stop it!'

I watched the muscles in her ears contracting, the flanges furling in on themselves as if she would shut out my words.

'They have proper pedigree ancestry, my girls,' she went on loudly, to prevent me saying more. 'The blood of show champions runs in their veins – they have generations of fine breeding behind them. Unlike you, Orlando, a son who never even knew his own father. How could you even think I would mate with you?' The venom in her voice was shocking.

I was nonplussed, then angry. 'But Liddy, you cared for me once, enough to invite me aboard your boat. Enough to lift your tail for me!'

She flew at me then, claws out, meaning to hurt. Her eyes were blank with menace. One of her paws caught me a raking clout across the nose, drawing blood. Another sailed over my head, but her elbow caught me a painful, glancing blow on the ear. She bit me on the shoulder; she bit me on the leg. With the strength of a seasoned tomcat battling for its life, she pushed me down. In a frenzy of loathing, she got underneath me, grasped me around the neck in a horrible semblance of affection and then battered at me with her hind feet, her talons harrowing my belly as if she would disembowel me. She hissed. She spat and bubbled. When she could make words – or I could distinguish them from the venomous sounds with which she attacked me – she cursed me: for my stupidity, my gall and my love. And all the while I lay there, foolishly, and let her buffet me, unwilling to fight back for fear I would forget myself and, reverting to my primal self, hurt her in return.

At last she fell back exhausted. I pushed myself painfully to a crouch. I was bleeding from a dozen wounds, could feel where her teeth had met in my hock. My muzzle smarted where her first blow had fallen. Water was seeping from one of my eyes. It stung so badly I wondered for a moment whether she had caught a claw in the delicate skin surrounding it. Then I realised the other eye was doing the same thing. Mortified, I turned away from her.

I sat there, blinking furiously, little afterwaves of shock making the muscles tremble in my flanks. What could we say to one another now? How would we even share the same house from this point, let alone the same food bowl? I groomed my torn neck and tried to think of calming phrases that would make light of the situation, but the vehemence of her attack withered the words before they bubbled out into the air. At last, I decided on my approach. 'Liddy,' I started. 'You're upset. I can see that. It's understandable –'

My face composed into mild forgiveness, I turned round, but Lydia, stealthily, silently, had gone.

Her absence hurt more than the blows.

She did not return that night, nor the next. She had never left Nonesuch before, never gone anywhere on her own, to the best of my knowledge. She had been cared for and cosseted all her life – except for that one brief spell she would not speak about; that sore wound in her life that I had so thoughtlessly pressed upon, out of shame of which she had fled. The house became a tense burrow of anxiety. I heard John walking the gardens when the moon came up, calling her name, but she did not reply. Anna went outside and banged a spoon against a tin, an action which always caught Lydia's rapt attention; but she did not come. The girls and I scouted the gardens, quartering the area carefully, noses to the ground. I found a lingering trace of her scent near the orchard wall, but there it disappeared.

I walked the human roads of the village of Ashmore, in the day and by the light of the moon, but no cat whom I questioned had seen a beautiful golden queen close to, or from afar. And when I went to see the Besom, to ask her opinion and her advice, she was gone, too. It was as if all my friends were deserting me, one by one, leaving me with a hard task to perform, a task that would either prove me or break me. I half expected old Hawkweed to manifest before me, a gleam in his single eye, to explain the rules of this new test. It would have been a blessing if he had.

I took to the wild roads. I hunted up and down them, though I could not imagine Lydia entering the highways. I stopped each cat I came upon there and sniffed at them carefully: for in her primal form on the animal highways, who knew what Liddy might look like? I went further afield, out of Ashmore and towards Drychester and the towns that crept out over the plain, and into the chalk hills that bore strange patterns carved into their skin, like tattoos upon the earth. I met travelling cats there: jaunty gypsy cats without a care in the world, strutting lads in the skins of tigers and pumas; feisty queens sashaying along with the proud, swinging gait of lynxes and caracals, rag-eared toms and their retinues; a pride of lions; gaggles of girls – in a fabulous assortment of guises – out for a lark and feeling themselves very daring and grown-up to be swept up in the cold compass winds, not knowing quite where they might emerge.

Not one of them had seen a cat who answered my description, on the highways or off, though a few of the lads looked at me askance and said they'd have a good idea of what to do with such a one if they came upon her. Then they would cackle and cast knowing looks at each other so that I did not know whether they had indeed encountered Liddy, or were having me on.

I ran my feet raw during the days following Lydia's disappearance. I ran till my pads were bleeding and my neck ached with the tension of staring rigidly into howling winds and bright lights. I ran till I could run no more. Then, one night when the moon hung huge and full and bloody-orange in the sky, as swollen as a dream sac that bears the worst of nightmares – a hunter's moon, they call it, though I brought no bounty home with me – I limped back into Nonesuch and found that just when I thought I was feeling as guilty and as sorry for myself as I possibly could, things had taken a turn for the worse.

Belly and Letty were sitting on the front doorstep, peering out into the darkness, so still and intent that at first I did not realise they were there.

'Oh, Uncle Orlando!' Letty's eyes lit up at the sight of me so that they blazed like two lamps in the shadows.

'We're so glad to see you. Something dreadful's happened,' cut in Arabella.

'Squash's gone,' finished Letitia.

'Caterina,' corrected Belly, 'not Squash, she's not a baby, you know.'

The relief on their faces at being able to pass this information on to someone who might pass for a responsible adult was clearly visible. But instead of responding with the calm reassurance – that all would be well – they so longed for, all I could do was let an ear-splitting wail roll out into the night air.

They quailed. 'She said she had to follow a dream,' Letty said hurriedly, disturbed by my reaction.

'But we thought that was stupid,' Belly added. 'It's the sort of thing you hear in stories.'

My heart sank even further.

Letty looked askance at her sister. 'She told me more than that. But I didn't understand what she meant.'

'Let's go inside,' I said wearily. 'Tell me exactly what happened while I eat.'

I had been away from Ashmore for three nights. On the second of these Caterina had woken her sisters with the declaration and had disappeared through the cat door. Letty, who had come into the world some seven minutes before the other two and therefore regarded herself as the eldest – the one in charge when things suited her; the one to chastise when they didn't – went after Cat and found her outside in the garden, staring fixedly at a point in space about five feet above and in front of her. When she had enquired as to what exactly Caterina was playing at, making such a drama and waking them all up for no good reason, Cat had replied enigmatically that the baby was having a bad dream and since Uncle Orlando was not around to deal with it, the onus fell on her to sort it out. None of which, of course, made any sense to Letty, who had complained bitterly at the interruption and had tramped back into the house in a bad temper. And when she and Belly had woken the next morning, Cat had not returned. Nor had she come back the previous night; and they had been waiting outside ever since supper in the hopes of spying her.

I could see little point in explaining matters further to the girls, so all I said was that they should on no account leave the house; that if Cat came back they should keep her with them and that I would be back before dawn. I gulped down whatever drying food was left in the bowls. It had gained an unappetising crust and gone as dry as sawdust, and it might as well have been the latter for all I cared.

Out I went again into the night. I leapt into the first highway I came to and let the compass winds have their way with me.

I fetched up, as I had known I would, on Ashmore Common. There, with that grim moon hanging overhead, in the shadow of the isolated oak that stood in the centre, where once I had buried a human tooth, I sat and considered my options. I could trudge the highways till dawn and miss Cat by sheer bad luck. I could follow the flow of tonight's dreams and see where they led me, in the hope that the currents were working much the same tonight as they had the previous night. Or I could locate myself in the middle of the knot of highways that converged on the common and pray that she would drift past.

The trouble was she could be anywhere by now. The wild roads can cover immense distances in a disconcertingly short space of time, for the planes of the inner world and the outer visible world do not always mesh; and the highways have a tendency, also, to convolute and disorientate. Some of them can become so contorted – doubling back on themselves where disturbing events lie heavy on the land and dreams have thinned the walls so that the integrity of the highway is lost – that they can deliver an unwary cat into other time periods entirely.

I stared desolately into the nothingness and felt only despair. First my poor sister Vita; then Liddy and now Caterina. It seemed that every female cat who came close to me was doomed to be lost.

I had just made up my mind to insert myself into the knot of highways where a dozen of Ashmore's wild roads converge and hope for a miracle, when I was granted such, without even the formality of a prayer to the Great Cat. From the far corner of the common, where the goat willow and hawthorn abut the hidden pool where the yellow flag-irises bloom, something was moving at a smart trot.

The bloody cast of the moon was deceptive this

night; for it seemed to me that the thing approaching me was a large dog with a coat of the most impossible russet-red. I could not see its face, for something was swinging around in front of it. As it came closer, I realised it was a fox, carrying a large, plump rabbit; no doubt heading for the bramble thicket on the other side of the common in order to eat its kill in peace.

I stood up and fluffed out my fur to give myself a bigger profile. Foxes are unpredictable animals: neither quite *Canidae* nor yet *Felidae*, it seemed to me, but an uncomfortable mixture of both. Though I had only known friendship and bravery from the one fox I had ever encountered, I had heard stories about other cats who had being attacked by foxes – some, even, who had been killed – and I had no intention of being traded for the rabbit.

I was so intent on scaring it off that I failed to be at all observant of the newcomer. Then, suddenly, there it was right in front of me: a large, handsome, long-backed, reeking beast with sharply pricked ears and powerful haunches. A patch of grey fur lay about one flank and ran down into the hock joint on that side. It had intelligent eyes. It winked at me and laid the rabbit at my feet.

Impossibly, the rabbit leapt up and started calling me by name.

'Orlando, Uncle Orlando!'

My eyes had deceived me, for it was not a rabbit at all: it was Cat.

Her muzzle was more bloodied than my own, and unspeakable fluids had gushed and dried upon her face, down her neck and on to her shoulders. She reeked of something pungent and vile. She was grinning from ear to ear, but when she tried to stand, her front foot folded under her and she whimpered in pain.

'I found her,' the dogfox pronounced, 'chasing one of your dreams.' He grimaced, his big red tongue lolling out of his mouth in his most humorous expression, and the vigorous, gamey smell of him rose up and enveloped me.

'I caught a dream,' Caterina said, sitting upright, her injured paw held drooping in front of her. 'It was a big fiery one, but I caught it all the same and I fought it and fought it for ages. But it knocked me down and got away, and even though I hurt my foot, I still chased it. It went for miles, in and out of all these little highways, as if it was trying to confuse me, and then we were somewhere else. Though it looked like the village, it wasn't right – the cars were all gone and all the big houses – there were fields all over the place, and women in funny long dresses, and the men all wore dull clothes and strange hats, and I didn't recognise any of the people I saw, and they didn't know me. Isn't that odd?'

Before I could say anything, she burbled on, her eyes alight with the hunter's moon. 'Except for one thing and that was weird. There were a man and a lady sitting on a bench in the churchyard and he had his arm round her, and he looked like John, but he wasn't. And the woman wasn't anything like Anna at all: she had all this black hair and these green, green eyes –'

My intestines went cold.

'And they were doing that strange thing with their mouths like humans do –' Caterina closed her eyes and made loud sucking noises, like a landed trout. 'You know. That thing. And then this woman comes by and I couldn't see who she was, because she had her back to me, but she was very angry and she stood there and shouted at them, and then ran away crying with her hands over her face. And the man got up and looked all uncomfortable, and he reaches into his pocket and gives the black-haired woman something, and then he runs off after the other woman.

'And then the dream came to a halt and I managed to grab it and stand on it; and when I looked into it, I could see exactly the same thing, except this time it was as if I was the woman on the bench, because all I could see were her big human hands and this little black box thing in them. And then the hands opened the lid and it started to make this horrible chiming noise – like the church bells only not as loud – and she started to cry. I could see the tears falling all over her hands and staining her dress. Then the fox came and helped me hold it down while I ate it up. It tasted awful, but I knew I had to do it because you weren't here.'

I knew that box thing: it was the baby's new toy. I shuddered. An unpleasant pattern was beginning to emerge, but I didn't know what it could mean.

I turned to the fox. 'Thank you,' I said inadequately. 'Thank you for rescuing Caterina and helping to run down the dream. I should have been here.' I paused, as something occurred to me. 'You haven't recently happened upon a golden-furred cat by the name of Lydia, have you?'

Caterina looked very serious. 'I asked him exactly the same question as soon as we got off the highway,' she said. 'But he said "not a whisker".'

The fox shook his head. 'Not a whisker,' he repeated.

Cat looked up at him adoringly. 'Will you carry me home, Loves A Dustbin?'

'No chance of that, you fat little squab. It was all I could do not to chew you right up there and then. I might not be able to resist again.' He lunged his sharp muzzle at her and she recoiled with a giggle.

I stared at the dogfox. 'Loves A Dustbin?'

The fox nodded. 'It's what many of my friends call me. A throwback from my urban past, though I've learned to eat better now.' He mused, then after a moment added, 'Or should I say, more healthily. Even now I've acquired a taste for fresh food, it's still hard to beat licking out a tinfoil tray of vindaloo. I don't suppose . . .'

I had no idea what he meant by any of this. All I could think of was that in all the time in which I had been acquainted with him – when he had pulled me away from the scene of my grandfather's desperate demise and had helped me and Millie run the dream to ground in the heart of the knot garden on that awful night; when he had lectured me on my lack of native wit – I had never thought to ask his name. He was just 'the fox' to me, as if all the vulpine race were indistinguishable from each other.

'I'm sorry,' I said.

'Don't suppose there's much you can do about the lack of take-aways on the Crowbury Plain, son.' He grinned.

'I'm sorry that I never asked what you were called.'

'It's only names, Orlando,' Loves A Dustbin replied. 'Here's a name for you, though.' He paused to make sure he had my attention.

I looked back, narrow-eyed, wondering what he had in store for me next.

'Vita.' He quirked his head at me.

'Vita? My sister?'

The fox nodded. 'A little tabby with white paws and pretty eyes; and a ragged little hole in one ear.'

My heart stopped. Then, 'But she's been gone for seasons past, lost, dead to us all –' I cried.

'Be that as it may,' the fox said, 'I've seen her.'

'And I saw her too,' crowed Caterina, not to be outdone. 'She was in the old place, the knot in the house where time gets caught up and everything is white and cobwebby.'

I sat down hard, feeling dizzy. It was as if the world had just changed shape.

Chapter Seven

'I JUST FELT a sort of dread,' Anna admitted to Alice, a few days after Eleanor's curious first words.

'Most people would be proud,' was Alice's opinion.

'I know.'

'Then what's the problem?'

'I can't explain it. There she sat, in that awful room with its rubbishy old furniture, chattering away to herself, and all I felt was that it was wrong.'

It was a nice day and they had decided to get Ellie out into the fresh air. Anna, in her cautious and cumbersome way, drove the Volvo up to Cresset Beacon, where the three of them settled themselves on a lawn of sheep-cropped turf and sat gazing out across Ashmore, compact as a model village in its curve of pasture land. Behind them the downs rolled away into bracken dells, feathery woods, hidden villages with names like Lower Highmore and Gallowstree Common; and Anna went on, in the voice of someone still unable to account for her own puzzlement, 'The articulacy of it was astonishing.'

Alice considered this. 'Wittgenstein didn't speak until he was seven.'

'Who?'

'You know. Wittgenstein, the philosopher.'

'Ah,' said Anna. 'Him.'

'He didn't speak until he was seven, then he said, "We appear to have run out of marmalade." Those were his first words.'

Anna stared at her. 'And –?'

'Those were his first words. His pronunciation was perfect. An adult could have been speaking, his parents were clear on that. "We appear to have run out of marmalade."'

'Alice, she's not two yet.'

Alice shrugged. 'What do I know?' she admitted.

'It's not so much what she said,' Anna tried to explain. 'It's that she seemed to turn on and off like a tap. Just like a tap.'

Eleanor pulled up a handful of grass and examined it judiciously. She had allowed herself to be bundled into a warm jersey and tights, and was wearing her woollen cap askew. This, combined with cheeks reddened and shiny from the outdoors, helped give her the look of some amiable but mad old woman. Eventually, after making sure that everyone was watching her, she gave a coy little gasp and sprinkled the grass into the air to watch it fall.

'Very nice,' said Alice. 'Show us your music box, then.'

Eleanor looked vague.

'That's another thing,' Anna told Alice. 'We lost that some time ago. I can't think where.'

'She doesn't seem to miss it,' was Alice's opinion. 'After all those tantrums!'

It was a perfect day on the downs, blowy, with a bright blue sky across which clipped vast white cumulus clouds. The sandy heath was at its best, dry, warm in sheltered spots; bracken and birch trees hummed with insects. They stayed for perhaps an hour and saw a hare – 'Look, Eleanor! Look. No, that way! Oh dear. *That* way,' but too late, Eleanor had missed it – then went off to get lunch at the Crooked Billet in Cockley Cleye, where an aunt of Alice's, all of twenty-eight years old, kept the bar. There, Eleanor made an exhibition of herself over the little paper sachets of tomato sauce and a worse one when they wouldn't give her chips.

Nonesuch was the largest space Anna had ever occupied – although the term 'occupied' didn't seem exact enough to describe the present circumstances – and the most complex. Pleased with what he thought of as her success in deciding what to keep and what to throw away, and determined to push on with the clearance work as fast as he could, John now sent her almost daily to look at this or that and bring back an opinion on it. The result was that, despite her two-year relationship with the house, she often found herself in rooms she had never seen before. It was in one of these, some mornings later, that she came upon Orlando sleeping in the two long bars of light from a casement window.

He looked so tired, sprawled out on the wooden boards, that she sat with him a moment or two. 'You do have a bit of a life with her, don't you?' she whispered, not knowing quite whether she meant Eleanor or Lydia. Then, out of a rush of feeling in which love and regret seemed equally mixed (because, after all, from the day of his birth – from before that day – Orlando's existence had been shaped, whether he chose it or not, by the perils and pleasures of her own) she said, 'You've had a bit of a life of it all along, haven't you?'

If this was an apology, Orlando seemed willing to accept it. He opened his eyes, purred suddenly, slept again. For a moment he was safe from both his tormentors – though Anna thought he would pine if Lydia really had finally wandered off.

Reassured, she looked round the room.

A shabby old carpet in faded pinks and greens. A single upright chair, across the seat of which rested a broken violin bow trailing festoons of horsehair. There was a nice walnut bureau, its writing desk hinged down to reveal bundles of papers, dusty old pens and pencils, a jar of perished elastic bands, a few shabby books. Anna left Orlando to his dreams and poked about among these things. She was leafing through one of the books – *Alchemy*, written by someone calling himself Johannes Fabricius – then out of its pages dropped first a tinted Victorian picture postcard, then a piece of writing paper of the same age, folded in four, stiff and faded at the creases, and covered on both sides with handwriting which must, in its day, have been thick and black, but which had long ago faded to a brownish tint barely darker than the paper. She could make out only the words – '. . . the Great Light. I am not to tell you this, but Dance itself comes from the Light.'

Anna examined the picture postcard, which showed a half-clothed boy with flowers in his hair, holding up a violin; behind him a balcony, sea, ships, two doves kissing on a balustrade. She turned it over. 'Orpheus,' explained the minute printed text, 'by Domenico Frilli Croci, first half of the seventeenth century.' In the blank space above this were two or three lines of much more modern handwriting she recognised instantly.

God, John, I don't think I can stand here looking out of this bloody window at the endless bloody gardens and the bloody, bloody rain for a minute longer. If you –

There it stopped. There was no address. There was no stamp. It had never been posted. Anna shivered, hearing the voice of an intelligent, passionate young woman, trapped in a house which had turned from an opportunity into a prison, someone so unable to contain her own frustration that she would write it down on the back of a Victorian postcard to send to a teenage boy –

Stella Herringe, twenty-two years old.

And 'John', of course, was John. By then, he would have been at Marlborough, a quiet boy barely in his teens, decentred by the deaths of his parents, not really a Herringe but already fiercely excited by his new life at Nonesuch, where his cousin had begun to open out sexually for him like a flower. 'What do you

163

think happens between a bored, power-hungry woman and an adolescent boy?' he had once asked bitterly. Although Anna often reassured him – 'I don't mind, honestly. I know what you felt for her. I just feel sorry for her now' – she still wasn't sure she had forgiven him those shaping experiences. She tore up the postcard in a methodical way and put the pieces out of sight. ' "This bloody, bloody rain," ' she whispered to herself. Orlando, sleeping curled up like a shell, responded with a comfortable little chirruping noise.

She glanced around. Something caught her attention, glittering in the floss of dusty, rosin-impregnated fibres from the broken violin bow. Anna went over to have a look. Tangled up there, as if it had been deliberately woven into the horsehair, was a necklace of small, black, multifaceted beads – each facet polished to a mirror finish – from which depended some kind of locket.

As she reached out to take it, Orlando got up and left the room.

When she followed him out a few minutes later, the necklace was wrapped round her fingers. She found John in the kitchen, playing some ridiculous game with Eleanor in which he pretended to hide his face behind *Round the World with Ant and Bee*, while Eleanor made a noise like a duck. Anna put the necklace on the kitchen table in front of her husband. 'Present for you,' she said.

She left him looking puzzled and went to do the weekly shop.

On the way back, the sky turned the colour of tobacco. Lightning flickered. A steady drenching rain began to fall. As if in response the Tank, so long a byword for reliability, coasted slowly to a halt and would not go again however hard she banged the steering wheel with the heel of her hands. There was petrol. There was oil. The battery worked, but the engine did not.

'Damn,' said Anna.

She wished she hadn't broken the mobile phone, which had been as useful to her as it was to John. Behind her the lane stretched away down a gentle incline between unkempt hedges and empty fields; not far ahead it turned abruptly right beneath the branches of an old chestnut tree, which spread out across the road in the wet light like the groined vaults of a church ceiling. She sat there waiting for the rain to stop. If anything, it came down harder. After five minutes or so a movement caught her eye and she was startled to see a silent white-faced figure standing in the shelter of the tree. For a moment she had no idea what to do. She rolled down the side window and called loudly, 'Hello? Excuse me?' and then, understanding suddenly who it was, 'For God's sake, Francis, what are you doing here?'

He stood awkwardly beside the front passenger door while she leaned over to open it. He was holding his old tweed jacket together at the neck with one hand. His trousers were black with water. He ducked his head into the car and said vaguely, 'I was out walking. I'm soaked, I'm afraid.'

Before he would get in, she had to tell him it didn't matter. 'Really, Francis. It's only a car. Just get in. Have you been here all along? Why didn't you come over when I stopped?'

He considered this. 'I was trying to sort some things out,' he said, with the air of someone answering a different question. 'Life is never quite what you think it is, is it?'

'Francis?'

He sneezed. 'Sorry. Do you know, I think the sky's brightening over there.'

It was. As the rain slackened and the thunder grumbled off towards Drychester like an old dog tired of barking at the front gate, Anna tried the Volvo again. To her surprise the engine turned over, coughed, caught. *Yes*! she thought. To Francis she said, 'You'll be ill if you don't get dry. I'll take you back to Nonesuch –'

'Oh no. Really. I'd rather go home.'

'Suit yourself.' She banged the Tank into gear. 'You're being very eccentric.'

'Do you believe in life after death?'

She stared at him. 'Don't you?' she asked.

'Of course –'

'Then why ask me? You're the Christian here, Francis. I've never heard anything so ridiculous.'

He didn't reply to this and they drove the rest of the way in silence; but as she dropped him outside the vicarage something prompted her to touch his hand and ask, 'What's the matter? Really?'

He smiled. 'Oh, you know.'

'But I don't. I don't see what it is you want.'

'From you?' he said quickly.

She hadn't meant that at all. He had the air of someone about to make an admission. To forestall him – because she knew better than him how difficult it could make things for them – she said firmly, 'From anyone. From me or anyone else. From life.' Remembering his white face, passive and blurred with rain beneath the tree, she added, 'You mustn't be unreliable or too demanding, Francis. That's not what people want in a friend.' She tried to soften her voice. 'Now go in and get out of those clothes, and have a hot bath.'

He waited for her to finish and turned away, smiling painfully.

Oh well done, Anna! she congratulated herself as she drove away. *That was really well done.*

When she got back she found the silver-grey Mercedes drawn up on the gravel apron by the main doors, and Mark and Oliver poking about in their graceful, slightly futile way in one of the rooms along the corridor from John's office. They were wearing pastel-coloured polo shirts with faded designer jeans, boat shoes without socks, classic Swiss airline-pilot watches. Their wrists and ankles were tanned and slim, as if they had just come back from a month sailing in the Aegean. They had managed somehow to open the padlocked door of a white Kelvinator freezer cabinet John used to store out-of-date paperwork and were eyeing its cluttered shelves disappointedly. Every so often one of them pulled something out and put it back again. They had the air of people who, their agenda having received a setback, were uncertain how to proceed.

Anna stood in the doorway with her arms folded, watching them. 'What do you think you're doing?' she enquired after she had let a minute or two go by.

They looked up, then at each other.

'Ah,' said Mark. 'Mrs Dawe. I wonder if you could help us.'

She had expected them to be down the corridor in the office itself, talking about business plans in bland voices, pausing every so often to consult John's computer screen or the tiny display of a WAP phone; not going through their old employer's things like a pair of Fulham antique dealers. 'Does John know you're here?' she asked. 'Do you think you have a right to be here, rummaging about like this? Because you haven't.'

Before he could answer she warned him, 'There's nothing of hers left.'

'Mrs Dawe, we –'

'The freezer's not even plugged in, you can see that. Everything that survived the fire we buried. Even if you dug it up, it wouldn't be any use to you now.'

She remembered a smoky winter afternoon, failing light, a trench in the garden, the barely healed palms of her hands blistered by the shovel. Then all those freezer bags going into the ground, labelled in Stella's careful handwriting as if they were pots of jam. The worst thing to remember was how the contents of each bag had softened as they thawed. John had turned away and cried; but Anna,

thinking she must bear witness to the deaths of so
many animals, had watched with dry eyes. They
were both just out of hospital at that time and still
not well. Anger had kept them going. Anna's anger
was boundless, but what can you do with anger like
that? You cannot vent it on the past. The past is
beyond your sense of justice.

'Mrs Dawe –'

'I know what you want,' she said.

Oliver, who was standing nearest the Kelvinator,
quietly pushed it closed. 'What have you got there?'
she cried. Even to herself, she sounded shrill and
panicky. 'Have you got something there? Give it to
me!'

'It's my phone, Mrs Dawe. It's just my phone.'

She swept it out of his hands and stared at it.
Eventually she gave it back. They were looking at
her as if she were mad; as if her attitude were too
inexplicable and too unreasonable to deal with.

'We're here on behalf of the Estate, Mrs Dawe –'

'I know what you want,' she repeated. 'Even if
John doesn't.'

'– just to make an inventory.'

'I'm going to tell him,' she said.

It was an empty threat. She had already told him
and he didn't want to know. John understood as
well as she did that something was going on. But he
didn't want to remember the events that had led up
to the fire, or the things they had found out about
themselves then. That was how he had decided to
deal with it all. He was in denial and she couldn't
dent the hard shell that made around him.

Seven in the evening. Eleanor Dawe, who could barely keep her eyes open but wasn't quite ready to give up on the day, yawned and blinked at the ceiling lamp. She had refused to leave her high chair, or have her Lion King crockery removed. Her parents sat, waiting her out with a kind of torpid patience, on opposite sides of the kitchen table. While Anna tried to read a novel, John played with the necklace she had found that morning, running it repeatedly back and forth across his palm. Anna found this vastly irritating. To make him stop, she put down her book with a sigh and asked, 'What do you make of it, then?'

He stared at her. 'What?'

'Wake up, John. The necklace.'

He rubbed his eyes. 'Oh, this,' he said. 'It's really quite a find. Early Victorian mourning jewellery.'

Anna took it from him. The necklace itself was made from alternating black beads and lozenges, all highly faceted so that they glittered under the kitchen light. The pendant, however, was a single flat teardrop half the size of a hen's egg, unfaceted, polished to a mirror finish. It lay heavy and cold in the hand.

'It's Whitby jet,' John continued, 'very good quality. And look!' He showed her two minute gold hinges, and a catch so small that Anna had to work it with the end of a fingernail.

'God, John,' she said. 'That's disgusting.'

'What?'

The pendant had swung open suddenly in her

hand, revealing an oval cavity into which was sealed a small lock of thick black hair, tied into a curl with the most minute piece of blue ribbon.

'*This*.' She held it up. 'Why have you put this in here?'

He looked hugely amused. 'Nothing to do with me. It's not mine, though I can see how you might think it was.'

On closer inspection, the hair had a dull, desiccated look. It was far too old to be John's; the ribbon that secured it was faded and brittle. Still, the shock of recognition remained, mixed up with an unreasonable distaste for – what, precisely? Anna didn't know. It was a distaste for the very act of memory the locket implied, grief and loss overacted, allowed to spill out inappropriately, on to an inappropriate object. No one mourned anyone that much, surely? You tried to leave the past behind and get on with your life. Memories were one thing, but deliberately to make a setting for someone's hair, then wear it so near your skin . . .

'I wish I hadn't found it,' she said. 'I don't like it.'

John stared at her, holding the necklace out to him, her face turned away as if she couldn't bear to look at it. 'Are you all right?'

When she didn't answer, he took it from her and turned it over in his hands. 'It is a bit necrophilic, I suppose,' he admitted. 'They were an odd lot, the Victorians.' He opened the locket again and stared into it. 'Some family story attached, I expect. The hair of a favourite child. Or a lost lover.' He touched the ribbon. 'Blue for a boy.' He smiled. 'I hope you don't find *my* hair disgusting,' he teased her. Then he snapped the locket shut. 'It's only a necklace. And' – dangling it in front of Eleanor – '*I* know who'd like to play with it. Don't I?'

'John, no!'

Too late. Eleanor, who had followed this exchange with growing interest, wasn't going to turn down a gift from the man in her life. In any case, she enjoyed the way the light glanced and glittered off the faceted jet. 'Gidgie,' she said in hushed and breathless tones, and snatched it from him quickly before he could change his mind.

Anna was appalled. 'John, we'll never get it off her!'

He was too amused to hear the exasperation in her voice. 'Did you see that?' He pretended to blow on his fingers. 'She's got the reflexes of a barracuda, your daughter.'

Anna scraped her chair back from the table. 'How could you be so stupid? You know how difficult she is. She's too young to have anything that small! And to give her something with a dead person's hair in it, that's just –' Words failed her. 'How could you?' Then she went on, 'Mark and Oliver were in the house again today, rooting through Stella's things. I don't want them here. I don't want them here, John.'

John's smile faded and he turned away.

What's in a name? says Izzie. And I say, how should I know?

Up and down the stairs I go. I find a thing here, a thing there. The nights are soft, the passages shift and turn.

Moonlight brushes the walls like fingers. I know what walls are now, I know what stairs and passages and doors are. I look out of the windows, I see the gardens in the rain or sun. I see the sundial. I see the light creep across the grass. I find the things, I hide them carefully where I'm told.

Good girl, Izzie says. You're a fine quick study. You and me, we're nothing like the rest of them and you can believe that or not just as you like.

Let's have a christening, she said, so she took me up under the roof, and we had a christening, up there with all the old abandoned things and spiderwebs like wedding dresses draped across corners. We were as secret as women among those old used things. Izzie put dirt on me. She put wax and said some words.

One word came towards me, faster and faster, out of the moonlight, out of the earth where Izzie lives and everyone else goes. One word rushing out of the Nonesuch gardens and the sundial, the passing clouds. One familiar word shook this old house.

That word's my name, it came to me from a long way off. I could taste it on my tongue before I said it. I know my name now, but that doesn't mean I know who I am. (On the Nonesuch lawns at night, you can see a darker stripe in the moonlight, water flowing underground.) What's in a name? Not much, Izzie says, but it's a start. You know your name now, but there's a lot more to do a lot more things to find, before you're you again. Oh and another thing she says: woe betide you if you fail. Your name's at stake, my little; one of those things gets out of place and you'll lose it again.

And we don't want that.

'I hated her after she was born.'

Anna Dawe sat in Dr Russell's consulting room, looking down over the little garden with its careful architectural values. Rain was falling softly on the leaves. The air was darkening visibly. Soon there would be a storm, the Drychester streets would empty of women while the cafés and teashops filled with steam and damp coats and laughter.

'Everything seemed to change between the two of us the moment I got her home from the hospital. Now I don't know what I feel, except that I'm a little afraid of her. She seems too . . . *formed*, somehow. Too adult. She learned to walk without bothering to tell us and wandered about the house in the dark. Now it looks as if she learned to speak as well. We feel shut out.'

Anna thought for a moment, then corrected herself. '*I* feel shut out. John just seems to love her whatever she does.' She shook her head ruefully. 'He gives her unconditional love. I can't and I feel guilty about that too. Am I just a bad mother?'

Martha Russell stubbed out her cigarette. 'I can't abide self-pity, Anna,' she said with some asperity and then went on more gently, 'Look. Children, even the best, even the nicest, even the most beautiful – come to think of it, especially the most beautiful – children, are manipulators. How could they be anything else, when they rely so completely on adults for the most basic, the most fundamental of things? Ellie's found a good way to play the two of you off against one another, that's all.'

'But she was such a lovely, uncomplicated little

thing when she was born! I remember looking down at her and feeling the most happiness I've ever felt in my life –'

'Children are people, Anna. They aren't dolls. They have a will of their own.'

'She was never wilful until she got to Nonesuch –'

Martha Russell thought for a moment. 'You know, something else changed then. That was when you had to begin dealing with her on a day-to-day basis.' She leaned forward. 'She didn't stop being ideal, Anna. That was when you realised she wasn't ideal. Do you see?'

'No,' said Anna. 'I don't. I don't want to see her like that. In fact, I don't want to see anyone like that, young or old.' She stared mutinously at Martha Russell for a moment, then looked away. Rain beaded the leaves of the hostas in the little garden; the beads ran together suddenly and dripped off on to the stones. 'Your TV's not on today. I quite miss it. I quite miss the digging.'

The doctor gave her a sideways smile and waited.

'All right,' said Anna. 'I'll think about it. I promise.' She got up to go. 'How *is* your excavation going?' she enquired. 'Have you dug up any more lavatories on the downs?'

John had been putting off his confrontation with the knot garden. His plans for the space were grand and perhaps because of that he lacked the confidence to see them through on his own. He needed advice. His expert – a local man, tall, grey-haired and rather elegant in an old-fashioned way, whose only gardening qualifications seemed to be a Barbour jacket and an Oxbridge Classics degree – turned up a couple of mornings after the incident with the necklace. By eleven, the two of them were still out there in the drizzling rain, waving their arms at one another and energetically scuffing up the ground between the box hedges with their wellington boots, while the builders – who had taken to using Joshua Herringe's pride and joy as a rubbish tip – worked around them and a desultory fire of ancient lath sent smoke signals into the wet air.

'Will you take them their tea?' Anna asked Alice Meynell. 'Otherwise they won't get any. I'm damned if I'm going out there.'

Alice had arrived at the same time as the rain. It was one of those days when she seemed to fill the kitchen. Her motorcycle leathers creaked. Her boots clumped on the tiled floor. She made bacon and egg sandwiches and cups of instant coffee; propped up her feet on the Aga and checked her phone for text messages; leafed through the latest issue of *Superbike Monthly* magazine, saying 'What crap!' in a voice of contemptuous authority. Eleanor gazed at her with undisguised wonder; while Orlando's children followed her about, begging for scraps of bacon. Now, her curiosity piqued, she put down *Superbike Monthly* and asked, 'What's he like, the gardener?'

'Find out for yourself. Kettle's boiled, tray's over there. I've put some digestives out too.'

Alice got up and touched Anna's cheek. 'There's no need to feel –'

Anna brushed her hand away. 'I don't feel anything, Alice,' she said defensively.

For a year after the fire she had dreamed nightly of flames – to wake with a cry, her partly healed burns sore and red, remembering something she couldn't possibly have seen: Stella Herringe, her skin charred, her beautiful face ruined, flopping and weeping and dragging herself towards the centre of the knot garden, hands scraping at the earth like blackened claws. Anna shivered. She had avoided the place ever since. It made her feel strange, it made her feel sick. Even in death, Stella had somehow polluted the ground she touched. 'I don't feel anything.'

'Hey,' said Alice gently. 'Come on.'

Anna tried a smile. 'Sorry Alice.'

'No need to apologise. Where's this tray, then?'

'Over there. On second thoughts, don't take him any biscuits. I'm still angry about that damned necklace.'

Alice was gone for about half an hour. In the meantime Orlando slipped into the kitchen and took up his place by the Aga. Anna picked him up and stroked his head. He didn't seem lonely without Lydia; in fact, he seemed relieved. Anna, now a little worried, whispered, 'Where's your wife, Orlando? Where's she gone?'

Eleanor, who sat in her high chair with a rag book, two Lego bricks and a gnawed piece of bread in front of her, held up the jet pendant in her sticky fist, turning it against the light like an item of food she enjoyed but didn't entirely trust. 'La la la la,' she said dreamily.

The door banged open on a gust of wind. Alice stood grinning and scrubbing her feet on the sisal mat while the rain blustered in around her. 'Recognise this?' she asked. She held out her hand. In it was an old-fashioned plastic doll's head.

Anna's heart beat suddenly. She was too hot, but her skin felt cold. 'Alice, where on earth did you get that?'

'From the knot garden. Don't you think that's amazing? Ellie's favourite thing! We all thought it was lost!'

'But how –'

'It was so weird,' Alice said. She had dropped a teaspoon. When she bent down to pick it up, there was the head, tucked in among the roots of one of the little box hedges, with some other stuff the builders had dropped. 'They must have come across it in the house and decided it was rubbish.'

'It *is* rubbish,' said Anna more definitely than she had intended.

'I was only down there for a moment and there it was.'

'Alice, give it to me.'

'I thought Ellie –'

'I don't want her to have it. It's just rubbish and she's forgotten all about it now. Let's just get rid of it.'

Alice looked disappointed. 'Oh well. Fair enough.'

An old galvanised dustbin lived outside the

kitchen door. Smelly, heavy, coated inside with ancient household ashes, it had been the servants' dustbin when there were still servants. Anna went out, lifted the lid quickly and dropped the head in on top of a layer of potato peelings. It lay looking up at her, cheeks beaded with rain, worse for wear than ever, as if another fifty years had passed since Eleanor lost it. Beneath the shiny surface of its jaw – pink as a scar – lay material of a fibrous grey consistency. The bland blue eyes rocked open and shut, open and shut. Anna touched the eyelids lightly, felt herself recoil. She was still staring down at it when she heard her daughter shrieking. She banged the lid back on the dustbin and went inside, to find Eleanor straining back in the high chair away from Alice, making pushing motions with her hands. Tears were rolling down her face.

'What's the matter now?' Anna wanted to know.

'I offered her this, but she doesn't seem to want it. Listen, Ellie! Listen!' A tinny, reluctant rendering of 'Für Elise' filled the kitchen. 'It's your *music box*.' Eleanor only shrieked louder.

Anna took the offending item out of Alice's hands. 'Oh, do shut up, Eleanor,' she ordered. 'No one's going to make you have it if you don't want it.'

She sat down weakly at the table. In the silence that followed, Alice looked at Anna. Anna turned the music box over in her fingers. Eleanor regarded them both with a kind of miserable wariness.

'Did you find this in the knot garden too?'

'Right next to the head,' Alice confirmed. 'Isn't that weird?'

That night Anna was restless. If she dozed, it was only to start awake from some dream disturbingly close to real life and discover that no more than two or three minutes had passed. Too hot, she pushed the quilt away from her; too cold, she drew it back up again. Never fully asleep, she was never fully awake. At two in the morning she got up, retrieved the music box from her dressing-table where she had placed it that afternoon and, after assuring herself that Eleanor was asleep, left the room.

She had intended to go to the kitchen, make hot chocolate, eat a piece of toast; she ended up sitting in front of the IBM in John's cold untidy office, remembering her life in Ashmore as it had been before she met him. She switched on the computer, dialled up one of her old financial connections, then, as soon as the screen filled with figures, switched it off again. A brief, light squall of rain pattered against the window. She realised that she had been listening all night. What for she hardly knew. It was listening so hard that had kept her from sleep. *My daughter*, she thought, *hides her own development from me. My husband has thrown in his lot with people whose actions are at best unethical. While Francis Baynes, who was such a good friend, talks to himself, and lurks under a tree in the rain and, if I am not careful, will soon nerve himself up to some declaration that embarrasses us both.* When she considered these events she could make nothing of them, but she had begun to think that they were all one thing.

She raised the lid of the music box and let the

wavering, unbearably sweet notes of the 'Für Elise' fill the room, reminding her of some childhood music teacher at the piano on a Saturday afternoon. Almost immediately she began to feel drowsy and, obscurely comforted, took herself back to bed.

The next morning she found that some animal – a fox or a dog perhaps, because what cat would be big enough? – had tipped over the old dustbin in the night, ransacked it for whatever seemed edible and scattered everything else over the small kitchen garden. Anna put on a pair of yellow rubber gloves and wasted half an hour picking it all up again, stopping every so often to massage the small of her back, stare round at the scattered eggshells and sodden orange peel and shake her head. It was a morning of absolute stillness. The clouds were down. Fine rain hung in the air, beading the washing line and the branches of the Bramley apple tree in the corner of the garden. Distances slipped into the mist, yet she could hear everything – the call of a rook circling above the tower of St Mary's; a car making its way up to Cresset Beacon; then, from inside the house, the scrape of a chair leg on the floor, the clatter of Eleanor's dish. The radio played light classical music, the new washing machine moved smoothly into its spin cycle, Eleanor laughed suddenly and Anna went in.

In the kitchen they were having grapes.

Eleanor liked grapes. Her idea of eating them was brutal, direct, inefficient. She made a fist round the grape, then stuffed the fist in her mouth. Much of the grape fell out. John never seemed to tire of this. 'Oh,' he would say, picking up bits and popping them back in again, 'you like that, do you?' Occasionally he would try to get her to eat a piece of apple instead. This she would give back to him instantly, glaring at him until he made a face and ate it himself. Breakfast time was fun for them and not the grim struggle Anna often faced. They got on so well together. She watched them for a moment, then said in a voice of amused despair, 'What am I doing wrong?'

'Oh, she loves her father,' John replied. He pulled Eleanor's nose. 'Doesn't she?'

'That's very helpful advice, John.'

'Don't mention it.'

Anna banged some pots about in the sink. 'I was serious,' she said, even though she knew she hadn't been. 'Sometimes I don't know where to turn with her.'

When he didn't respond to this, she threw the washing-up cloth into the water and stared indignantly out of the window.

Eleanor chose this moment to speak again. 'John,' she said. She paused for a moment to appreciate her father's astonishment, then, squirming around in the high chair, reached her hands up ecstatically towards him. '*John.*'

'My God,' said John. 'She can talk. Anna, she can talk.'

Anna gave him a blank look. 'I told you that.'

He seemed disconcerted for a moment; then laughed. 'Ah yes, but that was different.' Sweeping his daughter out of the high chair, he lofted her above his head until she giggled and squirmed. 'Now she can *talk*.'

Anna repeated, 'I told you she could talk. I heard her talk.'

'Well, I'm not sure about that,' John said.

'Oh, I see. You're not sure. Why, John? Because I was the one to hear her? Because she didn't say her first word to her daddy? Because she didn't say your name?'

'Of course not.'

'Why don't you believe me, then? Because you obviously don't.'

He had Eleanor high up in the crook of his arm now and she was pulling at his ear, trying to stand up so that she could blow into it. 'John?' she said and, when he replied, 'What?' only shrieked with laughter and pulled his hair. They played this game – 'John?' 'What?' 'John?' 'What?' – for a round or two. Then, appearing to tire of it, Eleanor turned away and caught Anna's eye. As soon as she was sure she had Anna's attention, she put her arms round her father's neck and gave him a wet, possessive kiss. 'Dada,' she said.

John chuckled. 'You can't argue with that. Two words in a morning.' He looked more delighted than Anna had ever seen him. He held out his hand to Anna. 'Come on. Come and give us both a hug. You should be happy.'

Anna was astonished to find tears in her eyes. 'Excuse me,' she said. 'I think the washing's finished.'

She darted past him, dragged a huge damp tangle of sheets out of the washing machine and buried her face in them, breathing in the cheap, strong, comforting smell of fabric conditioner. She would have done anything at that moment to cram down her feelings of rage and jealousy and exclusion. But it was too late for that. She thought of her recent conversation with Martha Russell. 'How can you be so stupid?' she heard herself demand. 'Not to see it? Your precious daughter is a manipulative little cow.'

She dropped the clean washing on the kitchen floor in front of the two of them and stormed out.

Chapter Eight

THE DOGFOX HAD said some interesting things, though it took me a while to make sense of many of them. Sitting there, on Ashmore Common, by the weird yellow light of the hunter's moon, with Caterina by my side grooming the last viscous traces of the dream out of her fur, it had seemed edgy and strange to be in conversation with the great russet creature. To an onlooker we must have appeared a bizarre group, much like two mice listening to the counsels of an owl; or lambs curled close beside a wolf. For all his care, I never was able to forget that he was a potentially dangerous predator who might turn upon the two of us like a dog: that long jaw was made for cracking bones, I found myself thinking more than once, he'd snap through a cat's neck with a single bite. Yet he showed no sign of such intent. All he did was offer his advice, rather than his teeth, and for that I was grateful – he was a wise beast and experienced in the odder ways of the world. He certainly had the years for it and the eyes, too, deepset, pale and penetrating: eyes that had seen too much. I found I could not look away from them, however much I might have wanted to, and the advice he gave me while I was held by that unwavering tawny gaze, though cryptic, haunted me for days.

'Look to your own,' Loves A Dustbin had said. 'The threat is close to home.'

But when I questioned him further all he would say was, 'It's coming back, Orlando. Quarter your own ground; check your own territory. Go to all four corners of the knot and take the path that gyres. Dig deep; then deeper still. Seek it out and run it down. We're none of us safe until you do; least of all the ones you care most for, the ones who are already adrift.'

He fixed me with that unsettling gaze, then he grinned: quick and sly. Those sharp white teeth glimmered for an instant in the starlight and a moment later he was gone, loping silently into the tangle of nettles and bramble runners from which he had emerged.

'What did he mean by that stuff about "quartering your own ground"?' Caterina asked me distractedly as we padded back to the house. She was limping, her injured foot held bobbing in front of her, but she appeared determined not to complain. Sometimes she tried so hard to be grown-up that it made my heart ache.

I shook my head. 'I can only take it literally.'

Neither of us knew what he meant by 'the path that gyres' and I had not liked to ask.

We walked in silence for a time. It was a still night and scents hung heavy on the air, but I was too preoccupied to pay them much heed. The fox's mention of my sister had ambushed me, coming as it had out of nowhere. Vita. My nestmate, my fellow orphan, my poor, despised, neglected sister. I had not been very nice to her when I thought myself an important dreamcatcher's apprentice and she was nothing but a silly kitten, forever tagging around after me in the hope of some game or another. I felt guilty that she had been lost on the wild roads in her attempt to impress me. Millie had left me in little doubt as to that.

'So where is this "white, cobwebby place" where you saw my sister, the tabby cat?' I asked yet again.

Cat sighed. 'I don't know. I sort of fell into it when I was following the dream thing. One minute I was chasing it down what looked like the Long Corridor, the next –' She stopped, frowning.

'What?'

'It all went . . . freaky.'

'How?'

'The house. It looked . . . the same, but different. It was sort of light and . . . fuzzy, and it smelled . . . foul . . .'

'Foul? In what way?'

Cat gave me a melancholy look. 'Stop asking me. I don't know.'

'Bad? Rotten?' I persisted.

'Oh, I can't remember, Uncle Orlando. Dusty and old. And some sort of nasty human smell, all salty, like blood.'

187

We were both quiet after that. At last we turned into the lane that led up to the gates of Nonesuch and threaded ourselves beneath them. We made our way up the long, soft lawn, skirting the rhododendrons, and headed for the dark kitchen.

Caterina said no more till we arrived at the cat door. This she sniffed with interest. 'Mum's back,' she declared and, butting the flap open with her head, manoeuvred her injured paw, and then the rest of her, carefully into the house.

I sat outside for a little while to collect my thoughts. Liddy had returned, of her own accord, it seemed, though I had searched for her assiduously up and down the village. Then I had quartered the ground, as the fox put it, the physical ground of Ashmore. I had run back and forth along the lanes, skirted the main road, sniffed my way between every tombstone in the churchyard. Had she watched me, I wondered, sheltering behind the yew, or perched upon a roof, and said nothing? Had she even laughed at my anxious efforts? She had called me a fool and worse, and all the while she had been gone I had been plagued by the sense that she had withdrawn herself from me as a form of punishment for my failings. So it was with some apprehension that I insinuated myself inside the cat door, braced for a confrontation. Instead, I was greeted by a tableau of almost excessive domesticity. In the warmest spot in the kitchen – directly in front of the Aga – was Lydia, submitting like a weary empress to the ministrations of her attendants. She lay there with her head tilted back, golden eyes reduced to hazed slits of pleasure, as Millefleur licked carefully around her ears and neck, and two of her daughters applied themselves to her feet and tail.

No one even looked up as I entered.

'So,' Lydia was saying to her audience, 'then it started to rain and you know how much I hate *that*, so I ran along the road till I found a likely refuge. Of course, I went straight past all those rather dilapidated council houses on the hill – you could hardly trust the people in them, could you? – until I came to that imposing place on the junction with Pond Lane; you know, the one with the ivy and the shutters, and I jumped straight up on to the windowsill and looked in. Such a smart drawing room; they even had a fire burning, which I always think is such a good sign, don't you? So I tapped on the window; not too hard, I didn't want to look too indigent, you know, and their little girl – smartly dressed, no jeans – came straight to the front door and held it open for me. Polished wood in the hall; very clean, and in the drawing room three big white sofas – gold fur always looks so good against white – and those lovely silk rugs that you can really get your claws into. I knew I should like the inhabitants right away. I could just *see* myself there. Do you know what I mean?'

She leaned her head back to look up at Millie, but the tabby and white gave her a flat-eyed look and stopped grooming. 'I thought you said you'd had a nightmarish time,' she accused.

'Oh, but I did,' Lydia cried. 'Do you know, they had no proper cat food in the house at all? I ended up having to eat salmon straight out of the tin . . .'

By the time she had recounted how they had made her up a bed of mohair sweaters spread in a wicker wash basket; how she had been fed properly from then on – fish boiled just so, with a little butter – and how she had met the extremely handsome and well-to-do cat next door, whose name was Tarquin and who had the most exquisite duelling scars around his ears, I could take no more.

I left the room, as unregarded by Lydia as I had been when I arrived. Millie flicked me a glance, then got to her feet and followed me out.

'So have you had a lovely vacation from Nonesuch as well?' I asked waspishly.

'Take no notice of Lydia, she's just enjoying boasting to us of how she's won herself a whole new cast of admirers,' Millie replied mildly. 'You know how she is: she loves being the centre of attention. For all her arrogance, she's really quite insecure, you know.'

I could hardly believe my ears. 'Insecure? Lydia? She's got more self-regard than a peacock!' I did not add *and no wonder*. I could not help looking past Millie and through the open door into the kitchen. Seeing Lydia lying there still, the buttery light of the kitchen lamp infusing her fur with subtle brilliance, made the blood run like fire through my veins. I felt suddenly dizzy with longing . . .

When my focus came back again, Millie was watching me, her eyes bright with hurt intelligence. Her chin came up and she looked me squarely in the face. 'As for me, I've been travelling around to see where best I might live.'

I stared at her stupidly. 'What do you mean?'

Millie dropped her head and began to clean a perfectly dirt-free paw. 'It's time I moved on,' she said simply. 'I can't just hang around here like a sort of surrogate mother. I want kittens of my own and I'm getting no younger.'

I sat down with a thud, as if someone had just sliced the sinews in my legs. 'Leave Nonesuch?' My voice sounded as if it were coming from someone else, someone far away down the tunnel of a long wild road, fighting against an icy compass wind.

'Leave Ashmore entirely. I thought of going south, actually, towards the coast; maybe even as far as Cornwall. I've heard it's nice there. A fishing port, perhaps. Eat fresh mackerel off the harbour wall –'

'Millie, you can't!' Now I sounded agonised.

'I only came back to tell you my plans . . . and –'

'Yes?'

She lifted her head from her grooming and held me with her amber gaze. It was an honest look. It pierced me to the heart and suddenly I knew what I had always known, what I had tried so hard to forget ever since that night when she had first accompanied me on to the highways and made me catch a dream for her. That night when she had offered herself to me, without games or duplicity: a generous gift which I had rudely spurned, obsessed with Lydia as I had been. As I still was. Despite it all, I had hoped we would be friends for ever, that we could all stay in our cosy group here at Nonesuch, watching

Lydia's kittens grow to adulthood, sharing their education, unruffled by jealousies and passions.

'And to say goodbye,' she finished sadly.

'Ah,' I said inadequately, shocked into incoherence.

For a moment there I had been sure that she was going to ask me to go with her to this seaside paradise. An image – as bright as a butterfly – had flickered through my mind's eye: the two of us asleep in a pool of sunlight in the crook of a granite wall patched with orange lichen, seagulls wheeling overhead against an endless blue sky, a greasy newspaper pushed to one side – two or three gleaming crumbs of battered fish still adhering to it – a long line of sparkling surf marking the margin between land and sea . . .

But you have never even seen the sea, came a voice in my head.

It was true: I hadn't, except in others' dreams and Millie's descriptions of the places she had visited on her journeys down the wild roads. *Besides,* that grim, sensible voice went on, *you have your duties here; you cannot just up and leave like some gypsy cat with no cares or responsibilities.*

And I realised that of all cats, Millefleur knew the enormity of a dreamcatcher's task and would never ask such a thing of me. She was just telling me her intentions; not asking me to join her, or even to dissuade her. I felt as if my world had suddenly folded in on itself.

We didn't speak much to one another over the course of the next few days. I watched her with

Lydia and the girls, as friendly and as gentle as if nothing had changed; and for them, I suppose it had not. Millie was at best an itinerant visitor in their lives, a bearer of news and teller of stories, and to Belly, Cat and Letty she was exactly what she had described herself as: a surrogate mother. They would miss her, I thought. But not half so much as I would.

This realisation came to me one afternoon as I lay upstairs in one of the unused rooms, trying to keep out of everyone's way. The baby had been tormenting me till I had grown tired of her insistent proddings and pokings; the builders were hammering away downstairs and there was dust everywhere. The girls kept squabbling and Liddy had snapped at me when I had tried to intervene, so here I was, feeling rather sorry for myself as I lay stretched out on the floorboards. There was a perfectly good rug on the floor beyond me, but somehow the bare wood against my limbs felt more appropriate, as if my internal discomfort should be echoed by my body being uncomfortable, too. Why was Millie leaving? I kept asking myself. Wasn't she happy here at Nonesuch? It was a large house and the food was good, the people, for the most part, attentive and friendly. Lydia – well, Liddy was Liddy: self-centred and greedy, beautiful and charming and chilly in equal measure. Everyone who knew Lydia knew this about her and accepted her as she was; even I had got used to the unpredictability and mood swings. I knew Millefleur loved the girls; she was so good with them, especially when their mother was oblivious or otherwise occupied, which was much of the time. But they were nearly full-grown cats now and less inclined to listen to others. Perhaps Millie was feeling superfluous here. The Great Cat knew I did, much of the time, when I was not hunting the dreams. I mused upon this unsatisfactory problem for a time, until I felt my eyes get heavy and my head grow soft. I was just drifting off into a listless doze when I heard footsteps in the corridor outside.

It was Anna. I could tell by the sound of her footfall. I heard her walk into the next room and cross to the window. A rattling noise meant she was fiddling with the window and a few moments later her footsteps came back out on to the landing. She entered the room in which I lay, shoes clacking first on the bare wood, then cushioned by the old rug. I pretended to sleep while she wandered about, examining the few dusty items left in the desk – books and papers, pens and oddments – and a few moments later, almost against my will, I found myself sliding into a dream.

In it, I had taken Anna's place and was myself walking the corridors of the house, lonely and alone. It was twilight; or maybe the hour just before dawn. The light was undependable, a sort of glassy grey that slicked off the surface of things but gave back little illumination or comfort. I had the sense that I was looking for something, but what that thing could be eluded all my mind's attempts to corner it. Anxiety burned cold at the back of my neck. I thought someone might be following me, but whenever I turned round there was no tangible sign of another presence, although little eddies of dust, transfixed by the grey light, swirled up behind me. No sign – except a smell.

There it was again: suddenly a strong whiff.

Something old and powerful, old and sad . . .

My eyes snapped open. Anna was standing with her back to me, facing the broken chair and the wooden thing that lay upon it. I was sure, without having any understanding of how I knew this, that some part of whatever it was that had smelled so strong to me in the dream was now in her hand, close to her face. In a minute she would turn and I would see what it was she had found, and I knew then with absolute certainty that I did not want to see it at all. A convulsion of disgust shook me, a ripple of reaction that ran from the crown of my head to the tip of my tail. Before she could move, I got to my feet and quickly padded out of the room, aware that if I were to look back over my shoulder, I would see Anna staring after me, the object held wonderingly in her hand.

I did not look back. Instead, I ran down the corridor, fled down the stairs and hurtled into the kitchen, where I surprised whichever occupant was in residence. There was a flurry of activity, then a small blue shape leapt past me and on to the table.

'What's the matter, Uncle O?'

I looked up. It was Caterina. She was sitting on a pile of cookbooks, her tail curled over the edge, her left paw, which was clearly on the mend, set tentatively before her on the table. Her eyes were round with surprise.

'Hello, Squash.'

At the sound of her pet name she grinned at me and relaxed. 'Your fur went funny,' she said. 'It was all spiky. I thought you were getting chased by something.' She paused, uncertain of her ground. 'A . . . dog, or something.'

I laughed. 'No dogs here, Squash.'

'Then what was it?' Trust Caterina to be so insistent.

I looked around to make sure we were not overheard. 'A smell.' It sounded ridiculous even as I said it, but Cat looked unperturbed. 'A musty smell,' I went on, 'musty, and . . . perished.' I stopped. That wasn't it; not quite. 'But somehow still alive,' I finished inadequately.

Cat looked at me oddly. 'Foul,' she supplied.

I stared at her. 'Dusty and old, and with a tang of human to it.'

We both shivered.

In the middle of the storm that afternoon, the two men who looked like one came back. Something about them – their sharp eyes, their quiet voices, their intent expressions; or maybe just their identical smell – made me uneasy; and not just me, for an hour or two later I heard Anna's voice raised against them and the angry sound of her quick heels on the wooden floor. Even when they had gone, pulling away down the drive in the huge silver machine that growled like a great beast, their presence seemed to linger in the house. There was some tension between Anna and John after that: the air appeared to crackle with it like the aftermath of the lightning I had watched from the scullery window. In the next couple of days this edginess seemed to insinuate itself into all the other occupants of the house. Scraps broke out between Belly and Letty, then between Letty and Cat, who had foolishly tried to intervene. The baby wailed and grizzled through the night, causing Anna to have to get up and tend to her, though it seemed that no matter what she did, Ellie would not be appeased. Dreams came thick and fast on the wild roads around the house, and I wore myself thin with exhaustion hunting them down and despatching every last one.

One night, disturbed by Eleanor's incessant howling, I watched John take his reluctant turn with the baby, and marvelled at how a child that had for hours been little more than a writhing, shrieking thing that would not be picked up and comforted by its mother could so abruptly become still and tranquil in the presence of its father. All he had to do, evidently, was to speak to her softly, then pick her up and she became as pliant as a kitten. They sat together on the chair by the cot, John looking out through the uncurtained window into the mysterious shadows of the garden and Ellie resting with her head over his shoulder, half asleep and half not, the moonlight making silver snail trails of the path of her tears. I sat there for a few moments more, soothed by the sudden welcome silence, and applied myself to removing an annoying burr that had lodged itself in the tangle of fur under my left haunch. I had just got the elusive thing between my teeth and was starting to prise its little hasps clear, when there was a movement in the room behind me.

'Shall we go and see Orlando?'

I heard John say something which involved my name, then he was moving up and away from the chair, and the baby was awake and watching me with those wide green eyes of hers. I observed them come towards me – a creature with two heads that moved quietly through the dark. Stilled by surprise, one paw poised between rest and flight, suddenly I found I could not move.

John knelt beside me and set Ellie down on her feet. She gleamed at me, then reached out with one hand.

'That's right,' John said. 'Pat him nicely.'

The baby lurched at me. Something cold banged down painfully into the top of my skull, then rattled away on to the floor. As I spun round to see what it was that had hit me there burst from behind me a monstrous giggle.

'Bad girl,' I heard John say. 'Naughty Ellie. Didn't you want your toy?'

On the floor before me lay a complicated shiny black thing. Part of it had sprung apart as if broken, and from inside it a handful of dark stuff had scattered across the bare boards like a grotesque collection of spiders' legs. I sniffed at the strange bundle, then jumped back, sneezing. It had a reek to it: musty but still vigorous, still imprinted with its own clear signature. Whatever it was had certainly once been alive. But it had nothing to do with spiders.

I knew the smell of it, but I could not place it. It haunted me for the rest of the day, but by dawn the next morning I knew only too well what it was and wished I did not.

That night I completed my first excursion around the village's highways, having dealt with a number of small and relatively harmless dreams. Most of them were children's nightmares, in which nebulous monsters loomed out of the golden dream sacs, then dissipated to nothing at the first bite; but some had been more serious. In one, a man had stood in the path of a thundering beast, bigger than a car by far, all hot metal and screeching and burning oil. He had remained there, unable to move, time and again as it had come for him. Time and again he went down in its tracks and turned to see the same event occurring from another angle, from his blind side, from behind, spinning to meet it face to face. It was a hard dream to catch and harder still to swallow. The metal beast, though it dwindled as soon as the sac was opened, tasted foul and bitter; and the man fought me as he passed. The ghosts of his screams haunted my inner ear for hours, even though I knew the dreamer whose nightmare I had swallowed now lay quietly in his bed, snoring in untroubled sleep. In another, a woman knelt before a tall, fully dressed man and began to divest herself of her clothes, her gaze never leaving his face. Off came her coat and her shirt, and the thin, strappy thing she wore underneath. Her breasts were large and golden-white, the nipples like flower buds. Through her eyes I watched him looking at her, calm and dispassionate, unmoved by her vulnerable pale flesh. She cupped her breasts in her hands and offered them up to him, but all he did was to blink and frown as if puzzled, then take a step backwards. With a moan, she pulled at the skin till blood came; then she reached inside the cavity she had opened and held out her hands to him. They were red and wet, and full of something that beat and twitched. He stared at it for a moment, then shrugged and turned away. I swallowed him first and he tasted of nothing at all.

After that, the wild roads had been quiet and I had returned home. All the lights were out and the moon was high over the house, gliding over the tall chimneys. It was just past waxing point, a strong three-quarter moon, and it lit my way as clearly as a winter sun. So when Grizelda leapt out at me from the cover of the rhododendrons I was not taken by surprise, much to her dismay. 'Hello, Griz,' I said, before she had even had time to hiss at me.

'Oh,' she grumbled, 'you're no fun.'

I grinned. Griz was a big cat and older than me by some years, but she was attractive all the same, with her slanting golden eyes and soft belly. 'Sorry.'

'On your own again, are you?'

I looked at her. 'Just me and my shadow.'

'Fancy some company?' She winked at me, her meaning suddenly clear.

'I can't,' I spluttered, suddenly as embarrassed as a yearling boy. 'I'm on duty . . .'

She roared with laughter so that her brindled coat jounced and gleamed. 'Chasing moonbeams again, are you?'

'I've got work to do,' I said carefully. 'Dream-catching.' She looked at me askance and I knew she didn't believe a word of it. Like many of the cats we'd rescued she'd been bred in the laboratory and knew next to nothing about the world outside. 'Making sure the dreams don't damage the high-ways. It's my task, as the Dreamcatcher of Ashmore,' I finished lamely. I sounded pompous even to myself.

'You should be concerning yourself with more than dreams, my lad,' she said, and her tail flicked with impatience. 'Fine fellow like you and no kittens to your name.'

I stared at her.

'Well, anyone with half an eye can tell that them little blue girlies ain't nothing to do with you,' she carried on cheerfully. 'Seen a lot of strange things in my time, but never a blue kitten come from an orange father. It wouldn't be natural, would it?'

I regarded her warily. 'So you know who their father is, then?'

'Oh, yes. We all do, the girls out here and me. Her ladyship' – she cocked her head at the house – 'may give herself airs and pretend she's the cream on the milk, but some of us know different. Bred her to the Russian, she did, the witch.'

'The Russian?'

'Big blue chap. Witch's best stud beast. Handsome in his way. Wouldn't have said no myself, in different circumstances, if you know what I mean. But not like that.' She shuddered.

I found myself trembling. 'Didn't she have any choice, then?'

The big cat gave a short laugh. 'Not the first time, she didn't.'

I looked at her stupidly. 'The first time?' I echoed. 'She went to him more than once?'

'She didn't take the first time. And, silly girl, suddenly all she wanted was kittens. So she offered to go in Fig's place the next time the witch came. Persuaded Fig to feign illness, then wailed and sang like she was on fire. She didn't know what the woman did to them, you see, the kittens, I mean.' Griz's face hardened at the memory. 'She soon lost her eagerness when she found out. Too late by then, of course, or it would have been if you hadn't come and rescued us.'

I remembered the cold room crammed with cages; the reek of urine and fear, the dull eyes of the prisoners. All those cats; all those lost kittens . . .

'What did the witch do to them?' I asked then, though I hadn't meant to. I didn't even want to know.

Grizelda's golden eyes were glazed now. She was staring at a point above my head and suddenly I could see the toll her experiences had taken on her. She was older than I had thought, for there was grey around her ears and the fur was thinning on her forelegs. 'She took three broods from me and four from Evie, before she died. Brood after brood after brood and no way out of it. I still hear my lot, each voice distinct, crying for me as she took them away. Never saw any of them again.'

I could think of nothing to say. A pause fell between us, lengthened, became uncomfortable. A night bird flew overhead, the moonlight making of its wings a silver cowl. I watched it circle the garden silently, then slip away over the dark yew hedge and into the woods beyond, and wished I too could soar up and away from the dark places of the world . . .

'Boiled them, she did.' Griz's voice cracked through my reverie and for a moment I thought I had misheard her, but when I dropped my gaze from the night I found her watching me with an intense focus, her eyes glittering as if rain had suddenly fallen from a clear sky. 'That evil woman. She boiled them, my first kits. Three of them, there were: a little girl same colour as me and two dark boys. She took them from me after their first feed. You could hear . . .' She stopped and after a moment I could hear her trying hard to stifle a sob.

I hung my head. I knew how the man had felt now, the one in the dream rooted to the spot as the machine bore down on him again and again. Something in me had known this – if not in the appalling detail revealed by Grizelda, then in the rough shape of things – something visceral in me, something without words, had recognised disaster when it chanced upon it, there in that grim courtyard. I stared at the ground and found myself selfishly wishing I had not come this way home, that I had skirted the lawn and run up along the orchard wall, and maintained my foolish ignorance. But even as I thought it, I felt the shame rise in me, that I could try to avoid this truth simply by not thinking about it, when Griz and Liddy and the other cats in the laboratory had lived through it and gone on living with the knowledge and, in Lydia's case, the results of the experiment. That took a great deal more courage than I had in me, I suspected.

After a while Griz regained her composure and started to speak again. When I looked up, her eyes were clear and sharp, her jaw set like a tomcat's ready for a brawl. 'The boiling didn't suit her purpose, though, it seems. She never bothered with boiling the rest, though I dare say something equally terrible happened to them. She boiled up something in that room, though, that much I can tell you. I'll never forget the smell of it, not if I live to be twenty.'

'The smell of what?'

It was Caterina, ears pricked and face sharp with attention.

Griz turned to face the newcomer with remarkable speed, given her size. 'Old chicken carcass I chanced upon behind the dustbins, Squash, so full of life that smell was, it could almost walk.' She laughed quickly; too quickly.

Cat regarded her suspiciously. 'I'm sure that's *not* what you were talking about,' she said primly. 'I can tell when adults think they're being clever in hiding things from me. But if you don't want to tell me, that's your business. However' – she fluffed herself up – 'I didn't come here to talk to you; I came to find

Orlando, to tell him something *important*.'

Griz gave Caterina what she would have called 'a look', then swished her tail from side to side to show her annoyance and headed back into the depths of the rhododendrons. 'Remember,' she called to me over her shoulder, 'if you need some company, you know where to find me.'

Caterina's eyelids composed themselves into two straight lines, and beneath them the warm amber eyes turned to hard topaz. I knew that expression from long contemplation of her mother: it was one that spoke of being upstaged, of having lost a carefully fought advantage; of jealousy.

'What was so important that you had to be rude to old Griz?' I asked.

Cat glared at me. 'I thought that since you're supposed to be our dreamcatcher, you might like to know that there's a big fiery dream caught in the Long Corridor.'

I looked at her aghast, then gathered my haunches under me and fled up the lawn. I pelted through the cat door so fast I skinned an elbow on the way through, slipped over on the quarry tiles and skidded into the maze of hallways beyond the kitchen. But when I reached the Long Corridor there was no sign of the dream that Cat had reported, or of any other disturbance. The newly plastered walls were bland and unthreatening, now that the rows of old portraits had been removed, and gave back nothing to my questing senses other than the pervasive smell of chemicals and something vaguely faecal, something that reminded me oddly of the fields beyond the canal on the way to Glory Farm where the large black-and-white animals moved slowly across the green, cropping the grass with their big yellow teeth. I was comforted by the smell, for it was not the one I had come to dread, but something more natural and somehow cleaner. And it was a relief to me that the paintings had been taken down. I had always found them disturbing in a way I could not explain – it might have been their age, the way the old surfaces had crazed and yellowed, and then darkened to an almost uniform black-brown so that it was hard to make out any details, as if time itself had deliberately laminated them, trapping the dirt and dust of centuries inside untold layers of grime in order to obscure and withhold the impressions they carried. I was particularly glad that the portrait of the woman with green eyes – which seemed to be the only portrait out of them all that had been regularly cleaned – had been put away; for I could sense that dead gaze on me whenever I walked beneath it, following me with a questioning smile, as if taunting me with a connection I had failed to make.

At the top of the corridor I turned the corner and found myself in the Painted Room. Here, I felt the air shiver as if agitated. A faint scent of char curled around my nose.

I opened my mouth to scent it better and was invaded. Acrid and violent, the smell of smoking hair and burning fur insinuated itself through me, and suddenly I was back in that same room, the girl in the big boots and her man in the leather jacket behind me, and the awful burning upstairs, and I was yowling at the top of my voice that Anna and John were trapped in the chamber with the witch, but the people were being dense and going the wrong way, and the air was thick with smoke, the fumes were in my lungs and my fur was on fire . . .

'Get up, get up!' Cat nosed at me furiously. 'What are you doing, lying down here, Uncle Orlando? The dream is getting away.'

And just as suddenly I was back in myself again, and the scent of burning was faint and distant: the scorching of a dream globe and no more, reminiscent of the whiff made by melted candlewax, though stronger, more animal. I followed the scent of it and there, in the top corner of the room, pitching itself awkwardly against the ornamental coving, my prey hovered unsteadily. If it had started golden, as other dreams do, it had long ago lost its innocence. It hung there, a baleful hunter's moon of a dream, all blood-orange and fire, its outer membrane crossed with veins of black as if poisoned by its own contents.

I could not reach it. Even the mightiest jump in my ordinary form would take me less than halfway up the wall. I stared up at it, then turned to Caterina. Her eyes gave back a doubled image of the dream and she started to growl. Little flecks of froth formed at the corners of her mouth; then suddenly she sprang up and ran at the wall, bubbling and spitting with fury. The plaster in the Painted Room was broken and uneven, little ripples and outcrops playing across its pale surface. To a lightly built cat

– especially one borne up by the power of an almost supernatural loathing – it offered sufficient foothold to enable Caterina to reach high enough to snap at the lowest bulge in the dream's sac. She caught it between her teeth, then tumbled to the floor, dragging the dream, swollen and reluctant, down with her. Without a moment's thought I leapt upon it, pinioning it beneath my hindquarters, where it lay as senseless and unresponsive as a punctured football.

I raked at it with all four sets of claws. I ripped my teeth into it, but the membrane was strong. I pushed my head blindly into it, but the sac simply gave under the pressure and re-formed itself around my shoulders. At last I managed to hook a thumb claw into it and tear a small hole. I bit and bit at this, enlarging it so that I could wedge my head into the ghastly opening, but as soon as I did so the dream rose with a whoosh, as if it had felt the wound. It jagged its way across the room and out into the Long Corridor, where it melted through the wall and disappeared from view. I followed it, feet skittering on polished wood, down the corridor and in and out of all the rooms on that side of the house. To no avail.

Outside, clouds had drifted over the moon, rendering the darkness complete. But a cat can see even in the pitch-black and I could see the dream. It was tottering over the orchard wall, heading for the knot garden. My heart sank, but I knew I had to catch it. Up and over the wall I went, my feet barely touching the old brick in my haste. Once on the other side, it skirted the straggling box hedges and veered to one side, as if trying to keep close to the house. At the corner it wobbled uncertainly, then made the characteristic dash of a dream entering a wild road, a sudden, elongating motion, followed by a pleating, as if it had met resistance, then it was gone.

I stared after it, puzzled. There was no highway where it had vanished – at least none that I knew of and it was my job to know every wild road in Ashmore.

I ran to the spot where it had disappeared and sniffed cautiously at the ground. About a bird's height above the gravel, my nose met a familiar resistance: the skin of a wild road. This was most bizarre, for surely there should never have been a wild road here, so close to the house. Nevertheless, I pushed my head inside and gazed around, eyes narrowed against the sudden icy blast. There was nothing about the interior of the highway that indicated it was anything less than a natural road, but even so I was taking no chances. Pulling my head out again, I found Cat sitting behind me, watching my performance with interest.

'Stay there,' I said sternly. 'Whatever happens, just stay there and wait for me.'

She made a face. 'I could help.'

'I know, but your best help would be waiting here.'

'What if it's too strong for you?' She got up hopefully.

'It's not.'

'But how do you *know*? It might be and then I could help.'

'Caterina, I haven't got time for this.'

The use of her proper name had its effect. She sat down again, looking hurt.

'If I don't reappear, fetch Millie. She'll know what to do.' I wondered even as I said this just how long I could rely on my old friend being around. Then, with a final apologetic glance at Cat, I leapt into the new highway.

At once, the winds caught at me, whipping my mane back and forth across my eyes in a confusion of cross-currents. I stood for a while, trying to take my bearings. There was something recognisable about this road, but at the same time something warped. I could have travelled every highway, each lane and tributary of the wild roads of Ashmore and its environs with my eyes shut; but now I had the discomfiting sense of being entirely lost, as if one false step would carry me over an unseen cliff edge, or down into the deepest pit. I trod warily.

Up ahead, dimmed by the ice flurries and a sort of swirling mist, I could just make out the fiery red of the dream, diffused to a radiant glow, like an autumn sunset. It was drifting away from me. I increased my pace. Beneath my feet I could feel solid ground, which was dry and soft and almost warm, unlike the frost-bound earth that always hurt my pads whenever I ran the highways. And the scents of the wild that helped me to orientate myself – the loam and mulch, the standing water, the tang of life – seemed muted and far removed, as if someone had shut a door against the outside world and trapped this road inside.

I turned a corner and found myself in the place Caterina had described. It was a tunnel, or a corridor, and it was dark. The mist was not mist but cobwebs, great hanging swathes of them, though of their makers there was no sign. The dream had suspended itself in the thickest part of them, as if settling itself into a nest. Fear came down on me then like a cold hand, for it seemed to me that the dream was in its natural element and I was not. Perhaps, I thought, I should leave it to destroy this strange highway and take myself back to the world I understood. It would be so easy to walk away and relinquish this hunt. I could almost feel myself begin to step backwards towards my point of entrance, but just as I was about to do so a movement behind the dream caught my eye. I craned my neck. Illuminated by the dream globe's carmine light I saw Vita.

I had not seen my sister for some six or seven seasons, ever since the highways had swallowed her, and she was much changed. But those white socks against her tabby coat were unmistakable; as was the reproach in her eyes. She sat upon what appeared to be a tall chair of black wood, and the light from the dream was in her eyes, as if a fire were raging inside her skull.

'Eat the dream, Orlando,' she said softly, though her voice carried easily to me across that open space. 'You must eat all the dreams she sends, or I will be trapped here for ever.' She stared at me for a moment or two more as if imprinting me with her fiery gaze, then she jumped down from the chair and ran away from me. In the gloomy light, all I could see of her as she fled was the flash of her white feet, the recurring image I had seen in my sleep time after time. Then I realised who it was I had sensed beside me all those nights as I dozed, whose hot breath I had felt upon my neck, whose scent had surrounded me when I awoke.

'Vita!'

My voice echoed hollowly in that place and I knew from the sound that I was somewhere in Nonesuch, but it was not a part of the house I recognised, or at least the house as I knew it, for there were silken runners on the floor beneath my feet, rather than the dark polished wood that was there now; and when I ducked under the white shrouds to run after my sister, the old portraits were back, rich with colour as if freshly painted. This was disconcerting, but I refused to be put off my pursuit of Vita. However, before I had gone more than a few yards down this odd version of the Long Corridor I found myself back where I had started, with the dream looming red before me.

I ran past it again, for surely I had missed my way. But even as I ran, I knew I could never have turned a full circle and not noticed it. And indeed, a few seconds later I was back where I had begun once more. Was I dreaming, too? But the dream I pursued here was real; I had felt the heat from it scorching my fur as I passed. I could see the shadows its fiery corona cast. My image loomed huge and attenuated upon the walls of that highway: a gigantic lion stalking its prey. Except that I had run past my prey twice and given it not a thought.

Eat the dream.

I did not know what she meant by the rest of what she had said, but I would eat this dream and every other dream I found. I would do my job as Ashmore's dreamcatcher. I reached up and pulled the fiery dream down from its nest of webs, and it came almost willingly into my paws, as if ready to give up the half-life it had found here. It did not resist me even when I bit into it and started to gnaw a head-sized hole.

Beyond the viscous membrane the dream contained one of the clearest scenes I had ever seen in any globe. I was inside a room panelled in dark wood, a gloomy effect only heightened by the lengths of black muslin that had been draped across the single mullioned window. Candles, tall and yellow, burned at intervals along the mantelpiece and from two ornate wall sconces, and these gave off the scent of burning tallow I had smelled in the Painted Room. No modern candles these, with their synthetic wax and clean tapers: instead, plumes of dark smoke coiled in lazy spirals from these towers of animal fat, to leave greasy spirals on the beamed ceiling. I was in Nonesuch, in one of the downstairs parlours, I realised, recognising the pitted wain-scoting, the carved pattern of ivy and roses along the central rail. But where this wood was dark with age, the wood in the room I knew had been lightened and limed to an almost buttery finish, and again I felt disorientated, as if someone had picked me up and spun me round many times before setting my feet back on the floor. The room swam. I turned round. Against the back wall stood a tall, ladder-backed chair in ebony wood and upon this was curled a small tabby cat with all its paws tucked neatly beneath its tail.

In the centre of the room a tall woman in a long dark dress – her glossy black hair pinned up into an elaborate knot – stood over the body of a man in a long wooden box. She was facing towards me and when I turned to regard her she looked up briefly. Her eyes flashed at me, green and dangerous, then she bent to her task again. A silver implement flashed in her hand as she worked and when she straightened she held a small twist of dark hair between her fingers, and this she first laid against her cheek, then stowed inside the pendant of the shiny black necklace she wore. Again that sense of disquietude came over me; for surely the woman was holding in her hand the same black necklace the baby had thrown at me that very afternoon? I began to feel distinctly queasy and, as I did so, the perspectives shifted eerily again, so that I was almost floating in mid-air; for when I looked down I found that I could see the man in the box. He was very like John: dark-skinned and thin in the face, though this man was older and tireder than the John I knew, his cheeks withered and fallen in, his hair greying at the temples. A high, stiff collar supported his lolling head and his hands were crossed upon his chest. I could see small cuts and abrasions on his knuckles and wrists. His eyes were open and staring.

They say a cat, staring into the eyes of a dead man, can make out the last image that the man saw, imprinted upon his retina. I do not know if this is true; but what I did see in the eyes of John-not-John was unmistakable.

It was terror, pure and simple.

I gagged as I ate the dream down, piece by piece, though for once the occupants went quietly, without a fight, as if this were the last, most peaceful, scene in a long and destructive dream. But as I swallowed the dream woman, the cat on the chair opened one eye, then winked at me and slipped away. I could not see her feet, but I knew that it was Vita all the same, checking to ensure I was carrying out my appointed task.

'You were ages; where have you been?'

As soon as I exited the strange highway, I found Cat waiting for me exactly as I had asked her to, though the gravel in front of her paws was churned up into little heaps and lumps as if she had dug her toes into it in frustration and impatience.

'I'm not sure it's a matter of where,' I said softly, 'but rather of *when*.'

Chapter Nine

'THE THING ABOUT a relationship', Anna explained to Alice, 'is that you patch things up. Everyone tries harder.'

John's idea of trying harder was to concern himself as much as possible with the repairs. He missed meals and she found him eating with the builders. Or he took the Tank into London and spent the afternoon looking at fabric samples in the V&A. In the evenings they kept off the subject of Eleanor and confined themselves to the day's other events. He was trying to assess the damage to the Long Gallery. He had saved some sixteenth-century oak panelling and ten walnut chairs in the style of Daniel Marot; but it looked as if water damage had rendered the famous Brussels tapestries unsalvageable. 'Not that I'll miss them,' he claimed. 'They always smelled of mothballs.'

Anna laughed and turned a page of *Mansfield Park*.

Eleanor, meanwhile, had new shoes. She tottered about in them matter-of-factly sweeping the books from the shelves and stuffing small things into the tape slot of the VTR; or toddled sturdily along the corridors of Nonesuch, leading her mother by the hand. She cared nothing about relationships, but out of some native shrewdness now encouraged Anna to join the fun at breakfast time. She had adopted two more words – 'ca' and something which might have been 'Orlando' had the first and last syllables not been so obviously absent. Most of what she said was nonsense, eked out with an amazing penetrative shriek used to signify anything from impatience to delight. This was so loud it often drew the builders from their work to scratch their heads over her. They seemed fascinated.

'She's a proper little girl all right,' Alice Meynell told Anna, as if there had been some doubt. 'Twenty-two months old and she's already got that lot wrapped round her little finger.'

But it is always nice when people find your child engaging; and as most of the workmen had children of their own, Anna found herself reassured by their goodwill. There couldn't be too much wrong with her daughter if these ordinary and decent men liked her so. When Eleanor turned up to visit them one day without her necklace, they unearthed for her a silver spoon of obscure purpose and uncertain provenance. It had been a bit bent, they explained, when they found it, down between two of the huge old floorboards in the Yellow Dining Room, and a bit blackened with age, but it had polished up well. Would she like it?

She would.

It was as long as Anna's middle finger, with a small deep oval bowl curving into the elegant upward sweep of the handle. Wear had given it a soft, blurry sheen, a deeper colour than you would expect from silver, and – as John said – the feel of something properly old. He thought that it might be from the Regency, or perhaps a little later; he had no idea what it was for. Eleanor loved her spoon; and no one regretted the loss of the necklace, with its tawdry Victorian glitter and hidden twist of hair.

St Mary's vicarage, a cavernous structure built in 1912 in patent brick glazed to resist weathering, looked less like a house than the annexe of some Edwardian junior school in Birmingham. Arriving there mid-morning to find the front door open, Anna propped her bicycle against the wall and, entering without a thought of what she would do next, pushed her way past the coats and along the narrow hall where a row of Francis's shoes lay motionless at the base of the wainscoting like very large black beetles.

'Francis?' she called.

She knew he was at home, because she could hear him upstairs somewhere, talking. When he didn't answer she waited irresolutely in the kitchen, looking from time to time at her watch. Finally, she went to the bottom of the stairs and stood with her hand resting on the mahogany banister, listening. She could hear his voice, modulated and rhythmic, argumentative and hesitant by turns. It never rose louder than the buzz of a fly trapped in a bedroom on an October afternoon. She gave him a moment more, then called, more loudly than she had intended, 'Francis? Hello?'

His voice stopped immediately. In the silence that followed, faint sounds filtered in from outside.

'Francis!'

Nothing.

Just as she was beginning to turn away, she heard him begin to talk again, picking up, it seemed, exactly where he had left off, his voice still rising and falling conversationally though, quite clearly, he was alone up there.

Anna had no idea about religion. She had no clue what a vicar might do when he was on his own. Perhaps he was praying. She formed a sudden image of him kneeling on a bare floor, his hands locked together in front of him, the expression on his face not one she associated with Francis. She took her hand off the banister as if it had been burned and stepped quickly back into the kitchen, which greeted her with ingrained smells of carbolic soap and vicarage cooking. Everything spoke of an unlikely dedication. The Formica-topped table was littered with squares of crumpled butchers' paper on which Francis had been trying to draft a sermon. Even the kitchen appliances had the worn-down air of women who give their lives to the Church.

Anna smoothed out the first bit of paper that came to hand, wrote hastily on it in pencil, 'Why don't you come to tea any more? I do miss talking to you,' and left as quickly as she could.

Passing them in the hall, she averted her eyes from his shoes.

When he heard Anna's voice, Francis Baynes felt himself stop speaking. He felt the kind of spasm go through him that goes through old plumbing when a tap is turned off and he raised his head to meet the amused smile of the woman who lay on his bed.

She had laughed at him from the beginning. She found endless ways of teasing him: she took up the position of an effigy on a tomb, hands praying on her chest; she threatened to raise her skirt or show him a nipple (which, he knew, had a wide brown aureole surrounded by faint downy black hairs). Francis was afraid of her. Her level gaze, with its frank will to power, reminded him of something he couldn't quite remember. Her rank sexuality attracted and repelled him. She continued to smile at him for a minute, perhaps more, in the silence in the room; then, looking towards the open door, shrugged abruptly, as if to say, 'So what?' While from the bottom of the stairs, where she stood trembling, Anna Dawe called out, 'Francis!'

The woman on the bed smiled and shrugged.

Francis Baynes, relieved, smiled back and spoke again. ' – the mystery of it,' he continued, as if he had never left off.

She raised her hand, palm outwards. 'Do you want to understand that mystery?' she asked. 'Or do you want to *know* it?'

'I want to know it.'

'Then you must be more committed.'

From childhood his faith had been rooted in ideas, never passion; ideas had sent him to the Church. He had turned to ideas because the world made him squeamish. That was why he was so vulnerable to the woman on the bed. It was as bitter – and exciting – and simple – as that. She was sex. She was life. She was risk. She was everything he had shied away from; everything he had wanted from Anna Dawe, under the guise of love. He didn't know what he wanted now. He didn't know whether he had been damned or freed. He supposed that you never did. He opened his dry mouth to say this, but she was already warning him.

'You must be more of everything.'

'And yet –' he said. He meant, 'To live fully is to admit that you will die.'

'Life is not death,' she said. 'Neither is death.'

He tried to laugh. 'We have no choice about that.'

'Everyone has a choice.'

He would not be convinced. They talked and talked, to and fro, until late afternoon tinted the light between them. At that she rose to her feet in a motion somehow floating and energetic at the same time, and put on her gloves. Her long brown skirts settled themselves with a smell of dust, flowers, menstrual blood. When she approached him, he backed away. She smiled sadly. 'Oh, Francis,' she chided, 'Francis.' He watched her descend the stairs and go along the hall. He always left the front door open for her, though he suspected she did not need him to. He left it open because he didn't like to think of her coming and going without using it.

Physics had robbed Alice Meynell, however temporarily, of some of her sturdy qualities. Her enthusiasm had diminished. She rode the Ducati about the lanes with no less confidence – because at the speeds Alice travelled, diminished confidence would certainly have brought about injury to herself or others – but there was a morose determination in the note of its engine, and calculation had replaced brio in the rhythm of its gear changes. She hung about in Anna's kitchen, quoting from magazine articles with subtitles like 'Is Celibacy the New Promiscuity?'. To get her own back on her physicist, she decided not to go to America to see him; then, as soon as he wrote to her from Baja, full of the poetry of something called 'critical state theory' – a kind of mathematics which, he claimed, could explain everything from earthquakes to stock exchange crashes, although 'explain' was clearly not the right word in this context – changed her mind.

'He's just so *excited* by this stuff,' she said.

Anna, who had had enough of obsessional men to last a lifetime, was dubious about the whole thing. 'You must make sure you have a really good time and not let him set the agenda.' This sounded feeble, so she added, 'I mean, with some men it's so easy to lose yourself.'

Alice grinned. 'Can you see me letting that happen?'

'Of course not,' said Anna, who could see it quite clearly.

Originally, Alice had asked for a lift to Drychester

station, where she could catch a train to Heathrow. But that would have meant changing twice and catching a later plane, so Anna had offered to take her all the way, insisting, 'It would be a change for me. Honestly, Alice. I can see Drychester any day, but I haven't been to an airport in years.'

'You *must* be bored.'

They found themselves on the bustling concourse of Terminal Three, two women and a toddler, in everyone's way, feeling provincial and not entirely sure what to say to one another. Anna's cotton print dress was already a little the worse for wear. Eleanor had been sick in the car; now, round-eyed and diffident in the face of it all – especially when she caught sight of the huge coloured tailfins of the aircraft manoeuvring stealthily about on the tarmac outside – she was clingy and demanding. 'John,' she whispered, 'Dada' and clutched her spoon in case anyone tried to take it away. She had never seen so many people. None of them knew who she was.

'Well,' said Alice. 'I'd better be off.'

'Have a really good time,' Anna repeated.

'I'll do that all right,' Alice assured her.

'Don't forget to send us a postcard.'

'I'll do that too.'

They stood uncertainly for a moment in the rising tide of travellers at the departure lounge, then Alice smiled and kissed them both, and strode off abruptly. Anna held Eleanor up in the air. 'Wave,' she told her. 'Wave to Alice!' Eleanor blinked. To give her the idea, Anna stood on her tiptoes and waved energetically. Eleanor stared at this display, then at her own hand, then at Alice's retreating back and scuffed cordura softpack luggage. Eventually, with great effort, she waved. But by then Alice had vanished into the crowd.

'Well.' Anna sighed. 'That's that, I suppose.' She looked at her watch. She was in no hurry to face the motorway again. She showed Eleanor the row of coffee shops that stretched away, steamy and warm, smelling of mocha and warm cream, in both directions from where they stood. 'Shall we have a cake before we leave? At one of these places?'

Eleanor beamed. 'Muffing,' she said.

Without Alice to distract her Eleanor became difficult again. She tried to keep her father in view at all times and showed anxiety if he left a room without her. She didn't want to toddle, and the builders made her shy and speechless. Still chastened, perhaps, by her encounter with the world outside Nonesuch, she clung to Anna's shoulder and firmly clutched her spoon. Anna consulted the baby books: *Setbacks*, she read, *are common. Be encouraging*.

If Eleanor was preoccupied, Anna felt restless. The airport had been a shock to her too; living in a village so long, she had begun without knowing it to miss the bustle of things. With Alice gone and only Eleanor to talk to the day seemed empty. To give herself something to do, she sat down at the computer in John's office, and – withdrawing the last of her savings from an e-banking account – began day-trading again, buying mainly into companies that specialised in sustainable low-tech solutions for third world problems.

Soon she was up there every afternoon, gaining a little more than she lost, watching the numbers scroll, trying to feel her way back into the life of money. But though day-trading was fun, and reminded her she had talents and qualities of her own, it wasn't the rough-and-tumble she had been used to at TransCorp and it hardly filled an hour. The rest of the time she poked about in the rooms along the corridor from the office, fastidious as a cat – her nose wrinkling with those smells of dust and fire damage and ghostly 1940s Brylcreem – but hoping perhaps to understand why Mark and Oliver kept coming back to Stella Herringe's things. That was how, kneeling in front of the abandoned Kelvinator surrounded by bundles of estate documents tied up in green string, she found the little screw-topped jar of white emulsion, labelled, in Stella Herringe's distinctive childish hand, like Women's Institute jam.

Someone had pushed it right to the back of the shelf, behind two or three old Eastlight box files, an ordinary little jar which had originally contained supermarket honey or peanut butter. Anna took it from the shelf. She held it up to the light; gave the lid a half-turn anticlockwise. That was enough. The room filled suddenly with a perfume so distinctive, so authoritative, it was less like a smell than a voice. It 'turned your head' in the old sense of the words: you couldn't wait to see who had entered the room, laughed, spoken your name . . .

It was always Stella Herringe. Stella, six months before the fatal fire, leaning over to touch Anna's wrist and whisper, 'You should take care of that skin, dear. I can recommend something.' Stella at a dinner party in a one-sleeved Amanda Wakeley frock and Manolo Blahnik kitten heels, looking up suddenly in the candlelight to laugh. Stella smoking a cigarette, always laughing and turning the men's heads, always eighteen years old, whispering, 'How old are you now? Thirty-five? Thirty-seven?' and 'Are you afraid yet?' and 'I promise you, dear, that it works.'

Anna held in her hand the balm to every woman's nightmare. A cream that really could make you young.

Engelion.

'Oh, my God,' she said. She sat back on her heels, breathing as if she had just cycled up to Cresset Beacon. 'Oh, my God.'

She found John in the kitchen.

'Where's Eleanor?'

John indicated the baby intercom, winking cheerfully in its corner. 'Upstairs,' he said. 'She was tired this morning, so I thought I'd get her down for an hour or two.'

'Good. I want to talk to you.'

'What's the matter?'

'Did you know this was still here?'

'What?'

She put the jar on the table in front of him. 'Open it, John.'

He did as she asked, blinking as the perfume enveloped him, its more obvious elements – traditional flowers, the bloom on old English orchard fruits – barely masking whatever coiled, thick and musky and animal, beneath. He studied the even white surface of the cream; brushed it with the tip of his finger. Anna knew how it would feel. Though lightly textured, it would have a consistency which made it seem as thick as oil; it would be surprisingly cold to the touch. John raised his finger to his face. Anna gasped and caught his wrist. He stared at her for a moment, then stumbled over to the sink and began washing his hands. After he had washed them three or four times, he bent down to the cupboard under the sink and came up with a wire-wool scouring pad and washed them again, using that. 'Christ,' he kept saying. 'Christ.'

She touched his shoulder, but he didn't notice. Eventually, when he felt he could stop washing, she said, 'This is what they're here for, John.'

'Who?'

'Oh, for God's sake.' She brandished the jar in front of him. 'I don't want this in my house.'

He looked defeated. 'Do you think I do?' he said. 'Throw it out, Anna. Throw it out.'

'That's not enough. I want Mark and Oliver Holland thrown out too.'

'They're not *here* today.'

'You know bloody well what I mean!' She went out to the dustbin, dropped the jar inside, banged the lid down as hard as she could. Perhaps hearing the clatter from her cot, Eleanor woke up and began to cry, her voice, relayed to them by the baby intercom, sounding tinny and distant. 'I'll get her,' Anna offered. 'It's my turn.' Then, 'This is what they've been after all along, John. I never want them here again.'

Busy, busy, always busy. The hedges wind round and round, and I go to the heart of the hedges, also up and down stairs, up and down the corridors, busy as you like in the moonlight. (And busy when you get there too, says Izzie.) Stair, wall and corner, I open each cubbyhole and niche, and I draw out all their little secrets. It's easy now. Knowing secrets makes them yours. Knowing secrets makes you theirs.

I got my own secrets now, I said, and Izzie said, you watch that others' secrets don't find you out. You get above yourself and there'll be enough secrets out there to bury you.

Then she says, What's your name? once, and I tell her. What's your name? twice, and I tell her. What's your name? three times, and I tell her. Never forget that, she says. But what's in a name, when you don't know who you are? I say. Busy, busy, my girl, is Izzie's advice. That's the answer to that conundrum: you get busy. You'll know who you are all right, when Izzie's good and ready. You've got to earn your identity in this life.

Anna wondered what was happening to Alice in America. *I miss her,* she thought. *I even miss the sound of that damned motorbike.* She speculated about Alice's physicist, to whom she gave brown hair, then black, then a smile which, reminding her strongly of Jake Wishart's, caused her to blush while watching TV on the sofa with John. John didn't notice. He had been withdrawn and distant since the discovery of the Engelion cream. She knew how disappointed he was. If Mark and Oliver went, their money went with them and John's hopes along with it. He was blaming her a little for bringing it to his notice, for making his choices so stark, but she had been prepared for that.

That wasn't what puzzled her. It was something else.

She thought for a day or two, then asked at breakfast, 'Why are you avoiding me?'

He was trying to do the *Guardian* crossword puzzle while Eleanor massaged a slurry of Coco Pops and full-cream milk into her hair and shouted, 'Tooty! Tooty tooty tooty!' He put the paper down and stared at Anna with exaggerated patience for some time before replying, 'Anna, we're sitting here at the table together.' He looked at his watch. 'Two minutes ago you asked me if you could have the marmalade.'

'I don't care.' She got up. 'You're avoiding me and you know it.'

John, out of his depth, got up too and tried to put his arm round her, while Eleanor gazed at them both with interest.

'It isn't the same,' Anna said, slipping away from him and going to stand by the sink, her arms folded under her breasts. 'It isn't the baby or the house, or being tired all the time or having no money. It's not even Mark and Oliver, though I know you're upset about that. You're avoiding me even when we're in the same room, and I can't work you out and it just isn't the same between us.'

He shrugged helplessly, as if to say, 'How could anyone deal with such high levels of irrationality?'

Several days had passed without answer since Anna had left the note in Francis Baynes's kitchen, but she rang him up anyway and invited him to tea on the lawn. She wanted one of those old, safe, comforting teas, during which he would eat most of the scones, complain about his bishop, then look across at the house, with its Flemish gables against the blue sky and, after a period of satisfied silence, say, 'And what about your life, Anna? What's happening in your life?' In the event it rained, forcing them to have tea in one of the ground-floor rooms, where most of the furniture was still under dust sheets.

They sat with a spindly little gatelegged table between them, while Eleanor slept in her car seat on the polished floor and Orlando watched the milk jug like a hawk. The builders, who were working not far down the hall, kept driving some kind of drill into the brickwork with a low, gloomy, grinding sound, which got into the bones of Anna's chest. Francis crossed his legs like a younger version of his own father and balanced his cup on one knee. Every so often he cleared his throat deliberately, or rubbed his hands and said, 'Tea!' She looked at his out-at-elbow tweed jacket with the paperback copy of *A Glastonbury Romance* in the pocket and thought, *Whatever will he do with himself in ten years' time, fifteen? In that great box of a vicarage?* This made her remember the last time she had called there; also how he had stood alone in the rain, under a tree, in full view of her Volvo.

'Are you sure you're all right, Francis?'

He looked puzzled. 'Of course.'

'Good,' she said hastily. 'That's good.' She waited for him to ask, 'And how are things with you?' but found she hadn't been able to wait long enough and had already gone on without planning to, 'Things have been a bit hectic here.' She was immediately full of contempt for herself.

But Francis didn't seem to notice. 'How's John?' he asked. 'How are you coping, you two?'

Relief flooded through her. 'Oh, Francis,' she answered. 'I can't make him *listen*.'

Orlando, who knew how to choose his moment, leapt up next to the milk. She tried to brush him down, but he clung. The table rocked and everything was close to being spilt. The noise woke Eleanor, who looked around for her spoon and, not finding it, grizzled until Anna found it for her. 'For God's sake, Orlando,' Anna said, blinking through real tears. 'Can't you once behave?' Orlando looked hurt, but retreated only as far as the legs of Francis's chair.

'I'm sorry, Francis,' Anna said. She was horrified to hear herself sniff loudly. 'I don't know what's the matter with us today.'

Francis – who greeted most domestic upsets with a formality which, Anna thought, disguised real distaste – said, 'You mustn't worry,' then stopped, his expression stiff with something he couldn't articulate, and cleared his throat again. Suddenly he looked less like Francis than a version of himself – the version who would end his career at St Mary's, tired, gaunt, passed over for promotion because of his old-fashioned ideas. On the phone he had spoken as if nothing had happened since they last met. But she wondered if he had caught a cold that day in the rain under the chestnut tree, one of those colds that stay with you week after week.

'Francis,' she said. 'You are looking after yourself, aren't you?'

'Yes.' He sounded vague. 'Yes, I am.'

'You're sure?'

'Oh, yes.'

The way he said this caused her an anxiety she couldn't explain. 'You *are* sure?' she insisted. 'Because if you're not feeling well or anything –' She let herself trail away. He was looking out of the window, as if he had seen something on the sodden lawn. 'Francis?'

Francis cleared his throat again. 'No,' he said. 'I'm fine.'

'Good.' Now she had his attention, however, she didn't seem to know what to do with it. She tried to tell him about Mark and Oliver. But how could she describe them? Without bringing in Stella Herringe and the events that had led up to the fire it was difficult to make them seem anything more than businessmen; and she ended up by saying, to her surprise, 'I feel as if they're edging me out of my own house.' She paused. 'I mean,' she corrected herself, 'that to get what they want they would edge me out.' This sounded even more ridiculous, so she continued, 'I don't know what I mean.' She shivered, wishing she could tell him all she knew, and – not really referring to Mark and Oliver at all – asked, 'Do you think people can be evil?'

'Yes,' Francis said. 'Good, too.'

This wasn't much comfort.

'I sometimes wish we could give up on Nonesuch.'

'What would you do?'

She shrugged. 'Sell up, take the loss, move away. I could easily get us somewhere else to live. This is so much more John's project than mine.'

'And have you suggested this?'

'Oh, yes. But I don't know if I mean it anyway. It's not so much the house,' she said, hearing the builders through the wall, 'it's all the mess and noise.' She looked around vaguely. 'The uncertainty,' she added. 'If it weren't for John and Eleanor –' Not sure what she was about to say, she sighed, and went on, 'They're so close, those two, I sometimes feel there isn't room for me any more.'

'You aren't being very clear.'

'I'm not, am I?'

In the end, it was half past four, and she hadn't said anything sensible, and he would soon have to leave. She caught him glancing out of the window again. 'Francis, you aren't listening.'

His head moved as if he were following someone's progress across the empty lawns and he smiled. 'It isn't your husband (who strikes me as a very decent man). It isn't his business associates, who will soon get what they want, or not and go away. It isn't the house itself. Or the builders, or, really, the money, because you are too strong, both of you, not to overcome irritations like that.' He looked into the bottom of his cup, swilling the residue around like a fortune-teller. 'Whom does that leave?' he asked Anna. 'Anna,' he answered for her and gave her a moment to think about it. 'I wonder if you've simply let yourself become dissatisfied with your life. I wouldn't blame you if you had.'

'That's not very helpful,' Anna reproached him.

'Isn't it?'

'I thought God –'

'Ah, God,' he said. He stood up.

Anna stood up too. 'Francis, don't go yet.' She took hold of his hand. 'Look, I haven't said half of what I wanted to say. All of a sudden I just feel lonely and not very loved in my own house, that's all.'

He smiled. 'It seems like a lot to me.'

'It does, doesn't it?' she agreed. 'And you're right, of course, I've let things get the better of me. I feel oppressed by the sheer effort of it all, resentful at giving up my career, and from time to time ragingly jealous of my own daughter. Do you suppose that's normal?'

'Perfectly.'

Somehow the afternoon pivoted on this one word.

Anna thought, *How can you say that? How can you know anything about that?*

Suddenly she had no confidence in him, or in herself. In a panic she brought the back of his hand to her lips, kissed it. She knew that this gesture offered more than she had intended. But if she lost his attention, whom would she have left to talk to? 'Dear Francis,' she said. 'I don't know what I'd do without you.' Which, as she told herself later, was not something you could say safely to a twenty-six-year-old boy who already had a crush on you. You didn't need the expression on his face to tell you that.

She stood on the front steps to watch the little Rover make its way slowly down the drive – 'Wave, Ellie. Wave!' – then went back inside to the kitchen, where she ran warm water on the tea things. The afternoon was almost over. Eleanor sat in her high chair, toying drowsily with spaghetti hoops in 'tomato' sauce, then fell asleep quite suddenly.

A little later John came in from the knot garden, bringing with him a smell of waxed cotton, damp air, gathering dark.

'How was the vicar?' he asked.

'Don't say it like that, he's never harmed you. Anyway, he was fine. A bit vague. Do you want tea?'

'Desperate for it.'

'Well, you know where the kettle is,' she told him.

He laughed and Anna began to make tea anyway, using the last two Assam teabags and a spoonful of loose China. 'This is all I ever do,' she said. 'Make tea and clean up Coco Pops.'

'You too?'

'Piss off, John.'

He hung his wet Barbour jacket on the back of the door. Then he said, 'It's the strangest thing.'

'What is?' she enquired.

She found the tea strainer and poured the tea into two large mugs, looked in one of the cupboards for biscuits. She could hear him busily emptying the pockets of the jacket, then putting things down on the kitchen table behind her. She arranged three or four stale chocolate digestives on a small plate, picked up the mugs and turned round.

'Well, look what I found,' he said.

On the table he had lined up Ellie's plastic doll's head; the little lacquered musical box Francis had found in the builders' rubbish; the Victorian mourning locket with its secret twist of hair. From the musical box issued a few wavering notes of 'Für Elise'.

Anna stared at it. She stared at her husband. She felt a curious warm weakness in her legs, as if they were reluctant to support her any longer. It was like the rush of sleep when you have been up all night, like an unexpected depression on a November afternoon. She sat down suddenly. 'Where did you get these things?' she whispered.

'Anna,' he said. 'The tea.'

She put it down carefully, so as not to spill any more. 'Where did you get them?'

'That's what's so odd. They were in the knot garden.'

'Show me,' she ordered. 'Take me there.'

'Now? Why?'

She struggled to her feet, still staring down at the objects on the table. She tried to be calm. 'Because I threw these things away.' She separated the pendant from the other items. 'I don't even know what happened to this,' she said wonderingly. She shook her head. 'I keep throwing these things away and they keep turning up again. They just keep turning up again. Can you explain that to me?'

'Anna –'

She went over to the kitchen door, opened it and stood there waiting silently for him while rain blew in round her.

He made a fuss about bringing Eleanor, who had to be dressed for outdoors – waking briefly, she looked puzzled, whispered 'Dada', fell asleep again with her head lolling against his shoulder – and another about finding her hat. He made a fuss about looking for a torch. He didn't want to go out again. 'Don't you even want your coat?' he asked.

'For God's sake, John, just take me there!'

She followed him along the side of the house in the rain, through the old parterres and rockeries. He wouldn't slow down for her and there was no comfort in the bulk of him, silhouetted against the torchlight, which illuminated in random, chaotic flashes a mossy brick path; sodden, impenetrable rhododendrons; the leaning orchard wall, its spalled orange lip fringed with the branches of medlar trees and dripping like the lip of a drying waterfall. He stopped to unlock a gate. She felt a terrace open out on her left; smelled smoke.

'I hate this place,' she said.

Builders' rubbish had obscured much of it, but it still made the eye restless, and you could just discern in the clipped lines of germander and box, the knot, the maze, whatever you properly called it: the roiled whorls and spirals, the curves and re-entrants, that disguised Joshua Herringe's initial – the 'hidden J' he had devised in 1482 to celebrate his fortune, impress his new wife, encode his own self-esteem. There were so many ways to describe the knot. A half-solved puzzle, a clock which told only Herringe family time. Anna took one step forward, felt the nausea of her own past well up, saw the house blaze, the madwoman crawl out here to die. Two years might not have passed. She felt her burns again: when she looked down, one hand cradled the other to ease the memory of pain. I don't want this moment, she said to herself, although she wasn't sure yet of everything it contained, everything she knew. She made herself take another step and felt the stickiness of the past dissolve, release.

'They were over here,' John said.

'Where? Show me.'

He pushed back part of a box hedge with his foot, so she could see the shallow depression scraped at its roots. Torchlight lay in there, like cheap gold paint on twigs at Christmas time. It lay across his boot. 'I don't know why I noticed it.'

Anna knelt down and touched the wet ground. *Who would do this*? she asked herself. Her mind felt completely empty. She stood up and looked around. As her eyes grew used to the gloom, she saw that the smouldering builders' fires had layered the wet air with white smoke. She examined the tips of her fingers. Only earth.

'Well?' enquired John.

She wiped her hands on her skirt. 'There's nothing to see,' she answered. 'We can go back.'

He gave her a disgusted look and, turning his back on her, carried their sleeping daughter towards the house in the rain and thickening dark. After a moment she ran after him and caught up, and tried to put her arm through his. 'You're avoiding me again,' she said as lightly as she could. He was like a piece of wood, nailed across himself to keep her out. 'Something is going on at Nonesuch,' she continued firmly. 'We just aren't ready to see what it is.' When he wouldn't answer, she made him stop and look at her. 'John?' But she couldn't think how to convince him.

'It's a wet night, Anna,' he said. 'Ellie should be inside.'

'John –'

'Don't include me in this. Because it's stupid.'

'All right.' Anna's voice was bitter. 'Stay in denial, if that's what you want.'

She bathed Eleanor and put her to bed while he cooked tagliatelle and made a sauce with some leeks and cheese he found in the fridge. 'This is nice,' she told him and he said, 'It could have done with a minute or two less.' By the end of the evening they were talking to one another again; but true to her word she stayed in the kitchen after he had gone to bed. With a sense that she was taunting something much bigger than herself, she threw the doll's head back in the dustbin and locked the back door on them both, hid the musical box on the highest kitchen shelf she could find and arranged the necklace in plain view on the table overnight. All three were gone by morning, which was how she came to be certain she was right. She had no idea what she would do next.

Chapter Ten

THE WAY THE 'false' highway had opened itself only to me – the way it had revealed my sister, trapped in its environs, like a goad or a gift – haunted my every waking moment. Time and again I had been back to look for that elusive road, but it appeared to have removed itself as effectively as if it had never existed, until I was unsure whether it might have been no more than a dream within a dream. At night the dreams of Ashmore – insistent and increasingly strange – kept me so occupied that I soon felt worn thin and ragged in the head.

Eventually I decided I was in need of help, but at whose feet I might lay my parcel of worms I did not know. The dogfox probably knew more about the nature of the wild roads than any other creature alive, but, even if I had known how to find him, I did not feel comfortable taking my concerns to him. His abstruse pronouncements and wicked grin were almost as disorientating to me as the strange road itself, and I felt I needed another cat's eye upon the matter, one who perceived the same patterns in the world as I did, rather than one who saw more than I ever wished to comprehend.

In the end I decided to see whether the Besom had returned to her cottage, for if the wild road that had appeared at the far western corner of the house had ever existed before, she would surely know of it. I went in search of Millie, as I thought she might like to join me on a visit to the old girl, but there was no sign of her anywhere in the house and no one had seen her in the grounds that morning, so in the end I took Caterina with me. Ever since I had banned her from accompanying me on my last journey she had been so cool and reproachful towards me that I thought inviting her to meet a real female dream-catcher might in some way mollify her. After all, I reasoned, I was hardly the best role model for her in the affairs of the highways, since I appeared to have so little understanding of their mysteries myself.

We walked along the main road through Ashmore, then took a detour through the churchyard, for it was a bright, crisp, sunny day and the leaves of the horse chestnuts were resplendent with colour, each tree afire in the autumn sun. When the chill of November began to bite in earnest, they would all detach themselves and float down through the air like so many great hands; already there was a scattering of gold among the graves. They were so big and slow that even the clumsiest cat could capture them before they hit the ground. Millie said you should make a wish for each one you caught – one for the Great Cat, one for a friend, one for the people who fed you and one for yourself – so we always tried to catch four.

I sat on the gravel path and stared upwards into the maze of branches. The sun punctured the canopy with dazzling shafts of light and the fiery colours burst upon my eyes so that for a moment I was overcome by sensation and could barely make sense of what I saw: so many arms and twigs, so many bifurcations and offshoots; broken limbs, the patchwork bark. Details would fix themselves in my mind, then run together in a blur when the dappled light changed with the passage of a cloud, or the wind stirred the branches and the pattern broke apart again. Nature contained a complexity I could not comprehend. How could a dreamcatcher make sense of the world if he could not even make sense of a tree? But even as I did so, a seven-fingered leaf broke free of its anchor and began to drift down towards me and weightier matters dispersed like a mist.

'Cat! Quickly! The leaves are falling!'

I looked around.

While I had been staring up into the chestnut's canopy, Cat appeared bent on some kind of mission. She was nosing around the gravestones in an abstracted way, her tail stiff with concentration, and she did not even look up at my exclamation. The disappointment I felt was brief and rueful, but keen all the same; she might not be a kitten any more, ready for a foolish game at a moment's notice, but I had hoped at least she would humour me with some small show of interest.

I walked slowly up behind her. 'Autumn's here, Cat,' I said softly.

This time she whirled round, her concentration disturbed. 'What?'

'The leaves.' I gestured vaguely up into the branches above us. 'I thought you might like to catch them. For luck . . .'

'Oh, that,' she said contemptuously. 'Don't be silly.' And, when I looked crestfallen, added, 'Come here and smell this. Tell me what you think. I'm sure I recognise it from somewhere, but I just don't seem to be able to place it.'

I bent to the corner of the grave she had been examining and sniffed cautiously. At once, the scent hit the back of my throat so that I recoiled with the shock of it. Acrid and musty at once, it was that old, familiar smell that had dogged my travels and my dreams for so many weeks now, but somehow – out here in the open, where it should have dispersed by the movement of the wind, with the passage of feet and the traffic of wild creatures, and been mingled with the natural odours of decay, with the leaves and the mulch – it was stronger, more alive. Unnaturally so . . .

I stared at Caterina and she gazed back, wide-eyed and expectant. 'Can you smell it, Uncle Orlando?'

I shook my head and the scent seemed to roll around inside me as if now that I had smelled it in this powerful form, I would never be rid of it. A sudden fear came over me. I backed away, on to the sharp pale gravel of the path, my feet digging in so hard that I left little crescents of soil showing through the stones; and from there I ran away into the lych-gate, with its clean scent of new wood and wet tile.

From the corner of the sheltered seat, I watched Caterina coming after me slowly, her paws reluctant, her face contorted with bewilderment. *Mad old Uncle Orlando, behaving weirdly again . . .*

By the time she reached me, my skin was trembling with some primal revulsion, though my poor slow brain still seemed unable to tell me exactly what it was that had caused me such a violent reaction. 'I don't know what it is. I don't want to know –' I stammered, already feeling foolish.

'It's the smell from the dream roads,' Cat said. 'I just wondered why it was here, so far from the house.'

The smell from the dream roads. The smell of the black thing with which the baby had hit me; the smell of the hair inside it and of the Long Corridor when last I had been there. The smell of the woman with the sharp green eyes –

I jumped down from the seat and walked smartly out on to the road, hardly caring whether there were vehicles coming or not. 'We're going to see the Besom, Cat,' I said grimly. 'We're going to see her now.'

We walked swiftly and in silence the rest of the way and by the time we reached the holly hedge that surrounded the old brick-and-flint cottage on the hill my jaw ached from being set in its most determined expression. I was looking forward to being soothed by the wild serenity of the pretty garden I knew was on the other side of the hedge; but when we wormed our way through the cat-sized hole, I was not prepared for the sight that awaited me. What earlier that summer had been charmingly disordered, with its rambling briars and rampant honeysuckle, its twining clematis and windblown roses, was now a wasteland of neglect. Dead flowerheads hung brown and rotten from the bramble runners and rose bushes; the lavenders had grown out all leggy and untidy; the clematis had yellowed and died, and the ferns that had stretched up through the other foliage towards the light were now for two-thirds of their length frondless and woody. Many had fallen back on themselves, their stems too weak to bear the weight of the heads. Goosegrass had strangled every delicate plant in sight, then withered and died back itself. Everywhere you looked was a tangle, a chaos. My heart sank. Where was the Besom? Her trim, groomed elegance surely had no place amid all this disorder.

The answer, when it came, gave me little comfort.

Caterina, upon entering the garden, immediately found a scent and started burrowing her way into the undergrowth, head down, at a crouch. 'Hello!' she was calling. 'Can you hear me? I'm coming!' And with that pronouncement she disappeared.

I followed her, of course, though the path she found through the dense runners was so narrow and so low as to require me to crawl for much of the way on my belly. In and out of brambles with thorns that caught the skin and grass with burrs that tangled in the fur, between the roots of shrubs and arms of rogue holly, among ground elder and wild mint we went, until at last we reached the end of the tunnel and emerged into a tiny clearing. There, curled into a tight, miserable ball, sat a mangy old creature, at first sight appearing more dead than alive. The bones of its shoulders were hunched about its ears like the elbows of an ancient, leathery bat. It smelled terrible.

'Never mind,' Caterina was cooing. 'We're here now. It's all right, now.'

The creature shifted uncomfortably at our arrival and turned its head to regard us. Its eyes were as dull as currants. It regarded us grimly, uncomprehendingly, then turned away again as if negating our very presence.

It was the Besom. The last time I had seen her she had certainly been old and worn; but now she was little more than a wraith. The spirit had – in the weeks since our last meeting – simply gone out of her, leaving behind this terrible, dying husk, less cat than carcass.

'Ma,' I urged. 'Ma, it's Orlando. Speak to me.'

Again the uncomfortable shifting of weight and this time there emerged a whisper as scratchy as teasel.

'What did you say, Ma?' I encouraged.

The old cat blinked at me and her eyes were dull with reproach. 'Go away,' she said more distinctly. 'Go away and let me die in peace.'

The old lady who fed the Besom had mysteriously gone away, it turned out. She had last been seen one evening climbing awkwardly, with the aid of two tall men in dark clothing, into a large white van whose blue light had strobed quietly through the holly, casting a bewildering maze of jagged shapes across the already neglected lawn. She had not returned. No one came. The house had remained cold and closed. Those who prided themselves on knowing such things said she'd died, but Ma, who had a nose for death, was unconvinced. She'd waited patiently through the first week, sleeping in the front porch to ensure that she would be the first to welcome the old woman home, but she had not reappeared. Ma grew hungry and weak. She drank rainwater out of the deep, furred leaves of umbellifers. She ate slugs and late-summer beetles worn to a slow daze by the passage of the year. A rabbit run over on the road outside sustained her for a week, even though she had to stand off two magpies and a crow for the unappetising leavings. The crow had eventually given up and flown off, unimpressed by the increasingly flattened corpse, leaving the magpies to leer at her from the hawthorn opposite the cottage. The knowing gleam in their blue-black eyes gave back the clearest of messages: *we can wait; you'll be next.*

Driven as much by a determination to thwart the carrion birds as by any true wish for survival, Ma – a proud cat not suited to the indigent life – had been reduced to making door-to-door calls to the nearest houses to beg for food. She had been chased off by dogs, bullied by farm cats a quarter her age and terrorised by children with fireworks. Pickings had at best been slim and even sleep had offered no escape from her plight. Within moments of closing her eyes, exhausted after another day spent on her nerves, she dreamed of food. These were not comfortable dreams. Increasingly, the food that came to her at night, or in snatched naps in daytime hedges, reversed the natural order of the world upon her. Tins of cat food gloatingly revealed their nightmarish origins; sardines reared up out of saucers and tried to swallow her head first; the long-dead rabbit, scoriated and dried to a dark-red jerky, lifted its mashed skull and gnashed gleaming white jaws at her. It was all too much to bear.

At last she had crawled away into the thickest undergrowth, determined that the magpies should neither be able to see nor pick at her, and willed herself to die. She had been there for four days now, but death was evasive.

Caterina was stricken. 'I saw the rabbit,' she said at last. 'On the highway that runs across the Common, just after full moon, about a week ago. It was horrible, and it laughed at me, all stretched and red, all sinew and exposed bone, but I ate it down all the same.'

The Besom opened her mouth as if to cough, but no sound emerged and at last I realised she was smiling.

'Little dreamcatcher, eh? I wondered why the rabbit hadn't been back to taunt me. Come here, child, let's have a look at you.'

Cat darted a glance at me, then moved closer to the ancient cat, who reached out a slow paw. I saw where the hair had come away in patches along her arm so that you could see the mottled black-and-pink brindle of the skin beneath. It was so thin it looked like a stick, an old and weathered stick marked by fungal growths. Gently, she touched Caterina on the face and although Cat looked briefly alarmed she did not flinch.

'Bless you, child,' the Besom said. 'I can see it in your eyes. It's a noble profession, though a tough one for a girl.'

'Come back with us to Nonesuch,' Cat said suddenly. 'There's plenty of food at the house and warm places to curl up. I'll watch out for the dreams; you'll sleep easier there. And you can tell me stories. About dreamcatching.'

Ma Tregenna blinked. She resettled herself as if contemplating the proposition. At last she spoke. 'En't nothing to look forward to. Best leave me be.'

Cat looked appalled.

'We can't just leave you,' I interrupted in as reasonable a voice as I could manage. 'It wouldn't be right.'

'It's my time,' the Besom said obstinately. 'You're too young to understand.'

'You're right,' I agreed. 'I don't understand. We can help you: we *want* to help you. I spend my time trying to ward off the bad things of the world, to preserve life and health: I *won't* leave you here to die.'

'Death's not so bad when you reach my age,' Ma Tregenna returned, her tone maudlin. 'I feel him coming to me, like an old friend . . .'

This was too much for me. With a huge effort I grabbed her by the back of the neck and picked her up. She was as light as a kitten, all her substance gone to heat and bones. Her dusty fur filled my mouth. For a moment she wriggled like a worm on a hook, then, as if sensing her struggle was useless, subsided. It was not until I got her safely back to Nonesuch and laid her down in the warm kitchen that I realised that, maybe in some instinctive response to the pressure of my jaws on the scruff of her neck, some memory of the way a parent had once carried her about, she had relaxed so entirely into my care that she had fallen fast asleep.

When she awoke, though, it was a different matter entirely.

I was dozing peacefully in a little square of sunshine on one of the upstairs landings when there came a piercing howl from down below. At once I was on my feet, my spine tingling as if someone had drawn a hot wire through it. I did not recognise the voice of the cat who had howled; was not even sure at that moment that it was a cat I had heard. I skittered down the uncarpeted stairs and dashed along the corridor, my feet slipping sideways on the polished wood, only to collide in the kitchen door-way with the Besom's scrawny rump, emerging backwards at speed.

We fell over one another in a tangle of limbs; then, despite all her weeks of malnourishment, the Besom gathered her feet under her and bolted past me as if pursued by all the hounds of hell.

I stared after her. A voice from the kitchen made me turn back.

'Here, cat, come here –'

It was the baby. It giggled. In one chubby fist it held a long-handled silver spoon, which it waved purposefully at me. An innocent enough object, the spoon, yet I found I could not take my eyes from it. The light gleamed dully off its scratched surfaces, offering reminders of its many pasts. I shivered and with effort drew my eyes away. Ellie grinned at me. There was a strange expression in her green, green eyes. Her other hand reached out to grab me. I ducked my head away from it and at the same time found myself backing away in awful parody of Old Ma Tregenna. Then I, too, took to my heels.

I caught up with the Besom, finally, under the rhododendron bushes in the garden, being comforted by Griz.

'There, Pol, there. Don't shiver so. Never thought to see you again, not after all this time, not after that fox come and drug you out. Left us all behind and never a word, but we didn't begrudge it you, not after what you went through.'

My amazement must have been clear, for Griz now turned her attention to me, though she still spoke to the Besom. 'Poor lad. He doesn't have a clue what he's dealing with here, does he?'

It was true: I didn't. I sat down and listened as Grizelda and Old Polly Tregenna told me their desperate, tragic tales.

*

The witch kept coming back, they said, though she stayed as long as she possibly could, making magic out of the kittens she stole, magic she made in pots in the laboratory behind the courtyard full of cages, where both Griz and the Besom had once been imprisoned. I remembered what Old Ma Tregenna – Pol – had said to me when I first knew her: that she had no kittens of her own and regretted it bitterly. She had no kittens of her own because the witch had taken them – as she had taken Griz's litters – time after time. The terrible thing, according to the Besom, was that the kittens who had a dreamcatcher both for father and mother were the most efficacious in the magic the witch made, so that the more litters she bred from Ma and the blue stud cat, the stronger and apparently younger she became. The irony of it all was hard to bear; for the woman had no understanding of the significance of the bloodlines she was thus abusing, no knowledge at all of dreamcatching or the inherent power it produced in the offspring. It was a burden the Besom bore in misery. Mated time and again to Circassian Gogol II, the witch's handsome familiar, a dozen or more kittens removed from her care, she had gone progressively mad, until at last the russet fox with the grey-spotted haunch had come and blasted a wild road through the very wall of the courtyard, as he had again some years later – as Griz reminded me – to rescue my own mother, and had borne her away. It was something he could do only in the cause of dreamcatchers, he had said, though she had no idea what he meant by this at the time.

I listened to what they said and let the terrible significance of it all seep through my skin, down into my heart and bones. Then I went back into the house and sat in the Long Corridor, to ponder further over those images, to weave connections – tenuous and unlikely though they seemed – between what the old cats had told me and what I had seen for myself and failed thus far to understand; and to wait for the inevitable dream to come and find me, as I knew it would.

I did not have long to wait. I even knew, this time, what I might expect to encounter, in theme if not in detail.

So when the first frayed, fiery globe howled over me, I was ready for it; ready, too, for the dizzying descent through the dream corridors of Nonesuch, the tumble not only through place, but time. The dream, too, seemed to recognise my increased awareness of the game, for it feinted and dodged away from my great paws like prey from a predator, instead of bumbling, insensate, along walls and ceilings, till caught up into the flow of the highway's energies. Through a Nonesuch that I could identify – the house immediately before its current renovations – it drew me first across landings redolent with a heavy, musky perfume, so that I half expected the tall, green-eyed woman – pale-skinned and unburned – to slip round a corner at any moment, that taunting half-smile on her face, her hands ready to scoop me up and take me to the place of cages; but soon the landscape changed its nature. The house darkened. First there were shutters on the windows; then musty thick curtains; then a stretch of bleak, cobwebbed passage in which the night sky showed through holes in the raftered roof; but always the highways we travelled were lit by the febrile light given off by the flaming aura of the dream.

At last, after many twists and turns which finally disorientated me, the dream swooped down through a low arched doorway I had never previously encountered anywhere in the house and disappeared into the chamber beyond. There I knew it remained, for the reddish light it emitted pulsed intermittently, but always at the same intensity. I entered the chamber cautiously, my whiskers bristling with anticipation at what I might find within. My anxiety was not misplaced. The dream globe hovered in the far corner of the room as if to provide me with the very illumination with which I might best appreciate the scene before me. In the middle of the chamber, half turned away from me, stood a woman. From her stance and frame, and for all the elaborate generosity of her full-skirted brocade costume, I could tell that, like the Besom, she was a creature at the end of its mortal tether, all worn out to skin and sinew. She was busy at something I could not quite see. A brazier full of glowing coals, over which a large dark cook pot was suspended from an iron tripod, stood off to one side of the room, framed by a clutter of stacked boxes and shelves lined with clay vessels, jars and scrolls of paper, barely visible behind the clouds of vapour that came belching up out of the steaming cauldron. So fascinated was I by the fact that for all the red-lit detail thus presented to me I could make out no scent at all, as if my nose had abruptly stopped working, that I hardly noticed the exact moment at which she turned to face me, but became all of a sudden aware – like the crawl of an insect upon the skin – of her eyes upon me. Her green, green eyes . . .

They were not the eyes of a crone, those eyes, but of a young, young woman. I blinked and my perceptions reordered themselves. The eyes – and indeed the face – were clear and smooth; but below the pale white chin the neck was all turkey-wattled and parched, mottled with liver spots and blue veins; and from there down, the body was that of a crone, as twisted and gnarled as an old ash tree that has seen too many winters and longs only to die.

Her jaws clacked at me then, emitting a torrent of words from which I could take only a tone of malice and contempt; then the dream globe floated down from its position on high to drift tantalisingly in the air before me, as if the old woman had commanded its sacrifice.

With one eye on the crone, I swiped the dream on to the flagstones and pressed down hard with my paw. The old woman sighed, as if the pressure of my foot were somehow squeezing the air from her lungs, but the dream resisted not at all, beyond the faint pulse of its half-life, even when I sank my lion's claws through its feeble skin. There was a sudden release of pressure, followed by a hot wet gush.

The crone smiled, then, and those full red lips drew back to reveal pale and withered gums, and stumps of teeth as sulphur-yellow as any rat's. *So*, I thought to myself, even as I bent to my task, *your magic may make its mark on the outermost skin, but it cannot reach through to the bones of you;* then I gulped the dream down.

The chamber spun around me, woman and words, pots and parchments, ceiling, shelves and stone floor all rearranged themselves until I felt myself both inside and out of the dream, and could barely discern one from the other, for it seemed the place in which I had stood now shivered in and out of time, through a darkness so complete I could see nothing beyond my own nose, to the burning light of a roofless day, in which neither chamber nor witch owned existence, and back to a space lit by the flickering of wall sconces and tall candles. There, as before, a woman stood tending a pot over a fire, her back half turned to me. Behind her, shelves lined the walls of the chamber, though the pots upon them were arrayed differently and charts now lay scattered across the floor. I was just pondering the subtle differences the scene was offering me when suddenly my sense of smell returned with a vile, invasive gust. A heavy musk filled the air, followed by something more unpleasant and yet more cloying.

The dream, I told myself, *it's only the dream.* Then I heard my grandfather's voice in the back of my skull. *Eat it down, Orlando,* he ordered me. *Eat the dream!*

I swallowed and swallowed, but even as I did so the smell became taste, foul and perverse, an offence against nature; and abruptly identified itself as the unmistakable flavour of burned hair, boiled flesh –

Bile scalded the back of my throat. I gagged and retched, but the dream stayed down.

'They say the lion is a noble beast,' the woman said. 'They call him the king of beasts.' Her words buzzed in my head like flies on a carcass. ' "Who contains the power of the sun, the fiery principle, but is also death." The Mother Goddess Ishtar rides upon a lion, for even his power can be mastered, and she is greater even than death.' She laughed. 'And my cousin Isaac the Alchemist has made his life's work the quest for the Animal Stone, for long life and the key to all knowledge. He has boiled down all manner of things to reach the purifying ingredient known as the Green Lion, whose blood may bring him to the heart of the mystery! How well I know that cats contain magic, when rendered to their essence and stirred with purest silver –'

Like maggots to the blowflies were the meanings to her words: they crawled about in my skull like the hatchlings from eggs that had been laid there.

Then she turned to face me and I saw that the woman was Stella, but not Stella: for she was small and compactly made, rather than tall and straight and thin, and that her hair was brown, not black; that she seemed less finely made than the woman I had seen in the life, as well as in the dreams. But the eyes: they were that same remarkable cattish green.

'But now, my little lion, you are no better than I. Worse, in truth, for I have never stooped so low as to consume the flesh of my own kind!'

And now she laughed long and hard, and I saw that in this dream, or whatever unreality it was, she had no teeth at all; but it was not this, nor indeed her bewildering words, that arrested me, but her outstretched hand. In its bony talons she clutched a gleaming, long-handled silver spoon. I recognised that spoon, though it was shinier and newer-looking than the one I had expected to see. I followed her gesture as she pointed with the spoon beyond me into the shadows of the chamber at my back.

There, in a cage of dark wood, was my sister Vita.

'I caught her skulking through the Great Knot,' the witch said. 'Through the shifting circles of the wild rides, and none are permitted to trespass there without paying my price. I have plans for this little one.'

'Oh, Orlando,' Vita wailed. 'Don't let her boil me.'

I opened my mouth to tell her all would be well, that she mustn't worry, for I would find some way of rescuing her, when the room started to spin once more, and harsh laughter and foul smells, light and dark, and up and down all became mixed into a sickening whirl and I found myself falling through a vortex. I fell and fell until the sensation of falling seemed endless, and then, quite abruptly, I was lying panting on the bare floorboards of the Long Corridor and someone was standing over me, mewing with distress.

'He's had one of his strange turns,' I heard one voice say. 'Fetch Millie; she'll know what to do.'

'No way,' the other said, 'she's with that mangy old thing Uncle Orlando and Squash brought in this afternoon. Have you seen her? Her fur's all falling out. I might catch something.'

'She's not a "mangy old thing",' came an outraged third voice. 'She's a poor old cat who's dying of starvation and you should have more respect. Besides, Uncle O's not having one of his turns; he's been chasing dreams. Leave him to me.'

It was with some relief that I heard Letty's and Arabella's voices receding away down the corridor.

Caterina nudged me vigorously. 'Wake up, Uncle O,' she hissed. 'You were shrieking; something about being boiled. It upset them.'

I opened my eyes, then gingerly sat up and looked around. Oblongs of bright daylight fell across the far end of the Long Corridor, where the door to the courtyard stood open. When I had entered the wild road in pursuit of the dream it had been barely midnight.

Chapter Eleven

ANNA'S NIGHTS GREW strange, coagulated. She no longer woke up in the hot room, with sleep still like curtains drawn inside her head. Instead, she was unconscious past dawn and dreamed all sorts of things. (John slept, too. They felt better for it, they told each other in the mornings, but not as much as they had hoped.) She dreamed she was in London, beside the Thames. John ran past her and jumped in. Once the water had closed over him he neither sank nor swam. She could see him down there under the water in a kind of wavering bubble, his arms clasped round his knees. It seemed clear he needed help, but she couldn't make herself act. He hung there for a long time, while she stood on the bank not knowing what to think, her feelings shifting slowly from irritation to dread, a voice in her head whispering, 'I have to save him from himself.'

She dreamed she was fat, fat and hard like an armadillo or half a barrel. She dreamed she was dead. After death, everything was a knotted wet mass. There was chaos – a life she did not recognise, clothes she had never worn – then flashes of light on a knotted wet mass.

Nightmares were nothing new in Anna's life, but these were so disorientating they hardly seemed to qualify as her own. Then one night she dreamed she was in California with Alice and the physicist, who – in the dream anyway – had blond hair and was teaching her to swim while Alice looked on, strong with approval. His hands touched her under the water and she could see that Alice approved of that too. She was embarrassed and amused to find a card from Alice in the post next morning. On one side was a photograph of the surf rolling in on some southern Californian beach. On the other side was written in a careless hand –

Hi its really good here, David says surf is the physics of pleasure, you ought to come out xxxs Guess Who?

It was a message from the dream, full of sunshine and music and sex, everything missing from Anna's waking life. She propped it against the rice jar on the kitchen counter, where its raw, optimistic colours signalled to her until mid-morning, when she left Eleanor with John for an hour and took the Volvo out just for the sake of it, driving round the lanes on her own and uncharacteristically fast. Eleven thirty: she parked below Cresset Beacon, walked to the top and sat in the cold strong sunshine, watching for a fox, a deer, a dragonfly, something special. Eventually, she realised she was looking out for Alice; or for some of Alice's qualities in herself. As if youth and durability and happiness could fly to her out of the air.

When she got back, she found John in the kitchen. He looked excited. 'The builders are starting to demolish the old cattery,' he said. 'I thought you might want to watch.'

Down in Ashmore, Francis Baynes was going about the work of the parish. Thursday: his day for feuds and buildings. This week it was Hetty Parker, who had placed poinsettias in big displays inside the church, and the Hewlett sisters, who thought them vulgar. Meanwhile, the parish hall, a wooden building two doors down from the Green Man, had been designated a fire hazard. After lunch the telephone made him late for a meeting with his archdeacon in Drychester. Later, he stopped off to sit with old Mrs Evans in the Daffodil Ward of Drychester General, whose flesh had the transparency of candlewax and who looked unlikely ever to return to her cottage outside the village. Margaret Evans – ninety-two years old and with an indestructible local accent – had been a follower of Bertrand Russell for much of her life and an atheist for all of it. Francis held her hand, which had the weight and papery feel of birds' bones, while she breathed stertorously for a bit, then warned him, in case she might have caught him praying, 'None of that rubbish here, thank you.'

All this left him feeling, in his mild way, savage.

'I can't see what I'm for,' he tried to explain to the

woman in his bedroom. Her hair was down over the pillow, thick, black, oily with life. She hid whatever she had been doing and put it up again. 'All these people' – Francis gestured around, as if Hetty Parker, the Hewlett sisters and old Mrs Evans were all somehow present in the room – 'I can't see why I was brought to the Church if it wasn't to open their lives to something wonderful.'

She gave him a smile from the side of her mouth. 'If you want to see something wonderful, follow me.'

She led him through his own lych-gate, into the church – where Hetty Parker's disputed poinsettias raged like fires up and down the nave – and into the tower. She filled the narrow spiral staircase, her dry brown skirts, which she had gathered up to make the stairs easier, brushing against the walls. Her feet were large, bare and dirty, her calves white, her thighs were round. Trudging reluctantly up behind, Francis could see the blue veins in her flesh. She was as pregnant – as massive – with herself, he thought, as she might have been with child. Her powerful smell came back to him in the confined space.

'Now!' she said, bursting out on to the top of the tower like a mare released into a field. 'Look! All this could be yours!'

Francis looked. A cloud like a tower of smoke was beginning to spill over the edge of the downs and roil out towards Ashmore, its gilded underside, carmine and Japanese black, discharging great rods and beams of afternoon sunlight. 'It's beautiful,' he said.

'Not that!' She was contemptuous. 'This.'

Two blowflies, borne up from the graveyard below on some updraught of which they were barely aware, had settled on the worn stone parapet and begun to copulate. Francis studied them with revulsion. Locked together in the horizontal light, they looked like an iridescent enamel brooch. Every so often they buzzed groggily and lurched into a new position. He looked away. Then he turned back deliberately and crushed them.

'Ah dear,' said the woman from the graveyard and shivered as if she felt a cold breeze around her. At the same time her eyes were full of triumph. 'Ah dear, vicar, you're a fastidious man. Was their pleasure too great for you? I show you the mystery and you look at clouds instead.'

Francis rubbed his fingers together. 'Why have you come here?' he whispered.

'Oh, I'm here to help.'

'But why me? Why visit yourself on me like this?'

'What? Do you think I'm here on your behalf? Is that what you think, my cherub? You're a sideshow for me. You're the entertainment. I never come for the men.' Her great coarse laugh rang out across the churchyard, driving two or three surprised rooks from the branches of an adjacent yew. 'The men always want me, but it's the women I come for.'

The Nonesuch cattery – centre for the breeding and commodification of generations of animals – occupied the site of a pleasant little courtyard constructed by Joshua Herringe in 1482 so that his fragile second wife, Elizabeth, could enjoy the sun.

With his death a few years on its use had changed beyond recognition. Clara de Montfort had roofed it over. In his turn, William Haut-Herringe, a sly and overweening man, hid it from his peers behind a triumph of *trompe l'oeil* art in what came to be called the Painted Room. By the time Stella Herringe took up the family traditions it was open to the sky again – but her regime was the least forgiving. A ribbed, unfinished-looking concrete surface drained into a central grating. The pens themselves were little more than galvanised metal shelves, enclosed and partitioned with rusty wire. Two years after her death, the courtyard remained saturated with the sad, ammoniac smell of trapped animals. Two or three nights in every month its former inhabitants abandoned their new lives in the Nonesuch shrubberies and returned in search of their half-forgotten kittens and, failing to find them, sat among the shadows with their eyes hard and narrowed until dawn.

'We've got problems here,' John told Anna. He seemed pleased. A problem gave him something to work against. 'Stella seems to have had the floor poured to Ministry of Defence specifications.' He had borrowed a yellow site helmet from the builders, along with some hardened safety glasses which made him look boyish and studious. 'So we got this stuff in.'

They had brought in a compressor and two heavyweight pneumatic drills. The courtyard was thick with diesel fumes. Air lines snaked between the ripped-out cages, pulsing with each cycle of demand. The builders strode about covered with cement dust, sweating hard as they bellowed at one another over the roar and hiss of the compressor. Anna stared down into this throbbing pit for a while, hoping to feel something of John's energy, some sense of justice being done. But there was still something sour and unpleasant about the place, and she experienced no relief.

It had been a mistake to watch from the Painted Room. Too much had happened to her there. She had been made a fool too many times by that room, right up until the moment, temper gone and caution to the winds, she had smashed through the depicted courtyard of the painting and into the real courtyard beyond. She had ignored for six months the faint cries of the trapped cats. She had watched Stella Herringe, dressed in kitten-heel shoes and a three-thousand-pound frock, triumphantly serving rotten medlar for supper a hand's breadth from her victims. Staring now at the remains of the *trompe l'oeil*, with its curiously stiff, awkwardly lit rendering of Joshua Herringe's original vision – a place of tranquillity and meditation, a place to sit in the sun – Anna was left with the feeling that nothing had ended. Perhaps nothing ever ended, perhaps the consequences of things just kept ringing on and on, poisoning the life that came after.

Leaving, she heard herself say, 'I want this destroyed too.'

John began to argue, but by then she was in the

corridor where the picture of Clara de Montfort had once hung and she didn't hear him.

Later, they argued again.

Unable to afford more than twenty-four hours' equipment hire, John had asked the builders to work under arc lights until the job was done. Breaking through the concrete at about half past eight in the evening, they made a curious find in the sour earth beneath: a little mud-coloured drawstring bag of chamois leather, so hardened and distressed that it could no longer be opened but had to be pulled away from its own contents in strips. It was obviously very old. They switched off the compressor – silence pressed up against their ears – and stood, passing the bag puzzledly from hand to hand; then shrugged and called for John Dawe, who arrived with his daughter riding on his shoulders.

Eleanor stared around the courtyard with a kind of sleepy hauteur, taking in the workmen, the ploughed-up concrete, the dust drifting about under the glaring lights. 'Poo,' she said. But she was fascinated by what they had found and, by the time John carried her back into the kitchen half an hour later, he had already given it to her.

'I wish you hadn't done that,' Anna said. 'I really do.'

John looked mulish. 'What harm can it do?'

'We haven't got any idea what it is or how it came to be there –'

They persuaded Eleanor to swap it temporarily for two squares of organic chocolate, so that Anna could turn it over in her hands – the figure of a squatting woman, three or four inches high, carved in cream-coloured bone, feet placed squarely apart as if for purchase on an invisible floor, her thighs, pelvis and partly exposed vulva massively proportioned, crudely worked yet detailed enough to have an immediate impact on the viewer. Everything else seemed unfinished, sketched-in, as if the sculptor had lost interest – everything, that is, but the expression on the face, which was both disturbing and inexplicable. The mouth opened as wide as it would go to admit some formless cry, the lips pulling themselves back and down, the eyes staring but unfocused. What had she been designed to signify, this icon of some vanished culture? Not anguish, precisely. Not pain, not effort, not rage, not sexual exultation. Something without a name, something that bore a resemblance to all those things. In the end you were left with those two impressions – the open thighs and planted feet, the enduring roar of . . . what?

Loss, Anna thought. Some kind of triumphant loss. Can you have that? How appalling. She weighed the figure in her hand. It seemed, on reflection, too heavy to be bone. She thought it might be flint, a coated flint, creamy white, out of the chalk downs. But how would you carve flint? Unless, she thought, it hadn't been carved at all –

She made up her mind suddenly. 'I don't want her to have it.'

'Oh, come on, Anna. It's ugly, but she doesn't know that.'

'That's not the point,' Anna insisted. 'She gets these things, she keeps them for a while, then they turn up in the knot garden, John. What's happening to them? How are they getting there? Don't you want to know?'

He opened his mouth, then shook his head as if he couldn't think what to say. 'Anna –'

'You don't,' she said, 'do you? You don't think this is important.'

He put his arm round her and tried to calm her down. 'The things that happened in this house are finished. All that ended two years ago. You're right. I don't want to think about Stella, or reincarnation, or what that might mean for us. But it's not denial. It's that I have a wife and a child and a house to look after. Look at me, Anna. No, look at me. I love you and I love Eleanor. There isn't a day on which I don't puzzle over everything that happened to us here. What we learned was wonderful and strange. But how can we go forward if we let it fill our minds? And how can we ever be free of Stella if all we do is see her in every little thing that happens?'

'John –'

'Anna, these are just objects Eleanor picks up and puts down, like any kid. They're just toys. While you're worrying yourself sick about them, someone has to look after the ordinary stuff, someone has to do the real work. And I think you're in danger of forgetting that.'

Anna stared at him in disbelief. She pulled away. 'That's so unfair,' she said. 'That's just so bloody unfair!' She threw the figure down on the table in front of him. It fell oddly, spinning and flickering in the kitchen light, making a noise like the rattle of dice. Anna blinked and reached out her hand to stop it. 'You're the dreamer, not me.'

I learned how Izzie's other name is the Fat Lady from Under the Earth, and how important she is for everything around here.

This is how it came about: it's night and I'm busy, busy, busy about the place – what's new? – hiding a secret here, a secret there, and I see how the corridors are suddenly elongating in the shadows, elongating and opening out until they don't look like corridors any more but like roads. (What do you know about roads my sweetling, Izzie says, but she doesn't see everything I do, and I know, I know.) In a flash they lead everywhere these roads, outwards, outwards, outwards. It would be a crazy ride on any one of them, you would speed like in your dreams.

This is it, though:

I see where they lead outwards from, these roads. I see the big knot under the garden maze, trapped and pulsing, the knot that Izzie made a million years ago, before this was a house at all.

No one sees my knot, Izzie says, except those who will benefit. Those who see without permission soon see no more, she says, and they welcome that, because I put the knot in their bowels, tightening and tightening, and everyone covers their ears against that scream they make trying to push it out again, too late for that.

Poo, I say to that. You won't catch me trying to expel a knot in my bowels.

Hoity-toity, says Izzie to that, also Little Miss Know-all. You know what happened to Little Miss Know-all. Little Miss Know-all soon came to grief, she caught a disease.

Best be careful you don't catch a disease.

So I'm very careful when I crawl between the hedges, where the Parts of Izzie I got will soon be the Parts of me, and she will go and I will stay and that will be the end of her, with her hoity-toity. That'll be the end of her all right, the day I know who I am.

Anna continued to dream. Her dreams were full of strange anxieties. She dreamed she was a white bird flying out, a black bird flying home – she had been the same bird all along. She dreamed she had gone up to the Beacon so John could show her a fox; neither of them turned up. She dreamed of Francis Baynes, standing in the middle of the vicarage kitchen with his trousers down round his ankles, his mouth open on a kind of vacant sigh –

This dream caused her to start awake with a noise in her ears.

She thought it was Eleanor. She thought it was someone in the house.

'Did you hear that?' she asked John.

'It was you, Anna,' he answered. 'You called out.' He leaned over her to look at the alarm clock and groan. 'It was more of a scream, actually,' he said. 'Can we go back to sleep now?'

But it turned out he couldn't sleep, so after an hour's irritable tossing and turning he got up to make a cup of tea, sit stunned in front of the Aga for a few minutes, then go back upstairs to confront his financial problems. That was how, already in a difficult mood, he discovered Mark and Oliver Holland making themselves at home in his office. They had pulled out all the drawers of the old steel filing cabinet so that it leaned perilously away from the wall. They had scattered coloured folders everywhere. The computer was on and a search programme loaded from an unmarked CD was busily munching its way through John's secure files.

John looked at his watch: 7.30 a.m. on a wet Friday. 'This is a little bit out of business hours,' he commented.

'Ah,' said Mark.

Oliver added, 'We thought it would be all right.'

'I don't think it is, you know,' John pointed out.

The first Anna knew about the situation was when, ten minutes or so later, standing by the front door in a grubby white towelling robe, she glanced up from the morning's crop of junk mail to see him escorting them towards her. They looked as discomfited as she had ever seen them.

'You could regret this,' Oliver said.

Mark began, 'The Estate –'

John bunched up the lapels of Mark's suit jacket and used them to push him against the wall. He was really much taller than Mark, Anna noticed, and his face was dark with anger. 'Fuck the Estate,' he said quietly. 'Fuck them all. They knew as well as you did what was going on here in Stella's day. It just wasn't quite profitable enough to keep their attention.' He let Mark go. 'You won't be coming to this house again. Will you?' He thought for a moment. 'In fact, before you go, you can give me whatever keys you have in your possession.'

Mark adjusted his jacket, some buttons of which had come off. He and Oliver exchanged a quick glance. 'I'm not sure the arrangement would have suited us anyway,' he said.

Oliver added, 'I don't think, given the figures, we can support your business plan.'

'Get out. Just get out.'

Anna went outside to watch them drive away.

When she came back John was sitting at the bottom of the stairs, looking dejected. 'That's fucked that then,' he told her.

She sat next to him and took his hand affectionately. 'You were brilliant and I love you dearly, even when you give me lectures about parental responsibility.'

He looked comforted for a moment. But then he said, 'Was I brilliant? The next time the phone rings it will be the bank manager, to review the loans. Or someone from the Estate, congratulating me on having the courage to go it alone.' He shrugged. 'How brilliant is that?'

She put her arms round him and hugged him fiercely. 'It was the right thing to do.'

'I found them going through my office,' he said tiredly. 'You can't have people doing that. The rest of it – all this other stuff about them and the Engelion cream – well, you might be right and you might be wrong.' He stood up. 'I think you're wrong.'

'John –'

'At least we've seen the last of them,' he said.

But even that was too much to hope for.

Walking Eleanor slowly around the grounds two or three days later, on a morning so quiet you could hear the traffic miles away on the main road, Anna witnessed an event curious enough to seem like something from a film.

The sun, pushing through a layer of pearly cloud, had melted the night's frost. Fine beads of moisture were left on every blade of grass, turning the lawns into silver carpets – stretching away from Nonesuch in magically heightened perspective – on the receptive surface of which every passing footprint stood out clear and delineated. The little tracks of birds beginning and ending in nowhere. The wincing, fastidious trudge of cats. A narrow meandering swathe like the spoor of a small mechanical digger, punctuated every so often by an abandoned stick – Ellie Dawe in her red wellington boots.

Eleanor was collecting sticks. She was practising her new word. 'Norty!' she shouted.

An echo flew back off Nonesuch like a white bird.

'Norty norty norty!'

Echo echo echo.

Eleanor's technique when she saw a new stick was to approach it with a fast, cumbersome, tottering motion; then, breathing heavily through her mouth, plant her feet, rock forward with one arm outstretched and, overcompensating, fall over backwards on to her bottom. The effort caused her face to become as red and shiny as her wellington boots. 'Oh, dear!' said Anna, who had never seen a funnier thing in her life. 'Upsy daisy!'

'Norty.'

They were making their way across the Great Lawn in this manner when several cats shot out of the thick bank of rhododendrons fringing the drive. For a fraction of a second they paused as one animal, haunches down, fur up, to look back the way they had come. Anna drew back nervously. Eleanor had no such qualms. 'Wor,' she said. She brandished her latest stick. 'Ca'!'

This was too much. Hissing and spitting and falling over one another in their anxiety to escape, the cats scattered in all directions. Shortly afterwards the figures of Mark and Oliver Holland burst out on to the lawn. They had caught one of the cats and were trying to force it into an old fertiliser bag. Seeing Anna, Oliver stopped to brush at his clothes, while Mark continued to struggle with the cat. After a moment they turned and ran back into the bushes.

Anna, suddenly terrified they had taken Orlando, abandoned her daughter without a thought and flew after them shouting, 'How dare you!'

The rhododendrons were a nightmare. Branches whipped at her face. She fell to her knees in the sodden, fibrous earth. Every time she found an easy way through the tangle, it led back to the lawn. Filthy and out of breath, she burst out on to the drive an instant too late and had to watch the silver Mercedes pulling away right under her nose, one Holland dragging the rear offside passenger door shut even as the other floored the accelerator pedal. The stolen cat, meanwhile, had escaped the bag but not the car, and was throwing itself desperately against the rear window. It wasn't Orlando: she had time to see wild eyes, scrabbling claws, a pink nose pressed up against the glass – then a little crest of tabby fur.

They had taken Tufty.

Anna watched car and cat get smaller and smaller. She dabbed at her cheekbone where the rhododendron branches had cut her. 'You bastards,' she whispered. 'You absolute bastards.' Then she pushed her way through the rhododendrons and back on to the Great Lawn where her daughter sat, a picture of misery. 'I'm coming,' she called. 'I'm coming.'

'Norty, norty,' wailed Eleanor.

With Tufty gone the dynamics of the household changed. The kittens missed her and could be found at all times of day sitting where she usually sat. They were bad-tempered with one another, although not perhaps as bad-tempered as Orlando and Liddy, who had to be separated by Anna after a confrontation in the kitchen.

Anna felt unsettled and irritable too. She was reluctant to tell John what had happened; he would only look patient and long-suffering, and somehow hold it against her. How could Mark and Oliver be pursued anyway? Even if she could get him to confront them, they would simply deny it. The question she asked herself again and again was, *Why would they do this*? In her heart she already knew. They had failed to find Stella's formula and now, with the house closed to them, they were after the next best thing: the bloodlines, the genes, the most recent subjects of the four-hundred-year Herringe experiment – the cats who lived in the shrubbery. They had got Tufty by accident. It was an example less of their malice than their futility.

Two or three days later, events drove the incident out of her mind. Eleanor's latest toy went missing. One minute Eleanor was clutching it as forcefully as ever while she sat on the floor, breathing heavily over the counters for a game of Flounder, the next – Anna had turned away to pull a saucepan off the Aga – she was empty-handed. She didn't seem to have noticed. A search of the kitchen revealed nothing. The unpleasant little bone figure, with its obese thighs and indescribable expression, might never have been. Anna nodded to herself. 'Right,' she whispered.

Midnight: she made sure that John and Eleanor were sleeping soundly. Then she got out of bed, dressed and made her way downstairs. In the kitchen she set the kettle on the Aga. While the water was heating up, she collected her old fleece jacket from the hall and put that on too. From a downstairs cupboard she took the goose-down sleeping bag she had last used as a student. It looked a bit crushed and smelled faintly of damp, but when she shook it out it seemed perfectly warm and dry inside. The kettle boiled. Anna filled John's steel Thermos flask with hot chocolate, to which she added two or three good measures of dark rum. Then she shrugged into her oiled-cotton jacket, and provided herself with gloves and a torch. She opened the door and stood there staring out, the sleeping bag under her arm and the flask stuffed into one of the pockets of the Barbour. 'Come on,' she told herself. 'The sooner it's done the sooner it's over.'

It was a bright cold night in the knot garden, with a promise of frost. The contrails of airliners sketched themselves high up across Orion and his dog. There were no builders' fires tonight. Much of the rubbish had been hauled away. Everywhere else in the grounds the chiaroscuro was fluid, shifty, moon-driven; here, the light fell across the sharp outlines of the box hedges in such a way as to bleach them white, at the same time strengthening the shadows so that things stood out with hallucinogenic clarity.

Making her way to the centre of the maze, the only moving thing in a static landscape, Anna looked like a silent paper cut-out, a strange, gliding figure waist-high in hedges. She bent down, scraped with her foot in the loose cold soil, then shone the torch on what she had uncovered. They were all there. The doll's head, its blue eyes rocking open–closed, open–closed, open–closed, gazed up at her, bland and babyish. Torchlight glittered off jet necklace and silver spoon. From the music box came a ghostly flutter of noise, 'Für Elise', incredibly distant yet receding even further as she listened.

For a moment something in her tried to follow it. There was a brief vertigo, a sense that she was being drawn down into this nest of meaningless but significant objects. She felt the presence of something, another world perhaps, somewhere she had never been and yet knew as well as Nonesuch, somewhere central to her life. She heard a voice call – it was her own! – then it was gone and she was herself again. She shivered. Nothing would persuade her to spend the night sitting next to this ill-starred stuff. In the end she found a corner from which she could watch over it uninterrupted. She shook out the sleeping bag, poured herself a drink from the Thermos and settled down to wait for whoever would arrive to bury the bone figurine.

'Someone must be doing it,' she told herself. An hour later she was asleep.

The dreams were senseless, debilitating. She woke into them as if they weren't really dreams at all, just another way of being awake. The house – it was Nonesuch but not quite the Nonesuch she knew – was dark and hot, and she never had any idea where she was. The corridors seemed to lengthen away from her in all directions, though she didn't know how. The stale air wrapped itself around her like an unwashed blanket. Nevertheless, she was making progress and always to the same appalling place. All the time she could hear a voice she half recognised, childish and unformed, murmuring things like, Busy, busy, busy and Up and down, up and down the stairs. On and on it went, in a pleased sort of way – Seven secrets, only two to go. I put these parts together and they're the parts of me – while Anna struggled to identify it. As soon as that seemed likely, fear overcame her and she dragged herself awake with a shout, only to find herself still in the same house, the same endless dark corridor, tilting up and back on itself. She had woken into the same dream, only she was a little closer to the knotted, throbbing heart of it. Seven secrets under the maze, the little childish voice congratulated itself. Seven secrets to make me who I am.

She opened her eyes. The moon was down. The knot garden looked vague and brown, cobwebbed with the residue of the dream. Anna lay fuddled and exhausted, her left arm, trapped beneath her, useless with pins and needles. She looked at her watch: a quarter to five. Soon it would be light. She pulled herself feverishly out of the sleeping bag. Two strides and she was shining the torch under the box hedge, hacking at the earth with the heel of her shoe –

Too late. The figurine was already there, nested among all the other stuff, its awful little face wrenched into the configurations of a loss no one alive now could understand.

'Damn,' said Anna.

At the sound of her voice the garden seemed to shift, gather itself, settle. There was a rustling noise, quite close to her. She swept the torch across the hedges, calling, 'Hello? Orlando? Liddy?' As soon as she spoke, the noise stopped. She switched off the torch, tilted her head to listen. Nothing. She toured the maze, shining the torch into every corner. It was empty. But for a moment she had gained the clear impression of something small pushing through a hedge, then moving away, trying to be as quick and silent as possible. This impression stayed with her even after she had taken herself tiredly back to the house and fallen asleep without even checking Ellie's cot.

She had been so close! She thought about it all morning, then, leaving Eleanor with John for half an hour around noon, returned to the knot garden, which lay deserted under a brittle gold light. Anna stood for a moment at its centre, trying to feel the things she had felt in the night. But it was just a garden, a bit scruffy and uncared-for. Now that the rubbish was cleared away, you could see the clever, cursive lines of it. In a day or two, Joshua Herringe's curiously enduring monument to himself would be gone for ever, four hundred years of history grubbed up and hauled away in an afternoon. John had already ordered the mechanical digger. Anna sighed. She remembered the first time she had come to Nonesuch in the company of Stella Herringe, how she had fallen in love with the house, the light, the soft heaviness of the air beneath the cedars. A shadow flickered briefly across the knot garden. Anna looked up. Three wood-pigeons flew over in a long, banking arc – she could hear the creak and quiver of their wings.

After a moment she found the right place, stirred the earth around the box roots with her foot, then bent down and quickly sifted it through her fingers. It was greyish, dry and crumbly, mixed up with bits of leaves, bleached sticks, a feather. She stared at this innocuous stuff for a moment, thinking, *Why aren't I surprised?* She dusted her hands. She thought, *At least I know I'm not mad. That's something. I don't know what I'm up against yet, but I know I'm not mad.*

The hole was empty.

Everything had gone and that was the last time anything appeared there.

A growing panic sent her to Dr Russell's consulting room. There, of course, she could admit nothing. She needed to talk. But of her daughter she would only allow herself to say, 'I'm sure she still gets out at night,' as if they were discussing some problem pet. All this accomplished was to cover up the fears Anna desperately needed to share. Martha Russell's psychiatric toolkit barely penetrated the surface of Anna's world, where the hidden strata of the personality were little more than a superficial membrane stretched over the nightmarish truths of reincarnation and death. The knot garden and its contents were packed tight behind everything she said, like the stuff in some overloaded cupboard, ready to fall out the moment the door was opened . . .

Her relationship with John was safer ground, so she talked about that, while the afternoon drifted away with the smoke of Martha Russell's cigarette and in the corner of the room images of weekend excavations in the damp, receding downland flickered across the flat wide screen of the Sony television.

'I wonder if I should leave him now,' she said. 'I wonder if it's weak of me to stay.'

Martha Russell considered this. 'You aren't someone who gives up,' she reminded Anna. 'You said that yourself.'

'You can love someone too much.'

'Can you? Even if that's true, it isn't weakness that keeps you there. It's strength.'

'This desperation,' Anna said, 'to recoup what you've invested? When really you'd be better to cut your losses and walk away? In business they used to call it "sunk cost error". My grandmother was more direct: "Anna," she would advise me, "never throw good money after bad."' Anna laughed sadly. 'I didn't expect to be thinking about my life in those terms.'

'Never do!' the doctor said with a certain energy. She lit another cigarette. 'Perhaps there are good, constructive reasons for leaving John,' she added. 'But the better they are the more important it is not to couch them in the language of defeat. Do you see? You are a strong person.'

'Am I?'

'I think so. You remain undefeated.' Martha Russell thought for a moment. 'You remain. That in itself counts for a lot.' She blew smoke towards the television screen. 'I want you to look at this.' She did something with the remote control and the tape reversed itself with a gentle whine. 'Here's something we found this weekend.' Thick male hands again, this time in fingerless mitts. Thumbs working at a clod of earth until it broke apart suddenly to reveal an ivory-coloured shape. It was the figure of a crouching woman, perhaps two inches high. At first it seemed to be carved from bone or ivory. Then you saw it was flint and not carved at all. 'It's the local Iceni goddess. Isn't she impressive? Now there's a metaphor for persistence in the face of things! Loss or gain, birth or bereavement, love and death: it's all one to her, she just digs in and endures. We've been finding her all over the downs this summer, at every excavation. She goes all the way back to the early paleolithic. And yet you don't see her worshipped anywhere else in Britain. Ashmore's own goddess!'

Anna Dawe got to her feet so hastily that her chair fell over. 'I have to go,' she said.

'Anna! What's the matter?'

Anna indicated the TV screen. 'Dr Russell, you're wrong about that thing. I have to go.'

She stumbled out of the consulting room and drove back to Nonesuch at what was, for her, a reckless pace. When she parked the car she was still shaking. To calm herself before she faced her husband, she walked back through the grounds of Nonesuch. How would she convince him? How would she make him understand that all these events were linked? In the end, she didn't have to, because things got worse and her new fears were driven away by older ones.

Pale sunshine fell across the herringbone paths, dusty brick walls and espaliered fruit trees. The kitchen garden was full of a faint, familiar musky smell Anna couldn't quite identify. At first she thought it was drifting in over the orchard wall, where the medlars had been left to rot on the ground every year since Stella's death; then she realised it was coming from the open kitchen door. When she left, the kitchen had been full of shouts of laughter. Now it was quiet. Anna thought nothing of that. John often took Eleanor on a tour of the renovations in the afternoon. Eleanor liked to inspect the workmen and it gave Anna a rest.

Alone at last, thought Anna. Beans on toast and a quiet cup of tea.

But what she found inside drove that out of her head. Eleanor Dawe was sitting square in the middle of the kitchen table, breathing heavily and talking to herself in a little sing-song voice of absorption and self-congratulation. Open in front of her was the pot of Engelion cream Anna had thrown in the dustbin and she was smearing it confidently if haphazardly over her pudgy face. It was in her hair. Her hands were thick with it. The kitchen reeked. Her father was nowhere to be seen.

'Eleanor!'

Eleanor gave a girlish laugh. 'Gidgiee!' she said in her most affected voice. She offered the pot to Anna, then, seeing immediately the inappropriateness of the gesture, pulled a face instead and began to sob.

Anna swept her up, carried her to the sink, turned on the cold tap and ran the water over her head as hard as it would go. Eleanor, who had never experienced anything like it, took a huge breath and choked. Her arms and legs, emerging plump and reddened from her sodden dungarees, jerked disconnectedly. The wetter she got the more difficult it became to hold her. She writhed out of Anna's grip and fell into the sink. 'Oh no, you don't,' said Anna, reading this as an attempt to escape. 'Oh no, you don't.' Eleanor's screams redoubled for a minute or two; then the fight went out of her. Anna sat her down and used the washing-up liquid as shampoo. 'Well, close your eyes, you stupid thing,' she said mildly. 'If it hurts. There now. That's got it off. You're all clean now.' Eleanor, seeing that the threat was past, remembered her dignity and began to howl again.

That was how John Dawe found them – Eleanor slumped sobbing in two inches of cold water in the sink; while Anna, soaked from the waist up, rocked her daughter to and fro, saying over and over again, 'All clean now. All clean now.'

'What's happened?' he asked.

Even the sound of his voice made Anna want to hit him. She indicated Eleanor, slumped unhappily in the sink. 'This is your daughter,' she said. 'I came back and found you had left her here on her own.' She snatched up the almost empty pot of Engelion cream and brandished it at him. 'I found her with this. She had it all over her face. You were in charge of her, John. How could you leave her? How could you?'

'It was only for a moment. The builders –'

' "The builders",' she mimicked, ' "the builders".'

'It's quite important at the moment that we –'

'Oh God, John, just shut up. There isn't any excuse. Don't you see that?'

He turned away from her angrily. 'At least I didn't

leave that foul stuff around for her to get hold of.'

This was too much for Anna. 'I threw it away! I know I did. I've told you; I keep throwing these things away and they keep coming back again!'

'Things don't just "come back", Anna,' he said. 'That can't happen.'

'What do you mean?'

'The rest of us live in a world of cause and effect,' he replied. 'For you, things just "come back". I think you should see someone. I think you should ask Dr Russell to refer you to someone. I think you need help.'

'What?'

There was shocked silence. Then she said, 'You can't imagine how useless that makes you sound –' at exactly the same time as he said, 'I'm sorry, I didn't mean –'

But they both knew he had gone too far. They stared at one another mutely, wondering if this was how things broke for good and could never be mended. Anna began to cry quietly. He knew what had happened to them at Nonesuch in the terrifying moments before the fire. He knew what they had learned from Stella Herringe, about themselves, about the nature of the world. He had been a dreamer himself when she met him, someone prepared to believe he had lived other lives, to acknowledge what Francis Baynes would call the 'mystery' of things. Now he was denying all that in the cheapest way she could imagine. She had a sudden vertiginous sense of her whole life leading here, to this moment of blank, willed, nauseous misunderstanding.

'Is that what you think?' she asked. 'That I'm mad?'

'No,' he answered. 'I suppose I don't.' Then he said, 'One of us ought to dry her and find her some clothes. Would it be better if I did it?'

'Don't you dare touch her, John.'

'Anna –'

'I'll take her away, John. Something's happening here. I'll take her away if that's the only way to save her.'

Chapter Twelve

Dusting and dusting: the dust never stopped accumulating. Even as Mrs Parker has finished cleaning the china, making the mantelpiece spick and span, down it comes, spiralling in the sunlight, each mote sentient, intent, determined to settle and stay. She sweeps here and there with the duster, until her hand is a blur of movement, but it just keeps coming; more and more, until there is a scurf of it on every surface and more snowing down from the ceiling, billowing in through the window. Ankle-deep, now she runs for the Hoover; but it is already up to her knees before she reaches the cupboard; thigh-deep as her hand touches the handle. She staggers to the door, opens it, only to admit an avalanche of the stuff, rolling down from the bedrooms. The children, upstairs, have gone ominously quiet . . .

Thunder, rolling heavy overhead: a storm come out of nowhere. At the general store, Reggie Candleton watches the lightning it has generated flicker intermittently over the pond, making nightmare shapes of the willows; looming super-real, then gone back into the darkness.

Orange clouds have started to gather to the north, orange as if lit by fire. No sooner has he thought this than he hears his cat outside (a cat he has not shared a house with for twenty years or more) howling piteously. He runs downstairs and opens the door to it. In it rushes, fur alight with flame, which he beats out with an old coat. When he takes the mackintosh away, the fur comes with it, to reveal inside the child he and Hilda had in their youth, which died at only four days old . . .

The wailing went on and on without respite. She covered her ears with her hands, but even this barely deadened the shrieking noise of it. She felt abruptly furious, hateful: full of hate and animal violence. It wasn't her baby; how could it be? It was a beast, a creature, unnatural. The screaming rose by a note, as impossible to turn a deaf ear to as fingernails on metal, claws on glass. Hadn't she buried it well enough the last time? Clearly not. Up she got, in a tangle of sheets – wet, somehow, clinging – and lumbered out into the garden. There, beneath the hedge, the baby had indeed resurfaced. There was dirt on its face, in its hair. Its eyes were black and indignant, its mouth a huge red hole of protest. She went to fetch the spade again . . .

John stood back to admire the builders' handiwork. The new plaster gleamed, smooth and clean: a brand-new wall, which would dry to a surface perfect for the Farrow & Ball Casein Distemper (English Primrose) he had ordered and which would arrive next week, a properly traditional, rustic paint which would dry to a satisfyingly matt and chalky finish. Unable to resist the temptation to touch, he brushed his fingertips against the wall, then drew them back, disappointed to see the trailing marks they had left in the new plaster. Even as he watched, the shallow depressions deepened, became holes. Plaster began to slough off the wall, revealing the old brickwork, mottled and age-eaten underneath. He stepped back just in time. With a sigh, the wall caved in and fell in slow motion, each brick detaching itself from its fellows and pirouetting to the floor, which also began to break away under this new weight. Behind and beneath the brickwork lay a void, dark and evil-smelling. Second by second, the rubble grew. As the last brick toppled, he looked up just in time to see a crack searing its way across the newly plastered ceiling like lightning in a clear sky. He opened his mouth to scream; but before the sound could emerge, the house fell upon him and took him down with it, into the darkness.

I chased down a lot of bad dreams over the nights that followed, but one nightmare breeds another, it seems, and it was hard for a single dreamcatcher to keep up with the dreams of an entire village. I wore myself ragged going after them, racing down the highways till my lion's heart was ready to burst, sleeping only during the bright hours of the day; and even then, my own dreams were disturbed and unrestful. In the end and after many arguments, in which the advocacy of both Millie and the Besom were engaged, I allowed Caterina to accompany me on to the wild roads at night, and together we hunted and swallowed down the dreams of Ashmore before they could do their pernicious damage to the highways.

Thoughts of Vita haunted me. I saw her again and again in the wooden cage, her eyes pleading at me; the witch, laughing. At last I took myself off to see the Besom. Fed on the food that Cat and I stole for her from the kitchen – Anna had been so pre-occupied she had not noticed that she was missing, over the days that Ma Tregenna had been with us, a packet of bacon, two chicken drumsticks and a good-sized lump of cheese – she had put on some of the weight she had lost and a gleam of vitality had come back into her glazed old eyes. She and Griz sat and swapped reminiscences under the rhodo-dendrons; I could hear them cackling together whenever I brought my latest bit of thievery, though sometimes when I appeared they would fall abruptly silent, as if I had intruded on the discussion of a subject too close to the bone for comfort.

This time, my offering consisted of four pork sausages, still joined by their twisted rubbery casings. (The other four had fallen on to the floor when I had dragged them from the cold white cupboard before anyone was up, but between us Cat and I had managed to bundle them back in on to the shelf again, and Cat had licked the dust from them so that they looked as clean as ever.) But if I had expected Griz to leave us to speak in private, the sausages soon put paid to any hope that she might quietly wander off. Instead, she eyed the gleaming pink packages, licked her lips and grinned at the Besom.

'This is the life, eh, Pol? Handsome young lad fetchin' and carryin' for us. Bet you never expected such luxuries in your old age, eh?'

'Never expected to live so long,' Ma said lugubriously. 'Nor wished to, neither. I've seen too much in my time.'

'Ma,' I started, tentative.

The Besom had her head down to the sausages now, was chewing with the side of her mouth. 'Mmm,' she said indistinctly.

'Ma, I've seen my sister Vita. On the highways. Here, but not here. There's a sort of knot in the roads that run through the house, but it's as if they twist back on themselves, and every time you think you know where you're going, they snake around on you and suddenly you're not where you thought you were at all, or when. And then there's the objects, you see, the things the baby has collected. They mean something, something more than themselves, if you see what I mean, and every time a new one arrives the roads seem to change again, and if I chase the right dream, I know it will take me somewhere the object wants me to be –' I stopped, partly from lack of breath, partly because my speech seemed foolish and garbled even to myself, and indeed, when I looked up, Griz was staring at me as if I were mad. The Besom carried on her slow, methodical chewing. I gazed from one to the other. Obviously I was going to come by no help here after all.

But just as I stood up and made to walk away, Ma reached out with a paw and patted me. 'I can eat, listen and think at the same time, my lad,' she said. 'It's something you learn to do, over the span of the years, with application and practice and cunning.

You might learn the art yourself some day. Sit down.'

I stared at her. She gazed back, her face a mask. I sat down. She winked at me, showing more of her pink old gums than I'd have preferred to see. It was clear now why eating took so long: she had barely any teeth left beyond the yellowed atrocities at the front.

'It's the Great Knot, Orlando. The wild rides. *She* makes them; or rather, she has the power to take them and shape them.'

'The witch?' I asked, shivering. 'I saw her down there, she was –'

'No –' The Besom was impatient. 'Not *her*, though she's gaining strength again, the Great Cat curse her. No, it's the one who came before; the Big Woman. Got a taste for life, she has, that one, stronger than all the other Old Ones put together. She'll push so hard, she'll turn the world over, given the chance.'

'Who will?'

The glossy green foliage parted to reveal Lydia, with Millie in her wake, looking resigned and a little irritated, as if she had been dragged out here against her will. I felt my heart lurch.

At the sight of the half-eaten sausages lying on the dusty ground, Liddy's head lunged forward. 'Where did you get those?' Her voice was sharp with recrimination. A line of spittle had started to form at the corner of her mouth.

The Besom looked at Grizelda. Griz looked at me. 'He brought them,' she said, careless of the consequences of such an admission.

'I knew it!' Lydia turned to Millie with an expression of triumph. 'You see, my instincts are always right. I told you I could smell sausages on Caterina; I knew she'd been stealing. And I knew she wouldn't have done it unless he'd made her, for I've brought her up properly, her and my other two, my treasures, all on my own –' She turned gimlet eyes upon me and finished, 'He's always had the common touch, has Orlando, oh yes. He has far more care for these old ragbags than he has for me!'

I opened my mouth to protest, but it was Millie who stepped into the fray. 'Lydia!' She was furious. 'Do you have no shame? Do you have no fellow feeling at all? These cats have been through as much as you, shared the same fate, and yet you'd deny them food when you're as fat as butter! Look at you; you've all but doubled in size since coming to Nonesuch, as if you think you can keep the bad things of the world at bay just by eating till there's no more to eat. And as for bringing up the girls on your own, I've never heard such a shocking lie. Poor Orlando. All this time he's been here for you, loving you, taking care of you, raising your kittens as if they were his own, and all you do is turn your nose up at him, look through him as if he doesn't exist.' Her voice crackled with emotion. 'You treat him abysmally and he loves you all the more, as if he cannot help himself, poor idiot. I watch the two of you playing out these little dramas you love so much and my heart breaks to see a decent, brave, beautiful cat like Orlando – a tomcat who should be fathering kittens of his own with a queen who would give herself to him completely – twisted round your selfish, miserly paw. You are a cruel, cold trollop, Lydia. You should have stuck with the witch and that handsome stud cat of hers, and left Orlando for me, who loves him more than all the world!'

My jaw dropped open. I stared at Millie, who looked away from me, her eyes crazed and damp. Then Lydia began to laugh. She threw her head back and howled with it, a harsh, clattering sound that rose through the winter leaves like the mocking of a magpie.

It brought the child to our hiding place. Crashing through the leaves, she came at us, waving her stick gleefully. Anna was some way behind her, her face closed and pale.

'Wor!' Eleanor said. And, 'Ca'!'

At the sight of her Grizelda and the Besom quailed, then shot away, their fur standing on end as if they had been electrified. Millie hissed and ran right past me towards the lawn, followed by Lydia, bowling me over in her panic. Like a fool, I lay there and watched them go. My legs felt leaden, my heart as heavy as a stone.

Eleanor stumbled on, flailing her stick around, missing me by inches. That galvanised me. Getting my haunches under me, I leapt away after Liddy and Millefleur, but was almost trodden underfoot by another pair of humans emerging at speed from the rhododendrons, preceded by half a dozen of the cattery survivors, who scattered wildly across the lawn. I stared back at the pursuers. Two men, in identical clothing, one with a white plastic sack in his hand. Lydia and Millie had also stopped and looked back to see what the cause of this new commotion might be and the other cats streamed past them.

At the sight of the Two Who Look Like One, Lydia's eyes widened and she began to mew in consternation. Millie's head whipped round. I saw her take in the two men, saw how they came at her and Liddy, hands outstretched.

'Run!'

I heard the voice, shrill and desperate in my head, but no sound emerged. Of their own accord, it seemed, my cowardly feet bore me away and when I looked back all I could see was a confusion of movement, a blur of bodies, a struggle, and then the Two Who Look Like One were dashing across the lawn, heads down, and there was something in the sack, something that distorted the white plastic with desperate limbs.

Anna came running out on to the lawn after them, her hair wild and mud on her knees. She shouted something and one of the men glanced back, then urged the other on towards the big silver machine parked awkwardly half on the grass, half on the gravel. They flung themselves into it and roared away down the drive, spraying stones as they fled.

In the back window, a cat scrabbled desperately against the glass.

It was Millie.

*

'We have to leave. It's not safe here any more.'

'This is my home and the girls' home. We're not going anywhere.'

'The witch is on her way back,' I said, knowing I'd never be able to explain what I meant by this to Lydia, who refused to see anything beyond the plainly visible. 'Those were her helpers. Why do you think they were here, if not to prepare for her return?'

Liddy looked at me. 'By taking Millie? What good will that do them?'

I had no answer for that, of course.

'Anyway,' she went on, extending an elegant foreleg and examining a spot of mud that had dared to dry below the dew claw, 'what do you think we're going to do – sleep in a ditch?'

'You didn't manage so badly the last time you left here,' I said waspishly and immediately regretted it.

Lydia's face became closed and hard. Then she got up and stalked into the next room. There, the three girls lay curled together for comfort. They looked up as I followed their mother in, their faces identically inimical. I knew without a word being said that they blamed me, somehow, for Millie's abduction.

I blamed myself, too. Over and over I thought how different things might have turned out had I been able to croak out that single word of warning; if I had got in the men's way, tripped them up; if they had taken me instead. As it was, I had chased the silver vehicle down the drive, out of the gates and on to the lane outside. At the junction with Village Road I had almost caught it, though I thought my lungs might burst with the effort, but then it had leapt away from me with a tremendous surge of power and I had lost it as it sped away, fishtailing round the corner, and headed towards the main road for Drychester and the towns beyond. Millie's face as the car accelerated away was the face of a cat that has lost all hope.

I wandered far and wide on the highways, searching for any sign of her, but to no avail. I popped out into unfamiliar streets in towns I had never before visited. I asked every cat, dog, bird and rat I encountered if they had seen her; but many of them ran from me, and I realised too late that I had stepped into their path straight from a wild road and still wore my lion's mane. I tried and failed to find the fox, Loves A Dustbin, to enlist him in my quest. I quartered the gardens of country houses as old as Nonesuch, or so new they had no scent at all. Of Millefleur, or the Two Who Looked Like One, I found no trace.

The days that followed Millie's disappearance were terrible indeed. The girls squabbled with each other constantly. Bickering turned to hisses and howls; hisses and howls to sudden outbreaks of violence. Little tufts of blue fur drifted in the air; there were spots of blood on the mat in the kitchen. Lydia ignored me entirely and for once I did not care.

The things Millie had said before she was taken kept coming back to me. I lay in empty rooms and contemplated them. In the quiet moments between times – before I slept, when I awoke; exiting the wild roads after a night's work; while grooming the burrs and thorns of winter from my coat – her words echoed in my skull. I walked in the garden in the rain and thought about how she had described me. How she had described herself: *Who loves him more than all the world . . .*

The phrase went round and round in my head until I found I had to get up and do something, anything, to displace it. I explored the house from cellar to roof. I found rooms I had never discovered before, rooms that had been shut as if for centuries, for the dust lay as thick as fur on every surface. I disturbed spiders and mice, moths and woodlice. I watched John standing vacantly in the knot garden as though someone had switched him off. I came upon Anna, asleep, with tears drying on her face; I watched the baby crawling and toddling around the corridors when no one was paying attention to her.

The baby puzzled me. It was as much the way she smelled as her random behaviour, her odd out-bursts, her avid interest in us cats; even the bizarre and resonant objects she adopted. Some days her scent was the scent of a young creature: warm and softy and milky; but I began to realise that on the days following a particularly hard night of dreams, especially those times when I had been forced on to the labyrinthine highways of Nonesuch to tackle a witch dream, she had started to smell very odd indeed. It was not merely that she smelled adult, or that very occasionally, and for a fraction of a second, she gave off the heady aroma of a fully grown and willing female – all salt and tang – but that she had many scents all intermingled, so that if you approached from one side she smelled sweet and musky; from another like a thing dead in the earth for months, a thing that worms and centipedes have found, a thing with eggs laid in its belly; while underneath it all was the innocent baby smell that suited her appearance. She conformed to nothing in the scent map of the world my grandfather had so painstakingly taught me; yet all things were present within her, as if she represented the entire world, the old and new, the fresh and the rotten, both love and hate; gentleness and a black, tearing violence.

She scared me, if truth be told. The other cats kept out of her way without the slightest understanding of why they did so beyond a cat's natural avoidance of the unpredictable feet and grasping hands of an unsteady but curious child; but they had not seen the dreams she generated as I had.

Even so, I was nagged by the sense that she was the mystery to which all the other recent events – the discovery and dream life of the significant objects, the recent preponderance of nightmares in the village, the convolution of the highways through the house, my sightings of Vita, even the disappearance of Millie – were somehow connected and so I kept a close watch on her.

One afternoon, when Anna was working in the kitchen and Eleanor was playing beneath the table, I found myself drawn by the presence of another of the magical objects. From my vantage point, carefully out of hand's reach under one of the kitchen chairs, I saw that although the baby appeared to be engaged in a game that involved the throwing around of a number of pieces of brightly coloured plastic, amid much clapping of hands and shouting, the object of her true attention lay all the while in her lap. I could not see it as such, but I could feel it, as though it were a pebble dropped into a pond, generating ripples that spread out and out towards the shore. Without moving closer it was hard to spy it out and I spent many frustrating minutes waiting for a clear sight of this new toy. At last, apparently aware of my interest, the baby picked the thing up and cradled it in her hands. She looked me squarely in the eye, a look at once blank and yet challenging. Then she held the object out towards me.

I felt the hairs rise on my neck and spine.

It was a bone doll. I had never seen one before in Ashmore, could not even explain how I knew this for a fact. They say that cats twine through time like the skeins that hold the world in place; they say we have been closely associated with witches, that cats and the craft have been intimately joined. They say that dreamcatchers in particular have lived many lives. Maybe once, in one of mine, I had encountered an object such as this, for how else to explain the repulsion I felt for it? I found myself backing away across the room, until my rump hit the skirting board and there was nowhere left to go. The size of a small kitten, it squatted in Eleanor's hand, a grotesque replica of a human woman, its fat, thick legs set wide apart and its mouth carved open in an obscene utterance. The baby turned the figurine back towards her and gazed lovingly at its crude, demonic face; then she turned it back to me again. Her own expression had taken on an identical form to the bone doll's: eyes slitted as if in some intense pain or pleasure, mouth yearning out a soundless cry.

I felt the room spin. A moment later, without the slightest idea of how I had got there, I found myself deep in the knot of Nonesuch's highways. Lights flickered and faded, chill draughts blew my fur in all directions, cobwebs brushed my face. Behind me, as if through a mist, I could still see the kitchen as a distant glow. If I squinted hard, I could make out the shape of Anna standing at the stove, her red jumper vibrant in the surrounding gloom of the highway. Of the child there was no sign at all. Slowly I turned round. There was nothing to see on either side except nondescript walls, as if the house were hiding its locations from me, making sure I had no starting point in the maze it had constructed. Ahead of me, however, there was a light, albeit faint and greyish, but a light all the same. Knowing that I was being herded into it like a sheep into a pen, still I went towards it. Cats are curious animals; sometimes we cannot help our natures.

The highway began to tilt downwards as I made my way forward so that when I looked back, the glow of the kitchen had disappeared and all there was behind me was darkness. I shivered then. This was the first time the highways had swallowed me without my permission, the first time I had entered them without a goal in mind: a dream to catch or a journey to make. I could not decide whether, like other wild roads, the highways of the house were a natural phenomenon, part of the Great Cat's creation, or if they had somehow sprung into existence as a result of the witch's magic; or whether their true nature lay somewhere between these two points. Whatever the truth of the matter, I gave myself up to their logics. It appeared that they had something to show me and I braced myself for whatever that might be.

I did not have to wait long for the puzzle to present itself. There came a peal of laughter from the lightening tunnel ahead of me. I picked up my pace. A moment later I was in what I could only describe as a cave.

Someone, or something, had hollowed a circular chamber out of the rock here, of a size to accommodate the height of a standing human and of a length to afford sufficient space for three or more to lie at full length. The floor was of soft earth, barely compacted by the passage of feet. The chamber gave back nothing more than an aroma of mulch and leaf mould, water upon stone; and the acrid scent of melted tallow. If I opened my mouth to flehm, to *taste* the smell, as it were, I caught the faintest echo of burned feather and cold ash. The walls of the chamber were lit by candles: tall yellow pillars, their surfaces roughly moulded as if by hand, the length of them matted with drip marks. Shadows leapt and jumped across the small space. I stepped boldly into the circle of light and there, in the centre of the floor, lay a burned-out fire. Criss-crossing it in a complex pattern were a number of long white bones, laid in a collapsed pyramid. A small heap of black ash sat in the midst of these, the centre of the pile disrupted, as if by a hand. The laughter came again, disembodied; above me, very close. I jumped back, just in time to avoid being hit by something. The object – heavy and pale – fell with a thud into the middle of the ashes, sending up a plume of dust. I looked up and saw above me a small hand, stark white against the ceiling of the chamber. For a moment it seemed to hang there, then it disappeared, as if it had been swallowed by the darkness.

The laughter echoed away into silence.

I moved forward into the light again. In the centre of the extinct fire lay the bone doll, but even as I bent my head to nose at it, the lights flickered as if blown by a great wind and all the candles went out.

Chapter Thirteen

ANNA SAT WITH two of the cats in the drawing room.
She had come upon them curled up there asleep in a
heap, their paws tucked into a neat pile near their
faces, but even so, Letty's pale star was just visible
above the white sock on Belle's paw.

'What do you make of these goings-on?' she asked
them, running a hand over that bizarre blue fur.
'Not much, I bet.'

The drawing room had a deep window recess, a
ceiling decorated with lions and roses in chequer-
board squares, all the tranquillity of a place worn by
use and then abandoned. Life had left its mark as a
patina of use, on the oak floor, the silverware, the
blackened seats of the Jacobean chairs. Along with
that soft dull shine came the gentle, predictable
curve of wear – the curve, John had always said, of
human occupation. He said you saw it wherever
people had lived, but never at Heal's, where every
curve was designed. Not that he was saying
anything like that now.

They hadn't talked much after Eleanor got hold of

the Engelion cream and hardly at all since John sold the *Magpie*.

Her new owner, a cheerful man from the Midlands, arrived to take possession the day after his cheque had cleared. John and Anna watched from the towpath as he swung the boat away from its mooring for the last time. It seemed to take for ever. The *Magpie* was slow to manoeuvre, her engine chugged heavily in the wet air. John shouted advice, while Anna stared numbly at the willows on the far side of the canal. The first time she met John he had been on the water, she had been on the land and that opposition had set itself into the relationship. They had fought immediately, though over what she had forgotten. She remembered saying contemptuously, 'No one owns a cat.' Or had that been him? *You were rude then*, she thought, *and self-absorbed, and you had no idea how to live. We argued over the slightest thing, but at least you cared about something other than a house.*

After the *Magpie* had vanished into the Drychester reach, Anna said forlornly, 'He was a nice enough man. Don't you think? But I didn't like to see him take her away.'

She had felt the best part of their life go with him. What John felt she could only guess, because all he did was shrug. He had made more out of the sale than he expected, but it wasn't enough. If he kept the builders on, he couldn't buy materials. If he bought materials he couldn't pay the men. The less he could afford to do, the harder he worked. It was beyond escapism now. It was beyond denial. He was in a kind of despair. He had to mend the house, because he hoped that would mend the rest of his life. It didn't matter how often Anna warned him; the more he invested in this activity, the more he had to invest. Sometimes even this wasn't sufficient to explain his obsessive determination and he seemed to Anna to be working less for any reason of his own than to prepare the place for someone else. Did he still expect the Herringes to ride up the drive in their expensive foreign cars and, at the last moment, save him?

'I don't know what he expects,' Anna told the kittens, 'because we don't talk about anything like that.'

Letty purred, half woke, slept again. Belle stirred and opened her eyes just enough for the barest sliver of light to show, then screwed up her face like a disgruntled pensioner and threw both paws over her head. Anna knelt up next to them and ran her fingers over them. She could smell their dusty blue-grey fur in the warmth of the sun that poured between the stone mullions and into the window recess. She had no idea any more what was going on in the quiet feline world they inhabited. She had no idea where Orlando was; she hadn't seen him for a day or more.

'I wonder where you've gone this time, Orlando,' she whispered. 'I wonder where you are. Do you still remember the cottage? And how we all lived in it together, you and your sister and Dellifer and me? And that bad-tempered old tomcat! Do you remember him? Sometimes I wish we were back there again.'

A moment later there came the soft, distinct pat of paws on the oak floor and she looked up hopefully, thinking he might have been summoned magically by the draw of her voice. But it was only Lydia standing on the threshold of the room, surveying the attention being lavished on her children with a rather belligerent expression on her neat golden face.

There was a problem with the courtyard. The builders complained that the ground they had uncovered beneath it was 'dangerous', that it was unstable in some way they couldn't quite describe. They thought there might be some much earlier structure down there – a passage, a cellar, the remains of some earlier building, perhaps even an old excavation, which had partly collapsed in on itself – into which the courtyard earth was subsiding. They didn't, they told John, want to get involved with anything like that: the complications, structural and legal, would be too much. Listed buildings, they complained, were difficult enough to deal with as it was; for him it might mean a postponement of the work while archaeological teams were brought in. It might mean further preservation orders. Whatever else, they advised him, it would mean pay, pay, pay. This he understood. It was less easy to understand their other complaint, which was that the ground was being tampered with before they arrived in the mornings, perhaps by an animal. Something had been scuffling about there, they insisted, trying to dig it up. John went down to look.

He couldn't see what they meant, though he had to admit that the earth appeared looser and dryer than it had before. He took some up and rubbed it between his finger and thumb, quickly let it drop. He hadn't liked the feel of it. 'This stuff hasn't seen the light of day in four hundred years,' he said. 'It might be that.' And the shrubbery cats were in and out all night, making a nuisance of themselves. Might one of them be scuffing it up?

There was some laughter.

'It would have to be a big cat,' they said.

He reported this exchange to Anna in his office. She had gone up to show him a postcard from Alice Meynell, now in Morningside Heights, New York. (Alice was happy: into America, into physics, heavily smitten. Though she would be home soon.) After the most dutiful of glances he had said, 'Mm' and left them both casting around wretchedly for something more to say. It was his turn to mind the baby. Eleanor, always happy to have her father to herself, hadn't even looked up when Anna came in. She was sitting on the floor by his desk, whispering secretively to herself, surrounded by soft toys, rag books, crumpled paper, none of which could compete with the object she was turning over in her hands. It looked like a coloured brooch.

Anna bent down quickly and took it from her. 'What's this?' she asked.

For a moment Eleanor was too startled to respond. Then she caught her father's eye and began to whimper, holding her arms up to him.

'Be quiet,' Anna warned. 'Or you won't have it back.'

It was an oval of some soft faux-silver alloy pressed into a shallow concave shape perhaps two inches by two and a half, on the upper surface of which someone had made an incredibly detailed and lifelike portrait of a young woman. She was seated, dressed in brocade and a ruff, staring boldly out at the portraitist. Her hands were in her lap, holding a pair of grey kid gloves. Her unbound black hair framed a face used to having its own way, and her green eyes were blank with greed. Anna stared. Her heart was pounding hard. She felt something approaching her purposefully from a long, long way off. It was a feeling of absolute disaster. 'John,' she said. 'This is a portrait of Stella.'

He studied it over her shoulder. 'No,' he told her. 'It's very striking, but it's not her. This thing's too old anyway. I'd put my money on one of the ancestors – Eleanor Knole, Clara de Montfort, someone like that.' He studied it again. 'Those women! They all look so alike, as far back as you can trace them. And God knows how far after that. Saxon women seducing Normans. Tribal beauties luring Roman notables away from their safe and civilised lives. I bet they looked the same when they were knapping flints on the chalk downs.' He handed the miniature back to Anna with a bitter laugh. 'The genes of the Herringe women, raging out of the Stone Age long before they had a name.'

Anna, who didn't find this at all funny, said, 'But how did Eleanor get this? Did you give it to her?'

'She picked it up,' he said vaguely. 'It must have been in here somewhere.'

'I thought we discussed this. I thought you were going to keep a better eye on her if I let you have her. That was the agreement.'

'I know. I'm sorry.'

'That was the agreement,' Anna repeated.

Her skin had crawled when she set eyes on the woman in the picture. She should say more, she knew. She should make more of it. Instead, she looked down at the miniature again. She could see that he was right. Though the colours were still rich, the varnish used to fix them had long ago decayed into a fine craquelure of tiny lines, lending a brownish cast to the light where it fell across the sitter's face and an oddly sexual look to her smile. It was very like Stella, but it wasn't Stella. How could it be? Anna returned it to Eleanor, who looked surprised and gratified. The ways of adults were certainly odd.

'Please try to keep an eye on her,' Anna said to John.

He looked relieved. 'I will, I will.'

Anna made a small gesture with the postcard. 'Well, I should get on, I suppose. I just thought I'd show you this.'

'Good,' he said.

'She's coming home soon but she isn't sure of her flights.'

'That's good.'

'I thought you'd be pleased.' Then she went on, 'We aren't really here, are we? You and me. Not for

Ellie, not for each other. Are we just going to let this happen to us?'

She waited for him to agree, disagree, anything, just so that he acknowledged the danger they were in. He let her get all the way to the door before he said, 'Anna, I wish –'

'What?'

But she had turned back too quickly and frightened him off. 'Nothing.'

Anna telephoned Francis Baynes. He didn't answer. There was an odd ticking sound on the line and behind that a sort of expectant hush. Anna put down the handset. On the table in front of her she had Alice's postcard from New York, showing a detail from the Cuxa Cloister at the Museum of Modern Art. She held it upright between her fingertips. 'Hurry up and come home, Alice,' she said aloud. Then she telephoned Francis again. This time he was engaged. She put on her coat, found the keys to the Volvo and drove it down to the village, where she parked it outside the front gate of the rectory and waited. The Hewlett sisters walked past, pretending not to look into the car. Ivy Compton followed. There would be talk later. After about ten minutes Francis came out, looking puzzled.

Anna wound down the driver's window. 'Hello, Francis.'

'Why are you waiting there?' he asked her. 'Is there something I can do?'

'You can come for a walk with me,' she told him.

He opened his mouth.

She opened the passenger door. 'Get in.'

She got the car moving and after about a mile said, 'If I don't talk to somebody I'll go mad. Francis, I'm afraid I've lost them. That damned house is taking them from me.'

Francis sat facing precisely forward, staring out of the windscreen like a trapped animal.

'Am I going too fast?' she asked.

'It isn't like you.'

'No,' she agreed, slowing down. 'It isn't. Where would you like to walk?'

'The downs are always nice,' he said.

It was a cold day, but with a brightness about it. They sat in the car for a moment in the empty car park. 'From up here you can see every church in the county,' Francis said suddenly. He rubbed his hands together. 'Well then, you've taken me from my sermon, so let's have this walk. You can explain to me as we go.'

But she could explain nothing. How could she explain an irrational fear? And phrases like 'a fatal error' kept coming to her; she kept wanting to say, 'I think I've made a fatal error.' In the end she managed, 'We just aren't talking to one another any more.'

'That doesn't sound so new.'

'I suppose not. But it's worse than it's ever been. He won't see what's in front of him. I can't make him care.' Suddenly she said, 'Francis, do I use you?'

He smiled at her. 'A little.'

'And do you mind?'

'A little.'

Shame emptied her out and she walked on in silence. Up there it was very bright, very bright and cold; a variety of paths meandered along between groups of stunted birch. They stopped where the trees thinned out and looked down over Ashmore, laid out between the scarp of the downs and the curve of the canal with the duckpond at its centre like the iris in the eye of a cat.

'Show me all the churches, then,' she said. 'Tell me their names.'

'Sanford Orcas, East Owler, Laxfield St Cross, St Margaret's, St Peter's, St Cuthman-at-Cookley.' He touched her arm, pointed out across the plain. 'And there! See? There's St Mary's in Burnham, the only round-tower church south of the Blackwater Estuary – Norman font, fifteenth-century bell, a porch with medieval faces of the sun and moon.' It was a litany. He loved these places. He loved the idea they represented. With the collar of his tweed coat turned up and his face shining in the cold he looked thin, undernourished, unbearably young. He looked like a survival from another age. *Only his naïveté*, Anna thought suddenly, *is keeping him here.* Without this astonishing belief in things he would fall away from the nice life, the acceptable life, be discovered years later living on the street in Birmingham or Bethnal Green, having made up his own religion, something appalling and occult, driven by the unspoken forces inside him. She was overwhelmed by a feeling of pity for him, caught up inextricably with her pity for herself. 'North Creake,' he was reciting, 'South Creake, Sedgeford-by-Attwater –'

'Stop!' she said. 'Stop now.'

She made him face her, brushed his hair out of his eyes. 'Poor old Francis, you do have a time of it.' She kissed him gently on the lips. She felt him jump like a startled child. 'Shh.'

A lion burst out of the air beside them.

Perhaps not precisely out of the air, she would think later, and perhaps not precisely a lion. But something huge, some huge cat; and it came, in a sense, from nowhere, assembling itself in an instant from the spaces between the birch trees, this huge, hot, golden animal running towards them. They could feel the heat of it. They could feel the bunch and unbunch of its muscles, how it was propelled tirelessly forward as if it need never, ever stop, through a different world from theirs. Then, 'Francis!' she cried, for it was at her elbow – at one and the same time infinitely distant and close enough to touch. It was a lion. It was a tiger. It was the couched Brazilian jaguar in its arboreal gloom. Its paws were the size of dinner plates. She could smell the rankness of it. It hung there in the air, then jumped down and paced jerkily about in front of them, roaring.

'Francis! What is it?'

'I don't know,' he said.

They were shouting like people trying to make themselves heard in a storm. She clutched his arm. Shaking with astonishment, they stared at the apparition. Its flanks heaved and steamed in the sharp air. Head on one side, it showed them white teeth, a mouth the colour of a rose. Its eyes had the flat gleam of a cat's at night. Then a shimmer went over its outline so that Anna seemed to be seeing it through water and as suddenly as it had come it was gone, and with it all Anna's fear.

'What was it, Francis?' she asked. 'What was it?'

He shook his head. They stared at each other, trembling.

Anna said, 'Where did it come from? Has it escaped from a zoo?' Then she laughed, a laugh of amazement, delight, sheer relief. 'I've never seen anything so beautiful. And what a smell!' She laughed. 'Phew.' She took his arm, looked around. 'We oughtn't to stay here. It won't come back. But wasn't it beautiful? Wasn't it beautiful?'

Francis said nothing. She walked him back towards the car, her arm through his. Everything looked sharper and clearer, as if she were seeing the world through some special kind of glass. 'I'll drive you home,' she offered and laughed. 'You needn't worry that I'll go too fast.' On the way back, a kind of calmness overcame her. 'It wasn't from a zoo.' What had happened? She would never know, except that something like that was the opposite of everything Nonesuch stood for. It was beautiful and real, but it was like any other event: you could not hold on to it. At Nonesuch they would never let anything go. And there was another thing. If you wanted an event like that to have any meaning for your life, you would have to make up that meaning yourself. You would have to learn its lesson, allow it to change you. So when she had stopped the car outside Francis's house and let him out, she said, 'Francis, I shouldn't have kissed you. It was unfair and silly, and I'll always feel guilty about it.'

'Anna, I –'

She gave him a sad smile. 'I know, Francis, I already know. But it isn't any good, is it? I love John.'

He let his arms drop to his sides. 'Of course,' he said. 'It's just that I wish –' He shook his head. 'I'm sorry.'

'It was my fault. It isn't anything for you to be ashamed of.'

'I'm rather afraid it is.'

'Oh, Francis, it was just a kiss!'

He shrugged and made his way into the rectory. Later, she would be reminded of how he had stared out almost desperately towards the Drychester churches like a sailor looking for one last landmark, something to navigate by after the fog set in. But now she was so full of her vision of the great cat and what it meant to her that, right or wrong, she forgot him. Suddenly she was parking the car at Nonesuch and running upstairs to John's office, and throwing her arms round him whether he wanted it or not and saying, 'We're being really, really stupid, you and me. We really are. Life is too short for this. Do you know that?'

Eleanor stared up at them from the floor.

Francis Baynes leaned against the wainscoting in the cold bare rectory hall. Greyish light seeped in round the partly open door, to illuminate his drawn features, baggy trousers, muddy shoes. *I look like my own father*, he thought with despair.

Try as he might, he was unable to see the afternoon's events as anything but ill-starred and minatory. They were a warning. Against what he wasn't sure. He knew that he shouldn't have allowed Anna to kiss him. He knew, perhaps more importantly, that he had failed to understand her joy. It was the characteristic failure of his life: with the mystery all around him, he had failed to meet it on its own terms. He had been unable to live up to it. What had happened anyway? She had kissed him. As a result, a huge animal had appeared. He couldn't separate one event from the other. He was twenty-six years old and he had been too hard on himself for most of them, and he felt as though he might be going mad. As the Volvo drove off, he thought he saw the great cat flicker briefly into existence again, lashing its tail and running away down the village street.

He took himself upstairs.

There he began to get undressed, staring down into the graveyard from his window and thinking, *I wish I had been born a thousand years ago.* The afternoon was almost over. Night was in the foliage of the yews. Rooks circled and cawed around St Mary's tower; they settled, flew up, circled again. Francis let his trousers fall round his feet, stepped out of them. 'Why must you always be here?' he said bitterly to the woman on the bed.

'Oh dear,' she answered. 'Have we had a reverse?'

He turned away from the window to face her.

'Why won't you leave me alone?' he asked.

She laughed. 'It was you who called to me,' she explained. 'You have a spiritual smell, men like you; you've never sorted sex from desire, desire from religion.' She pretended to sniff. 'Quite right too. Delicious!'

She was squatting on the uncovered mattress, her feet planted squarely as if for purchase. She had strewn her flowers on the bed and drawn up her brown muslin skirts, exposing her thighs and vulva. She looked roughly hewn, monolithic, cream-coloured here, a smoky yellow there, like some old figure carved in bone. She smelled as rank as a cat. She was smiling at him with the side of her mouth, not in contempt or triumph, or even sexual invitation. It was something that bore only a resemblance to those things, Francis Baynes thought, something lazy and without a name. In the end it was indifferent to what you called it. All he could see were her thighs, massive and open. The rest of her seemed to recede.

'I'll give you some advice,' she said. 'It's this: you'll get nowhere with that skinny bitch.' She laughed at his expression. 'Oh, I know. Do you think I don't know everything? But I do, my cherub, I do. There's nothing for you there.'

'I don't know what you mean.'

She laughed. 'Oh yes, you do, my cherub. Oh yes, you do. But come in here and have some comfort before the night.'

Francis looked down at himself. His erection was thick and painful. It made him feel foolish and encumbered, standing there with his socks and his shirt still on. He came as soon as he touched her, felt used, then didn't know what he felt. 'There, there,' she said. 'You'll soon want to go again, a boy like you.

'All the boys want Izzie.'

Busy, busy. Up and down. Me and Izzie we go from corridor to corridor in the night, corner to corner, nook to cranny, secret to secret. We have got some secrets between us, her and me. But here's the big one –

Izzie says, I'm the oldest one of all. I was here before anyone else. I was deep in the bones of this landscape. I was dug down deep here before the Herringes learned how not to die. She laughs. It was me taught them. I showed them how to make the maze. I taught them how to say the words. More than that, I stay with them while they're dead: I help them remember who they are. I pick the strongest. Only the strongest get the chance to live on. I'm a clever old Izzie, she says, I pick the ones with the most fear.

They're the ones ravenous to come back. They're the ones who'll do anything.

I watch them at the Johnny-and-Jill, the old in and out that never varies. I'm at the heart of all this. I'm the heart of this. Look at life, you find me hidden underneath it all, in and out, Jill and her Johnny, Johnny and his Jill. You go along now, she says to me, and do what must be done.

You were my best pupil, she says to me. You were always the most afraid. It's the next time round for you. This is your next time round, if you want it. Run along and find it now, the underneath, the underneath-it-all, and bring the things you already have to the thing you'll find there.

I say, But Izzie –

Oh, you'll find me too all right, my hinny, I'll be there. Don't you worry. Don't you care. You can take this little baby and be inside it fully. You can be you. You can be what you want. You can always be what you want. You can always have what you want. Come back now, my hinny. Come back now, my Stella. My lovely frightened Stella now. Come on. Come.

Izzie says this over and over again to me.

So I know who I am not. I know who I am. It'll be fucking between the hedges now, underneath the yellow moon. It'll be Johnny-and-his-Stella again now.

And that other bitch, and her damned cat, had best watch out.

Night.

Anna woke up suddenly, convinced she had heard something. She looked at her watch: a quarter to two. She yawned. Her dreams had been of Nonesuch – rain with a bitter grey light slanting through it at wrenched angles, the sodden pathways of the knot garden tangling and retangling themselves until she couldn't find the way out, smiles awry on faces heavily rouged over arsenic-white, notes of deceit exchanged by deft betraying hands – unpleasant encounters in period dress which, unresolved in sleep, flickered on in her head for an instant or two like TV drama and were gone.

'John?' she asked.

'No,' said John. He gave a greedy chuckle. 'But if it means more of this I can learn.'

'John?'

He was fast asleep.

He had come to bed earlier than usual, slightly bemused and already aroused. They had made love until she was quite sore and John couldn't do anything whatever she whispered in his ear. Nothing had been solved by this and it had rather puzzled her. But sharing the same pillow makes it easier to admit your grievances. John felt that everyone depended on him too much. This frightened him. 'If I don't get the house right, what will we do? Where will we live? I'll have let us all down.'

The honesty of this forced Anna to confess, 'I'm jealous of Eleanor. I don't know what I expected. That she would be a real person but somehow not change anything between you and me. I expected a doll; instead, she elbowed her way into our life. And why not? All she wants is a place. How can I blame her for that? Or for loving you?'

'She loves her father, it's true. Will you always hold it against me?'

'Only on wet days.'

'What a comfort you are.'

She had not told him about seeing the lion, or kissing Francis. That was her business. Now she looked down at him and whispered, 'Don't ever think you've let us down, John Dawe. You're not in it on your own. We're in it with you.' Then she thought, *This room seems hot. I'll drink some water.* But the glass by the bed was empty and a few moments later she had fallen asleep. This time the dreams were less pleasant. In them she was dead again. There were all kinds of death and this was the one like knotted wet sheets. She woke full of anxiety, with her mouth thick and dry. She was sweating. John lay half across her in his sleep, one arm flung out; his body heat made the bed seem close and airless, like some felt-curtained four-poster from the deep history of the house. She pulled herself from beneath him, looked at her watch. It was a quarter to three and the room was very dark. 'I'm going downstairs for some water,' she whispered. 'If I can still walk.' He grunted but did not wake.

Rather than disturb him by switching on the light, she felt her way round the end of the bed to Eleanor's cradle and reached in to make sure her daughter hadn't thrown off the blankets. 'Sleep well, little girl,' she said. 'Sleep well.' She felt around with her hands.

The cradle was empty.

Anna stood outside the bedroom door in her nightdress. Her head was full of sleep and at the same time mercilessly clear.

This is it, now, she thought.

She thought, *I'm so tired*.

The corridor stretched away in the dim glow of the temporary lighting. Abandoned ladders and stacks of lath projected long, expressionist shadows on the panelled walls. Beneath them scampered Eleanor Dawe, a little plump figure in a pair of pull-ups, clutching her latest object and talking to herself as she went.

'Eleanor!' called Anna. 'Eleanor, come back!'

If the child heard she took no notice, but turned the corner at the end of the passage and vanished from sight. Anna started after her, hesitated, half turned back to fetch John then thought, *Too late. I mustn't lose her. I mustn't lose her again.*

She reached the end of the passage in time to see Eleanor turn down the next one and that was how it was from then on: like a nightmare in which Anna could never catch up. Eleanor made all the running. Her agenda, though, was hard to understand. She slipped into John's office, to reappear almost immediately with something in her other hand – whatever it was, she dropped it soon after and didn't seem to notice. She squatted down suddenly at the smoke-blackened entrance to Jonathan Herringe's Great Chamber, and with a good deal of grunting and whispering, relieved herself into the nappy. She went up a floor by the back stairs, only to descend again immediately by the front ones – encouraging herself as she lowered herself backwards from step to step in the voice Anna had heard in her dreams. On and on it went –

Busy, busy, it said. *Oops, norty.* A small laugh, then: *Hidey and findy. Hidey a-n-d . . . findy!*

– while Eleanor climbed stairs, pushed open doors and, breathing catarrhally, clambered over the clever child-proof gates John had taken such trouble to fit. All along she had had the run of the house, but to see her actually do it was like a discovery in a nightmare – senseless, debilitating. And if Anna found the facts difficult to accept, they also made her wary – more than once she opened her mouth to call 'Eleanor!' only to shut it without speaking.

How can a baby do this? she thought.

In the half-hour that now passed, none of the answers to this question proved palatable; meanwhile, despite her familiarity with the building, Anna lost all sense of where she was. Staircases seemed to elongate themselves bizarrely. Stale air wrapped itself around her like an unwashed blanket. 'Cross a threshold here,' she remembered Stella Herringe saying, 'and you've moved two hundred years before you know it.' Eventually she recognised the Long Corridor and the oblong on the panelled wall where the portrait of Clara de Montfort had hung – Eleanor had brought her mother to the door of the Painted Room, that site of many defeats. Inside, moonlight struck in through the casement window, falling as a series of startling, sharply delineated bars; shadows hung in the corners like the cobwebs in a bad film; while through the ragged hole in William Haut-Herringe's *trompe l'oeil* could be seen a faint suggestion of the empty courtyard beyond. Eleanor rocked on her heels in a beam of light. 'Wor,' she whispered softly, turning her head as if at a fireworks display. 'Vootie.' She offered her toy to the empty air; snatched it back; then, chuckling to herself at this good joke, wriggled her way through the hole in the painting and vanished into the courtyard beyond, trailing behind her the distinctive smell of an unchanged nappy.

The courtyard, empty of machinery, looked bigger than Anna remembered it. Bits of broken concrete like recently excavated bones littered the loose dry soil across which Eleanor made her way on hands and knees. She seemed agitated now, a little reluctant, stopping repeatedly to look up into the air. Whatever she thought she saw there caused her to wince away. *'Phew,'* she complained in her not-Eleanor voice. *'Busy busy.'* She reached the centre of the courtyard, where the builders had found the old subsidence, and, murmuring with relief, knelt down. She looked at her hands, wiped them on herself and, using as a trowel the miniature of the woman in the brown dress, made a ragged mark in the earth. This she contemplated for a moment. Then she began to dig. Her idea of digging was to lean forward, scoop the soil towards her with both hands, then propel it back energetically between her pudgy legs. After a few minutes she didn't seem like a little girl any more. She seemed more like an animal.

Anna, watching from the Painted Room, couldn't bear it. Bad dreams still roiled about inside her like brown smoke. She tried to call out. To begin with nothing happened. Then she made a jerky, almost inadvertent movement of the head and neck – as if some physical gesture were necessary to unlock her vocal cords – and with great effort managed to whisper, 'Ellie.'

Eleanor looked uncertainly over her shoulder.

Had she heard something? Perhaps not. She gave a little shrug. The dry grey soil began to shift and slip away into the subsidence in front of her like the surface of the sand in an egg timer; a shallow depression formed. At this, Eleanor chuckled appreciatively, picked up the miniature and began scraping with renewed excitement. More soil fell away. Soon she was in it up to her elbows. She was easing herself forward into the position of a swimmer who prepares to slide beneath the surface.

At this, Anna's paralysis left her. 'Eleanor,' she cried, lunging through the hole in the wall. 'Eleanor, don't you dare!'

A comical expression passed across Eleanor's face. 'No, Mummy,' she said in a voice easily recognisable as her own and burrowed into the dirt until only her feet remained visible.

Anna grabbed them.

For a moment, things seemed to get worse. All around her the soil, undermined from beneath, was slipping away into whatever ancient cellar or passageway lay down there, making a quiet hissing sound as it went. Eleanor shrieked and kicked. Anna groaned and shouted, and hauled on Eleanor's ankles. There ensued a tug of war, not so much with the child as with the ground. The ground had become something in itself, something undisclosed and shy, powerful yet not entirely willing to show its hand. She felt it there, as a fully-fledged consciousness opposed to her own, and then it was gone. Anna lost her balance and sat down suddenly. Eleanor was pulled out of the earth like a cork from a bottle, roaring and struggling and calling, 'No, Mummy. No, Mummy.'

Anna made eye contact. 'Eleanor,' she said. 'You are a very naughty girl.'

Eleanor laughed. '*Let me go, you silly bitch*,' she said.

Anna slapped her and ran.

She ran with Eleanor tucked under one arm. She ran as if somehow she could take Eleanor away from herself. She ran for both their sakes, blundering through the Painted Room and out into the Long Corridor, where she turned right instead of left and became mired in Stella Herringe's old quarters. Here, the fire had burned so hot it consumed plaster as well as lath, stone as well as metal. The melted objects of Stella's tenure – lifestyle accessories from Heal's, Conran, Purves & Purves – lay underfoot like bruised and rotting medlars in the orchard. Anna slithered about among this stuff for some minutes, while the child murmured blandly, 'This won't help you. Do you think this will help you, dear?'

'I'm not letting go of you,' Anna said, determinedly looking for a way out. 'I'm not.'

Suddenly the topography of the house unspooled itself for her and she saw where she had gone wrong. Clutching her burden firmly, she took the nearest staircase to the ground floor.

Eleanor shrieked and pulled at her hair. 'Norty! Norty Mummy!' Both of them were sweating, crying, covered in greyish earth.

Anna ran, murmuring, 'Oh, Ellie, poor Ellie,' one

moment and, 'Shut up. Shut up. Shut up,' the next. Suddenly she was in the kitchen, sweeping things off the worktop in search of the keys to the Volvo, and a man was in front of her, his mouth opening and shutting like someone trying to make words underwater.

He had black hair. Half-dressed, bleary-eyed, puzzled-looking, he was still pulling on a flannel shirt. He clutched at her arm. 'Anna!' he shouted. 'Anna, it's me! It's John!'

She examined him. 'So it is,' she said in a moment of clarity. Her panic subsided for an instant, only to wash back again. He was no good unless he could help. And she had the keys. 'Don't you know what's going on here?' she asked. 'Your special little girl has had the run of this house for weeks. She's been out there every night while you snored, in and out of everything, digging up the courtyard, assembling that hideous collection of objects. It was she who overturned the dustbin to get them back. It was she who buried them in the knot garden –'

He put his hands on her shoulders. 'Anna –'

'John, for God's sake listen. Do babies do that? In your experience?'

'Anna, of course they don't.'

'Then *listen*. This has something to do with Stella. That bloody horrible little flint idol –'

'Anna, please –'

She shook him off. 'There's no time,' she said. 'We're leaving. Something awful will happen here if we don't. Listen to her, John.' She held the baby up in front of him. 'Just listen to the things she's saying.'

'Dada,' wailed Eleanor, holding out her arms.

'Why is she so upset?' he asked. 'Have you upset her? She's a tiny girl, Anna –'

Anna gave a bitter laugh. 'That's all you know,' she said. 'I want you to come too, John. We're better off out of here. We should never have come back.'

He tried to take this in. 'But this is our house.'

She stared at him in complete disbelief. 'It's *Stella*'s house, John,' she told him. 'It always was.' She looked at her watch: almost morning. 'I've got to go now.' She caught a glimpse of herself in one of the hall mirrors – a woman with her car keys in her hand, already turning away. Her hair was disordered, her life toppling off the edge of itself. She was still in the unbleached cotton T-shirt she used to sleep in – it was one of his, oversized, bearing the legend 'Green World'.

He followed her to the doorway, clutching at the hem of it. 'Anna, you're overwrought. You can't just run off like this.'

They struggled briefly and in the confusion Eleanor managed to get her arms round his neck. 'Dada, Dada,' she screamed.

Anna dragged her away. 'Get off, John,' she said and, when he tried to catch hold of her again, pushed at him as hard as she could. He lost his balance and fell over backwards. 'Leave us! Leave us alone!' she cried.

She ran past him, down the steps, into the dawn.

Chapter Fourteen

ONCE THE CANDLES had gone out the blackness of the chamber was absolute. In all my life I had never known such intense darkness; it felt almost a physical pressure. Cats have good eyes: it's said we can see in the dark, and to an extent it's true, for we can find and focus whatever small light there may be in our surroundings. But no one can see light where light does not exist and in that pitch-dark there was none for my eyes to find. I sat crouched, waiting for whatever might happen next.

For a long time there was nothing. Nothing, that is, except for my own sense of apprehension and a growing suspicion that something was watching me; or if not watching me, exactly, that something was aware of me and was biding its time. Then there came a subtle change in the air pressure and a strong scent filled the cavern. It came from all around; it seemed to engulf me. It was every dead thing I had ever smelled; it was rotting fungus and hatching flies' eggs; it was soft flesh and old fish; it made my eyes water. And then a rumbling came that shuddered through the bones of my skull, through my chest and down into my legs. Where I touched the ground the vibration redoubled, till shudders of sound ran up and met the ripples running down and turned my limbs to liquid. I spun this way and that, as if I might somehow surprise the source of the noise into revealing itself, but all that followed was laughter. It was not the laugh I had heard before, which had been high and light; a child's laugh, wayward and impish, rather than this sound: a deep, malicious roar, which made my skin crawl with such repulsion that my bollocks retreated up under my fur and the ridge of fur along my back sprang so high that I could feel the chill of the air on the naked skin between the peaks.

Then whatever it was spoke. The rumbling continued through the chamber, but the voice sounded inside my head: 'Don't meddle in things that don't concern you, little beast,' it said to me. 'You are trespassing in the first place they made for me here. All this is beyond you; *I* am beyond you – for I am age itself; I am life.'

That it should address me so, angered me and somehow I found the gall to respond. 'I don't know what you are,' I said into the darkness, 'but to me you smell of death.'

'A cat – you are a cat, aren't you? It's always the cats that give me most trouble – a cat should know better than to judge me so,' it replied then, and I knew from the tickle that its scent made in my head that the thing which addressed me was female, 'for do not cats die many times, yet cling so tight to life that they return over and over again?'

'It is the way the Great Cat made us,' I said, not knowing where the words came from. 'She abhors waste.'

'The Great Cat!' The laughter reverberated around me. 'The Great Whore, more like. *She* certainly knew how to spread her gifts widely. We have much in common, she and I.'

The smell of decay grew stronger as her poison seeped into my head. 'I will not listen to you,' I said loudly and closed the muscles of my ears hard against the sound of her voice. Yet even though I could feel my ears furling inwards, the muscles contracting as tightly as an eyelid shutting, I could still hear every word.

'We want it all,' she continued, 'the Great Cat and I: the power and the glory, for ever and ever. The glory of living on and on; the power not to cease to exist; the glory and chaos of the sexual act, the energy and stench of it all. That's what we seek, this power over others, and to create ourselves again and again through them. You will never understand this urge. You should leave well alone, for you will never understand – you have no greatness in you, you males.'

'Who are you?' I called into the darkness.

There was a laugh; a pause. Then, 'Me? Oh, I have many names and many forms. Long ago, when I was strong and many worshipped me, I was known as Ishtar, the great mother, and the world trembled at my feet. The Phoenicians named me Balaath and

Astarte, and amid the barren hills of Sinai they prayed to the Mistress of Torquoise. Others called me Isis and brought their dead for me to revive. The fools – I ate their souls and grew stronger again. They learned, after a time; and for a time I slept and made dreams for them. In Europe, they knew me as Isar and named rivers for me. Perhaps it was for the cargoes I sent them, in the night. The Iceni tried to make me theirs; but I was not for the taking. Other people carved white symbols in the chalk to summon me; or made a pyramid of bones licked by fire. I like children to call me Izzie, or the White Lady. It seems – how shall I put this?' I could hear the sneering smile she made. 'More *friendly*, shall we say?

'And you, little beast. What will you call me?'

All I heard in my skull was the buzz of flies, then the scent in the cavern changed, subtly at first, so that the aroma of putrefaction lost its rankness, gradually becoming sweeter and more enticing so that my nose twitched in spite of itself. At last it became a wave of intoxifying musk that made the blood buzz in my head. It was the smell of a cat on heat, a female ready to mate, a queen offering herself to me. It was quite intoxicating.

'You see,' the voice went on, 'see my power and what I can offer you; and perhaps I shall, if you leave this place, leave the Great Knot alone and go away from here. The time is at hand. It will not be for long; then you may claim your reward.'

I opened my mouth to respond but that heady perfume enveloped the scent organ which we cats have there that enables us to assess smells with the greatest accuracy, and whatever repudiation I was forming in my mind evaporated. The walls themselves seemed to press in on me then and I knew I was lost.

The air wavered minutely. I thought for a moment that I was about to lose consciousness and fall into the power of that smell, that voice, but just as my joints started to wobble a spark of brilliance fractured the gloom, then became a glow that spread out from its source in the same way as do the concentric wavelets made by a raindrop falling in a lake. The effulgence undulated and expanded, until it had filled that dark place with a spectrum of colour; then the fox appeared, shedding rings of light in mid-gallop, rings of light that broke as if on an invisible shore and melted away into the once more darkening walls.

'Come with me, Orlando!' he cried and when I continued to stand there like an idiot, he barked at me, and then I felt the nip of his teeth on my neck accompanied by a sharp, searing pain. 'Run, you fool!'

He reopened the highway through which he had come and the rainbow rings swept round me like a sea. Suddenly my feet were my own again and I followed him away from that cavern and into the shrieking winds of a wild road.

Behind us, a howl of rage rose and crashed like a storm.

'What was that thing?' I asked the fox a few minutes later as we lay panting beneath the great oak on

Ashmore Common. 'It said it was called the White Lady and much besides, but I did not understand it.'

Loves A Dustbin ran a long pink tongue over his long black lips and regarded me with a wary eye. He looked exhausted. 'I am not sure,' he admitted at last. 'I felt a greater disruption than usual on the roads around the village from a distance and came as fast as I could. Could it be the dream maker? I asked myself and at once dismissed the thought as a superstitious fancy. But now that I have experienced its presence, I do wonder . . .'

I had no idea what he was talking about, but the very mention of the word 'dream' made me even more uneasy. 'Who is this dream maker? Is it the White Lady?' I asked at last, though I could tell he did not really want me to question him further.

For a while he was silent; then he barked a laugh. 'I really did think all these tales were just nonsense to scare kittens with and it would hardly be fair for me to claim that I have much understanding of it; the thing derives, after all, from a cat's world-view. What little I know of the dream maker I heard from an old cat who was once my friend, the oldest and wisest of all the cats I ever met. He was known, among many things, as the Majicou, but I never knew whether or not it was his true name. He had many lives and I knew him in his last two only. For a long while he was the guardian of the wild roads, and his tale is a long one and only to be recounted at a safer time than this. He once told me what he called "The legend of the dream maker", though whether the story ever had any historical inspiration, or whether it derived merely from superstitions he did not know, but this is what I can remember of it:

'He said that the one you call the Great Cat created the world and everything in it (though we foxes have a different tale, as you may imagine). She dreamed herself into being in the midst of the void, so that light and dark, earth and water and air sprang from her eyes, followed by every bird and creature that we know. But human beings – being greedy and impatient – escaped from the Great Cat's eye and ran out into the new world before they were fully made, since they were still all pale and hairless, and able to walk only on two legs. They feared the One Who Had Made Them so much that they ran away from her light to make their homes in the caves and dark places of the world where they thought she could not see them. Woe for the world that she was not the Great Fox' – a pale golden light came into his tawny eye – 'for *she* would have gobbled them up without a second thought for their impertinence, and for the perfidy they would later commit against our kind. Lucky for them that the Great Cat was more benevolent, even towards her most misbegotten creations. In their caves, in the comfort of the darkness, the humans dreamed, having learned the skill from the One Who Made Them –'

'I know!' I burst in joyfully, for I had heard a version of this story before, long ago. 'This is the tale old Hawkweed told me, when we were out hunting rabbits for the first time. And there was something in it about the little yellow flowers called hawkweed too. And a lot about dreams and the highways . . .' I paused, feeling foolish, since I could not remember the rest of the tale at all, let alone the point he had being trying to make.

Loves A Dustbin regarded me wearily. 'Your grandfather always said you had the patience of a gnat and the brain of one, too. That you were forever interrupting and not paying attention. Now is the time to concentrate your mind, Orlando, for there's usually a kernel of wisdom in the middle of stories like these; and it may be that the fate of all of us, including your lost sister and poor Millie, as well as all those in your household, rests on the way we bring what little knowledge we have to bear upon the problem –'

'Millie!' I interrupted again, without a thought for what else he had just said, for the image of Millefleur was clear in my head and the memory of her stung. 'You said "Millie". Do you know where she is?'

'I do,' he said, but volunteered nothing more.

'Then tell me,' I pressed him anxiously. 'Tell me where she is so I can rescue her.'

'That can wait. It must,' Loves A Dustbin said heavily. 'For there are worse matters for us to attend to before then.'

I was aghast. The dogfox knew where Millie was and he wouldn't tell me. I felt my heart swell up until there was a terrible pressure in my chest, pushing against my ribs and up into my throat. 'But I love her!' I croaked at last.

'I know,' said the fox. He gave me a knowing look,

his long face grave and still. 'You've loved her for years. Even so.'

I stared at him. What had I just said? 'But it's really Lydia I love,' I started, then faltered, confused. Images of the two cats danced in my head: Lydia as I had once known her – lithe and golden and proud, lying stretched out across the deck of the narrowboat, her scent pervading the air, the epitome of the Great Cat's every line and grace, a very princess among felines, for whose favour a dozen tomcats would fight – Millefleur, the moonlight shining in her wicked eyes and flickering off the silver earring she had once worn. I thought about the strange little tuft she had on the top of her head; I remembered the way she had leapt and pounced in her lynx form on the wild roads, and how luminous her white belly fur had seemed to me that night when she had offered to lie with me. And then I remembered Liddy's many cruelties to me and to others. I thought of how she hoarded food when the shrubbery cats were starving, how she had neglected to teach her kittens well, leaving the hard work to me, how she had flown at me in fury and then disappeared for days without a word; and how all the while I had made excuses for her, telling myself that it was only the hardships she had suffered at the hands of the witch which had driven her to such meanness of spirit. But now in my truest heart I knew that Lydia had always been this way: selfish, manipulative and as vain and shallow as the canary that falls in love with its own image in the mirror that hangs in its cage; and that her traumas

341

had only enabled her to get away with ever greater lapses of behaviour.

Last of all, I recalled Millie's words, spoken in anger and sadness just before her capture: how she had called me 'a brave, beautiful cat' and said that she loved me . . .

The dogfox looked at me askance. 'Well,' he said at last. 'Am I right, or am I right?'

It was as if a cloud cleared in my head. 'You're right,' I said.

He gave me his long, lopsided grin. 'I usually am,' he admitted boastfully. Then he grew solemn again. 'But things are as they are, Orlando. We must leave Millie where she is until we have untangled this knot –'

'But she is in danger!' I cried out wildly. 'She was taken by the witch's servants, the Two Who Look Like One.'

'She is in no immediate danger. Trust me in this, Orlando.'

I gave him a hard look. 'I will never forgive you if anything happens to her.'

'I will never forgive myself.' He gazed back at me steadily and I found my panic subsiding. After a while he took a deep breath and continued, 'Now, back to the story. Back to the dreams. The Majicou told me that some of the humans dreamed up a creator of their own to worship, one they imagined in their own image: pale and two-legged. But they dreamed her massive and powerful, to challenge the Great Cat, and so she became. She made them fertile and those who yearned hardest – and it was usually the females – were granted many dreams to fuel the fire of their desires. Those dreams are damaging to the highways, as you know; and the White Lady – or whatever else she calls herself – revels in that damage. Her favourites she rewards with long life: once, the Majicou said, he came upon one of her followers – a woman who had lived many lives, such as cats enjoy. At the beginning of her life, many centuries ago, she was the niece of a queen's sorcerer, who came from a place called the Dead Lake: Mortlake, on the River Thames. There, under his tutelage, she learned of the existence of a substance humans called the Elixir of Life, which was said to elongate their lives infinitely and to maintain beauty. She made her search for this stuff her life's work – or rather, the work of all her many lives.

'Through the breeding of cats, and the potions she extracted from them and their young, she made her magic, though I do not think she ever perfected her recipe. I have come to believe that we have seen these magics at work, you and I, Orlando.

'The Majicou did not know her name. But we do: Stella Herringe, the witch of Ashmore.'

'But she died in the fire at Nonesuch,' I said at once, frowning. A large idea was forming in my head, but as yet it was shapeless and confused.

'She did. In that life, at least . . .' Loves A Dustbin glanced hesitantly over at me and I thought I detected anxiety in his gaze, as if he were concerned that I might think him mad. 'I once encountered something of this sort for myself. It was a man, that time; or it had been, once. I knew him as the Alchemist and by various foul means he had managed to preserve his life for far longer than its natural span.' He shuddered. 'Humans can be terrifyingly ruthless and unscrupulous in their pursuit of power, or in fleeing their fear of death. The worst of them allow nothing to stand in their way.'

There was a tiny click in my head as if an air passage had just unblocked itself. 'It's the child,' I said.

'The child?'

'My people's baby,' I clarified at once, suddenly sure of my ground. 'The witch is trying to come back through it.'

The fox frowned at me. It was, I conceded to myself, a bizarre statement, especially to anyone who had not lived in the presence of Eleanor and seen the things I had seen. For much of the time the baby seemed quite normal, as small humans go. It cried and smiled, and chased us cats about the place as any child might, but sometimes its natural liveliness and curiosity would be replaced by a kind of demonic energy. There was also the smell of it, that wavered in and out of recognisable range; sometimes the softy milky scent you'd expect from a young creature, then, within moments, the ferocious musk of the calling female. And when the smell was strongest, its eyes would change: brown-green as a fresh hazelnut they were most of the time; but when the child's scent changed they flashed as green as a rose-chafer's wing case, as green as malachite. I had been close to that eye colour before, held up by strong, hard clawlike hands when the witch had caught me outside her knot garden.

There was also the strange matter of the dreams: contorted and fiery, dreams in which my sister seemed to be trapped.

I had not paid enough attention, I realised, to the baby, in the midst of my own difficulties.

I told the fox all this. A long silence followed while he digested it and then I added, 'Also, it collects things, the baby.'

Loves A Dustbin narrowed his eyes. 'What sort of things?'

So I told him about the bits and pieces it adopted, the things which disappeared, only to reappear in the knot garden – the doll's head, the wailing tin box, the shiny black object which contained strands of black human hair that smelled disturbingly of John, the spoon, the bone doll – and then I told him about the dreams that had followed. 'It was as if the objects generated the dreams. And each time they did, the wild roads around Nonesuch warped in such a way that I could move through time to see where the things came from.'

The dogfox nodded rapidly. 'That'll be the disruption I came upon,' he said in a matter-of-fact sort of way. 'A great tangle of highways, many of them indistinct; some of them blocked. It's where I saw Vita, too.'

'She said I must chase down all the dreams and eat them up, otherwise she would stay trapped there.'

A change had come over the fox following the conclusion of this discussion. Where before he had seemed weary and old to me, now his eyes shone bright as topaz, his whole frame alive with energy. He seemed impatient, fidgety, eager to be off. 'There's a relationship between all these things, Orlando: the wild roads, the objects, the dreams and the witch; and between all of them and whatever it was I just rescued you from,' he said briskly, standing up and stretching out his legs. He pushed with his nose in an irritated fashion at the haunch where the fur had paled, as if it were not responding as he would wish, then turned back to me, his gaze fierce with determination. 'The end is in sight, Orlando. I can feel it in my bones. The child will have another object any day now, I'd say. Keep your eyes open. Chase down whatever dream it makes. I'll be back.'

With that he was off, loping smoothly into the undergrowth.

I watched him go with a shade of annoyance. It seemed to me that he had discovered something of his own in what I had just related to him and had decided not to share it with me; rather, like my grandfather in his own high-pawed manner, he had treated me like a kitten and refused to entrust me with something he did not think me ready to deal with.

A few days later the next object turned up, just as the fox had predicted. I found the baby preoccupied with something in the kitchen one morning. It was sitting on the floor, crooning. Every so often it would lift the small object to its face, kiss it and murmur something to it. Then it would bang the thing on the ground, where it made sharp contact with the flagstones. I could not see, from my vantage point in the doorway, what it was, so I waited until Anna carried Ellie to her cot for her afternoon nap.

When I knew the child was asleep, I jumped up on to the chair beside the cot and craned over the wooden bars, my front paws braced carefully on the top rail to ensure I could make a swift getaway if it was required. In Ellie's hands the thing gleamed dully; but her fingers obscured the larger part of it. Frustrated, I stretched a paw into the cot and snagged the coverlet with a claw. The drag of the fabric moved the sleeping child's hand a fraction, but still I could not see. I pulled again, harder this time, and the object slid free. I found myself staring into the face of a green-eyed girl in a rich, elaborate robe, whose hands rested in her lap, where lay a pair of soft grey gloves. It seemed innocuous enough. I blinked and, as I did so, the picture shifted almost imperceptibly, so that where I had glimpsed the pretty girl, I now thought I had glimpsed an ancient, naked woman clutching a pair of unhappy-looking blue-grey kittens by the throat so hard that their eyes bulged. I recoiled, horrified.

With a wail, the baby woke up.

I was so transfixed by the painted miniature that I did not react fast enough, and suddenly Eleanor had grabbed me by a leg and had dragged me into the cot. I twisted and fought, but she was appallingly strong. A moment later her chubby hands were around my throat and she was squeezing with a strength that belied her apparent nature. I stared up, only to find the eyes of the witch upon me.

'Ca –' she said and squeezed harder.

I felt my limbs go soft and useless in her grip. This is it, I thought then. Inconsequentially, I heard a car start up outside and then pull away, the sound droning off into the distance. Anna going out some- where, I thought, leaving me with her monstrous child. This is my death. But not my first death, the thought came to me, and probably not my last. Will I come back? I wondered, and was still pondering this when the door to the room came fully open and John walked in.

I knew this because the baby greeted him.

'John,' she said, quite distinctly. And again, 'John.'

It was not a child's voice, but that of a fully mature woman: low and soft.

At once, the pressure on my neck relaxed so that I could suck in a breath. The inside of my head went from soft and muzzy brown to a series of electric blues and reds. White-yellow lights shot across my vision; then I was assailed by a powerful sexual scent and, when I looked up, the child's eyes had taken on that disconcertingly piercing green.

I leapt out of the cot.

John watched me leave the room with a bemused expression on his face, as if he were not quite sure where, or even who, he was.

*

I ran and didn't stop running till I reached a series of highways I knew like the back of my paw, highways I was certain were uncontaminated by the strange disruptions at Nonesuch. The freezing winds scoured through me, a series of vicious, icy combs removing from my fur every trace of the vile scent that had clung to me.

I lost myself for a while in my lion form, let my mind meld down into pure sensation as my massive paws struck the iron-hard earth and my muscles bunched and stretched endlessly, on and on. I turned sharp corners, took minor tributaries, let the compass winds blow me where they would. Outside, I could see glimpses of a pleasant afternoon, a land waking from frost, mists burned off in the hollows, the sun low and bright across a sky so pale it was almost white. I caught snatches of birdcall:

Too cold; fly south.

Yes, yes! To the lake!

A brace of barnacle geese.

My berries, my berries!

No mine; keep your thieving beak off them!

A pair of male robins, puffed up with belligerence facing each other off on the top of a hawthorn, glimpsed as a double blur of vermilion.

I heard the caw of crows circling an ash tree in which a barn owl sat hunched up and disorientated, its hoots of protest a haunting counterpoint to the rasping chorus of its attackers.

Dead rabbit still warm; come eat! A magpie to its mate.

I thundered on till my lungs ached from my

exertions and at last burst out of the wild road on to the summit of Cresset Beacon, my head swimming with images, alive and clean again with the tastes and scents of the natural world.

I took a couple of paces forward, shook my mane in the chilly air.

There was a gasp, then the sound of voices.

Standing right in front of me, very close together, were two people. Shocked by their proximity, I let out a roar and took a step forward. The woman was staring straight at me, her eyes round with surprise and a sort of savage, triumphant delight. Her companion looked entirely terrified.

It took a moment for me to realise that they were seeing me in my wild form, which no human should ever witness: it upsets their sense of their place in the world.

It took another moment after that to recognise them as Anna and the man from the church, who smiled and was kind to us cats, but who had lately begun to smell very odd. I turned at once and leapt back into the highway from which I had issued.

That night the dreams came thick and fast. The folk of Ashmore were beset by nightmares of rot and pain, and the taste of them was bitter. But still I did my job. My old grandfather would have been proud of me, I thought. I dragged the last of the smoking dream globes down from the roof of the wild road and trod upon it hard. It squirmed beneath my toes, but I was used to that. The first dreams I had caught, under Hawkweed's stern eye, had disconcerted me with their writhings and attempts to escape – I had lost more than one of them into the highway winds and had to chase them like a fool – but I was rather more proficient now. I bent my head to the gelatinous casing and bit into it so that its liquids spilled out over my toes in a hot gush. I knew now that the solution in which the dream swam was not the crucial element; rather, it was the matter of the thing that must be despatched before it could flee out on to the wild roads. I examined the contents. Another corpse dream: this time a woman, standing over her own dead self, her face a mask of disgust and panic. Such a fear of death that humans have. Such a horror of the grave. It is so easy for the cruel to terrorise them. I was almost beginning to feel affectionate towards the people of the village, for they were my charges and I their guardian: to me fell the task of keeping them safe from the harms that came by night. I remembered my grandfather making pronouncements like this, and had always thought him arrogant and self-deluded for doing so. But now I saw the truth of it and for the first time in my life I felt as if my role of Dreamcatcher of Ashmore held something of value after all. It was a strange feeling. I ate the dream down, corpse, woman and all; and just as I was swallowing the last morsels a great wind came and with it something that roared past, scorching the very tips of my ears.

My head shot up at once. There, in the ceiling of the highway, a fiery dream globe blazed and hissed. It had an aura of dark-red flames that shaded almost to black where they joined the main sac and glowed an incandescent white at the head of each leaping tongue. It hovered overhead as if to taunt me; then, against all possibility, turned once more into the howling wind and headed back in the direction from which it had come.

Every time it got out of my sight I would round a corner and there it would be, idling its time as if waiting for me to catch it up, bobbing in the turbulence overhead. Yet as soon as I leapt to catch it, it would disentangle itself from the twisting energies of the highway and dodge away from me to continue its journey.

I trailed it all the way back to Nonesuch. There, the highways made their usual weird, contorted transitions through the history of the house. I glimpsed previous incarnations of rooms as I ran: windows shuttered and curtained; undraped and broken with the moon shining through on to dust and dereliction; chandeliers and candlelight; people dancing across rich carpets; banqueting at long tables; couples grappling with one another in dark corners, bent over furniture, on all fours on the bare floor. I saw cats, too – real cats and ghost cats – a skein of life winding its way between the human inhabitants. Some watched the people with undisguised curiosity; some sat nervously grooming themselves, ears twitching, ready for flight; others were more shade than substance, their eyes wide and haunted. After a while I realised that one of them, amidst this tide of events, was always still and as solid as myself.

It was a neat-looking tabby cat with a slightly

ragged ear. 'You'd better hurry,' it said, 'or you'll lose your dream. It would be a shame to come so far and then fail, wouldn't it, Orlando?'

It was Vita.

'She didn't boil you, then, the witch?' I found myself asking stupidly.

'She'd like to,' Vita said. 'Isn't it what she does with all cats?'

'Can't you come with me?'

Vita shook her head sadly. 'The highways are all tangled up. The Great Knot is tightening. You have to eat the dreams, Orlando, or I'll be tied right up in the middle of it. Now hurry after the dream. She's drawing it to the courtyard.'

I must have looked puzzled, for she added, 'The one with the cages. Where the witch kept her breeding females.' Her eyes went misty and her voice dropped almost to a whisper. 'I saw Mother there. She was pregnant with us, but she knew me all the same. "Tell Orlando I'm very proud of him," she said. Then she added, "He will avenge us all."'

I stared blankly at her for a moment, trying to digest this latest strangeness, but she got up and, with a flick and a twist of her now adult body, dived into a tributary of the wild roads that made up this part of the Great Knot.

I followed the main highway along the Long Corridor, to the room where one wall had been painted with a garden scene. There, the walls were flushed with jumping red light and I knew I had found my prey. It was waiting for me there, unsteady with some trapped emotion, some intention to wound and damage. As I entered the room, it swooped down like a hawk and set my mane alight. Suddenly, my head was engulfed in fire. I couldn't think straight. I could feel my heart thundering in my chest, as the awful smell of burning hair brought back to me the memory of the last fire I had been in – in this very house, this very spot almost, the winter before last, when the witch had burned along with many of her cats. I had barely made it out alive. So it thought to burn me, did it? We'd see about that. A combination of fury and smoke was making my eyes water: I blinked fiercely, but by the time my vision was clear, all I could see was the dream coming at me again. This time I gave a mighty leap and pinioned it between both front paws. Even with the flames blazing into my scalp, I held on for grim death.

The dream twisted in my grip like a maddened rat. It was horribly strong. Just as I thought I had the better of it, it drew away from me so hard that I thought my teeth would be pulled from my head. Over and over we tumbled, until I was not sure where I was; all I could see was the blur of the dream sac before my eyes and a wild mist of dark smoke. I could smell myself burning: not just the awful acridity of charred hair, but the sweeter smell of scorching flesh. With all the effort I could muster, I bit harder and after what seemed an age, the dream made a sighing sound and relinquished a gush of sticky liquid that burst out over my head, extinguishing the flames in my mane.

I threw it down then, as roughly as I could, and trapped it between my paws. I snarled at it; I roared my hatred and triumph as I felt its life force dwindling. At last it gave up its contents to me. A man sat in one of the upstairs rooms at Nonesuch on a tall chair. His dark hair was caught back in a tail; but I knew him instantly as John, or some earlier version of John, even though he had his back to me. He was hunched over, his right hand working with a fine brush at a tiny oval picture. Beyond him, where rays of pale afternoon light filtered through the thick diamond panes to illuminate the far side of the room, I could see the head and shoulder of a woman, framed by a fall of long black hair. I pushed my head further into the dream, the better to understand what I was seeing.

The man was painting: a tiny portrait of a young woman, richly dressed. He worked with his face close to the painting, adding minute strokes of colour to a glorious brocade robe. Without the brown and crackled patina it had acquired over the intervening centuries, the detail of the work was miraculous. I moved in closer, for something nagged at me, something out of true; and there, beyond him on a plush settle, sat the witch.

Naked and wrinkled she was, and as old as the hills, her skin stretched tightly across her thin frame like the skin on a chicken's carcass. Her lips were moving, for she talked soft and low to him throughout this whole procedure, and her eyes – as green as a spell – never left his face. In her lap there cowered two kittens, a pale blue-grey. She held them tightly around their necks, so that they struggled for air. Their little eyes bulged with panic. One of them managed to free a tiny paw and strike out at its captor, drawing a long thin line of red across the back of her hand. The witch swore in fury and looked down at her wound.

As soon as her gaze was averted from him, the man stirred from his stuporous task, looked up and shook his head. He seemed confused, disorientated. He glanced once at the woman on the settle in front of him, then down at the painting he had made. He frowned and opened his mouth to speak, but at that moment the witch looked up and said something to him and he settled back to his task without a word.

Then those wicked green eyes met mine, and she said something to me and laughed, showing me her empty gums. There was a thin wail, a sickening crunching sound, and then silence. I dragged my eyes from her face. The kitten that had scratched her lay limp as a rag in her lap, its head skewed awkwardly, its neck broken.

With a rage I had not known I could summon, I opened my jaws wide and flew at her. With fangs and claws I tore at her and the rest of the fabric of the dream until there was nothing of it left.

Then I lay where I was in a daze.

When I finally came back to myself, I was lying in a room I had not seen before. It was roughly circular in design and white, with thick plasterwork into which small holes appeared to have been hollowed out, and someone seemed to have been storing odd bits and pieces in these rough niches. I went up to one wall where the plaster was coming away to reveal patches of shining rock and sniffed cautiously. Back came the age-old scent, the aroma of mulch and leaf mould, water upon stone, that I had smelled not so very long before. But now, instead of the pitch darkness I had endured here when the candles were burned out, the room was illuminated by a single shaft of pale moonlight from a small hole high up in the roof, out of which a slow drift of soil was falling. *Another time entirely*, I thought; and when I looked down at the ground, I found that my paws were no longer those of a lion, foursquare and great-clawed, but those of a cat and a filthy one at that. The wild road which had caught me and the dream in its toils had spewed us out on its contorted passage and left us here, in the White Lady's room. A huge, complicated knot pattern covered most of the surface of the floor and at one end, where the gloom deepened, I could just make out the first steps of what appeared to be a narrow staircase. *A later addition*, I thought disconnectedly, *made when the house was built to enable the witch to come and go in peace*. I was about to see where the stairs would take me, when there was a great commotion overhead, followed by a small avalanche of earth. Then a pair of child's hands – incongruously white – appeared through the hole in the ceiling, followed by Eleanor's head.

Her eyes gleamed as she saw me. 'Ca'!' she cried, and, 'kill you!'

She lurched down, her face demonic with

triumph at having cornered me at last; then her expression changed to one of panic. 'No, Mummy, no!' she shouted, and there was a struggle in which Ellie appeared to be the loser, for a moment later she was visibly hauled backwards. With fury, she waved her arms around. Something flew out of her hand and struck the ground a few feet away from me. A second afterwards she was gone and the moonlight filtered down, serene and uninterrupted.

I approached the object with a heavy heart. I already knew what it would be. There it lay, face up in the dust and cobwebs: a tiny miniature painting encased in silver. Under its cracked brown glaze a pale, tranquil girl in a rich robe sat with her hands lying in her lap, demurely clutching a pair of soft grey gloves.

Chapter Fifteen

SIX THIRTY IN the morning and Anna Dawe, wearing a 'Green World' T-shirt tucked into a pair of oil-stained Levis rather too large for her, had stopped to use the toilet in a Little Chef on the main road about thirty miles west of London. Commuter traffic was beginning to build up on the dual carriageway outside, but as yet the restaurant was empty except for a man in a business suit warming his hands on his cup and smiling wanly out of the steamed-up windows at the rain. Anna sat where she could keep an eye on the Volvo and ordered tea, with a double chocolate muffin and a newspaper she would eventually leave on the table unopened. Every time a car pulled into the car park outside she looked up, expecting to see her husband getting out of a silver-grey Mercedes. This was unfair, she knew.

Eleanor, who had fallen into a kind of exhausted trance the moment they were away from Nonesuch, now sat obediently in the high chair provided, gazing round at the fairyland of the Little Chef, which she described to herself in hushed and confidential whispers – '. . . an' flahrs,' she said. 'Flahrs.'

She was dressed in the motley of bits and pieces Anna kept in the Volvo for emergencies. Her cheeks were flushed, and there was a stain on the front of her OshKosh dungarees where she had thrown up in a fit of rage, but at least she was speaking in her own voice again. Anna, whose memory of the night's other voices was unpleasantly clear, thought, *If I can get her right away from that place she'll stop it. She'll stop doing those things and just be an ordinary little girl again.* As a corollary, she thought, *Something awful is going on back there. I can save us, but I can't save John.* The bleakness of this went through her like a crack in glass. Everything he was, everything they had ever been to one another, seemed to fill her – until she was like a tumbler of cold, clear water on a summer afternoon – then, in the same instant, drain away again. How she would spend the rest of her life without him, she couldn't imagine.

This decision, already made a dozen times, gave her no comfort. She considered it for a moment or two, then drank the rest of her tea as quickly as she could. There was nothing else to be done. 'Come on, miss,' she said, lifting her daughter unceremoniously out of the high chair and going up to pay.

Eleanor waited until they were at the cash desk, then began to shriek at the top of her voice, clutching piteously at the hands of the woman behind the till. 'Dada!' she cried. 'My *Dada*!'

Anna managed to laugh. 'What can you do with them when they're like this?' she asked.

'I'm sure I don't know, dear,' came the bland reply. 'They're a lot of effort at that age, aren't they?'

Anna nodded hastily. 'Yes, oh yes. Yes, they are.'

'She looks tired if you ask me,' said the woman at the till, eyeing Anna's clothes. 'Was everythink all right for you?'

'It was very nice, thanks.'

Anna filled the Volvo's cavernous tank with petrol. She cleaned its windscreen. She sat in the driver's seat with the engine turned off and thought, *I can't save him. Not when he insists there's nothing to be saved from. I really can't.* Then she put the Volvo in gear and drove out into the traffic, where instead of taking the carriageway to complete the journey to London she performed an illegal U-turn and, to the accompaniment of blaring horns and shouts of rage, turned back towards Ashmore.

By the time she got there Eleanor had fallen sound asleep in her car seat and the rain had turned to a kind of Scotch mist, a thickening of the air that left tiny cold beads of moisture on everything it touched. Low cloud lay along the edge of the downs. The village street was quiet, the churchyard grey and sodden. Anna let the Volvo coast to a halt and switched off the engine. Silence, but for the muffled call of a rook. She sat there tiredly for a moment, thinking, *This is the right thing. It's the right thing to do.* Then she got out and went round to the passenger side to try to extract the car seat without waking Eleanor.

Francis Baynes must have heard the Volvo arrive,

because when she looked up he was already opening the rectory door.

Anna waved. 'Hello!' she called.

Francis seemed tired and nervous. He hadn't shaved and he was still in the clothes he had worn at Cresset Beacon the afternoon before.

'You look worse than I do,' she said. 'Can I come in?'

'No. No, I don't think that would be a good thing.'

'Francis?'

He managed a smile. 'After yesterday,' he said quietly, 'it wouldn't feel –' He shrugged. 'Well, it wouldn't feel like the best idea.'

'You're taking this too much to heart,' she told him. 'You mustn't be silly.' His expression made her add, 'I'm sorry. That was patronising.' She put Eleanor carefully down on the front step and took one of his hands in hers. It was so cold that the touch of it threw everything else out of her mind. 'My God, Francis,' she said, 'you're freezing. Are you all right?'

'Quite all right, thanks.'

'Do you ever heat this place?' she asked. 'Or don't they give you any money for that, either?' Tired, she saw now, wasn't quite the word to describe him. It was more than that. All the youth – all the certainty – seemed to have leaked out of him. Had she done this? It was ridiculous. 'Francis,' she admonished him, 'stop this. It was my fault. And it wasn't anything anyway.'

He withdrew his hand. 'No,' he said. 'No, I see that, I quite see that.'

He would have added more, she thought, and they might have got to some better understanding of how he felt, but at that moment two things happened. He seemed to hear something which caused him to turn round and look back into the house behind him. And at almost the same instant Eleanor made a small, fractious noise and stirred in the car seat at his feet. Waking up, she transfixed him with her bright green eyes. 'Gidgiee,' she announced.

Francis looked startled. 'Ah. The baby. Isn't it rather damp for her to be out?'

'They're quite sturdy, Francis.'

He smiled again. 'So I'm told.'

'She's why I've come,' Anna said. 'Francis, I need you to look after her for an hour.'

'I'm sorry,' he said. 'I can't do that.'

'Francis –'

'No.' He took a step or two backwards, shaking his head rapidly.

Anna pursued him. 'Francis! This is absurd.'

A faint stale smell filled the hall, as if he was keeping an animal somewhere else in the house. He had actually tried to close the door in her face. 'Francis, look at me. What's the matter with you? I can't believe you're doing this!'

'It isn't the place for her,' he repeated, 'just now.'

'What are you saying?'

'That I can't take her. Is there someone you can call?' He offered Anna the telephone, which he kept buried in a litter of church leaflets on the hall table.

'How pathetic your life has made you,' she said.

'You were frightened of me. You were frightened of the lion. Now you're frightened of looking after a baby.'

He stared away from her.

She took his hand again quickly. 'I'm sorry. I'm sorry. Francis, please. I have to have an hour without her. All I want is an hour. Half an hour, Francis. I promise I'll be back in half an hour. Look, here's a bar of chocolate. She'll do anything for that. Or just switch the television on – do they let vicars have television? Francis, she's asleep anyway. Give me half an hour, Francis. Please? I'm leaving Nonesuch, but I can't go without talking to John.'

The rectory door slammed behind her.

She ran back to the Volvo, started it up and, rather than waste time turning it round, plunged straight into the maze of lanes north and east of the village. These she would normally have avoided. They were ill-kept and unevenly surfaced. Summer storms washed loose gravel across their adversely cambered corners, which farm machinery then larded with mud. You were always unsighted by some hedge or bank, confused by the way the sunlight flickered through the trees. Still, she drove as fast as she dared; and as she drove, she rehearsed the things she was going to say to John Dawe.

'We could leave all this behind. Live in London. I could work again, I could get us a house. I'd love to do that. We could be an ordinary family together, with a house of our own and a garden, and you could write your book about dreams.'

Her eyes stung with sentiment and self-pity. 'Oh, John,' she said aloud. 'You're so useless.'

This made her think of Francis Baynes.

'It wouldn't hurt you to help,' she had insisted. 'And it's important, Francis, it's so important.' If he had understood he didn't show it, but only looked down at Eleanor (now fully awake and studying him with a sort of disinterested amusement) and said heavily, 'All right. But this is a mistake.' When he met Anna's eye again his expression had been so at odds with itself, so difficult to interpret, that Anna wondered if he wasn't right. But what was the alternative? Eleanor mustn't go back to Nonesuch. If anything was true, it was that. 'It will only be half an hour, Francis,' she had promised. Now she told herself, *I couldn't have done anything else. And men always plead to be let off. It's one of the least attractive things about them.* Just as she was thinking that, a woman stepped out in front of the car.

'Christ!' said Anna and jammed her foot on the brake.

Francis Baynes's room smelled strongly of sex. The sheets were half off the bed and on the floor all around it were scattered empty cups, plates of half-eaten food and discarded Kleenex tissues. Two large church candles were burning on his writing table. Francis stood at the window with the child in his arms. It seemed to be asleep again. He cupped its head gently in the palm of his hand and said, 'I won't do it.'

'Oh yes, you will,' said the woman on the bed.

When he came back upstairs he had found her sprawled out with her legs open, eating tomatoes, biting into them so carelessly that the seeds in their greenish jelly dribbled down her chin and into the bed. Now, though, she was squatting up near the pillows in her characteristic posture, looking alert but distant. The muslin dress had rucked itself up round her waist. Her breasts had fallen forward and spilled out. 'You'll do it,' she stated.

Francis stared at her huge brown nipples. He swallowed. 'I won't.'

'Shut up.' She closed her eyes and concentrated. 'Izzie's up to something, sweetie. She doesn't want it spoilt.' A brief, inturned smile flickered across her lips, as if, somewhere inside herself, she were looking not at the room, or Francis, but some other part of the village. 'There. Two places at once. If you want cleverness, leave it to Izzie. There! See? But you can't, can you? Because you're a religious man, Francis, you're such a moral man. Anyway, we've got the kiddy now. And this will keep your skinny bitch out of the way –'

There was an instant of slow motion – a weightless moment in which Anna, narrowing her eyes in puzzlement, was able to see quite clearly the long brown muslin dress the woman wore, how her arms were raised in that meaningless, rehearsed-looking gesture, how she seemed to be carrying a bunch of primroses – then the Volvo gave an elephantine shudder, spun sideways and slid towards the hawthorn hedge at the side of the road. Anna steered into the skid. Nothing. 'Oh God,' she thought. 'Now I'm for it.'

It seemed to take for ever. The Volvo tilted up on two wheels, pondered things for a moment, then smashed its way through the hedge and toppled over the edge of the thirty-foot bank behind it. Anna hung on to the steering wheel until a sudden change of direction banged her head into the side window. She saw badly tuned TV shapes. She had already forgotten the woman in the brown dress. She felt ashamed of the self-pity which had overcome her a few minutes before and remembered, oddly enough, some advice her father had once given her: 'Only ever cry for someone else.'

But her last thought was, *What a bloody stupid thing to do*.

Millefleur lay in the darkness, remembering the saddest sight she had ever seen: the old manor house receding away from her through puffs of dust kicked up by the tyres of the car in which she was trapped, and Orlando, brave, sweet Orlando, pounding down the drive after her, his face, appearing and disappearing through the swirling exhaust fumes, a mask of pain and horror. If sheer willpower had been stronger than reinforced glass, she would have melted right through the back windscreen there and then, and tumbled out on to the gravel in front of him.

Instead she was here, in some lightless, sealed room in which a dozen or more cats of all ages, and both genders, slept and quarrelled and complained of the cold. She had been here for several days. They all had. No one had fed them in that time; no one had even opened the door. Every time self-pity threatened to overcome her, Millie would conjure up in her mind favourite places she had visited; friends she had known; fish she had eaten. She remembered a headland, whipped by salt-bearing winds, on which the sun beat down so hard that the patches of lichen on the speckled rocks glowed the same orange as the buoys that bobbed in the sheltered bay below; lying in a beech forest amid a haze of bluebells, watching small birds dart from branch to branch, unaware of her presence; stalking the pebbly foreshore of a sleeping fishing port at dawn, catching hard green crabs with claws that nipped and pinched. She remembered an old brindled female to whom she had poured out her heart. And most often of all she thought about a certain marmalade tomcat and wondered if she would ever see him again.

It seemed to be some kind of holding pen they were in, somewhere to be kept on the way to somewhere else, but where they were headed none of them knew. For the first couple of days there had been an excitable air to the place. Cats had exchanged greetings, talked about themselves and boasted about their comfortable homes; their regular meals; their extensive territories; their kittens; the usual stuff of chatter. The second day, hungry and with nothing to sustain them except a bowl of stale water and a dripping tap, they had talked about nothing but food. Lately, though, anxiety had bred rumours and those were the worst.

'It'll be for our fur,' someone said; but this was immediately refuted by a gruff male voice.

'If they wanted us in good condition, they'd bleeding well feed us.'

'Perhaps it was a mistake and they'll come and let us go.'

'More likely we'll be left here to rot.'

'They're going to use us for dog food, that's what I reckon.'

A chorus of wails followed this.

'I'd heard it was for cosmetics – perfume, that sort of thing.'

There was a silence. Then, 'That's nice,' came a hesitant female voice close to Millie.

Someone explained exactly what that might mean, and Millie felt the shape next to her curl itself into a ball and begin to tremble.

After that, Millie could stand it no more. She got up, stretched her legs and made yet another inspection of the room. She had done this every day, as much for exercise as in the genuine expectation of finding an escape route. The place seemed to be constructed of featureless concrete, windowless and with a single wooden door, locked with a key high up. Bolts Millie could manage. A lock was a different matter. She made it through to the back wall, after much bad-tempered shuffling and muttering from the cats she disturbed, and started to work her way along the seam between the wall and floor. Nothing. She turned the corner towards the dripping tap and walked into an immovable object.

'Watch where you are going, clumsy daughter of a sewer rat!' The voice was deep, accented and rather upper-class.

Millie felt her hackles rise. 'I beg your pardon?'

'To think I should be reduced to this – left to rot in a filthy sty with the hoi polloi, as if I am a nobody, a nothing. It is a nonsense; a tragedy.'

Millie, despite herself, was amused. 'And just who are you, then, to think yourself so far above the rest of us poor hoi polloi?'

'My name is Circassian Gogol II, Supreme Champion Russian Blue of countless shows, winner of Finest Stud Cat, prized for my beauty and for my legendary staying power. I have serviced a thousand females, sired a million perfect kittens. Ah, the kittens, they would all have been show winners, had they . . .' His voice tailed away to a mournful drone.

Something clicked in Millefleur's head. 'Excuse me, Circus – whatever you're called, you don't happen to have a father who lived out Drychester way and was the local dreamcatcher there, do you?'

In the darkness she saw his eyes flicker briefly as if she had caught his interest. 'I might,' he conceded. 'But I had rather not tell more of my tragic circumstances to someone whom I have not even been introduced.'

'My name is Millefleur; though friends call me Millie.'

'Millefleur. French for "yarrow": a common

weed, found in hedges, I believe. Someone went to a lot of trouble to make silk from a sow's ear.'

'You are either naturally rude,' Millie returned cheerfully, 'or you are so handsome that you have always let your looks speak for you and never bothered about being polite. Which is it, I wonder?'

A frosty silence fell between them. Then, 'I apologise. I am not much used to the company of other cats,' the Russian Blue said stiffly.

'I thought you said you had sired a million kittens.'

'It does not take long to service a harnessed female.'

An unpleasant image flickered across Millie's mind's eye. 'So you are the witch's cat, then?'

'For years I was her familiar and stud cat. But she seems to have grown tired of me. Her boys took me from one place to another, but they did not seem to have much idea of what to do with me. For some time I was kept in some awful laboratory; then they brought me here two – three? – weeks ago. They kept bringing in bundles of scrawny streetmogs and throwing them in here, but the devil knows what I'm supposed to do with them. Apart from the fact that that pair don't even seem to be able to tell the difference between male and female cats, they can hardly expect me to show an interest in such miserable specimens, can they? But since they brought you in there's been no sign of them. How my mistress can allow them to treat me so I can't imagine.'

'She's dead, the witch.'

There was a long pause. Then the foreign cat said sorrowfully, 'I had thought she had found another to replace me. Now I'll be dead before she returns.'

Millie was puzzled by this. 'What do you mean? She's dead, I said. She's not coming back.'

'She always comes back.'

'I saw her body,' Millie said through gritted teeth. 'It was all black and burned.'

'Ah. They burned her, did they? I see. It'll be another body, then, that she seeks to return to this time. Tell me, did they burn the house, too?'

'The house?'

'Nonesuch. Did they burn Nonesuch along with its mistress?'

'Oh, yes,' Millie said. 'Though it wasn't completely destroyed. More's the pity.'

'And the knot garden and the Chamber of Secrets?'

'I have no idea what you are talking about. Various parts of the house were badly burned, but Orlando's and Lydia's people have been restoring it. Not that it seems to be making them very happy.'

'Lydia, you say? Not the little golden beauty?'

Millie sighed. 'Is she so memorable, among your thousands of conquests?'

'Ah. Do I detect a note of jealousy?'

'No you bloody well don't. She had kittens, you know.'

'They all do.'

'No. I mean, she still has them. They escaped.'

Millie felt a frisson of reaction, then, 'Kittens,'

Circassian Gogol II said ruminatively. 'Well, well, well. I say. How many?'

'Three. All girls. Letitia, Arabella and Caterina –'

'Pretty names. Very elegant. Very . . . proper.'

'– better known as Thug and Beetle and Squash,' Millie finished spitefully.

'How perfectly dreadful. It sounds rather as if they are missing out on the finer things in life. Yet, as I recall, their mother was a rather refined little queen.'

Millie snorted. 'Yeah, right. She's about as refined as a shark, that one. Same sort of appetite, too.'

'Even so, I should like to see her again,' the witch's familiar mused. 'And the kittens, too. How remarkable that they should avoid the Boiling.'

Millie felt her fur bristle. 'They were the lucky ones,' she said grimly. Then, 'Just how much did you know about what the witch was doing, anyway?'

'Not much, for a long time. She became less discreet as things progressed, however. Less discreet and . . . more . . . sleek, somehow. Terrible smell, though. No noses, these humans; no idea at all. The last time I saw her she stank of that vile concoction she made, despite all the rose tincture she added to it to disguise the scent of boiled kitten. I've smelled it on other women since – not the most refined version, of course; she kept that for herself. It would not do to slave so long in search of perfection and then allow others access to it, would it? There can only be one Queen of the Night, after all. And she could hardly afford for the other one to steal her man again, not after defeating her time and again down the centuries.'

'Centuries? Even *I* know humans don't live so long –'

Millefleur sensed the other cat's smile as a ripple in the air between them. 'She has had life after life,' he said at last. 'They all have, those three. Whether they want to return to Nonesuch or not, it draws them back into the pattern again and again. So my grandfather told me, and his grandfather told him. The witch and her familiars, defeating the plain little woman so that she may keep the Dark Man for herself.'

Millie felt a sudden warmth of fellow feeling for 'the plain little woman', by whom he seemed to mean Anna, who had gentle hands and eyes the colour of a burnished chestnut, and had never shown her anything but kindness, and tin after tin of tuna in brine. 'She had a child, too,' she said, a little dreamily. 'A baby with green eyes.'

Circassian Gogol twitched. His head went up. One of his long whiskers brushed her own. 'Does it gather . . . things?' he asked obscurely.

'What sort of things?'

'Oh . . . unusual objects. Things you might not expect a child to play with.'

Millie frowned. 'A black tin box that made a noise. A necklace thing. An old spoon –'

'She's coming back,' he said excitedly. 'My mistress is seeking to return. We must leave now. I must go back to her!'

'And just how,' Millie asked with the merest

touch of sarcasm, 'do you imagine we're going to get out of here? Melt through the walls, maybe; magic up a little door? I've searched this damn place from top to bottom and not found so much as a crack.'

Circassian Gogol made a strange creaking sound that Millie realised belatedly was a laugh. Then he stirred himself and stood up. He was taller than her: she could feel his warm breath on the top of her head. Where he had lain, the place felt different: cool and shimmering; somehow mutable, undependable . . .

Millie pushed a paw into the coolness, felt it swallowed, felt it grow. Freezing air, moving furiously, caught the lynx fur and flattened it to her skin. She drew the paw back, licked at it curiously. Tiny ice shards burst like scintillant lights on her tongue. She laughed. 'A wild road!' she crowed delightedly. 'You've been sitting right over the entrance to a highway all this time!'

'I felt it was my job to guard it,' Circassian Gogol said austerely, 'until I was certain of what was required of me. Now that I know, I must leave at once.' And with that he leapt into the wild road.

Millie looked back over her shoulder into the darkness, where a buzz of sound was beginning to spread excitedly through the room. 'Wild road,' she called softly. 'Right over here. Take your chance while you can and good luck!' Then she followed the witch's familiar into the highway.

Later that morning, not far from the rectory, two or three acres of rough pasture were turned over for winter wheat. The tractor – driven by an old boy-friend of Alice Meynell's, christened Dave but known to the village at large as 'Geronimo' – groaned its way up and down, then rumbled off into the mist, trailing the sounds of country music and leaving the gulls to wheel and screech above the juicy furrows, which now had the colour of Green & Black's chocolate and smelled a little like it too.

Some lapwings came and went. The turned earth lightened in colour as it dried out. Mid-morning, a fox crossed it east to west, deft and confident, unconcerned by the gulls planing and diving over its head. After that the field remained empty for some time, until the vicar of St Mary's Ashmore appeared.

He was dressed in the tweed jacket and Fair Isle pullover which always made him look as mild and fatuous as a Labrador dog. Progress was more of a struggle for him than it had been for the fox. The sticky earth forced on him a lurching, abnormal gait. He was out of breath, his shoes were caked with mud and in his arms he was carrying a small child tightly wrapped in a threadbare pink blanket. If he knew anything, he knew this gesture to be muddled and inadequate.

The child, however, did not care. She had already managed to disengage one arm, which she used to point at things. The circling gulls had aroused in her a particular interest. 'There!' she said. 'There!'

Francis Baynes paid no attention, only continued to skate and stagger across the furrows, his voice hoarse in the damp air. He was weeping and he seemed to be arguing with a third person, someone only he could see. Every so often he stopped, turned himself round as if manoeuvring some heavy, ill-designed vehicle, and with considerable effort started back the way he had come. Sometimes this disagreement lasted a minute or two before his internal voices faced him in the required direction again and set him off towards the north edge of the ploughland. From there the going would be much easier, all the way to Nonesuch.

Had Francis tarried but a little longer, or turned to look behind him, he might have witnessed the remarkable sight of a golden-eyed European lynx and a vast Siberian tiger bursting out of a wild road into the middle of the ploughed field he had just passed, their hot breath sending plumes of vapour towering up into the wintry air. As it was, by the time they had come into his line of sight, running fast and Ashmore-bound, Millefleur and Circassian Gogol II had dwindled back to normal cat size and were now visible only as two fleet shadows in the lee of a hawthorn hedge.

Chapter Sixteen

ANNA WOKE HANGING against her safety belt. When she moved her head hurt and a dark spinning movement began around her, going faster and faster until she was sick. After that she felt a little better and was able to open her eyes.

The Volvo had ended up on its side at the base of the bank. Through the driver's side window could be seen the greyish, leggy stems of gorse bushes; a patch of sky. The windscreen sagged inwards, frosted and crystalline, surrounded by loose ribbons of rubber. There was a smell of fuel. Anna kicked and wriggled to get her weight on to the transmission tunnel, then undid the safety belt and slithered out through the windscreen. The effort of this caused her to throw up again, so she sat in the wet grass, looking around at the gorse bushes and thinking, *I'm all right. I'm alive.* The relief she felt was exuberant but distant. She couldn't quite get in touch with it. Nothing seemed broken, though her upper body was bruised and sore. She looked at her watch. It was quarter to four in the afternoon. *Oh my*

God, she thought. *John. John and Eleanor. I'd better get going.*

After tearing its way through the hedge, the Volvo had rolled down the bank, turning over once or twice before it settled into the gorse. From up in the lane where Anna stood swaying and holding her ribs, you wouldn't know it was there. As she turned to go the world spun briefly – she reached out without thinking for something to hold on to – and she had a sudden clear memory of the accident. In it, the woman who had stepped out into the road in front of her seemed to be floating, perhaps a foot off the ground. 'The things you think,' Anna admonished herself.

She stared around vaguely. 'I wonder where she went? At least I didn't hit her.' This conclusion seemed to release her and she set out for the house. She had a less than clear idea of where it was from here. Also she was very thirsty, but she could have a drink when she got there.

At the back of the chamber in which I had been trapped, a staircase had been cut into bare earth, but it led up to a solid ceiling and I could make no escape that way. I hunted around the room; I even tried to leap for the hole through which the child had reached down to me, but to no avail. It took some finding and a bit of digging, but at last, behind the staircase I finally managed to locate the entrance to the wild road the fox had blasted through to reach me when last I had been here, diverting it from its time into his own. Now it felt musty and abandoned. It had not, I suspect, been used by cats in my lifetime, or probably even that of my grandfather. It was thin and weak, and when I stuck my head into it, the compass winds there were barely more than a chill breeze carrying a haze of souls whose energies had never been redirected. My lion form was slow to come upon me in this place, and my thoughts felt tired and sluggish. It took far longer than it should have done to find my way back into the world.

Late afternoon, Nonesuch.

Mark and Oliver Holland emerged from the rhododendrons on to the Great Lawn, where they stood for a moment energetically brushing each other's Guernsey pullovers and pressed blue jeans. At their feet lay a blue polythene fertiliser bag, inside which something seemed to be making angry but furtive movements. At one point, while they were cleaning the leaf mould off their hand-made Australian jodhpur boots, the bag rolled to one side and became quite violently agitated.

'Lively little devils,' said Mark.

'Yes, they are, aren't they?'

'But not as lively as the other one.'

'No, not that lively,' Oliver agreed. He stopped what he was doing to watch a magpie fly across the lawn. 'Was that a jay?' he asked. 'Because it certainly looked like a jay to me.'

The last time they came to Nonesuch they had only managed to take the one cat and that one cat had been more trouble than most of the rest put together, since it had bitten and clawed them both, and then howled unmercifully when they had shut it away. Now they had come back for more. As many cats as they could get, that was what they wanted. As many of these cats as they could get, for the product development people at English Lion to work on.

'We could look over there,' said Oliver.

'We could,' Mark agreed. He picked up the fertiliser bag and swung it over his shoulder. 'Well, shall we do that?'

'Yes.'

They were in the centre of the lawn when the earth seemed to rearrange itself in front of them and a woman came out. The lawn bulged and shifted in a sort of optical illusion, just a brief delusory rearrangement of things, and the woman popped out, massive and bone-coloured, to tower above them in her eternal open-thighed squat. Her yellow feet were planted in the earth. They knew her. They knew her of old. They were relieved to see her. 'Put those cats down,' she told them. 'Forget all that rummaging around. You're not here to poke your noses in. You never were. You're here because she needs you.'

'We wondered why we were here,' Mark said.

'She needs you now.'

'We thought,' Oliver said, 'she was dead.'

'Never think, boys,' she reminded them. 'Never think, my nice boys.'

So they dropped the fertiliser bag and trailed off across the lawn towards the front of the house, their voices rising and falling as they went.

'I'm sure it was a jay.'

'I don't think it was, you know.'

The fertiliser bag heaved for a moment or two, then disgorged two female tabby cats who, barely able to believe their luck, exchanged a single puzzled glare before running off in opposite directions.

I became so disorientated that I followed the old highway for miles as it doubled back on itself like a dying grass snake and when at last I regained the presence of mind to abandon it I found myself way out past the northern side of the village and had to enter two further highways in order to make my way back to familiar territory. Within minutes of using wild roads that were kept powerful and clear by regular use, my head had cleared and I navigated my way back to the lane in front of Nonesuch. I was just about to enter the gates when a fleeing tabby cat almost bowled me over. I dodged out of its way and turned to watch it scurrying down the road, its ears flat to its head and its hind legs bunching and leaping like a scared rabbit's, and when I looked back again I was confronted by the sight of Grizelda, making her own urgent but rather more stately progress down the drive towards me.

'I'm leaving,' Griz informed me matter-of-factly. 'So don't try to stop me.'

'On your own? Where will you go?'

'Anywhere away from here is good enough for me. This place is becoming far too strange for an old cat like me to stand it any longer. Nightmares all the time; people stealing cats; great white figures rising out of the ground. I've had enough of it and if you'd got any sense you'd not be coming back while you have the chance to get away with your skin intact.'

'Griz – I have to see the Besom. Do you know where she is?'

Griz shook her head sadly. 'Silly old mog. I tried to persuade her to come with me, but she wasn't having any of it. Said she was too old to move again and that if you weren't there to sort out the White Lady she'd have to do it herself. So I said to her, "Pol Tregenna, I've known you most of my life, which is far too long for most cats to remember, and you've always been as stubborn as a mule. Have it your own way." And off I went.'

'But where *is* she?' I asked, suddenly chilled.

'She and Caterina were on their way to the knot garden when last I saw them –'

Without another word I fled up the driveway.

Anna sat at the side of the road with her legs tucked up and her arms clasped round her knees. Every so often she applied her dampened handkerchief to the bruises round her right eye. *It's so ridiculous*, she thought.

She had wandered into the shadow of the downs, where the tangled lanes slipped down the escarpment before fanning out into the valley like the veins on the back of a hand – a maze of ancient greenways resurfaced with tarmac in the 1920s but still following the vanished commercial logic of the Middle Ages. Little clear identical streams ran beside them.

Every barn, hazel coppice, or intimate fold in the hillside looked the same as every other.

I'm lost. I don't know what they'd all think of me.

She was too dizzy and disorientated to be quite sure whom she meant by they, but the thought made her feel she wasn't doing enough. After a minute or two she got herself to her feet again and began to walk. She was too far north now and it was late in the afternoon. John was one of *them*. Francis was, too. They were all depending on her. *Poor old Francis*, she thought. *Eleanor will have worn him to a shred*.

After she had been walking for some minutes she heard a dull whining noise, intermittent and indistinct, somewhere off towards Ashmore. It grew rapidly louder, turned from a whine into a roar and a bright-red motorcycle burst round a bend in the lane in front of her, front suspension bumping and boring as its rider fought the understeer. Anna shrank away; then, understanding what she was seeing, stepped back into the road and waved her arms. 'It's me!' she cried. 'It's me!'

There was a shriek of brakes, a strong smell of burning rubber. The machine slewed past her, mounted the grass verge, from which its enormous rear tyre tore great clods of earth, then, fishtailing wildly, disappeared round the next corner.

'Oh dear,' whispered Anna.

There was a silence. After a moment, the motorcycle came back into view, moving much more slowly. It stopped in front of her. 'Bloody hell, Anna,' said Alice Meynell with a grin.

Alice had been back in the country for two hours.

She was in love, she admitted, and jet-lagged, and the only cure she knew for either of those things was motorcycling. 'Best fun in the world, these lanes, as long as you keep your wits about you.' She was pleased to see her friend – though, as she put it, 'a bit arse-over-tip' to find her wandering about concussed like this in the middle of nowhere. She had no idea what was going on and she wasn't sure she wanted to know. But – love or not, jet-lag or not – she was still Alice Meynell, who at the age of eight had driven her father's Land Rover into Ashmore Pond. So when she heard Anna's garbled tale, she only shrugged and revved her engine. 'Hop on,' she commanded.

Anna, awash with relief and affection, hugged her and hopped on. 'Oh, Alice. Thank God.'

The motorcycle bellowed. The world erupted into speed lines and began to rush past her on either side. Alice Meynell was in charge now. Things would be all right, at least for a while. Then the ice-cold airstream blew Anna's headache away and her sense of urgency returned. 'Can you get me to Nonesuch before dark?' she shouted.

'This is a Ducati 916, Anna. It could get you to Edinburgh before dark.'

Nonesuch, late afternoon.

Joshua Herringe's courtyard was an empty well, its ancient shadows drawing away from the walls with the onset of evening.

Three figures, bulky-looking yet difficult to identify in the milky, rather beautiful greyish light, squeezed through the hole in the Painted Room wall and made their way to the centre of the littered space. Ahead of them, somewhat more than life-sized and leaning forward like someone walking into the wind, floated the woman who called herself Izzie.

Francis Baynes's progress was slow. He held his head at a strained, reluctant angle, as if he were trying to dissociate himself from his own actions.

In his arms Eleanor Dawe chuckled gleefully to herself. There was the faintest flicker in the air above her. She stared up at it, transfixed. 'Aaah,' she said, in a voice more like a child's. She kicked her legs to be let down, and as soon as Francis Baynes had unwrapped her from the pink blanket and set her on the ground, she began to burrow. Her plump little arms and legs made energetic swimming motions. A dimple of sour dry earth formed quickly around her, slipping away like sand pouring through an egg timer. Then she was gone.

The three remaining figures stood about vacantly, staring at one another, then down at the disturbed earth. One by one, they settled on to their hands and knees and followed the child. As they swam into the ground their expressions wavered between distaste and puzzlement. Mark Holland got his mouth full of soil.

The woman called Izzie hung in the air above them. Then she wrapped herself in a kind of dark bubble and she too vanished like a dream.

There was a clammy mist wreathing around the house and no sign of any cats. When I called out, all that answered me was a weak and muffled echo of my own voice. I was just about to round the corner to the back of the house where the knot garden was situated when there came a suddenly mechanical, rumbling sound ahead of me and, a few moments later, a higher-pitched roar from the vicinity of the road, which grew ever louder in volume as it approached. I hurled myself into some bushes, and landed on something soft and warm.

There was a yelp, then, 'Where have you been? I've been looking everywhere for you,' a voice hissed.

It was Caterina and behind her, half hidden by the shadows and the mist, was the Besom.

It transpired that Loves A Dustbin had been looking for me, too. Instead, he had found the Besom, who had been half frightened to death by the sound of a large dogfox addressing her. She had been trying to face him off with a show of spiked fur and a terrifying spread of toothless gums, when Caterina had intervened to explain he was not there to eat her.

'He said some pretty weird stuff,' Caterina finished, 'then he went to look for you.'

'I'm glad to see you, Cat,' I said, licking her swiftly on the cheek, 'but I have to ask Ma something. Something important. Anna's and John's child,' I went on quickly. 'Have you noticed anything odd about her?'

The Besom froze. She batted her eyes rapidly, as though the question had confused her so much that she was unable to focus. 'The child,' she said slowly. 'Ah, yes. The child. With the eyes . . .'

'Green,' I prompted.

'Her eyes.'

'Whose eyes?' Cat stared from Ma Tregenna to me and back again.

'She's got *her* eyes all right. And soon she'll have the rest of her.'

'What are you talking about?' Caterina was almost bouncing with irritation.

'She kept collecting these . . . objects,' I said. 'The baby, I mean. Strange objects; not what you'd expect a child to want to play with. And every time a new one appeared the dreams came . . .'

The Besom nodded wisely. 'Ah yes. Witch must have stuffed them things full of herself and buried 'em around the house for when all her lives ran out and she needed to find other ways back. Must have called on the dream maker when she died to send her dreams, help her retrieve her memories.'

'Stuffed herself into the objects?' I frowned, bewildered.

'Aye, I reckon. Seen it before, I have. Previous life, though. 'T'ain't really her *self*, as such,' the Besom continued. ''Tis her spells and craft. Her memories and the like. To keep other folks' thieving hands off them, apart from anything else. I knew a witch once kept all her childhoods in a little blue egg. Weasel ate it in the end and she went quite mad. Forgot how to speak and such . . .' She mused on this for a moment. Caterina and I exchanged glances. A little later she said, 'Tell me what she got. I need to know how many.'

'An old doll's head.' I remembered the horrid

thing with the flickering blue eyes I'd dug up in the knot garden.

'A black metal box thing,' Cat offered, 'that made a noise when you opened it.'

'A black shiny object full of old hair,' I added, 'and then there was a long silver spoon.'

'I remember that thing,' the Besom said with a grimace. 'Come at me with that, she did, just like her ladyship. Stirred the pot with that spoon, the witch did, stirred the pot and supped from it most like.'

I closed my eyes. 'A small doll made of bone, too.'

The Besom puffed out her chest. 'Witch's mannikin,' she declared sagely.

'And a tiny picture that changed when I looked at it.'

'Six objects.'

I nodded.

'There'll be seven,' Ma Tregenna stated. 'There's always seven. Numbers matter in magic, you know. Some numbers are stronger than others. The last object will be the oldest and the strongest: the first thing she started with. And when she's found that one and offered it up to the White Lady the babe'll be hers and that'll be the end of all of us.'

'Whatever it is, we must find it before the child does.'

'That's what the fox said!' Caterina piped up. ' "I must find it before she does" – that's what he said before he went.'

'So where did he go?' I asked with a sinking feeling. I had hoped he would be here to advise me.

I did not much want to be responsible for a situation that bewildered me so thoroughly.

'I don't know. He said he might be gone a while, and then he just . . . disappeared.'

'He did say one other thing before he went,' the Besom added almost as an afterthought.

'What?' My tone was sharp; I couldn't help it.

The Besom looked affronted. 'No need for rudeness. The young are so impatient. Wait till you get to my age,' she rambled on, 'then you'll see how annoying it can be.'

'None of us will have the chance to reach your age at this rate,' I grumbled.

Luckily she was too deaf to hear me, though she gave me a hard look. 'He said something about "the power of three". That it would take three of the old blood to stop her, three who became great cats on the highways; three who guarded the world from dreams.'

'And now you're here!' Caterina cried happily. 'So there are three of us, three dreamcatchers.'

I regarded her dubiously. 'That's all very well,' I said. 'But what are we supposed to do?'

The mechanical clanking that had been going on in the background all this while came to a sudden halt and I could hear voices. My ears pricked up. 'Anna's by the knot garden,' I declared with some relief. 'She must have the baby with her.'

The three of us made our way through the mist to the back of the house. But what we saw there gave us no reassurance at all.

*

When Anna arrived at Nonesuch the light was fading. A few of the upper windows reflected the faint eggshell colours of the western sky. The rest were like shutters, and whatever lay behind them remained as uncommunicative and dark as the cedars in the grounds. The roar of the Ducati blatted back off the front of the house, then turned itself off like a tap. In the silence that followed, Anna took a few unsteady steps across the gravel to ease the trembling in her legs, staring up at the curiously angled roofs and gables.

Alice Meynell, meanwhile, propped the motorcycle on its stand, prised off her helmet, ran her fingers through her cropped hair. 'I'd kill for a cup of tea,' she said. 'Anna?'

'Shh,' said Anna absently. She tilted her head to listen.

She had heard the sound of machinery moving backwards and forwards somewhere behind the house. She looked at her watch. The builders would be long gone. *It's the knot garden*, she thought. *John's going to grub up the knot garden, on his own in the dark*. Her heart went out to him suddenly. She couldn't bear the thought of him there on his own in the fog of sunk cost error, throwing good money after bad, hoping to turn his life round by doing something which had never worked anyway. Out loud she said, 'Alice, will you do me a favour? Will you wait here while I go and talk to him? Then you can make us all a cup of tea.'

Alice rubbed at an imaginary mark on the fuel

tank of the Ducati. 'You go and give him hell, ducks,' she said.

'I'll do my best.'

It was colder behind the house. White mist pooled in the knot garden. The digger, a yellow JCB hired for the day, clanked and roared, sawing backwards and forwards in short, ungainly bursts. Its black energetic outline loomed up against the afterglow, ramming into a line of hedge, reversing away with a festoon of box roots hanging like severed electrical cable from its raised scoop. Diesel smoke poured into the clear air. Anna could see John hunched up in the cab, wearing his precious site helmet. She called, but he couldn't hear. She waved, but he didn't notice. What was new? In the end she waded knee-deep into the mist – it was as white and cold as milk from the fridge – and stood in front of the lumbering machine, waving her arms until it jerked to a halt so suddenly that the engine stalled.

John sat there for a moment, rubbing his eyes with the heels of his hands. Then he opened the cab door and stuck his head out. 'That was a bit stupid,' he said.

She smiled back. 'Wasn't it? And it's the second time I've done it today.'

He frowned. 'I was going to try to get this job done before the light went.'

'But will you come down and talk to me? Just for a moment?'

'I don't know what we'd talk about.'

'About Eleanor. I thought we'd talk about Eleanor.'

This brought him out of the cab and they stood looking at one another awkwardly in the hot, oil-smelling gloom by the engine. It was hard to judge his expression. She wanted to put her arms round him, but she knew she must keep a clear head. Perhaps he wanted that too. In any case, neither of them could think of anything to say.

Then he narrowed his eyes, reached out to touch the bruises on her cheek. 'What on earth have you done to yourself?' he wanted to know. 'And where's Eleanor?'

Anna told him what had happened. 'Eleanor's all right,' she said. 'But the car's a write-off.'

'I can't believe this. I just can't believe it.'

'John, we have to talk.' Anna tried to make eye contact with him, but he wouldn't look at her. 'Please?'

'You left your daughter with someone we hardly know,' he accused.

'It isn't quite like that, John.'

'What is it like?'

'I don't want her here, I told you that. And Francis Baynes is perfectly reliable.'

John shrugged. He turned away abruptly and swung himself back up into the cab. 'I'm sure he is,' he said. 'It's you I have my doubts about.'

Anna bit her lip. 'John, Eleanor's your daughter.'

He gave a quiet laugh. 'I remember that.'

'So won't you come away with us? For her sake? Don't you want this sorted out?'

'Yes,' he said.

'Then –'

'It's just that I have my own view of what needs sorting out. Do you see, Anna? I won't have you take my decisions away from me by presenting your view of the world as the only correct one.'

'John!'

He did something in the cab; then, when the engine of the JCB burst into life, revved it until the ground shook and the air stank of burned diesel. As soon as he was certain it would keep running, he let it idle and stuck his head out again. 'What I want to do is get this job done. What I don't want is to have my choices made for me. Can you understand that?'

'Nonesuch is making our choices,' Anna said. 'Not us.'

'You just won't give up, will you?'

He put the digger into gear. It coughed, hesitated, then lurched forward suddenly, its rear wheels throwing up earth.

'You won't either,' Anna whispered. 'You won't give up either.'

With her arms folded under her breasts and her shoulders hunched against the cold, she walked away. When she stopped to look back, the JCB was still visible, rolling busily about like a Tonka toy in the low white mist. She stood watching until the darkness swallowed it, and she could follow its progress only by the irregular squeak and clank of the shovel, the hiss of the hydraulics, the snarl and groan of the exhaust. Eventually she wiped her eyes and turned away.

At that, a comforting arm went round her shoulders and Alice Meynell said, 'Don't cry, love. Don't cry.'

'Oh dear. Have you been here all the time?'

'No,' Alice said. But she had clearly heard most of the exchange, because she added, 'Come on. He's not worth it.'

Anna sniffed and wiped her eyes. 'He is, Alice. That's the problem. He is worth it. Will you take me back to the village? I want to see Eleanor.' Then she said, 'What's that?'

The JCB had shuddered to a halt. On his last pass, John had set the angle of the shovel too steeply and instead of peeling up the remaining hedge it had buried itself in the earth. Anna and Alice heard the cab door open as he got out to look at the damage. Torchlight skittered across the knot garden to reveal white mist, churned earth and uprooted vegetation, then the front of the vehicle itself, which seemed to have sunk into the ground. John moved forward cautiously and dropped the torch. For a second he was visible in its yellow beam, his face a pale, drawn blur under the site helmet. His whole body looked puzzled.

'Are you all right?' called Anna.

He made an irritated gesture, as if to say 'Don't bother me now', then, as he picked up the torch, vanished again. Shortly after that, Anna heard a low cry. The torchbeam bobbed about meaninglessly, settled on something she couldn't quite make out, some movement at the base of the silent vehicle. Then she understood. All around him the ground mist had begun to move. It was flowing across the knot garden at an unhurried pace, rippling and parting here and there like shallow water over stones, speeding up a little towards the centre where the JCB had stranded itself, then pouring smoothly and silently over the edge of the hole which had opened up there. The knot garden was emptying itself like a bath.

'Anna, come and look. Come and look at this!' He bent down and peered into the hole. 'I can see something down there,' he said. 'I'm just going to have a look –'

'John, no!' called Anna. 'Wait!'

But by the time they got there he was gone.

Standing at the edge of the hole, they watched the mist slipping over and into the darkness. Alice Meynell – wondering aloud how much harm a bit of fog could do – knelt down to have a closer look. 'I can see what he meant,' she said. Her voice echoed back from the hole. 'There are stairs in there. Steps. Can you see?'

Anna shook her head. 'I don't want to see.'

But she knew she would be made to in the end. She waited miserably for the last of the mist to drain away and vanish. A cold, stale smell filled her nostrils. It was the smell of history – the headless doll, the twist of hair, bad dreams in the night. Old photographs she couldn't understand. Lives she had already lived, which, though she remembered nothing of them, would never let her be.

'Why did he have to go in there?' she whispered, more to herself than Alice. 'It's just one more horrible bit of the past.'

She looked up at Nonesuch, looming above her,

its queer gables and gambrel roofs black against the sky, then down again into the hole – from which issued suddenly the hollow, echoing cry of a baby.

'My God,' said Alice.

They stared at one another. A noise came out of Anna's mouth, a kind of muffled whimper in which you could barely discern the word 'Eleanor'. *What's happened?* she asked herself. *I can't cope with this, I won't be able to cope.* The thought made her instantly calm. 'I can see the steps,' she told Alice quietly.

'Anna –'

'I'll go first.'

It wasn't far.

The stairs were narrow and steep. Worn into John's beloved curve of use, slick with moisture on every tread, they had an acoustic of their own, which fetched up echoes and refractions of voices, and what turned out to be music. Near the bottom a faint light wavered on the damp walls. There was a smell of candle-wax. Anna paused and felt behind her until she found Alice Meynell's hand.

'I'm still here,' Alice reassured her.

'Alice, listen!'

It was the 'Für Elise'.

Anna shivered. With the old melody dripping a reluctant sweetness into the air around her, she stepped into the candlelight.

The room in which she found herself was circular in plan, perhaps twenty feet in diameter. *Useless to ask yourself who had built it*, Anna thought. Something had already convinced her this was the wrong question. It was as old as Dr Russell's paleolithic finds on the downs, just another temple to that malformed Iceni goddess, a chamber of worship echoing with her groans of loss and defiance in the face of time. *It's been here from the beginning*, she decided. *Since* before *the beginning*. Successive Herringes, locked into the past yet somehow unable to cope with the idea of a time before themselves, had rebuilt it to try to obscure this obvious fact. Even now, sugary Victorian plaster was falling off the uneven walls to reveal rough limestone blocks, thick with calcium deposits, eroding at their unmortared joints. There were dozens of niches and recesses at head height, waist height, and niches you would have to lie on the floor to reach. In them were objects collected to no good purpose by the same Herringes; and older things which Anna did not wish to look at. Here and there great thick grey cobwebs swept up, like net curtains layered three or four inches deep, towards a ceiling which seemed too far away.

There was no furniture.

A knot-shaped design took up most of the floor.

On the other side of it, in a loose, shifting group in the candlelight, she recognised the Holland brothers and Francis Baynes. Mark and Oliver were busying themselves about, moving from niche to niche like shop assistants searching for a difficult item. Francis looked ill and exhausted, and under some appalling strain. He had her daughter in his arms. 'Francis?' Anna said. 'Francis?' At this, the baby chuckled; the candles flickered (was that another figure, there in the shadows? If it was, it had vanished in the instant she saw it); and Francis stood forward of the others. Awkwardly, he raised Eleanor Dawe up in his arms, as if presenting her to the room.

'Oh, you bastards!' Anna shouted. 'Eleanor, stop this!'

Chapter Seventeen

THOUGH THE DESIGN cut into the flagstones bore some resemblance to the knot garden of Joshua Herringe, its complexities left even less for the intelligence to grasp. Each line of it seemed to shift continually. Everywhere Anna looked, patterns seethed away from her eye yet rushed towards it at the same time, so that she was forced to blink and wince, and turn away. Halfway across the knot, her husband struggled in slow motion, caught fast like a fly in a web, facing away from her with one hand raised. He had been running towards his daughter, she saw, when the design reached up to entangle him. *It had taken away his time*. His cry of despair was still dragging itself out of him, in a kind of formless, never-ending groan.

Mark and Oliver were amused. Every so often they stopped what they were doing to laugh at his slowly flailing limbs, his expression of anger and terror; or to look slyly across at Eleanor – who, one of her pudgy little hands held up in a curious, hieratic gesture, seemed to have brought all this about.

'Eleanor!' Anna cried. 'I won't tell you again!'

A soft laugh filled the room. The child leaned forward. 'To be honest, dear, I never liked "Eleanor",' she said, in the voice of Stella Herringe. 'You could have done better.' Suddenly she seemed to notice her father, suspended there between two of his own moments. 'Poor old John. Always so intense. You should have seen him at thirteen. He shivered like a pony when you fucked him.' She laughed. 'Just like a pony.'

John Dawe forged on into nowhere, groaning. Anna could bear it no longer and plunged in after him. As she slowed down, the world accelerated around her. Every sound in the chamber shifted abruptly into a higher register. Even the quality of the light seemed to change, brightening, becoming bluer and sharper. But she never found out what would have happened if she had continued. Mark and Oliver, exchanging the high-pitched squeals of bats as they flickered and skipped from niche to niche, found what they were looking for. Their enraptured cries caught Eleanor's attention and she lost interest.

For Anna – though not for John – things slowed down again. The world spun. The knot expelled her. She found herself on the floor, being sick for the third time that day, with a white-faced Alice Meynell bending over her. 'Help me up, Alice,' she said. 'We're going to sort this out.'

Alice, though, shook her head, lost less for words than for a description of the world she now found herself in –

On the other side of the room, Mark Holland took a small Victorian folding card table out of one of the niches and brought it forward. On its discoloured baize surface he set: the plastic head of a 1950s doll; a jet necklace with attached mourning locket, also Victorian; the small German musical box Frances had given to Eleanor, from which dropped the sweet tentative notes of 'Für Elise'; a silver spoon, no later than the Regency period; a miniature painting of one of the Herringe women, perhaps Clara de Montfort; and the carved bone figure of a crouching woman, to which no possible date could be affixed. These he arranged on the table according to the instructions of John Dawe's daughter who, after studying each placement for a few seconds, clapped her hands inaccurately together and indicated that Mark's brother could bring forward the object he had taken so reverently from its cobwebbed niche.

It proved to be a brown muslin bag, stiff and fragile with age, about six inches long, having a drawstring closure at one end. With great care, Oliver Holland worked the drawstring open until he could shake out the contents of the bag.

Eleanor, breathing heavily through her mouth, hung over his shoulder. 'Kitcheee!' she squealed.

A few small bones tumbled out on to the baize tabletop. They were brown with age and none of them was more than five inches long. Nevertheless it was easy to identify a tiny femur, two or three ribs, a little skull that had lost its jaw. They were the bones of a child less than a year old.

'Aaaah,' said Eleanor, in her most sentimental voice. 'The *baby*!'

She put out her hand as if to stroke it. Then she looked up at Anna again. 'You have to give up something if you want to live for ever, dear,' she said. 'This is what Clara de Montfort gave up. Her first child. Smothered at midnight, buried under the garden. She was never entirely sane after that.' She laughed. 'But don't you wish you'd done the same?' She looked up into the air above her own head. 'Izzie!' she cried. 'Ishtar!'

Instantly the candles were extinguished and the room filled with an unsteady leaden light that seemed to issue from the air itself. Along with the light came a sensation Anna was quite unable to describe – a buzzing in her jaw, a metallic taste which filled her mouth. Both. Neither. The closer Eleanor's hand approached the bones, the more pronounced this sensation became. Small motes of blue light began to leap between the objects on the table – as a kind of visual echo, splashes of much brighter light exploded soundlessly high up in the room like flashbulbs going off. In response, the design on the floor shifted and changed, the lines that composed it filling and increasing. After a moment, the space in the centre of the room was occupied by a knot of pulsing tubes each as thick as a woman's arm and filled with a tobacco-brown substance the consistency of city fog.

What is that stuff? Anna thought. *It's like smoke.* Then, sadly, *It's been here so long. It's alive. It's* alive. *It's supposed to flow, it's supposed to be free.*

But whatever it was, it had long ago become static and gelid. Ages before the building of Nonesuch, something had turned it against itself so that it festered. Who knew what its proper purpose might be? You could only tell that it was some basic process of the world. Generations of terrified women, empowered by their ghastly little flint idol, had helped knot it up. Anything to hold back the flow, hold back time. She remembered John saying, 'Those women! They all look so alike, as far back as you can trace them. And God knows how far before that. I bet they looked the same when they were knapping flints on the chalk downs. The genes of the Herringe women, raging out of the Stone Age long before they had a name!' Now those women had trapped him somehow in this place. Worse, he had trapped himself.

The knot tightened.

John Dawe groaned and struggled. He was obscured.

Anna bit her lips. 'John!'

'Izzie,' whispered Eleanor Dawe. 'I'm ready to come back.'

She looked up.

In its upper reaches the room now stretched away indefinitely, up through its own ceiling into a night no one observing from Ashmore would ever see. Up there, something moved, faint and huge. Eleanor kicked her legs in excitement. 'Now, Izzie!' she cried. 'Now!' She reached down, fumbled among the collected objects, and came up clutching the bone figurine of a crouching woman, which she banged repeatedly on the tabletop.

'*Izzie!*'

Smoke roiled in the flickering air. It writhed and contracted. There was a brief, sharp cry; an earthy smell, at the same time animal and metallic, which Anna remembered from the birth of Eleanor; a sense of pain. The figurine vanished.

Eleanor, who had perhaps not quite expected this, stared puzzledly at her empty hand for a moment. Then she laughed. 'And now,' she said thoughtfully in the voice of an adult, 'what am I going to do about you, my dear?'

'You're going to give me my daughter back,' Anna said. 'For a start.'

There was a silence. The child stared at her. 'Who do you think I am?' it said quietly.

Anna shrugged. 'I don't know, but I never liked you when you were alive.'

Stella Herringe's laugh rang through the room. 'Oh my dear! Hoity-toity. Do you think I care?'

'You were a drunk and a snob, and terrified in case other people knew something you didn't. Are you always like that underneath, whoever you're pretending to be at the time? Whoever's life you've stolen?'

Stella gazed absently into the air in front of her. 'Hoity-toity gets a disease,' she said, after a moment. 'Hoity-toity gets cooked in a pot.' She arranged a coy smile on Eleanor's face. 'When I was Clara de Montfort, I killed my own baby,' she continued proudly. After a moment's thought she squeezed out a tear or two. 'It was rather awful, dear. Still, after I'd killed her I had your husband every way I could think of. I wore the pony out.' Another laugh. 'I forget what your name was in those days. You were a dry little thing.'

'I feel sorry for you,' Anna told her.

'A dry little thing. His words.' Stella sighed. 'His very words.'

'Was it worth it, all of that?' Anna asked. 'Just so you could hang on and hang on like this?'

'What else can you offer me, my dear?'

Anna had an idea. 'Can't *you* help me, Francis?' she appealed.

Francis Baynes stood there awkwardly holding the baby, much as he might have done on the lawn at Nonesuch two or three months before. Anna remembered him then, eating cake with a fork, wincing away from the smell of Eleanor's nappy, trying to hide his fastidiousness behind his smile. *Poor Francis*, she thought. *You weren't cut out for me and Eleanor, or for all the opera and mess and bad judgements and honest mistakes of the world. All you ever wanted to do was talk. You wanted to look at the sparks of sunlight coming through the cedars and ask me about my inner life so that you could tell me about your own. Look what it got you.*

His inner life had led him here, then abandoned him. The short and bitter journey from Ashmore rectory had worked dirt into his clothes and his pores. His skin had a bluish, exhausted pallor. His fingernails were filthy and broken, and his eyes had the empty look of someone whose immune system has collapsed, someone who has fallen away from everything warm and supportive and ended up, without ever really knowing why, living in a cardboard box.

'Francis?' Anna said.

Eleanor laughed. 'Franciiis!' she squealed. Then in another voice altogether, 'I seen his little secrets.'

At the sound of Anna's voice, though, Francis seemed to recover something of himself. He gave the child in his arms a startled look, as if he wondered how he had come by her, then gazed vaguely about the room. The great pulsing knot made him pause and blink, but he showed no interest in anything but Anna. Despite this, she wasn't entirely sure he recognised her. 'I'm not very good with babies,' he said. Then he shuddered, passed one hand rapidly across his face and shouted, 'I won't do it!'

Eleanor giggled. 'Oh yes, you will.'

'It's all right, Francis,' Anna reassured him. 'It's all right.'

He looked at her again. This time his eyes were clear and direct. All his intelligence and delight in the world, all his sense of it as an essentially benign place to live a life, shone out through them. He was the Francis Baynes she remembered. He smiled sadly. 'It isn't all right,' he said. 'And it never will be now. But we can't have this, Anna. We can't have all this.' He stared at the knot. 'What *is* that thing?' he asked himself.

Eleanor Dawe grasped at his face with her cruel little hands. 'Oh yes, you *will*,' she repeated.

'Oh no, I won't,' he replied with a laugh.

Eleanor shrieked angrily. She squirmed round in his arms until she could face him. She bit and kicked.

'Silly girl,' he said in a preoccupied voice. 'Silly baby.' He approached the knot and examined it for a moment or two. Almost as if it sensed his presence, the knot pulsed. The longer Francis looked at it, the more its ugliness seemed to puzzle him, until puzzlement was replaced by a kind of mild irritation, as if he had discovered something unpleasant in the nave of St Mary's one morning before his favourite communion. 'But this is completely monstrous,' he said to Anna. He tucked the screaming Eleanor securely under his left elbow, knelt down and began to pray, 'Our Father, which art in Heaven –'

For a moment a light seemed to shine on his face and he looked like a twelve-year-old boy.

Eleanor stared around anxiously. 'Izzie!' she cried, redoubling her efforts to escape, 'Izzie!'

In response, something picked Francis Baynes up and threw him carelessly into the nearest wall.

He fell at the base of it as limp as a doll, with his hair and coat on fire. 'I don't think I can do any more,' he said. 'Sorry.'

He dropped the baby, who began to crawl rapidly away from him, calling, 'Norty! Norty!'

Alice Meynell, who had watched these events unfold with the numb incomprehension of a dreamer stuck inside her dream, shook herself and shouted, 'Anna! He's let her go!'

'It's not like that, Alice,' Anna began to say.

Too late. Alice had dashed forward, wincing

away from the knot, and swept the baby up in her arms. 'Come on, Anna! Let's get out of here!'

Eleanor writhed and screamed, 'Izzeeeee!'

In some way, Anna now saw, Izzie was less a goddess – spiritual mother or precursor of all those ancient, nameless Herringe women – than a sour and arrogant dream of the earth itself. Something that had lain here under the ground since the beginning of time, musty and yet full of appetites, savage with its own desires, savage with the desires of others. A permission, a carte blanche, an invitation that fed on all the insecurities of the human world. Izzie had tied her knot long before human beings came along to claim it as theirs and make it the living metaphor of their fear of age and death, their refusal to move on. Izzie was the knot; she was as much its substance – its meaning – as she was its caretaker.

So when Eleanor called, she came, condensing out of the air as a mist until she hung, surrounded by black space and the cold lights of the stars, feet placed squarely apart as if for purchase on an invisible floor, her eyes staring but unfocused, her mouth open as wide as it would go on a silent roar of triumph and loss. From one angle she was the flint figure from the downs; from another she was the ghost of Ashmore graveyard, the woman in the muslin dress; from a third they were only aspects of her and she was something else altogether, something huge, the bones of the earth, clad in earth.

'Bloody hell,' exclaimed Alice Meynell.

'I told you,' said Eleanor. 'You silly bitch.'

Alice let go of her, stumbled backwards and fell down, knocking over the card table as she went. Many of the objects Eleanor had so painstakingly collected over the last few weeks were lost immediately. The doll's head spun and danced, then rolled to halt in the shadows, its eyelashes fluttering. Baby bones rattled across the floor. The music box, which had been quiet for some time, started up again out of nowhere – a few tremulous notes filled the room and were gone.

'Izzie's here,' observed Mark conversationally into the silence.

'Yes,' agreed his brother. 'Yes, she is.'

They seemed reluctant and shy. They glanced furtively up at her, and away again. Then something passed between them, in a look and a shrug, and they began to climb up into the shadows between her massive thighs. She absorbed them as if they had been part of her all along and they were lost to sight, though for some time they could be heard calling in progressively more muffled voices, 'You first.' 'No, you.'

Eleanor, meanwhile, had got herself carefully to her feet. She stood for a moment in her OshKosh dungarees and maroon jersey, bottom stuck out for balance, then tottered over to the fallen card table and began to root around on the floor beside it, shaking her head and clicking her tongue. 'No good,' Anna heard her say. 'No good.' She bent down precariously and picked up the music box. Waving this in one hand, she approached Izzie. 'I earned my name,' she said.

She raised her pudgy little arms, as if she expected to be picked up.

Nothing happened.

'I earned my name.'

The bone goddess squatted and roared in silence, her image wavering in the black air.

Eleanor looked puzzled. She rattled the music box next to her ear, looked at it, rattled it again. 'Norty,' she said. She stared up at the thing that called itself Izzie. 'I earned this,' she repeated, in Stella Herringe's voice. 'I earned this and I want it.' Silence. 'I'm as good as you.' When nothing happened, she threw the music box at the goddess and turned to walk away.

Something shifted slightly in the room. It was nothing you could describe. A kind of settling of the light. Then, while Eleanor's back was turned, Izzie and the knot slumped into one another suddenly and quite silently, like two drops of oil merging. Eleanor's objects were drawn from all over the room, to be absorbed one by one. When the last pathetic brown fragment of bone, Clara de Montfort's dead child, had been taken home, a curious, rubbery sphere filled the space which had been occupied by the knot and Izzie was nowhere to be seen.

Eleanor turned. 'Aaaaah,' she said.

The sphere shrank steadily, until it was two or three feet in diameter. Oily patterns roiled across its surface, flickered, became clear pictures in which the same three people could be seen again and again: Stella, John and Anna, dressed in the

411

costumes of every television historical Anna had ever watched, and tied together in the same miserable knot of manipulation and betrayal. They were at Nonesuch. They were in the Painted Room. They were struggling and panting together in some bed, or on some floor, or in the knot garden in the middle of the afternoon. Stella laughed. Anna cried. Now Stella cried. John turned his back on both of them and sullenly walked away. Stella walked and John cried. Anna cried and cried.

'I'd rather die than go through that again,' said Anna.

'Would you, dear?' asked Eleanor in Stella Herringe's voice. 'How brave of you.' She tottered towards the sphere, reached out a little hand, as if she could touch the pictures on its surface. It dimpled beneath her fingers, shrank a little further. 'I love it, actually,' she said. 'I can't wait to start again.'

'Leave my daughter alone!' Anna shouted.

Stella laughed sadly. 'I can't, dear. I wish I could.'

She seemed to be preparing to step through the surface of the sphere and into the past – or, worse, into the present – when the air in the chamber ripped apart and several huge creatures leapt out.

The first was a lion, its mane a vast dark halo round its head. Muscle braided its chest and forelegs like a demonstration of anatomy. Its brassy orange flanks smoked with heat, as if it had run through a furnace to arrive there. You could hear the air go in and out of its lungs. It roared and the chamber reverberated with the sound. Everyone shrank away from its primal grace; everyone but Anna who, recognising it instantly as the great cat she had encountered at Cresset Beacon, felt no fear, only a kind of elation. Immediately behind the lion came a leopard, not yet full grown but gleaming with power and vitality. Last of all came a dusty-looking wildcat with a grizzled face and wicked-looking claws.

For a moment they stood there in the middle of the chamber, illuminated by the bizarre blue light like a mirage or a *Fata Morgana*. A moment later the great cats had gone and in their place stood a marmalade tomcat, a half-grown female and a geriatric brindled cat. These three fanned out to surround the child.

The sphere wobbled away from them, borne up out of Eleanor's reach by the waves of hot air generated by the rank energies of the new arrivals.

Ellie stared at them with a trembling lower lip. 'Bad cats!' she said, trying to back away.

The animals showed her their teeth and lolling tongues the colour of a rose. Then the air crackled with heat again. Concentric rainbow-coloured rings spread out across the roof and walls, and something else tumbled into the chamber.

'Orlando, the dream!'

The humans there were able to comprehend the sound as a wild and raucous ululation, but Orlando recognised the speaker at once. He spun around.

It was the fox; and with him were a lynx and a white tiger.

With a leap of his heart Orlando recognised

413

Millefleur in her wild form. 'Millie!' he cried ecstatically, his attention fatally distracted. 'He rescued you!'

'No one rescued me,' Millie retorted. 'I escaped –'

The fox ran at Orlando. 'There's no time for this, no time at all! Don't guard the child; take down the dream, you fools!'

With a roar lion, leopard and wildcat sprang upon their prey.

Eleanor sat down suddenly. Anna ran forward and scooped her up. The cats floated over both of them in a short steep arc, so close Anna could feel their tremendous heat and mass, smell the rank, savage smell of them. They came down with the full weight of their three bodies on the iridescent sphere, which now somehow contained both Izzie and the Great Knot. It writhed beneath them, pulsing with some delirious awareness of itself: dream within dream, within dream, within dream. It was like nothing Orlando had ever previously encountered, on or off a wild road: its texture was more slippery, yet at the same time more defined than the usual dream globe – less of a membrane than a skin – as if time itself had wrapped itself up again and again to congeal into this one tangible, solid mass of images and experiences. It seemed to be impossible to get a grip on it. But it was not as if the sphere was resisting them; it was more that it was shrugging them off, uninterested in their attentions, all its sentience turned inwards in complete self-absorption.

He tried to bite it but his teeth slipped agonisingly

across the surface. On the opposite side of the thing he saw Caterina and the Besom working in unison, arching their backs and digging all four paws in with a vengeance. The thing hunched and gave beneath them before repulsing them again. Orlando swiped at it with all his might. He felt a claw snag into the globe; then a second; and another. He gouged harder and the dream, as if waking suddenly from itself, gave off a jet of sulphurous gas that made his eyes water and his gorge rise. A wrinkle appeared in the previously slick skin. Seizing his opportunity, Orlando bit down hard and got the fold between his teeth. He worried at it like a terrier, twisting his head back and forth until his neck muscles ached. The sphere gave out another stinking emission that engulfed both cats and onlookers; then it seemed to gather its strength. With a lunge, it distorted, quivered and shot away. Orlando hung on for grim life. He tried to call to Cat and Ma Tregenna to help bring the sphere down to the floor of the chamber, but he dared not open his mouth for fear of losing his grip on the thing altogether, and his cry emerged as a muffled growl that only served to enrage the dream globe further.

He brought his hind legs up and started to scrabble at the iridescent surface. The glistening pictures of the lives trapped and knotted within writhed away from his mauling claws. They floated beneath his nose: first Anna, pale and austere in a high-necked robe, a white shift, a shroud; then John in a stiff frilled collar and a single pearl earring, a tall hat, a khaki uniform; and over and again the witch, green eyes blazing with the sheer desperation of maintaining her hold on life and on this grim eternal triangle. Her black hair wreathed about her head like roots, like snakes, like a deadly anemone, latching on to the other two figures wherever it could noose them, so that the three of them, in all their different configurations, were yoked together by black tentacles of the stuff. Orlando bit down and made another hole in the skin. Fluid gushed out, followed by a rope of hair which – as if it had a mind all its own – struck unerringly at its attacker and wound itself tightly round his neck. In the ensuing struggle he became aware of a number of things: the way the dream globe bucked and dived as Caterina and the Besom leapt heroically and attached themselves to it; how the air was filled with the bubbling and hissing of furious cats; how more hot liquid spouted out of their prey, followed by the scents of times long gone and never buried; how the hair wound itself more and more tightly about his throat; how his limbs began to feel as soft and heavy as waterlogged wood, and his vision speckled away into scintillas of black . . .

Then, with a howl of fury, something flung itself at his head. He felt it land on him, felt its claws rake his sides as they scrabbled for purchase. He felt its hot breath on his face and its teeth at his throat.

Suddenly he could breathe again. His eyelids fluttered once, twice; and on the third blink he found himself nose to nose with the blurry image of Millefleur, her mouth full of black hair, her eyes shining. Then she slipped away from him and in her place he could see a headless Ma Tregenna, all four feet braced on the sides of the dream globe, her neck disappearing into its interior. A moment later she re-emerged, with what appeared to be a large wet rat in her jaws.

The dream globe convulsed, as if the Besom had ripped away something crucial to its existence. Gouts of steam came up out of it, smelling of canker and rot, and some part of it turned itself inside-out, spilling a wreath of coloured vapours into the foul air. The Besom was catapulted backwards off the skin of the sphere, her burden adding momentum to her fall, which ended with an indistinct thud at the opposite end of the chamber. There was the murmur of voices, then something else was disgorged from the globe, something that shrieked like a firework and shot away into the darkness, trailing the stench of the grave in its wake.

'Mistress!'

Orlando heard an unfamiliar, deep voice; the unmistakable sound of a cat's hunting call; the scuffle of dancing feet; a mournful wail that chilled him to the bone; silence.

Then the world became inverted and Orlando found himself falling away from his prey. He hit the ground with an impact that shook the breath from him and when he came to himself this is what he saw:

The sphere, darting overhead, smaller now and somehow lighter. Beneath it, a blue-grey cat with golden eyes danced on its hind legs, clapping her paws together, striking out right and left. A fox –

long-backed, reddish, brindling towards its hindquarters and fine tail – wove himself in and out of
her dance. As he did so, the room appeared to
undergo a transformation. It shimmered; it twined
about as if everything in it were as insubstantial as
smoke. And where there had been a small grey cat,
now there was a young leopard, all muscle and roar
and arboreal splendour. It was an odd struggle. The
cat leapt and turned, and made artful, devastating
sweeps with her shining claws; while the sphere – its
surface as slick and iridescent as a soap bubble –
wobbled and bobbed out of her reach.

Anna watched this strangely graceful display
with something approaching awe. Into her mind
came a line from a book she had once read – '*Any cat
who wants to live for ever should watch bubbles. Only
kittens should chase them.*'

We can't expect to armour ourselves against change,
she thought. *Yet if we don't – well, this cat is as rough
as it is beautiful. Your life doesn't care how you use it,
only that you should. It doesn't care how it uses you.*

Even as she was completing this thought, the
sphere trembled and burst. Anna *heard* it burst, with
a sound like tapped porcelain. She clutched her
daughter to her. *Now we're for it*, she thought. *All
those rotten, knotted-up Nonesuch lives, all those crimes
against animals and human beings, all that fear and
desperation –*

But released, its contents weren't dark and foul at
all. They streamed upwards like coloured fire into
the night sky. A single female human figure
struggled hard to form itself and travel against the

flow of things, only to waver and sigh, and relinquish its hold at last. While Anna heard an old woman's voice whispering sadly in front of a mirror in some empty room, 'I only wanted to keep the nice things, dear. I only wanted to stay nice.'

Then it was all gone.

Anna felt bruised, astonished, elated. She felt herself all over. 'Well!' she said.

The next thing she thought of was Eleanor. She stared warily into her daughter's eyes, half expecting to see Stella Herringe staring back out in triumph. But look how she might, all she could see there was a daughter, a proper little girl who was looking rather puzzledly around the chamber, as willing to be upset as to be amused by all these *things* that were happening. Anna laughed delightedly. 'Hello, Eleanor!' She hugged her tight, smelling baby smells, feeling baby warmth against the side of her face. 'Eleanor, look!' She held Eleanor up as if they were at the zoo. 'Look, Eleanor! Look at all the cats!'

Eleanor laughed and extended her hand. 'Ca'!' she said. 'Ca'!'

For a moment or two the leopard who, with the fox, had somehow conjured a wild road into existence before their very eyes, continued to fling herself about the room, rearing up on its hind legs in a kind of joyful memory of the chase, batting with its massive forepaws at the strange lights fading and dying like fireworks around her. Then the dream globe filled the air with a grunting, coughing roar that Anna felt as much as heard, and it fell back to all fours again, trotting once or twice round the room, panting heavily and staring from side to side in search of an exit.

As it went, it shrank rapidly until it was the size and colour of an ordinary blue-grey cat, barely more than a kitten, with two little bony lumps on the top of its head.

'Good grief,' whispered Anna. 'Caterina? Is that you?'

Caterina wasn't saying. She scampered across the room to exchange a sniff with Orlando and a tall tabby-and-white cat who looked remarkably like the missing Tufty, and who, in a distinctly proprietorial manner, was grooming viscous fluid out of his marmalade fur. She then progressed to the fox and they touched muzzles in what seemed an almost ritual greeting. Beside him, curled in upon herself like the husk of a dead wasp, an ancient brindled cat lay where it had fallen in the midst of the conflict. All the life had gone out of her, that was plain to see. Caterina bent and licked the top of the creature's dusty old head. Then, with a curiously tender gesture, the fox nosed her out of the way, picked up the carcass so that it hung out of either side of his long, sharp jaws and sprang into the air. Rainbow rings shimmered across the room, and a moment later the fox and his burden were gone.

In the afterglow as the wild road closed in upon itself, Anna became aware of two more cats sitting in the shadows at the back of the room. One was tall and regal-looking, his fur the dense blue-grey of an August stormcloud, or the wing of an elderly nuthatch, and his eyes were the same deep gold as Caterina's. Beside him was a small tabby cat with neat white socks and a ragged ear.

'Vita,' breathed Anna, disbelieving. And it was, drawn through time from the centre of the pattern in which she had been trapped for so long, as if someone had taken the loose end of a knot and pulled it free, which in a way they had.

Meanwhile Caterina made an ambling personal circuit of the chamber, sniffing the empty niches, addressing various invisible items with her nose or, more cautiously, with one front paw. Her gaze passed briefly over John Dawe, Francis Baynes and Alice Meynell, who lay, huddled or sprawled, their limbs at odd angles, more or less where events had left them. Then she shook herself and returned to the centre of the chamber, where she sat down and began to groom with considerable energy, beginning with her left front paw.

Anna looked to where Orlando lay up with the cat she knew as Tufty. They had been joined by the tabby with the ragged ear, and each was licking the other in what seemed a paroxysm of relief.

'Orlando, have I understood any of this?'

No answer. How could a cat speak anyway? Anna shook herself. 'Obviously not,' she said.

Alice Meynell now groaned and woke up. 'I wish I hadn't done that,' she said. She looked at her own hand. 'Anna? Have we come off the bike?'

Anna laughed. She set Eleanor down next to Orlando – who paused for a second to give Eleanor a suspicious look before he acknowledged, by

421

licking her outstretched hand, that she was just a little girl again; then, in that companionable way cats have when they groom in groups, stuck one rear leg up in the air and redoubled his efforts – and went to help her friend up. 'Come on, Alice. I'll explain later.'

'I hope you will.'

'I'm just going to have a look at Francis.'

'Wait a minute,' said Alice. 'Didn't there used to be a design of some sort on this floor?'

Anna looked. 'So there did,' she confirmed. 'But all that's finished now.'

Francis Baynes was already awake. A considerable smell of scorched tweed hung about him. Anna helped him to his feet. 'Let me look at you,' she said. 'Oh dear, Francis, you have been in the wars.' But while his face still looked shabby and aged – as if twenty years had passed in twenty-four hours – and much of the hair had been burned off the left side of his skull, his eyes gleamed with energy and his spirits were remarkable. He wasn't what he had been, but you could see something of what he might become. Determination and intelligence had liberated themselves from the romantic in him – whatever had happened to him in the last twenty-four hours, he had exchanged one set of qualities for another and moved on. When she hugged him he winced.

'I'm afraid some of my ribs are cracked,' he said apologetically.

'And your inner life, Francis? Is that cracked too?'

This seemed to amuse him. 'It could be worse,' he told her.

They smiled at one another for a moment; then he gave her a long, thoughtful look. 'And Eleanor?' he asked.

Anna said quickly, 'She's fine, Francis, fine.'

'I'm sorry if I –'

'You did your best,' she assured him.

Any other answer would be too complex, requiring admissions, explanations, justifications that would better be made later and at leisure. Here and now, the events themselves were too close. What had happened to Francis? How had he come to be here? In a way she didn't want to know. She didn't want to pry. Francis's trials had been his own and he had risen above them beautifully. Anyway, Eleanor was Eleanor again and safe.

Half understanding this, Francis made a hesitant gesture, as if to explain himself, or begin explaining himself, then changed his mind and asked instead, 'Do you have any idea what happened here?'

'A little more than you, perhaps.'

He nodded. 'I thought so. You must tell me about it when you have a moment.' Then, 'You know, at first I believed some great evil was being brought to book.' He looked around the chamber. 'Now I suspect it was only a case of bad spiritual plumbing.'

'Francis!'

'Something was unblocked, anyway.'

There was a comfortable pause. Then she suggested, 'Come up to the house.'

He shook his head. 'There are things that ought to be done down here and they're my responsibility. I want to make sure this never happens again. I don't know how strong I am, or how much I can do, but I have to be a proper priest and try.'

She held his hands for a moment. 'Be careful, Francis.'

'I will.'

Arms round each other, Anna and Alice looked down at John Dawe. He was snoring.

'I'm tempted to leave him here,' said Anna.

'I know. But where would you get another one?'

They woke him up and a few minutes later the three of them stood in the remains of the knot garden in the moonlight. Alice was examining the foundered JCB with a kind of professional disdain. John, who had his daughter in his arms, kept looking puzzledly back over his shoulder. He seemed to retain little memory of the night's events and none at all of his episode of temporal fugue. He kept looking at his watch, shaking his head and saying, 'I can't believe it's this late.' Then he added, 'Something awful happened down there, Anna. Didn't it? I don't know if I remember –' Suddenly, he gave Eleanor to Alice and took Anna in his arms. 'A lot of this was my fault,' he said.

She shivered and laid her head against his chest. 'It was,' she admitted.

'Have I been a complete bastard?'

Anna laughed. 'You've been a complete idiot,' she said. 'If only you'd trusted the two of us, Ellie and me –'

'She wasn't Ellie, though, was she?'

'I think most of her was, John. She needed you to

encourage that part, not the other. Who knows how it would have gone then? But look, she's Ellie again now and we're going to keep her that way.'

'I love you,' John told her.

'I love you too.'

'Good grief,' said Alice Meynell. 'Kiss her or something, and then take this child off me so we can all have a cup of tea.'

John looked round puzzledly. 'What was I thinking of?' he asked himself. He hugged Anna again. 'I'm so glad you came back.'

'Think yourself lucky,' Alice Meynell advised him, 'that she did.'

'Alice!' Anna chided.

Indicating the digger, John said, 'I'll have to sort that out in the morning. It'll mean another day's hire, I'm afraid.' And finally, 'What exactly did happen here?'

Anna laughed and touched his arm. 'You fell asleep. Overwork. Bad driving. It's the usual old story.'

Bad driving, she thought, remembering the crashed Volvo – and, worse, the episode with Francis at Cresset Beacon. *Oh well, we've all done some of that*. Meanwhile she was anxiously examining her daughter's eyes. They were still green, but it was a green that inclined to the hazel now and, more importantly, they were Eleanor's. Each time Anna checked her heart turned over with relief and she thought of Stella Herringe, perhaps the worst driver of them all.

'Do you think she'll ever come back?'

John looked puzzled. 'Who?' he enquired.

'Never mind.'

Anna looked up at the crowded roofline, Flemish gables and tall octagonal chimneys of Nonesuch, behind which the moon rode the mackerel-coloured sky. They seemed less convoluted and threatening now, and she was already recovering some of the delight she had felt when she first came to the house, armed only with Stella's description of it as 'the Tudor building on the left at the end of Allbright Lane'. She remembered the languor of the afternoon sunshine in empty rooms; Stella's voice on the telephone – then suddenly, frost on the lawns on Christmas Day, her first Christmas as John's wife.

I can put up with the past, she told herself, *as long as it stays where it belongs. I can even learn to welcome it.* Out loud she said, 'Let's go in and have some tea.'

'Good idea,' Alice agreed.

John said, 'I want whisky with mine. I don't seem to have had whisky for ages.'

They were turning to go when Orlando the cat trotted up the steps from the hidden room. He sniffed the night air, gave the JCB an old-fashioned look, then made off rapidly, tail up, in the direction of the orchard.

Alice Meynell laughed. 'That cat knows something it's not telling.'

Anna laughed too. 'They all know something.' She gave the garden a secret smile. 'Orlando?' she called.

He stopped, looked at Anna over his shoulder. His eyes gleamed like gold in the night, then he was gone. What *did* he know? She had a sudden memory of him as a day-old kitten, struggling with an eye dropper of condensed milk, fighting so blindly to stay alive. What a long way they had all come since then!

Don't be silly, Anna, she told herself, but tears came into her eyes.

Epilogue

ALONE AS USUAL, Francis Baynes took Early Communion at St Mary's in Ashmore, then put away the paten and the chalice for the last time. He had grown to enjoy St Mary's for its bareness, its strong smell of lilies and wholesale wax polish, the echo of the dripping vestry tap, which no one seemed able to mend. He would miss it. It seemed to him a very real place. Good, ordinary light cut across its columns and pews. *But it's wrong of me to prefer it empty*, he thought, in a recognition of his own romanticism. He sighed, tidied the pamphlets in the rack by the door, and – casting one more glance over the battered pews before he turned to leave – saw he was not alone after all.

While he was busy with the pamphlets, Anna Dawe had slipped past him to stand at the other end of the nave, at the base of one of the great cylindrical Romanesque piers. The light from the side windows fell across her yellow frock. She brought to the cool air of the nave the smell of some light, flowery perfume. She had cut her dark hair in a new way.

For Francis, St Mary's was suddenly resonant with a faint full chord, as if someone had touched the keys of the organ, and the very air seemed filled with a kind of liquid gold.

Anna looked up at the east window, with its sweet, faded medieval glass and stout St Christopher. 'Do you think,' she asked, 'that God minds me leaving my bike in the graveyard?'

Francis pretended to consider this. 'He would rather you left your bike in the graveyard,' he answered solemnly, 'than your Volvo in a ditch.'

They embraced, then stood back and smiled at each other.

'So,' she said, 'leaving.'

Francis nodded. 'And not just me. I caught a brief glimpse of Alice before communion.'

'Oh yes?'

Alice Meynell had decided to go back to America as soon as she could wind down her life at Cambridge. She was going to marry her physicist and, after she had got herself a place at MIT, marry physics too. It was the only real pursuit for human beings, if you asked her. Meanwhile she intended to live, she said, in this amazing part of New York she had heard of, where Jack Kerouac had once carved his name in the tables of the bars and you could see *life* at any hour of the day or night. Anna was frightened for her friend and elated for her too: all that energy and commitment, all that faith in the world.

'Oh yes.' Francis smiled wryly. 'She was trying to get round Pond Corner at about eighty-five miles an hour.'

'I'll miss her.'

'The ducks won't. Or the older parishioners.'

They contemplated this for a moment. Then Francis asked, 'And how is John?'

'He's fine. He talked to the bank manager and they're going to back him after all. He's started working on his book again, *The Dream as Cultural Index*. I don't understand a word of it and I don't suppose anyone else will either. And of course he and Eleanor are like that –' Here she smiled and held up her right hand, palm out, first two fingers pressed tightly together. 'As for the rest of it, I don't think he'll ever remember much of what happened.'

'He's a good man,' said Francis.

'He is, isn't he?'

They went out of the church. Francis locked the door for the last time and they walked about the churchyard together, arm in arm in the early morning sunshine. Rooks circled and cawed. Starlings hopped about under the yew trees, bustling through the dark glossy turf and over the graves of those village stalwarts, the Millers, the Clements, the Rose Popes and the Herringes. Most of them had their epitaphs, their final attempt to control the way the world saw them. But Stella Elizabeth Clara Herringe's new South African granite headstone gave only her dates, 1947–1999. Primroses grew at its foot and there were fresh anemones in a little vase.

'And have you decided to take another parish?' Anna asked after a while.

He shook his head. 'No.'

'Then what will you do?'

'Travel. Learn more. In a way, Alice is right.'

'Don't let her hear you say that.'

'All we have is to ask questions of the world – physics is just a modern way of doing that. So much of the world is invisible. And so much of the visible world is wrapped up with the invisible. I was right all along: I was wrong.'

He thought for a moment. Some months after the fact, he had given Anna the edited version of his experience with the woman from the graveyard. Anna had seen through it immediately and delighted him by saying, 'Francis, I believe you had *sex* with her, whatever she was!' To which he had been surprised to find himself replying with some nonchalance, 'Oh, repeatedly, repeatedly,' which made her laugh out loud. Even so, he was a little nervous around the subject. 'That thing I encountered –' He stared up at the church tower and shivered. 'That woman or thing or whatever she was . . . Well, despite herself, she helped me to understand. Perhaps that was her function, for me.'

'In a way I wish I'd met her too.'

'In a way you did. We all did.'

She took his hands. 'Oh Francis! So you're off to see the world?'

'Yes.'

'I'm glad. You'll send me e-mails?'

'You know I will.'

They smiled at one another. Their walk had brought them back to the lych-gate. 'Look,' she said, 'here's my bike. Isn't it awful? All that rust. It clanks

431

so on the hills.' She looked at her watch. 'And I must go,' she added. 'Eleanor is making our lives hell about *Teletubbies*, toast and poo, and all that tends to happen at about this time of day.' She held out her hand, then put her arms round him instead. 'Oh dear. Goodbye, Francis.'

He watched her pedal away. He realised that, as ever, they had talked more about his life than hers. 'What will *you* do?' he called.

Anna Dawe, née Prescott – who had come a very long way from Pond Cottage, out of the jaws of certain death, not to mention the jaws of the past and of the money business and of her own inner life; who had defended both cats and men, and learned to lavish herself on the grubbiest daughter who ever swallowed a clothes peg, necessitating a race to A&E in Drychester at five o'clock on a winter morning in John's 'new' Volvo (which was more ancient) – only waved and pedalled harder. 'I'm going to make that house what it should have been all along,' she called over her shoulder.

'You're very quiet.'

The sun beat down, making a warm haze of the space between my ears, where the fur had been singed back to the skin and was now growing through again, downy and fine – as soft as a kitten's, Millie said, when she groomed me, and then she would fall silent and thoughtful, and her eyes would become unfocused for a moment or two and she would change the subject. It had taken me some time to recognise this silence and longer still to understand what it signified. My grandfather always said I was a fool, but I was only now realising the extent of my foolishness.

'I was just thinking,' I said, twisting my head to regard her and squinting through the brightness. The sun was silver on the sea, it made a halo of her fur, especially where it caught the tuft on the top of her head. 'About Letty and Belly; and Cat.' It was hard to think of her as Squash now, having seen the elegance and the power of her in her wild guise, making a finer dreamcatcher than I had ever been. 'And Lydia.'

'Ah, Lydia.'

I heard the resignation in Millie's voice and it made something inside me shrivel in shame. 'Well, Liddy and Cass,' I amended quickly. Initially, it had been hard for me to see the Russian Blue in Lydia's company, let alone usurping my relationship with the girls. 'Call me Cass,' he had growled at me once we had survived an awkward period of stalking around one another and he had ascertained I would not stand between him and his 'family'. 'I have had enough of this ridiculous Circassian Gogol II. The witch is gone and I must be a different cat now. I have certain . . . responsibilities.' Then he had leaned his great, angular head towards me in an uncharacteristic gesture of confidentiality. 'I shall do my best to make her happy; I know I have a great deal to make reparation for.' And indeed, he did seem to make Liddy happy – if anyone could. In his company her eyes shone – not the hard topaz gleam they had when she contemplated me, but the melting golden tone they took on when she was confronted by a plateful of whitebait: luxurious and sensual; nebulous with greed.

For their part, the girls behaved towards him as if they had always been together and none of the bizarreness of the situation touched them at all. Perhaps it was that the scent of him, that faint, exotic musk had been familiar to them from birth. It was a mystery to me. As it was, I passed through an interval of grim jealousy, until one night I was visited by a dream in which I was barrelling down a wild road, my lion paws thudding soft and rhythmic on the cold dusty ground, and light was spilling off my shiny fur. Beside me, a beautiful lynx, her coat barred with black and silver, great tufts sprouting from her ears like spring barley, bounded along on oiled limbs, her eyes like lamps in the darkness, and as she ran she called out to me, 'Leap and run, Orlando! Leap and run for ever!' and I had never felt so powerful or so free.

The next day, Millefleur and I left for a visit to her favourite seaside haunt and it had been all she had promised me – sunshine and salty air; fat hedgerow voles too complacent and slow to evade our teeth and claws; and flowerbeds full of fragrant marigolds in which to curl up and sleep.

We were lying in the lee of a garden wall now, a wall crowned with nodding heads of red valerian, its rocky crannies colonised by pennywort and rosettes of bright ochre lichen. Over Millie's shoulder I could see one of the fishing boats, tiny against the vast silver sea, making its way back to the harbour. There would be mackerel heads to be cadged there later.

'Millie,' I said, taking my courage into my paws at last. 'When I said I was thinking about the girls and Liddy, what I really meant was –' The enormity of what I was about to say made a hard lump of fear rise in my chest, fear that she would laugh in my face and leave me here, alone and stupid; but I swallowed it down and struggled on as best I could. 'What I was going to say, Millie – what I have wanted to say for some time now is: *kittens*.' Millie blinked at me but said nothing at all. It was as if the world were holding its breath. 'Kittens,' I repeated, reckless now the word was out in the open. 'You and I . . . Would you? . . . Could you? . . .' I blundered hopelessly to a halt.

In reply, Millie regarded me solemnly, then rolled backwards into the long grass. Her belly fur glowed in the sunlight. 'Takes more than fine words to make kittens, honey,' she said softly.

Her jaunty piebald mask twitched minutely. It was only when both eyes were open and shining again that I realised she had winked at me.

Available in Arrow

The Wild Road

Gabriel King

THE GREATEST JOURNEY OF ALL . . .

'Eat when you're hungry, sleep where it's dry. No one is ever what they seem.'

Sound advice. For Tag, stolen from his home to join a mysterious quest, it will be a lifesaver. Once tame, now he must navigate the wild roads, the animal highways which bind our world. He will be helped – by the old cat Majicoú; the urban fox, Loves A Dustbin; the magpie, One For Sorrow; and Cy, the tabby with a sparkplug in her head.

. . . IS ALONG THE WILD ROAD

It's a journey alive with possibilities, but fraught with danger, for the balance of nature is under threat. Gabriel King's remarkable début tells of the secret history of cats, and the perils of sharing a world with humankind.

'An entralling epic of a tale' William Horwood

'The ultimate animal adventure' Terry Pratchett

'I would recommend this story to everyone . . . absolutely magical' Richard Adams

The Golden Cat

Gabriel King

On a sunlit headland at Tintagel, the King and Queen are raising their three beautiful kittens. But which is the famed Golden Cat? And how to tell, when two of the kittens disappear suddenly, as if into thin air?

Other enigmas abound. In a research facility the cat known only as Animal X finds his misty dreams of freedom invaded by a mysterious force. Meanwhile, on another continent, the feisty feral cat Sealink finds herself caught up in a sinister conspiracy that threatens the wellbeing of the natural world.

And at the abandoned heart of the wild roads, Tag listens as a distant and chillingly familiar cry disturbs the dusty silence . . .

The Knot Garden

Gabriel King

When Anna Prescott, retreating from a doomed love affair and a high-pressure career, discovers the idyllic hamlet of Ashmore it appears to offer the perfect escape. With its pretty cottages, picturesque canal and intriguing inhabitants – Stella Herringe, mysterious lady of the manor, feisty Alice at the Green Man, and handsome, enigmatic John Dawe – it seems the ideal place for a new life.

When Anna finds herself adopted by two tiny kittens, Pond Cottage finally starts to feel like home. But dangers lurk beneath Ashmore's apparently tranquil surface, and Anna's arrival sets in motion a heady, nightmarish chain of events.

'It's brilliant: read it!' *Cosmopolitan*

'Gabriel King transports us to a magical, secret world of breathtaking suspense. I loved *The Knot Garden*.' Barbara Erskine.

8 00 →

AVAILABLE NOW IN ARROW

The Wild Road	Gabriel King	£5.99
The Golden Cat	Gabriel King	£5.99
The Knot Garden	Gabriel King	£5.99

ALL ARROW BOOKS ARE AVAILABLE THROUGH MAIL ORDER OR FROM YOUR LOCAL BOOKSHOP.

PAYMENT MAY BE MADE USING ACCESS, VISA, MASTER-CARD, DINERS CLUB, SWITCH AND AMEX, OR CHEQUE, EUROCHEQUE AND POSTAL ORDER (STERLING ONLY).

☐☐☐☐☐☐☐☐☐☐☐☐☐☐☐☐☐☐

EXPIRY DATE .... SWITCH ISSUE NO. ☐☐

SIGNATURE ....

PLEASE ALLOW £2.50 FOR POST AND PACKING FOR THE FIRST BOOK AND £1.00 PER BOOK THEREAFTER.

ORDER TOTAL: £................................. (INCLUDING P&P)

ALL ORDERS TO:
ARROW BOOKS, BOOKS BY POST, TBS LIMITED, THE BOOK SERVICE, COLCHESTER ROAD, FRATING GREEN, COLCHESTER, ESSEX, CO7 7 DW, UK.

TELEPHONE: (01206) 256 000
FAX: (01206) 255 914

NAME ....

ADDRESS..

....

Please allow 28 days for delivery. Please tick box if you do not wish to receive any additional information. ☐
Prices and availability subject to change without notice.